Copyright © 2

All rights rese

No part of this publication may be reproduced, distributed, or transmitted in any form or by any means, including photocopying, recording, or other electronic or mechanical methods, without the prior written permission of the publisher, except as permitted by U.S. copyright law. For permission requests, contact justinmurrayauthor@gmail.com

The story, all names, characters, and incidents portrayed in this production are fictitious. No identification with actual persons (living or deceased), places, buildings, and products is intended or should be inferred.

Book Cover by JD&J Design

To my family who put up with all my nonsense and the risk I took to write this story.

CONTENTS

Chapter 1	1
Chapter 2	13
Chapter 3	32
Chapter 4	47
Chapter 5	66
Chapter 6	83
Chapter 7	94
Chapter 8	113
Chapter 9	123
Chapter 10	133
Chapter 11	143
Chapter 12	151
Chapter 13	162
Chapter 14	174
Chapter 15	189
Chapter 16	204
Chapter 17	213
Chapter 18	224
Chapter 19	235
Chapter 20	250
Chapter 21	261

Chapter 22	279
Chapter 23	290
Chapter 24	300
Chapter 25	314
Chapter 26	337
Chapter 27	350
Author's Note	367

CHAPTER 1

"Do you think he'll come?" Jon nudged his friend Arne while dangling his legs off a barrel against the stable walls by the town's east gate.

Arne shrugged, "I dunno, but I hope he does."

The two kids had been watching the gate all day, looking out for the rumored Paladin to come through town. So far it was the usual suspects: farmers and the occasional adventurer party. Being at the ass-end of nowhere was rarely exciting. All they ever got were the trainee adventurers who came through to deal with goblins in the forests that encircled the village of Wren's End. Having impassable mountains west, north and south of the village with a major empire to the east didn't leave a lot for excitement. The residents of the town, who preferred to farm in peace, didn't share this sentiment with the kids. The greatest excitement they would see in a day was skipping stones at the river and finding one that made it across to the other side.

Jon and Arne had been there for hours. School was technically in session, but the two skipped for the day, along with every other classmate and the teacher, all who were positioned around the main drag in various vantage points. Some were even on the roofs of the tightly packed buildings. They weren't going to miss the arrival of a famed Paladin.

Sure, they'd love to see one of the rare holy order and even argued over which god was his patron, but they mostly wanted to scam him. Paladins had a reputation of being naïve and gregarious to a fault. The two boys dressed up in their finest rags to pretend to be orphan children. This was a joke because no one out in these parts was orphaned – the empire wasn't foolish enough to conscript from a major breadbasket to leave any abandoned children – but a Paladin wouldn't know this.

More people streamed through the gate going in both directions. Jon and Arne both began to wonder if the rumor was just that, a rumor. Sure, a few herders who had to chase some goats into the mountains came back claiming a strange crypt had opened up and some zombies were milling about the entrance. Were such lowly undead really a major concern for a Paladin? There were apparently only a hundred or so of the fabled warriors in the entire Quellis Empire. A minor mountain crypt outside a sleepy farming community could just as easily be handled by a few novice adventurers, assuming anyone cared to go all the way out where it was not harming anyone.

Still, the rumor circulated through the village, its source coming from the Adventurers in the Guild Hall. The village wouldn't be abuzz over some false rumor, especially since it originated from the Guild. They would have insider information on who was expected to show. Right?

The two boys' morale began to fade along with the day. It was late afternoon now and there was no sign of anyone other than adventurers in cheap padded cloth armor, a gambeson Jon thought they were called, returning from their training hunts. Nothing they hadn't seen day in, day out in Wren's End.

Jon slid off the barrel, adjusting his trousers that had stuck to the skin on his now sore bum, "That was a waste. I'd rather have spent the day in school."

Arne snorted, "It must be for you to actually want to be in class."

"Like you're one to talk," Jon replied, punching Arne playfully in the shoulder. This triggered an impromptu sparring match as the two wrestled on the ground, punching each other while laughing with joy. A few adults gave the two a wide berth while an old man sitting nearby glared at them.

The two wrestled in the dirt for a while longer when Jon put up his hand, "Stop. You hear that?"

Arne punched him, "What? You losing the fight? That's all I ever hear."

"You never win." Jon pointed toward the gate, "I meant THAT!"

Arne stopped and noticed that everyone had gone quiet. The two gate guards were staring into the distance with rapt attention, long shadows from the sun that was nearing the crest of the tallest peak followed their attention like pointing fingers.

Both boys stood and ran to the barrels they were previously sitting on, using them to climb up to the roof of the adjacent stables that were situated against the town palisade. They then jumped up on the high walkway ringing the palisade wall that was designed for archers during a siege, not that such a thing had ever happened in living memory here.

In the distance, the two saw a merchant caravan traveling down the main road leading from the heart of the Empire. Five figures traveled in formation around the caravan wagon on horses with a sixth one trailing behind. The one in the lead was what caught the boys' attention.

A Paladin!

His gleaming full plate armor reflected red in the setting sunlight. His massive war horse, white as a cloud, was clad in its own scaled armor barding. The man radiated a sense of power and skill from this distance. As he neared, more details became clear. His blond hair was nearly as brilliant as gold and was neatly cut to avoid getting caught in battle. His breast plate was emblazoned with the symbol of Tyrus, the God of Righteous Battle.

Closer still, his features were brought into focus. His face was chiseled and he had perfect skin. His piercing blue eyes scanned the town and he flashed a smile to the onlookers, showing off perfect teeth that shone nearly as brilliantly as his breastplate. A sword in an intricately carved sheath was strapped to the flank of the horse, long yet not so long it would require two hands to effectively wield. A heater shield was strapped to his back. It was made of metal, signaling the immense strength of the man.

The party with him paled in comparison, not because they, too, weren't impressive. They couldn't hope to match the Paladin's glory. Each rode in a protective formation around the merchant caravan wagon.

A thin dark skinned man with pointed ears, a Desert Elf, rode beside the wagon. He wore a sandy tan brigandine breastplate, brown trousers and a pair of sturdy sandals. Crossed on his back were a long spear and a shorter one. His eyes were dark brown and his long black hair was tied back into a series of intricate braids that streamed down his back. The boys suspected he was a Lancer, something the desert dwelling people of the southern coasts were masters of. He had to be a truly wondrous warrior to be party with the Paladin.

To the other side of the wagon rode a beautiful Leopardia woman, her pure white fur covered all parts of her body not obscured by cloth and was accented by black spots indicating her subrace was of the Snow people. Her sharp yellow eyes were split by a feline iris, narrow in the sunlight. Her pointed cat ears were forward and alert and her whiskers protruded from a short snout that hid the fangs that the race was known for. She was of the tribe that resided in the far north of the Empire. She didn't show a sign of weaponry and wore red robes inlaid with dark gold arcane symbols that hid her tail. Her hands had claws extended from the ends of the fingers as she gripped the reins and boots hid her feline feet. She must be a Mage and, considering her lack of obvious weapons, a powerful one.

The fourth member trailed behind the Desert Elf. He had dark blue skin and was completely bald, a Felkin, a member of a race that originated deep caverns of the world. His face was severe and spoke of a man who had little interest in social graces and was all business. He wore a leather chest plate over a thin white robe and carried nothing more than a simple dagger and wore an amulet of Refik, the God of Healing. He must be the Cleric of the group.

The fifth member of the party rode a smaller pony. She was a short Gnomish woman, standing roughly three feet in height. She, too, was unusually attractive. Red hair, pale skin and a curvaceous figure that would make most men stop and look. She also had a devious look in her eye. She wore a subtle brown tunic that would let her disappear in a crowd. Her soft looking shoes with padded rubber tree soles, small wrist mounted crossbow and two daggers screamed Rogue.

The figure trailing behind was forgotten by the boys, dismissed as a traveler that followed along out of convenience.

After the party passed through the gates, they made their way over to the stables. The boys jumped from the palisade walkway to the stable roof, scrambling to lean over the edge. Instead of the usual stable boy, the Stable Master deigned to greet the party in person, feeling his presence would honor the group.

The Paladin looked up and noticed the two boys. He gave

them a big smile and a wink before dismounting and handing his horse over to the stable master.

The Paladin turned to the pudgy man driving the cart, "Good merchant, I thank you for keeping us company on the long road from the capital. I'm afraid we have business to attend to at the guild. I hope you can reach the market without much trouble from here?" Jon and Arne both delighted at the honey smooth tenor that brimmed with confidence.

"Oh, thank you m'lord. I appreciate the escort. I don't know what I would have done in that bandit attack. Those guards turning out to be bandits, too, was a right surprise it was," the merchant said, handing out a small sack that looked like it contained coin.

The Paladin pushed it back toward the merchant, "No, my fine man. Keep it. Keeping innocents safe is reward enough."

Anyone not enamored by the Paladin's display of generosity would have noticed the eye roll from the Rogue, though no one in the growing crowd did.

The Paladin waved to the crowd and he, along with his companions, began making their way toward the center of town where the Adventurer's Guild Hall was located. The crowd dutifully split to allow the group to pass, no one willing to break the spell to approach or speak with the legendary group gracing the village with their presence. This event alone was enough to give the local bards something to sing about in the tavern for years to come, even before the tales of their inevitable victory in the mountain crypt.

Jon and Arne slid down from the roof onto a pile of hay bales then to the road, their plan to try and scam the party forgotten. The power that radiated from them was just too intense and the boys found themselves staring in awe as they walked deeper into the village. The cart rumbling past next broke them out of the stupor, as it did for the rest of the crowd that began to disperse.

"Wow, I can't believe what I saw," Arne said.

Jon nodded, "Me neither. It makes me want to become a Paladin, too."

Arne snorted, "The Gods pick their champions. Like you'd ever be one."

Jon shoved Arne, "Fine, I'll just become a Warrior to so I can travel with one."

"And I'll study to become a Mage," replied Arne.

"Someone has his eyes on that Leopardia babe, huh," Jon grinned at Arne.

Arne's face flushed red, "No, you moron. I'm just not that good at fighting."

"Finally admit you can't beat me. Besides, you're too dumb to be a Mage," Jon taunted.

"That's because I'm always with you and not in school. Mom says I'm clever. Maybe I should go to school and stop getting into your schemes."

Jon stuck out his tongue, "You'd be bored without me."

"Your friend is right you know, an education is important," a gruff voice said from behind the two boys.

The two turned and jumped back a few paces. Coming in behind the cart was the sketchiest looking man they'd ever laid their eyes on. He was an older man, possibly in his late 40s, with long, unkempt grey hair riding an equally pathetic looking grey mare. His face sported a scraggly beard in the same washed-out grey as sprouted from his head. He wore a tattered blue field worker's shirt with a rusted chain hauberk peeking through the holes with similarly worn brown trousers. A small, plain round shield was slung over his back. The only things on this man that looked to be in good condition were his hard leather traveling boots and the strange metal hammer hanging from a sling on his waist. The hammer was solid metal, roughly two feet in length and had a six inch spike protruding from the head opposite the hammer.

Worse still, he wore a simple amulet to Erinne, the Queen of the Gods. Only a total nutter would worship the Recluse Queen, who was such a joke that she didn't have a proper domain.

The two boys were relieved they were in town around other people. This is not a man they'd have wanted to run into in the forest or a dark alley. They suspected he was some weird vagrant that tagged along with the merchant and the Paladin's party out of convenience.

The man suddenly shouted to an empty space above the boys' heads, "I know, stop bothering me with that."

The two boys took a few more steps back.

Before either Jon or Arne could work up the nerve to either run or ask this strange man what he wanted, he reached toward his belt. The boys flinched and prepared to run and, instead of grabbing for his hammer, the vagrant dug around in a pouch and pulled out two silver coins.

"Here, for information," he said, holding the coins out at arm's length. Neither boy made a move.

After a moment the man rolled his eyes, "Yes, I can see that. Stop nagging me." He then tossed the coins at the boys' feet.

The boys each picked up a coin. Jon swallowed to move saliva over his suddenly dry throat, gathered his courage and looked at the man, "Uh, what can we, um, do for you sir."

"Point me to the Guild Hall."

Jon's brow scrunched in confusion. Everyone knew that Guild Halls were at the central point of cities. Who was this weirdo?

Jon pointed down the main road, "Just follow that street. It's the large building with the green door. You can't miss it."

"Thanks boys. And a word of advice? Your act needs more work."

The two boys looked at each other before Jon replied, "Begging your pardon, sir? Our act?"

The strange man pointed at their feet, "Your shoes. Remembering to smear dirt on your face and wearing old clothing is the easy part, but everyone forgets about the shoes. Yours are far too well-kept to be orphans. My older brother long ago got into trouble trying to run a similar scam."

The boys were too dumbfounded to reply. This weird vagrant saw right through them. Maybe it's because he was a scammer, too?

"Then why did you give us each a coin for something everyone already knows," Arne blurted out in response. Jon elbowed his friend with a shush.

The vagrant smiled, "Oh, you're not bad kids. I appreciate a good effort. I also used it as an excuse to give you a warning. You don't want to fall into that habit. It doesn't lead to good results."

The boys lost their voice and could only nod in return, scared of the prospect of disagreeing with this dangerous individual.

"Oh shut it. Don't you have someone better to bother," the man burst out yelling to the air again. He then sighed and rubbed his hand over his face in exasperation. "Sorry, it's been a long journey."

Jon replied in fear as he and Arne circled around to give the strange man a straight line toward the guild, "It's no trouble sir."

The vagrant looked back at the boys as if he had forgotten they were there. "Sorry boys, I'm not talking to you. I'll be on my way. Remember my words."

Jon and Arne watched as the vagrant dismounted and led his horse over to the stables. The stable master looked at him in disgust and called for the stable boy to come over and take the ragged mare. After taking it, the vagrant gave the boy a silver coin as well. Mixed emotions panned over the boy's face when he couldn't decide if he was happy with such a hefty tip or if he wanted to escape.

The vagrant moved down the street, periodically looking into the air and frowning. Other townsfolk took the same cue as Jon and Arne did and made sure to give the man a wide berth as he held a conversation with no one in particular and wandered away to the guild.

When he was safely in the distance, Jon felt himself release the breath he wasn't aware he was holding.

"I'm not sure I want to be an adventurer anymore," Arne said as he stared down the street toward the odd man.

Jon nodded, "I think I understand why Ma and Pa like living here so much. How many people like that do adventurers have to deal with?"

Arne shuddered, "One is one too many if you ask me. I think I'll just live here and be a farmer where it's safe."

"Me, too, Arne. Me too."

"At least we each got a silver out of it. I can buy Mom chickens she always wanted."

"Ha, I'm going to buy meat pies."

They both laughed and went back to the wrestling match they had started before the party arrived.

Had the two boys been more attentive, or at least less intimidated by the man's appearance, they would have noticed things far more strange than a raving lunatic talking to the air in the street. They would have noticed that this vagrant that looks like he lives in an alley had strangely perfect skin. Not perfect like the man in the gleaming armor from before, but true perfection. His skin didn't have so much as old smallpox scars, let alone a pimple, blackhead, sunburn, liver spot or wrinkle that a man his age should have developed.

Nor did they notice his eyes. They were not just intense; they were of a crystal clear emerald green with a dark, well defined limbal ring, making his eyes take on a youthful tone. There wasn't even a hint of redness from the rigors of road travel or the accompanying fatigue.

The boys further missed the man's teeth. Teeth so perfect and white that had they been in a portrait, the viewer would assume the artist is flattering his patron to keep on his good side. Not so much as a hint of yellow graced those pearly whites.

Most unusual of all, though, was his odor. Or, more specifically, his complete lack of odor. Even the magnificent adventurer party had whiffs of body odor and sweat that came from traveling the two weeks from the capital without a proper bath. This vagrant, who should have been so foul that his overwhelming funk would drive swine to madness, smelled of absolutely nothing. Even his breath was completely neutral, as if the rotting humors that lived in everyone's mouths decided to reside elsewhere. The air passed over the boys' faces but their nostrils weren't tickled by anything.

Being young and inexperienced in the ways of the world, overwhelmed by the combination of seeing bigger than life adventurers visit their sleepy town and bombarded by a strangely observant madman who talked to ghosts, the boys failed to recognize any of these incongruent elements. This odd man walked down the road and, by the morning, the two boys will have mostly forgotten about the encounter.

CHAPTER 2

"They were nice boys," a voice echoed in Gerold's head.

Gerold grunted in response.

"You know I can't read your thoughts," the voice continued.

"Yes, oh mighty Recluse Queen."

"You know you can just call me Erinne. We've been together for six months."

Gerold sighed, "I met you six months ago. We've only had, what, four weeks total together?"

"Pedantics," the voice huffed. Gerold imagined Erinne looked nothing like the rare depiction in artwork. Instead of the tall, sharp featured matron dressed in regal attire, her voice and mannerisms reminded Gerold of a girl in her late teens to early twenties dressed in the latest city fashion. The voice certainly didn't belong to a being that, at least according to her, was older than time itself, created the universe and even the other gods within it.

Not that anyone here was even aware of it. She was just a random member of the pantheon called a Queen and no one knew her purpose. At least according to her, she couldn't interact directly with the world because her powers are too vast to risk engaging much beyond talking to Gerold.

Gerold looked around the main street of Wren's End. He felt a painful sense of nostalgia rise up inside him as he looked at the well-maintained cobblestone road and thought of his own village. Unlike Wren's End, his village was on the frontier and its road was tamped dirt. It faced real threats from petty kingdoms, warring tribes and wandering monsters.

Still, it was much like this one. The wind wafted in from the east, carrying the smells of fresh fertilizer being sewn into the fields before planting interwoven with the pleasant smell of freshly baked bread and sizzling street vendor meat. A soft murmur of the crowd filled the air as people chatted with friends and loved-ones. He watched as a few rookie adventurers moved from shop to shop as they prepared for the next day's hunt.

Those days were gone. Has it really been six months? He barely had time to mourn when Erinne's voice touched his soul. He still didn't comprehend why he was chosen. Erinne had never had a Paladin before. There weren't even records of her having an Order of Clerics dedicated to her worship.

She said it was his soul. Something Erinne refused to elaborate on made him uniquely compatible with her. He tried to refuse, but Erinne had told him he could gain power to stop what had happened to his village from happening again.

He finally agreed and Gerold got the first taste of Erinne's more youthful demeanor when she squealed in delight as he felt his body filling with unexplainable warmth. It was short lived when Erinne said it was her first time doing this and she was glad he didn't explode.

"Hello, Gerold?" Erinne interrupted his brooding. He grunted in response.

"This again," Erinne whined. "I told you I can't hear your thoughts. I made that off-limits. Free will you know?"

"Yes, what is it?" Gerold responded.

"You're brooding again. Want to talk about it?"

"No."

"You should be happy that I talk to you at all. The other Paladins only get vague signs."

"I'm not, especially since I didn't want this to begin with."

Her voice booed in his head, "You know how to dig it in."

"Why am I here again?"

A long, drawn out sigh echoed in his head, "I picked up a strange surge of necrotic magic before it vanished. It's somewhere in this area."

Gerold knew perfectly well why he was in this village. Distracting the Goddess was the best way to get her to stop harassing him.

Gerold continued strolling down the road. His eyes wandered the village, though he refused to allow them to rest too long on families. The pain was still too fresh. His appearance and demeanor did make it easy to travel along the road with people parting as he moved. Despite being far removed from anywhere, it was surprisingly bustling here, between being the main training ground for the Guild and a major farming region. There is a benefit to being a safe, quaint place.

Worry grew in his mind when he overheard conversations by townspeople. They were excitedly talking about a Paladin having come to town. There was even coin exchanged to settle bets against those who didn't believe the rumors that one was on his way. How had they known? Had his disguise failed? No one was paying attention to him and everyone was focused in the direction of the Guild Hall.

Gerold knew it wasn't him. He was fresh out of basic training and told no one. When he strolled out of the Temple, it was obvious to anyone what he was – the stares he received confirmed it – requiring a special item to stop the attention. He even withheld his status from the Guild Hall, whom accepted him as a Warrior.

The Temple knew he was coming. Had someone there spread the rumor he was coming here and why? It didn't make much sense to announce his plans via random rumor and no one there was as enamored by the concept of Paladins as the regular public. Still, the town had somehow known he was coming even though they didn't recognize him on the street, confusing the head of the five man party as a Paladin.

Dwelling on it now wouldn't solve anything. Shoving those concerns into the recesses of his mind, he forged toward the Guild Hall.

Guild Halls in the Empire were almost entirely uniform. If you've been in one, you've been in all of them. What this did was make the building look out of place. A desert town? It would be made of wood instead of the surrounding sandstone. A major city? The Hall looks basic and ramshackle in comparison to the surrounding structures.

In a small village like this? The eight storey building towered over the surrounding structures. This Hall loomed over the central square, overshadowing the single floor Town Hall and two floor tall Pantheon Temple. It even loomed over the blue crystal sphere that sat at the center of the town square. Guild Halls were, also, located at the center point of a settlement to facilitate the maintenance of the Town Seed.

Gerold looked at the clear, gently glowing blue crystal, called a Town Seed. The crystal was a sphere five feet in diameter that floated a foot above a ten foot tall white marble column with grey speckles. The crystal lacked any flaws or marks, which led to debates where some observers could swear it was rotating in the air while others claimed it remained still.

The column the crystal stood upon was polished and smooth with a slight concave curve at the midpoint up the column. If someone were to run his hand across the surface, he would feel no lumps or imperfections. The column was unadorned with any other decoration, had no carvings and stood on a raised square platform made of stone.

The Town Seed radiated a minor sense of comfort. It was through this object that this town could exist without constant monster patrols. They required an absurd amount of Adventurer Coins to form, Gerold had heard from his Grandfather it took an Orichalcum coin, which was worth a staggering 100 million Copper. The man would know, he was the reason his home village had one.

The color, blue, was a sign of it being the weakest one. Wren's End, despite being a Guild Hall training location, was mainly a farming community, so most of the protective radius was reserved for the surrounding farmland. Even then, it still took a Gold coin to maintain each month, with another few Silver coins for the protective enchantments on the palisade around the town.

He remembered talking back in his hometown tavern about it. If this object was so important to a village, why not put a protective wall immediately around it or inside a protected vault? Apparently, it wouldn't work without sufficient open space around it. The square itself is a result of this as even packing buildings in too close can interrupt its function. The town palisade marks the closest point a protective wall can be built, though so much as a simple fence at the maximum perimeter of the effect with the same reinforcing effects would cost as much as the stone fortress in the Imperial Capital.

Gerold turned his gaze away from the Town Seed back to the Guild Hall. This Guild Hall did have an element not present in most of the others – the four acre training yard in the rear, leaving a large empty space in the middle of the village surrounded by a low log fence.

Gerold stopped for a while and watched the young trainees who came from all over the Empire to learn the basics of adventuring. Wren's End was a perfect place for this. The town was located far from the border conflicts and the dangerous frontier lands. It was nestled perfectly in a place that only spawned weak monsters.

Gerold momentarily thought how he would have spent his winter at the farm and not undertaking the intense one-on-one gauntlet he had to endure in the Temple's Paladin training course. The Temple taught him combat arms and honed his body, but it would be through combat experience where his true abilities would manifest. The Empire wished to maintain the image that its Paladins were living legends.

He was sure the patron Gods appreciated their efforts as well. Tyrus and Destus, the twin gods of war, wouldn't look good when their chosen, who are picked for soul compatibility, were felled by a simple monster. The small number of Paladins makes it easy to focus on a severe regimen since only a handful ever manifest in any given year. Gerold was the first Paladin the Temple had trained in over a year.

When Erinne first contacted him, he thought he was going crazy to have a voice claiming to be the Recluse Queen in his head. He ignored it for a while before acquiescing to its demands to go to the Temple for training. When he arrived at the Pantheon Temple in the capital and informed them he was a chosen Paladin of Erinne, the Head Priest called the guard to remove him from the premises. Before going, they interrogated him about how he knew the Temple trained newly minted Paladins since only the Gods, the Emperor, the Head Priest, a few select trainers and Guild Hall Masters knew. The divine physical gifts had yet to fully manifest at this point and everyone dismissed him because the Gods would never have missed him for so long and chosen him in his older years. Erinne had to tell him how to activate his first holy aura, Calm Nerves, which reduced stress and anxiety.

When he did, it gave the Head Priest a shock. While the Priest was convinced Gerold was a Paladin, he also felt Gerold was being deceptive. The Head Priest actually listed Gerold down as a Paladin of Pellius, the God of Deception, since everyone knew Erinne never took on followers. Gerold was enrolled in a few courses on etiquette, disguise and espionage work since, in the words of the Head Priest, "You're still new so the compulsion hasn't kicked in. Just because you're a chosen of Pellius doesn't mean you will be able to lie. We'll teach you counter-espionage and how to massage the truth to conceal what you don't want to reveal if you do choose to address a sensitive subject."

Erinne herself mostly found it amusing that the Empire formally registered him as Pellius' follower, even if Gerold did get a hint of melancholy in her voice. He was initially surprised that the Empire registered Paladins at all, though it made sense if they had to call on them in an emergency. He suspected it would cause issue if that roster ever leaked.

He watched the trainees taking advantage of the fading daylight work with a patient instructor who gently adjusted their grip on practice weapons, corrected wild telegraphed swings and helped their footwork as they hit wooden training dummies. Phantom aches from his own, rough training pulsed on his body where his corrections were less than gentle and the training dummy was his own flesh. His passive improved healing that was so flawless scars wouldn't form allowed his trainers to be rough on him. This was on top of afternoons and nights with spymasters and priests for training his mind and little sleep for weeks on end. The Empire didn't mess around with Paladins.

Gerold, in contrast, was unceremoniously graduated out the door. Even though the Empire was proud of its Paladin population, it was their policy to not help any of them beyond basic training. The Emperor didn't want the impression they were favoring any one God over another since the Empire worshipped the Pantheon as a whole. Provide assistance and it would introduce problems. Even equal assistance would seem discriminatory since some Paladins would inevitably excel more than others. The help would be seen as either insufficient or excessive depending on the viewer. And the Empire didn't want to compete with the Gods for the Paladin's loyalty.

So no one got any. All they got for a graduation gift was a simple weapon of their choice – Gerold took a hammer with a war spike on the opposite end since he figured it was a versatile tool for undead and monster alike – and a bag of holding. The bag was the one major expense the Empire was willing to part with since the items were immensely expensive to produce. The bag he received was not like the others normally for sale. It was plain and boring, looking like a normal leather pouch that would hold a few coins or herbs, which he appreciated since it hid its true nature. He also got an amulet of Pellius, though he sold this and convinced a craftsman to make one of Erinne to wear. He got a good deal on it because the craftsman thought he was crazy.

He also received some advice on the way out: register at the Adventurer's Guild and travel to Wren's End to build up his practical experience.

Gerold then went to the adventurers' guild and registered himself as a Warrior.

Normally, registration dictated the path an Adventurer would follow. A Warrior would develop skills related to Warriors, a Mage would learn how to manipulate arcane forces beyond basic cantrips and so forth. No one knew why this worked and there were rumors that other Guilds for less savory professions also existed. What was fact was membership conferred mystical abilities beyond those who didn't join.

Paladins were different. It was etched into the soul by the Gods themselves and couldn't be changed by a Guild. Rumors persisted that Paladins were not unique in this arrangement, though no one had any idea what those professions may be. So when he registered as a Warrior, the Guild saw him as a Warrior; the mystical process that changed a person wouldn't touch or override his status as a Paladin.

That's when Erinne informed him of the odd necrotic pulse from the far west of the Empire that she wanted him to investigate. Based on her description, it was the town he now found himself in. He was directionless and had no plans of his own, so he decided to follow along with the suggestion of the Goddess.

After buying his chain hauberk from a cheap second hand store and another item he splurged on, he was down to three silver coins. Two of those silver coins he gave away the moment he entered town and the third was spent on the stable boy. Gerold's charity got the best of him and he was now entirely broke.

The guild had a posting for a crypt that opened up near the area Erinne had pointed him toward and a five man crew had registered. This was the best clue he had going for him. He discovered a merchant was preparing to go to Wren's End and Gerold managed to convince the merchant to allow him to tag along, though he wasn't too happy given Gerold's appearance. He probably wouldn't have allowed it at all had the five who registered for the quest had not also suggested assisting in the escort.

He pulled his attention away from the training field and

moved toward the Guild Hall. He pushed inside and saw an identical layout to the one in the main capital. To his left was a request board. One request was engraved permanently on a bronze plaque attached to the board. This was for the goblin bounty the Guild Hall wanted the new adventurers to focus on for training. Others were on wooden boards. These were time or quantity limited requests, such as orders for medicinal herbs. The third type was a paper request. This allowed for parties to take them for registration since it made little sense to have people competing for them. They ranged from specific monster quelling requests all the way down to helping repair fencing for spending money.

To the right of the board was the guild reception. The remainder of the room was dominated by a common room with two dozen tables, set with five chairs apiece with five enchanted lights suspended from the ceiling above. A large fireplace dominated the wall to the right. Being early spring, it had small fire that was dwarfed by the cavernous opening that could accommodate more wood now that the harsh winter had ended. The rear of the building was the stairway leading to higher floors and a bar with a door leading to the kitchens.

The room was boisterous. Trainees were animatedly talking about the courses they took during the day, apparently the guild had a separate classroom building elsewhere in the village, and others were talking about encounters with goblins in the forest. The room smelled of cheap beer and cheaper food, sour odors spilled on the wooden floor mixed with the fresher smells. A friendly, harried server was moving between the tables providing food and drink to the trainees finished for the day.

Guilds served cheap fare for visiting adventurers. In villages like this, Guild Halls intentionally served only the most basic of fare to avoid competing with the local economy. In the capital, the Guild Hall was a well regarded culinary center, though they also restricted services to members only so no establishments in the capital felt any competitive pressure.

The walls were one element that was unique to each Hall with various trophies and engraved plates glorifying local achievements. This Hall, being a training center, had a large board next to the fireplace indicating training rankings for the season's class, broken down into magical, melee combat, ranged combat and support categories.

Gerold noticed a crowd gathered around a central table. It was the five adventurers that he arrived with earlier in the day. The man with the plate armor was regaling the crowd with stories of his achievements. However, his espionage training screamed that this man was a habitual liar. Gerold didn't think anything was nefarious about it. The man came off as an adult version of the two children at the gates, an underlying insecure man attempting to cover up his deficiencies with bravado and a show of wealth. Everyone had taken him to be a Paladin when it was obvious to anyone that paid attention he was not.

Not that he needed espionage training to spot the embellishment. Their fight with the bandits that accosted them on the road was, to be charitable, sloppy. The five of them only survived because the man's equipment vastly outstripped the poor bandits that ambushed them. Desperate men in rags with rusted blades aren't going to perform well against an inexperienced man in plate.

It was the four guardsmen that proved more challenging. They were better equipped than the party of five and more competent at that. Their big mistake, however, was assuming Gerold was just some weird bum along for the ride. They ignored his presence, which allowed him to attack from the rear, throwing their plan into confusion. His attack on two of the guards in the rear caught the attention of the Lancer Elf who turned just in time to dodge an incoming attack.

By this point, the guard and his remaining compatriot were overwhelmed by the party who had cleared the distraction and turned on the guards.

The man came off as a wealthy noble's son playing at hero and the party with him was no better. They were probably just his friends. The Leopardia woman was the most competent of the bunch. An idle mind is not capable of weaving magic. Still her spells were slow, her movements unsteady and her spells simple. She also failed to demonstrate any spells that required the expenditure of an Adventurer Coin. She used simple distraction cantrips, basic spells that used ambient magic and could be cast without taking on a Class at the Adventurer's Guild. She had the most promise of the bunch and would, in time, improve with confidence and experience.

Ignoring the group, he walked up to the registration counter. The man behind the counter, a young human in a guild administration uniform, barely hid his disgust at Gerold's appearance.

"Can I help you…sir," he woodenly droned.

Gerold pulled out his guild token from his pouch, a cheap wooden thing with an ID code wrapped in tiny numbers across the surface. The material signified he was the lowest rank.

The tokens were a marvel of magical creation. They could transmute themselves to different materials as they gained ranks with the guild, contained the identifying information of the holder and couldn't be lost or stolen. Throw the thing in a river and it would reappear in the owner's pocket within an hour. A guild token was the ultimate in proof of identity.

The man sighed, took the token and inspected it, acting as if it was a fake. He put his hand under the counter and looked for a few moments, "They'll let anyone in these days. What can I help you with?"

"A room please," Gerold grunted in reply. He wasn't upset by the treatment. If anything, he was silently pleased.

The man let out another groan, "Wood Rank. I take it you're here to train your skills? You'll have to wait until next season since the current classes have already begun."

The man clearly didn't want him around.

"Of a sort," Gerold replied, "I'd rather work on my skills in the wild."

The man's lips thinned, "Either way, Wood Rank is qualified for free room and board. Breakfast and supper only."

He turned and looked at the key board behind him. Over half the rooms were available with the top three floors completely empty. The man reached for a key on the fourth floor then paused. His hand then ranged to the top of the board to a key at the far right before turning it and dropping it on the counter. He wrote the information on the token down in a ledger along with the details on the key.

The man put both down on the counter, "Your room is the top floor all the way at the end."

Gerold felt a tinge of annoyance this time since he was being segregated as far away as possible and the man actively wants to inconvenience him. He held his tongue, knowing this is still intentionally invited on his part.

The man looked him up and down once more, "And if you can afford it, maybe after a few goblin ears, may I suggest visiting the baths? They are across the central plaza and only cost a silver. The barber can also work on that hair."

Gerold swept the key and token into his pouch, "I'll think about it."

He looked over the central eating area. Gerold decided to

take advantage of the free meal before ascending to his room, which he knew would annoy the arrogant administrator. The guild had an extensive subsidy system to help new adventurers get on their feet. Wood rank was entitled to free room and board while each subsequent rank-up became more expensive for the same services which stood in for guild dues. Not that it mattered much since the income higher ranks could command was more than enough to offset the small tax.

He found an open table at the perimeter of the area, well away from the trainees gathered around the popular party. The man was showing off his Iron token.

"How did he get that," a voice in his head startled him.

"He comes off as a rich noble. His family probably bought it," Gerold murmured quietly to avoid causing a scene in the room. He couldn't act too oddly like he did in the streets since that would attract more attention in the Guild Hall instead of repelling townspeople.

"And the guild allows that?"

"Money opens all doors. His family probably hired unscrupulous adventurers to gather the monster parts necessary to trigger a rank up. The guild doesn't have a system in place to know who killed the monster, only if the part is authentic or not."

"Where does that rank?"

"For a God, you're surprisingly ignorant of the world."

"You know we can't just look in. I can observe broad trends, movements of magic and other macro things you can't comprehend. Gods need a conduit like clerics and prayer to know anything about culture and events. I can't understand that stuff looking down on the world from above, at least until I was able to form our connection."

"I get it. Wood, Pewter, Copper, Iron, Steel, Silver, Gold, Platinum, Orichalcum and Mythril. That's the order."

"What's that hon," the server said to his side, concerned about this strange man talking to himself. She was a plain woman with a touch of fat and good muscle tone on her arms. She was in her late 30s, had brown hair and friendly eyes. She wore a blue dress protected by a stained apron.

Gerold pulled out his wood token and put it on the table, "Sorry, just reviewing the ranks. I'm still new."

She nodded in approval, "I get it. Everyone starts off new. I know Allan was rude to ya, but I figure you'll get on yer feet in no time and look more presentable. I'm impressed yer starting at yer age."

Gerold smiled, "Thanks. Can I get something to eat?"

"Sure, yer entitled to a free meal, but it's gonna be bad and the beer is barely more than beer flavored water."

It didn't matter if the beer was strong or weak, his passive resistance to common toxins had made it so he couldn't get drunk, much to his chagrin at times like this, "That's fine."

She smiled, "I'll be back in a bit."

Gerold continued to observe the Iron rank party, his training picking up on the constant lying coming from all of them, except for the Leopardia woman who looked uncomfortable being there. He also noticed another solo adventurer at a different table. Unlike the rest of the room enamored by the celebrities, this adventurer had taken to staring at him.

She was a Mountain Elf. Her skin was pale and she had rich brown hair that was tied back in a tail. Her brown almond eyes were fixed on him. She wore leather armor on her upper torso with a dark green shirt underneath. Her long, bare arms, thin, well toned and defined musculature were folded on the table along with an unstrung recurve bow and a rapier in a sheath.

Gerold was concerned by this attention. It was uncomfortable being stared at and she had an expression of anger and disgust plastered on her face. She couldn't have noticed his status as a Paladin since his only detectable aura, Calm Nerves, was inactive.

The server thankfully returned quickly with his meal of an oat gruel and thin beer. He quickly wolfed it down. Before retreating to his room, he noticed the Mountain Elf woman had quietly disappeared from the common room. Since he was positioned near the stairs and didn't see her pass, she had left the Hall entirely. He wondered where she could be going this time of night.

Climbing the stairs was more of an annoyance than a struggle after what the Temple put him through in Paladin training. Closing the door, he surveyed the room. It contained a simple bed with only a thin sheet covering a straw mattress, a small bedside dresser on which was perched a magic stone lantern. The lantern was set to a low setting, allowing ambient magic to recharge the device while still retaining dim light for those entering at night. Otherwise, the room was bare with nothing more than a single window with thick, light-blocking shutters closed tight.

Sitting on the bed, Gerold opened his magic pouch. He pulled out a hand mirror and a small wooden box. Looking at his reflection in the mirror, he pulled at his hair. It began to separate at his scalp, revealing close cut rich chocolate brown hair underneath. The healthy sheen of his natural hair conflicted with the ratty grey of the wig. He similarly pulled his beard off, revealing a clean shaven face.

"Why do you wear those things," the voice of Erinne echoed in his head.

"It's the curse."

"What curse? Paladins always look young, can live hundreds of years, never get sick, don't lose teeth and never get dirty. You don't even need to shave or cut your hair."

"I see that as a curse. I'm a 49 year old man that looks like an artist is trying to flatter me with an overly perfect portrait. I look like I'm 18, lived a life of a pampered noble and spend a small village's annual income on cosmetics."

"That doesn't explain why you look like a bum. You never had that long ratty hair even before the blessing fully activated."

Gerold folded the two hair pieces and slipped them in the box, sealed it and returned it to the bag, "It's how I feel. I don't want to look at a young, fresh face in the mirror. I still haven't had time to mourn."

Erinne didn't respond to that for a good while. When she finally did, her voice was somber and apologetic, "I'm sorry. I'm not good at understanding mortals. None of us really are. Death and loss are alien to us."

Gerold grunted, "It's fine. It takes time getting used to how we live. You never did say why you made the world this way."

Erinne's tone turned evasive, "I certainly didn't. I can't tell you."

"Can't or won't?"

"Can't. Sorry, even a supreme being has limits and this is one of them."

Gerold grunted.

Erinne continued, "Look, I have some major things to take care of. While I may not have a domain as you understand it, the fabric of reality does need to be maintained and that is my job. I'm going to disappear for a while and won't be able to respond. Just be sure to find the origin of that necrotic pulse. It's well beyond the parameters I'd expect to see on Alios."

Gerold grunted again, "Sure, I'll remember."

She didn't respond and was already gone. He was used to her lack of social graces which he assumed didn't exist in her realm. Erinne would only stick around to talk to him for a few days before vanishing again. Over the past six months, she only spent a cumulative four weeks occupying his brain. He couldn't expect a God, especially the one who created all of reality, to have nothing better to do than talk to him. Not even the other Gods had the capacity to hold conversations with random mortals.

Alone with his thoughts again, he felt both a sense of relief and sadness. It felt like a long time to him and he wondered how Erinne experienced time. Was it just a few moments in the life of a being that has been around for an unknown amount of time? Trying to comprehend the concept of existing for an infinite amount of time in the past, having no origin or birth and just "being" made his head hurt.

The loneliness then hit him hard. For the first time since being rescued from the wreckage of his home without brutal training or a nagging Goddess in his head to occupy his attention, his mind wandered back to that fateful day.

Everything about it was incongruent. It was a sunny, warm early autumn day as he surveyed his fields of carrots, peas and spinach that would be preserved for the coming winter. A crisp breeze blew out of the west and ruffled his scruffy hair. He had noticed the silvers were expanding across his brown mop. All things considered, silver was the best option it could turn. He figured it would make him look more distinguished, at least as distinguished a farmer could get. The crop was looking good and he was anticipating an excellent harvest.

His older son, Malrin, exited their two room farmhouse and stood next to his father. He had a goofy grin on his face. The twelve year old boy had helped plant the autumn harvest for the first time in his life. Gerold was proud of the boy for doing such a fine job. The two planned to walk the fields to search for signs of weeds. He had checked the fencing the day before and reported back no problems with the wire to keep out small animals. Gerold had gone in behind him later to confirm and was happy to see his boy did a thorough job.

Gerold's wife, Zelina, came out of the house with their four year old daughter Elli. Zelina gave a smile and Elli gave an exaggerated wave. The two were going to collect eggs over at the chicken coop.

Or at least that was the plan for the day. Before any of them could go about their daily chores, a low whine echoed over the prairie their farm was situated in. In the direction of the village center a few miles to the south, a strange black cloud erupted from the horizon and spread like a sinister canopy toward his farm.

At this point in his memory, Gerold tore himself back to the reality of his room. He couldn't continue thinking about it and shoved it down deep, hoping to forget. Tears came to his eyes and he put his face in his hands. He fought against a memory of his Father giving a lesson to him about men crying, choking on tears and refusing to allow any sound to come from his mouth. He never did take that lesson well.

Reaching over, he turned off the lamp then curled up in to a ball, ignoring the cooling night air seeping through the cracks in the shutters and not bothering with pulling his fur blanket from the bag. He went to sleep, hoping for a dreamless slumber.

CHAPTER 3

Thankfully, Gerold's night was uneventful. No dreams interrupted his sleep, though he didn't feel particularly rested. After spending a few minutes reapplying his fake hair and beard, he was ready to approach the day.

The first order of business was earning some money. Thinking back on his charity, he realized that was foolish given how far a silver coin stretched out in these parts. For all the benefits the guild provided, travel gear was not one of them. The reported crypt he wanted to investigate was three days travel from Wren's End. Provisions cost money. In the economy here, he figured that he'd need 80 copper coins – three days of provisions out, three days back and two days as buffer while on site. He would also need some coins to cast his healing spells.

After taking advantage of more thin gruel and stale bread for breakfast, Gerold wandered over to the Guild job board. The paper requests were mostly odd jobs and Gerold didn't think he could emotionally handle farm work. Wooden requests were herb gathering requests which Gerold knew nothing about. That left the sole engraved bronze plaque.

Goblin culling. Two copper coins for each left ear returned. Gerold already knew that this was unnecessary and any part would do. However, Guilds liked to request specific parts to reinforce a mechanism built in to the device used to convert the parts into money. It didn't like being cheated and if you brought back multiple parts of the same monster, it would cancel it out and produce nothing in return. By requesting a specific part of the creature, it would help adventuring parties avoid making the mistake of collecting random parts from the same monster, especially if it was hard to tell what was taken after mauling it in battle.

In truth, this was the optimal way to earn money. Sure, the paper requests and herb gathering paid significantly more and were safer, but killing monsters had additional benefits. While scholars don't know why, and Erinne refused to answer when he asked, killing monsters strengthens the body and mind. Not in the same way swinging a hoe on a farm will build muscles or reading a book will train the mind. There is something mystical.

The other reason was monster culling paid in Adventurer Coins, which were critical to activate abilities and fuel complex enchantments. The other requests usually only paid with normal coins that the common people traded with. Anyone who traded with Adventurers ended up with the more desired Adventurer Coins. Shops that didn't trade in adventurer gear or rely on enchantments would even give adventurers discounts since the coins would sell for more in mundane currency, not that Adventurers would regularly trade with a candle maker or woodcutter.

And that's where the Guild Token came into play. A traveler killing a random monster on the road did nothing. He had to have a token for his underlying power to grow. And the typical person never got a token because of how dangerous it was. This was because of Town Seeds keeping monsters out of established settlements. Frontiers still had farmers and other people who made a living outside the confines of a safe town and they would also train as adventurers. Those communities were becoming less common as the frontiers were tamed with Town Seeds.

Killing a mana-formed monster infuses a person with small amounts of power. The more powerful the target, the more power is infused in the individual who contributed to killing it. No one has been able to successfully measure how this works. It seems to fluctuate along a myriad of different factors. Some types of adventuring jobs, like Warriors, seem to accumulate strength faster than others. What is killed is important as is the relative difference in strength. Fell something tremendously more powerful, get a bigger boost. Conversely, a powerful adventurer hanging out at Wren's End killing goblins day in, day out will see nothing in return. Risk equals reward.

This process would enhance the body and mind beyond what mundane training could accomplish, gain insight on new ways to weave magic and even grant special abilities depending on what jobs the person undertook. A Mage would suddenly learn how to manipulate mana on a finer level or a Rogue would suddenly be able to subtly alter the movement of light to better hide in shadows. Spells and skills always came as a form of divine inspiration, though such inspiration didn't convey immediate competence. It also came with a gentle physical and mental feeling of refreshment, fatigue gone in an instant.

Erinne would only hint there was a reason why this was and she wasn't allowed to say. Gerold found it odd that an all-powerful creator of existence couldn't discuss things.

Setting that aside, he had another issue. One of the things he was not entirely honest about with Erinne was why he dressed like he did. Sure, there was truth that this is how he feels. His other reason was he didn't want the attention. Paladins were rare. They were worshipped almost like the Gods themselves in the Empire. And Gerold was a tremendous introvert. He didn't even meet Zelina until his mid-30s. The last thing he wanted was a group of people congregating around him like the party the night before. His flawless appearance attracted way too much attention since people ended up thinking he was a rich noble playing poor adventurer or, worse, properly deduced his true nature.

And his efforts at dissuading attention were too effective. He would have to reconsider disguising himself as a disgusting vagrant and go for below average adventurer. He couldn't alter his appearance now and avoid unwanted attention.

And why did this suddenly become a problem? His gross vagrant persona shut the door on getting a group. Hunting monsters solo was incredibly dangerous. Even simple monsters like goblins could potentially overwhelm an adventurer. Sure, he did train against skilled fighters and even had lessons on mismatched group combat, but the real world was always going to be more risky than even the harshest of training. His only saving grace was that goblins were little more than animals and were so savage that they couldn't form bands of more than five to ten individuals.

Sighing, he went up to the guild registration desk. A Dwarf was working the desk this time, who gave him a similar look as the man the night before. After what felt like pulling teeth, Gerold got a few locations in the forest a few hours from town where goblins formed. The Dwarf was easier to deal with than the man the night before because he had grown up with one and knew some of the tricks to getting on a Dwarf's good side.

Another one of the strange aspects of the world was monsters didn't just reproduce the normal way like people did. What made the wilds outside of the zone of a Town Seed was the fact monsters could manifest out of nothing. No one has ever observed this process since it seems that it doesn't work when actively watched. Go away for a day and a forest that was completely cleared of some monsters will be filled back up again. Leave it alone and normal reproduction, which adventurers have had the misfortune of walking in on, can eventually overwhelm an area. Oddly, those monsters never strayed far from their point of origin. Scholars couldn't ever figure out why, but it made identifying training and valuable Adventurer Coin generating regions easier.

Gerold walked out of town and headed further west toward the forest at the base of the Bear Teeth Mountains. The day was still early with the sun barely peeking over the eastern horizon, bathing the area in a warm, dim red light.

Walking down a well-trod road cutting through two fields that farmers were either maintaining or planting the spring harvest, Gerold made sure to keep his eyes laser focused on the road ahead. Even getting a glimpse of a farm reminded him of his former life.

To the north was a river that was fed by smaller tributaries coming out of the mountains. This time of year would have little to no activity at the small port since it was not harvest season. He had to take a longer land route since no barges were coming upriver. Farming communities were isolated from the outside world for much of the growing periods.

As he traveled, he kept getting the sense he was being watched. The few times he turned to look around, he noticed farmers staring as he passed. He turned on his Detect Evil aura, felt nothing and turned it off again. He disregarded the feeling as paranoia.

He reached the forest after two hours. The break between farm and forest was stark. Tilled fields stopped along a perfectly straight line and then the land was picked up by tall trees that marked the extent of the protective barrier of town. It was the same back at Gerold's home where his farm was at the outer border of the protective barrier.

The forest was the perfect setting for a classic story to scare children. The ground was thick with shrubbery and dry pine needles. The tall, thickly packed conifer trees blocked sunlight from reaching the ground below, casting the whole forest in a gloom. The gloom would likely get worse as the day drew on as the morning sunlight had a better angle to breach the interior from this point. Further in, the underbrush began to thin, marking the extent the morning light was able to reach.

Before stepping over the border between farm and forest where the road abruptly stopped, Gerold activated his Sense Evil aura and it expanded out 100 yards. Another strange element of reality he learned in his training is that all monsters have some degree of evil in them. There was no correlation between how much evil was present and the type of monster. Wyverns, which he also learned weren't related to dragons, were about as intensely evil as goblins. Yet wyverns were intelligent and crafty while goblins were chaotic and incapable of basic planning. He could, when he grew more powerful, evaluate the strength of an evil being through his aura.

Gerold hoped that this aura would mitigate his poor awareness. He wasn't trained in those senses and hadn't even stepped foot in a forest until passing through one on a road to the capital a few months prior. Using the aura to identify those meaning him harm wasn't entirely reliable since a good or neutral person could be deceived into believing a Paladin was an evil force and attack without evil intent, though that was unlikely here.

A year ago, he would have been terrified of stepping into a forest to seek out goblins, especially alone. After what happened six months ago, something changed his sense of self-preservation. Walking into this forest felt like nothing. Not like walking out to pull weeds in his fields, that either generated irritation or a sense of pride depending on the day. This was true nothing, as if his safety and well being was entirely irrelevant.

He dismissed the self-reflection on his emotional state, or lack thereof, and strode into the woods.

Gerold walked for an hour aimlessly through the forest. All the information he was able to pull out of the guild rep was that the forest due west of the town had the highest goblin activity. He didn't run across any bands and he left early enough to beat the later rush. This lack of density did, however, make this region a good training ground since there was little risk of being overrun.

He did, however, have that persistent sense of being watched. Nothing triggered his sense evil aura and his periodic scans around him noticed nothing. The forest gloom was difficult to see through, like a shadowy alley in a city, broken up here and there by rays of light that poked through gaps in the canopy. Where could anyone hide when there was no underbrush this deep into the forest? His senses had to be going haywire.

The only real evidence things were fine, along with his aura, was the chorus of birds singing in the forest. He also heard the occasional distant crunch of small animals fleeing his passing to go along with his own tamping on the dried needle carpet below. Additionally, there was an uncomfortable chill in the air as the sunlight failed to penetrate below, amplifying the already cold early spring.

He continued walking. Gerold almost missed a change when the birds stopped singing and the forest went deathly quiet. He mused how odd it is that a person will notice when a sound starts yet will never notice when a persistent sound stops.

Then he got a hit. In the city, he had to keep his aura of sense evil off. It was constantly warning him. A population that dense was going to inevitably have evil people in it. Worse, it only gave a vague direction of where the evil was originating and how intense it was. He could test an individual for evil by activating it nearby while looking at the target and seeing if he got a hit from that direction. Knowing who it is without having a suspicion? Near impossible. Not that he could walk up to a stranger and accuse him of being evil if he did know.

His aura produced a clear beacon in the forest. He sensed evil to the east, back in the direction of town. Knowing it was 100 yards out, he pulled his hammer and moved in the direction he sensed. He dispensed with any semblance of stealth since the needles were too dry and noisy to mask his approach. The forest was thick with trees and he wasn't able to see more than 20 yards out.

Gerold would periodically shift himself left to right to see how much the sense would shift. His training told him that this was the only reliable way to tell distance. He can tell direction but he'd have to estimate distance by the degree the sense moved when he did.

Not that he needed much because whatever it is heard his crunching. A loud, high pitched cacophony erupted in the distance and the crunching of footsteps started streaming his direction. Readying himself to engage in a fighting retreat, he waited.

The goblins streamed into view through the trees. The creatures were short, naked, hairless, gaunt and had ashen grey skin. Both genders in this small band were present, flapping ugly, shriveled mockeries of sapient reproductive features over thin bodies that showed exposed bones. Sharp yellowed nails sprouted out of their four digit hands and feet. The sharp teeth grew out of their mouths in an irregular, crooked pattern. And, had Gerold kept his sense of self preservation, the wild, bloodshot eyes would have been enough to make him flee in terror.

Instead, he waited. Goblins were savage, stupid creatures.

They each sprinted as fast as they could in his direction, creating a line as the different running speed of each individual created space between the goblins. Quickly checking a direction he could run through the trees with minimal side movements, he began slowly jogging sideways to reduce the relative distance the first goblin was closing on him. His evil aura now felt like he was surrounded because of how close they were.

As the first goblin entered his striking range, he picked up his jogging pace and quickly rammed the spike on his weapon into the creature's head. It fell limp on the ground and skidded to a stop. He continued jogging. A second entered his range and he repeated his move, then a third and a fourth. He wasn't sure how many were left. A fifth and sixth went down and he noticed no more were in pursuit. He had stretched the goblins over a 50 yard range.

Things were quiet now. A few moments went by with nothing happening and Gerold felt his adrenaline dump. While he still didn't feel fear, he was mildly nauseous from the unfamiliar experience of running and fighting. The real thing was fast, brutal and tiring, betraying the limits of even the most brutal of training in the face of real world experience. The feeling of evil didn't dissipate. He dismissed the concern of the sense of lingering evil when he remembered his training. Evil entities were detected by the mana in the body, which was subtly altered based on a person's base nature. When something died, the stored mana would continue to dissipate for hours after death until the internal mana everything was made of was exhausted.

There was another part of his training he forgot when he felt himself violently bowled over from behind – once surrounded by evil, he couldn't tell if new evil individuals approached. A high pitched scream pierced his ears along with sharp objects clawing at the side of his head. The attacker rolled off him from the momentum of the tackle and Gerold flipped over to his back. Before he could do anything, the mass was immediately back on him again.

Straddling him was another goblin. This one, for whatever reason, wasn't with its band and had returned from wherever it had been. His reliance on his evil detection aura proved his undoing. The thing straddled his chest and he found he was unable to get proper leverage to throw it off. He still held his hammer, but his arms were too long to hit his assailant. All he could do was use his left arm to hold the creature far enough away to avoid the swiping yellow nails, a sour odor that reminded Gerold of spoiled milk wafted from the creature and assaulted his nose.

He continued trying to buck the savage creature off him and continued to fail in his attempts. He felt his arm tiring as the nasty yellow nails started digging into his scalp and across his face. He felt oddly at peace. He wasn't quite sure how he could go on living. A Paladin's soul didn't mean much when it belonged to an aged farmer with nothing to live for.

Preparing to let go and accept his fate, he had just closed his eyes when the screaming mass suddenly went silent. Looking back up, he saw the creature slack on his arm, dripping black oozing blood on his face where an arrow had grown from the side of its head. Finally able to push the body off, he rolled over and stood up.

From around a tree stepped the Mountain Elf that was staring at him the night before. She was taller than he was and moved with practiced grace.

She looked him up and down, "You're crazy, you know that?"

Gerold shrugged, "I've been called worse."

Her eyes narrowed, "I knew it. You're not what you seem."

Gerold pulled out a utility knife from his pouch and kneeled over the goblin with the now broken arrow protruding from it and cut off the left ear. He extended the ear in her direction, "Here, this is yours."

Snatching the ear away she shouted, "Are you serious? You were almost killed and that's your response?"

Gerold was taken aback, "Thanks?"

"Not that. Well, that, but what's wrong with you? You don't seem to care about dying."

Gerold grunted, "Not much to care about."

"Uh huh," she bent down and picked something up off the ground and held it out, "It seems you do care. Why would you hide yourself with this silly thing?"

Gerold looked in her hand and saw the mangled remains of the fake beard he had been wearing. Sighing, he pulled his mirror out and looked at his reflection. A deep gash crossed his chin and he also noticed his brown hair poking out from under his now damaged wig.

He pulled it off and deposited the remains in his bag, "Great, this makes things more complicated."

"You're the Paladin, aren't you," the woman asked.

"Is it that obvious?"

"Only if you pay attention to the details. I picked up that something was off with you when you walked in last night."

"What gave me away?"

She tapped her nose, "You don't have an odor. Everyone smells of something. You? No one who tangled with something that foul should be clean. That goblin blood slid off your clothing. Plus, now that the disguise is gone, you're amazingly attractive."

Gerold nodded, brushing off the weird compliment at the end of her statement, "That is true. I can hide my hair, I can draw the eye away from my perfect skin and teeth, but I can't fake smell. I've doused myself in skunk spray and it just sloughs off. I can dip my clothing in it and the odor vanishes after I put it on."

"Why do this?"

"I don't want the attention. I didn't want to be a Paladin at all."

Her face screwed up in confusion, "What? Why would the Gods pick someone who didn't want it?"

He shrugged and pointed at his necklace, "Ask her."

"Erinne? What? No one would believe that. With that disguise, I figure you're a Paladin of Pellius. A bad one."

Gerold smiled sadly, "That's what the Temple said and made me take classes. No point in arguing it."

"You're a Paladin of Pellius then."

"I just said there's no point in arguing it."

The woman slapped her head, "You're infuriating. You don't care about your life but you care about hiding your identity and now you have this stupid story about the Recluse Queen being your patron."

"Believe what you want."

"Aren't you going to ask about me?"

"Why?"

"Isn't that what Paladins do? Be friendly, show interest in others, dive into trouble and help?"

"You want me to act like that puffed up noble from last night?"

She sighed again, "You're killing the mystique. You are one awful Paladin."

Gerold shrugged again, "As you've already said and I'm not debating it."

She put her hand out, noticed she was still holding the ear, shoved it in her hip pouch and put her hand out again, "I'm Niitty, rookie Ranger of the Hirvi Clan."

Gerold looked at her hand a moment before half-heartedly gripping it, "Gerold, Paladin of Erinne."

She winked, "Sure."

He left Niitty behind and began cutting ears off the goblins. He grumbled to himself. It was noon and all he had were six ears. He'd need 34 more of the things.

"Is that it," he heard her call.

"What? You want more of a reward?"

She stamped her foot in frustration, "No you idiot, I want to form a party with you."

He stopped cutting, "Why?"

Her mood suddenly shifted and her face reddened, "Because no one else wants to and it looks like you need one."

"That's odd. You're a great shot and I didn't hear you tailing me. I'm sure you can handle goblins just fine."

"Just the first one. When the rest notice me, I'd be in trouble."

Gerold moved to the next goblin, "I'm sure someone needs ranged support."

She had followed him and said something he couldn't hear.

"What was that," he asked.

She raised her volume to where Gerold could barely hear her, "No one likes me."

Gerold shoved the next ear into his pouch, "And you called me deceptive."

Niitty flushed again, "It's true. I'm a completely different person in town. I'm terrified of crowds and cities. I become withdrawn and prickly when in the city. The only reason I noticed you at all was you were a void in that place. All those odors were overwhelming and here you were sucking them in and erasing them."

Gerold thought that Wren's End was hardly a city and she would struggle in the capital. He did remember her having an angry expression on her face the night before.

Walking to finish up his trophy collection, Gerold said, "Let's try this out on a trial basis. I've quickly realized that if I'm to succeed at anything, I can't do it alone."

Niitty shrieked in joy, "Yay! My first friend. And someone my age, too!"

Gerold snorted, "I think friend is a bit too early isn't it? And I'm 49."

"What? No, you can't be."

Gerold shrugged, "The curse of being a Paladin. We can live hundreds of years and we look young the entire time."

She hummed to herself indicating she didn't believe a word he said, "Anyway, I think we need to get to hunting. You missed a whole mess of goblins tromping around the woods. You're not much of a tracker."

He cut the final ear off the goblin, "No, I guess I'm not."

CHAPTER 4

After sharing some nuts she scrounged up in the forest, Niitty suggested the two of them return to town for the day instead of swinging back to the missed goblin bands. Gerold's wandering had wasted most of the day and he had ranged far enough that he barely had time to get back to the protected walls by sundown.

As they approached the town, he noticed the growing discomfort of his new companion.

"I'm here for support if you need it," Gerold said in an attempt to sooth her concern. He only got a wooden nod in return.

"You know, I'm worried, too," Gerold confided in Niitty.

She looked over and replied in the same quiet, meek voice he heard earlier in the day, "What? Why?"

Gerold waved his hands over his body, "This morning, I walked out of town looking like an old vagrant. Now, I look like a city debutant wearing vagrant clothing."

She looked at his face, stared at his eyes and blushed, "Well, you do have pretty eyes."

Gerold grunted in response which got a small chuckle out of Niitty.

She continued, "I'm impressed that all that blood that dripped off the goblin on you just sort of fell off. Even the cut on your chin looks like it was dressed by a skilled medic."

"It's the curse."

"You keep calling those blessings a curse."

"Because it is."

"Care to share why?"

"No."

She dropped it there. Gerold wasn't sure if it was social graces kicking in or her fear of the town overwhelming her natural personality as they reached the gate checkpoint.

As they approached, the two gate guards at the edge of town stared at him, slack jawed. Niitty was a striking woman herself, but his own divine touched appearance overshadowed it. The two guards could only murmur as he passed.

Walking through town garnered a similar reaction and the unwanted attention that came with it. Here he was, dressed like a bum that stepped out of a salon catering to noblemen. He, sort of, understood how Niitty felt. He glanced over at her and noticed a sour, angry expression on her face, covering up her nervousness at being in town. Her eyes darted around and he noticed sweat beading on her forehead. Her chest heaved up and down rapidly as if she regarded herself as infiltrating enemy territory and any random townsperson would attack. Gerold knew his expression matched hers, but for a different reason. This at least kept the townspeople at a distance.

The two sour faced pretty people made their way to the Guild Hall and entered. It was late afternoon so the Hall was lightly populated with adventurers either still hunting in the forest or out in the training yard. Still, there were enough people present to notice the sudden hush as the two walked in and an uncomfortable number of eyes point in their direction.

Doing their best to ignore the attention, they walked up to

the counter. Gerold noticed Allan, the unpleasant man from the night before. Now his demeanor was completely different.

His face was one of concern when he laid eyes on Gerold, "Sir, are you well? Do you need medical assistance? Those cuts on your face look awful and your clothing is a mess."

Gerold grunted, "I'm fine, we just need to turn in some ears."

Allan pulled out a wooden box from beneath the counter, "Please, place them in here and I'll tabulate the payment."

Gerold shoved his hand in his pouch and willed the ears out of the strange space within. He always hated putting his hand in there, it felt cold and unwelcoming. He dropped his six ears into the box while Niitty added her own ear. Gerold glanced at her and her expression indicated that she thought of this as a party effort.

Putting his hand out, he said, "I'll also need your tokens to register the accomplishment."

Niitty put hers down first and the man pulled out a different object from below the counter. It was a strange device. A box made out of a pitch black material that shifted between polished obsidian and blackened metal. At the top center of the box were five depressions, each surrounded by a gold ring. They were shaped like the guild tokens. The bottom portion was a large, blank rectangular space surrounded by a thin gold border just like the depression. A strange wand made of the same material was connected to the device by a chain also made of the same material.

Niitty handed her token over first. It, like Gerold's, was made of wood. Placing it in the depression, information appeared in the blank space in fancy gold lettering.

Niitty of the Hirvi Clan, Wood Rank Ranger, ID 042778722526R92

Gerold though this must have been what Allan used the night before to check his guild status before allowing him to stay. Gerold handed his own over and Allan placed it in the second slot. Two more lines appeared and the slate now read:

Unregistered Party
Niitty of the Hirvi Clan, Wood Rank Ranger, ID 042778722526R92
Gerold of Hivastock, Wood Rank Warrior, ID 042778722525W41

Allan was taken aback when he saw this pop up, "How strange. You both registered at the same time."

Niitty found the wooden countertop more interesting and wasn't paying attention, so Gerold responded, "How can you tell?"

He pointed at the two ID numbers, "The numbers are sequential. There have been an immense number of adventurers in the world in history. Two people in line at one hall can register and have numbers hundreds of digits apart. Yours though? You two registered at different halls at almost the exact same time, it must be fate you're in a party here."

Allan waved the wand over the ears in the box. Gerold watched in fascination as the ears turned into an odd mist, faded out of existence and were replaced by 14 copper coins. He had never seen this process before. The odd box was a relic made of a strange divine material that converted monster parts into money.

Gerold had only ever used an Adventurer Coin once in his life for his Father's funerary rites. Simple farmers like himself would only ever use Imperial coinage. Guild coins were too valuable for other things to pass through a farmer's hands.

Allan pushed the box with the coins over, "Do you wish to

register your party?"

"No, I don't think so," Gerold replied. When he did, he heard a quick exhale from Niitty. He turned and he saw a mild look of hurt on her face.

Allan returned the two tokens, "And would you like a room, sir? Your companion has already indicated she has alternate accommodations."

Gerold chuckled, "I already have one."

"Oh? I'm sure I would have recalled one of your status coming through."

Gerold just smiled, took the coins and walked away with Niitty in tow.

After putting a few paces away from the counter, he spoke softly to Niitty, "Do you want to take advantage of the free meal or do you want to head out of town?"

Her eyes turned down toward the floor and moved back and forth a few times. She turned her face to his, "Food first, then I'll go."

"Then I'll join you. A friendly face, whatever it's worth, may help make this more comfortable."

Niitty gravitated toward an empty table at the perimeter of the floor in the quietest corner of the room. She positioned herself with her back to the wall so she could watch over the room, which included a view of both the stairway up to the rooms and the entrance. It was a typical five man circle table and Gerold sat with one chair empty between them to avoid crowding her. She seemed to approve of giving her a bit of space, quite different than how she preferred to stand close when outside of town.

The same server that Gerold had the night before came over.

"Nice to see ya again," she said, directing her eyes at Niitty, "I hope yer a bit more comfortable tonight."

Niitty nodded and put her token on the table without a word.

The server then looked at Gerold, "And it's nice to see a new…hmm, have we met before?"

Gerold put his token on the table as well. She picked it up and examined it. Her eyes then lit up, "My, ya look quite a bit different."

Gerold felt his eyebrows turn up in surprise, "You have impressive observational skills."

She smiled and pointed at her eye with a finger, "It's the eyes. An old man with those amazing eyes is hard to miss and this is the same token. The disguise is effective fer the most part, but I don't judge armor by its shine. Ya must have a good reason why yer not in it tonight."

Gerold looked around. People weren't staring as much since the novelty was wearing off. Still, he quietly said, "It was damaged by a goblin earlier today. Niitty here had to pull me out of trouble or I wouldn't have been here at all."

The server gasped, "Oh my! I'm glad ya managed to survive. It's not safe going out alone, even here. I'm so happy ya two found each other. And McVatter's General Store sells wigs. He may be able to replace yers."

Gerold sighed, "Thanks for the tip. I'm afraid I'll have to build up enough money to afford it. By the time that happens, everyone will be aware of who I am."

"Sorry that happened. Let me get yer food and outta yer hair," she said, bustling away.

The two sat in silence, looking like they were on a bad first date. Gerold took in more of the room. He was so engrossed in trying to be not seen the night before he didn't pay much attention to the other adventurers. Every one of them was young, between the ages of 18 and 20. A sense of exuberance permeated the occupied tables. Young men and women were enjoying freedom for the first time, treating the watered down beer like it was a rare delicacy and animatedly talking about the day's training or hunt.

Gerold's mind drifted back to his own son. In five and a half more years he would have been their ages. Gerold found himself closing his eyes and laying his forehead on his steepled fingers. He felt a pang of anguish building up and took slow, measured breaths to calm himself. He found himself yearning that Niitty didn't find him in the forest earlier in the day and how much easier it would have been to embrace the darkness.

The moment was lost when the front door slammed open. Niitty was startled and nearly tipped over back in her chair, Gerold's quick reflexes grabbing the chair back to keep her from going completely over. He looked to the entrance feeling annoyance building. It was the five Iron ranked adventurers.

A cheer rose up in the room at their entrance. They were quite the celebrities and were basking in the glow. The rookies were enamored with higher ranked adventurers in their midst. The higher ranked instructors kept themselves, amplifying the group's image in the eyes of the room. These five were comrades in arms and not some distant ideal.

The Felkin man peeled off and moved to the administration counter while the other four made their way to the common room floor. The man with the gleaming plate armor had signs of combat on him with the telltale stains of goblin blood as did the Gnome woman. Gerold wondered if this was calculated to help their image since they skipped the baths across the plaza.

The man scanned the room with a smile and gave a bow to

the crowd, which ate it up. When he came back up, his eyes landed on Gerold. The smile widened and the four of them made their way over to him.

The Desert Elf Lancer pulled over two additional chairs as the group cozied-up to the table. The man leaned back in his chair and looked over at Niitty, "I hope you are well today. Have you rethought my proposition?"

Niitty shifted closer to Gerold, gave the intruder a rude gesture and found something more interesting to look at on the surface of the table. The man smiled and turned to Gerold, "I haven't had the pleasure to meet you yet. You look like you're someone worth meeting."

Gerold frowned, "Oh, I'm a nobody."

The man laughed, "Please. I can tell a noble when I see one. My cousin is also playing the poor adventurer."

"Believe what you will."

The man didn't seem to notice Gerold's reply, "Introductions are in order. I am Sir Karl Schwartzstein, knight, eldest son and heir to the Schwartzstein Duchy."

Turning and pointing at the Felkin man turning in the bounty at the counter, "He's our cleric, a fine man and good friend by the name of Tulugaak. We have known each other since childhood and he is the heir to the largest arm's factory in the Empire."

Turning back he put his hand out to the Gnome woman, "This is Ellen, another fine friend of mine and excellent rogue. We have known each other since childhood and she is the daughter of a major merchant marine family." The woman gave Gerold a smarmy smile and a nod while spinning a dagger in her fingers.

To his other side he held his hand out at the Desert Elf, "This is Nader, yet another fine friend of mine and skilled lancer. He is the son of a Brigadier General of the Empire. We have also known each other since our childhood." Nader gave a subtle nod to Gerold.

Pointing to the Leopardia woman sitting on the other end of Ellen, "And, finally, this beautiful specimen is Gewa, our mage." She gave a small wave.

Gerold noticed that Karl had a different introduction for Gewa, avoiding bragging about her background and didn't call her his fine friend.

"Gerold, Warrior, and this is Niitty, Ranger. Now what do you want?"

Karl put his hand over his chest, "You wound me. I'll play along with your concealment of your family. I come with a proposition. As you probably know, we have taken on the request to investigate and clear the crypt that opened up near town. We are preparing and resting at the moment and intend to head out in five days. I noticed you and I'll extend the offer to join us in the glory."

"Karl," Tulugaak came over to the table and laid 32 copper coins on the table along with three guild tokens made of iron, "Here is our bounty."

Karl smiled and waved at the small pile, "As you can see, we are quite skilled. We dealt with two bands of goblins in the forest."

His friends all murmured and nodded at each other in approval and picked up their tokens. Save Gewa, who didn't have her token in the pile and looked embarrassed.

Gerold was not impressed in the slightest. He killed six by himself and, sure, he got himself in trouble, but with Niitty the two alone would have little issue hunting goblins the next day.

Gerold looked over at Niitty and she had shifted her body to point slightly out from the table, prepared to bolt.

Gerold sighed, "No, I don't believe so. Besides, the Guild limits parties to five for rewards."

"Oh, don't worry about that. Gewa here is a servant and we still have one party position open. Besides," he leaned in, "I'm secretly a Paladin and you'd be helping me out greatly."

Gerold noticed Gewa subtly shake her head no. Gerold already knew this man wasn't a Paladin. Sure, like Gerold, he could have been suppressing active auras to avoid detection. His soiled clothing gave him away and, while attractive, he had small imperfections not present on Paladins. Karl was someone of means, his attitude, equipment and the ability to have well-equipped members of his entourage. What concerned Gerold was his party. They were all, save for maybe Gewa, introduced as high born individuals.

Then it hit him. Karl was recruiting entirely based on appearance. Gewa was a Snow Leopardia and a particularly attractive one at that. His friends, typical of the highborn, were also attractive. He noticed the group, while basking in attention the night before, didn't try to recruit any of the other adventurers. Niitty was the only other one he approached. And Karl had assumed Gerold was a noble playing at adventuring, which is why he gave him a formal invitation to the fifth spot.

"No, I don't think we'll be joining," Gerold curtly replied.

Karl's face screwed up in anger. Gerold could tell he wanted to yell, but his highborn training reined it in for appearances, "I see. I'll assume you're deep in playing your role this evening and I'll let that slide. I will allow you to rethink your decision. I will only offer one additional chance. Just remember, the Schwartzstein family is not one to cross. Sleep on your decision, for your house's sake."

Karl kicked his chair back and waved his hand in a circle over his head. The rest of his party gave sneers, save Gewa's apologetic glance, and moved to the center of the room. Looking back one more time, he shouted, "Extra rounds on me! Except for those two."

A mug of watery beer was enough to buy the adoration of the room.

The server came in a few moments later. She put the watery gruel and mugs down before each of them, "Sorry about that. We get nobles through here from time to time and a lot of them like throwing their station around. I also hear he's a Paladin. That's not very becoming behavior."

Gerold picked up a spoon and poked at the food, "Don't apologize, it's not your fault. Besides, he's no Paladin."

The server looked over in shock, "What? Really? Look at him."

"Just take a closer look."

She squinted across the room at the party at the central table and examined Karl. Her eyes went wide, "Well I'll be, yer right. Ain't no Paladin that would walk around with blood stains on his clothing."

She then looked at Gerold, "Looking at ya though, maybe yer a Paladin?" She then laughed at the absurdity of her joke.

Gerold laughed with her, "Yea, that would be ridiculous. With these rags and struggling with a couple goblins? I'm even less believable."

"In any case, more rookies are starting to come in and I have a lot more tables to get to. Enjoy yer meal, or at least don't let it be too miserable," she waved and went to the next table.

Gerold didn't want to be in the Guild Hall anymore,

mirroring Niitty's discomfort. Karl kept looking over at his party and giving them an ugly glare. The man was angry, though Gerold didn't feel like he was going to do anything crazy. He had an image to uphold.

Niitty kept her head down and quickly gobbled down the gruel. Gerold did the same. She stood up immediately after finishing her beer, "I'll be heading back to the forest now. Thanks for the company."

She started to move without waiting for an answer. Gerold reached out and grabbed her arm, "Hold on, I'll escort you. The Hall has suddenly become stifling. Give me a moment."

Niitty nodded in relief and went to wait by the door. Gerold, thankful he kept his worldly possessions in his bag of holding, found the decision he just made easy to carry through.

He walked up to the counter and Allan came up with a smile, "How can I help?"

Gerold tossed the key on the counter, "I won't be needing this. I'm finding the Guild Hall beneath me."

Allan looked confused, "But sir, the sun is setting and a village like this doesn't have other accommodations. Where will you stay?"

"That doesn't matter."

"Let me register the return and you can be on your way," he said. Taking the key, Allan looked at the number and was surprised, "What inconsiderate fool would put you up on the top floor when we're only half booked?"

Looking in the ledger, his face went through a series of expressions ranging from shock to confusion, "Where did you get this?"

Gerold smiled and reached into his bag. Willing the mangled

beard and torn wig from the container, he threw them on the counter, "Dispose of that would you?"

Allan saw the materials and Gerold could see the man's brain making connections. Gerold's training wasn't able to identify the strange mix of emotion Allan was going through. It could have equally been anger, confusion and embarrassment when the man realized that the Gerold before him and the foul vagrant the day before were one and the same.

Gerold didn't wait for a response. He gave a wave and walked toward the exit, "Come on Niitty, let's get out of here."

Niitty's hands balled in fists as the two navigated their way out of town while her breathing was fast and shallow. She looked like she was ready to break down into a full panic. Risking exposing himself, Gerold decided to activate his Calm Nerves aura. Niitty immediately calmed and looked over at Gerold and whispered, "Thanks."

Whatever Niitty was going through was so deep-seated that the Calm Nerves aura was only a temporary salve that let her function enough as they left the settlement. The gate guards attempted to warn the duo that the gates would be closing at sundown, which was rebuffed when Niitty curtly told them to mind their own business.

As they worked their way back down the road that Gerold had traveled earlier that day back toward the forest, Niitty visibly calmed more. The aura Gerold was maintaining hit its one hour limit and winked out.

Fortunately, the two had put enough distance away from the village that the fear didn't hit Niitty with the disappearance of the aura. Gerold did find out the aura worked on him because his anxiety at seeing farms kicked in.

"I have questions," Niitty said more confidently than she had spoken back in Wren's End.

"Ask."

She was silent for a moment, collecting her thoughts, "Why did you turn down forming our party?"

"That's a big step to link ourselves like that," Gerold responded.

"But you said we can be a party yesterday."

"On a trial basis."

"But you promised."

Gerold sighed, "Look, we just met. Forming a formal party is a huge leap. Maybe we should learn more about each other. And now's a great time because I just gave away my room at the Guild Hall, insulted the guy who hands out the keys and got myself locked out of town for the night."

Niitty laughed hard enough she snorted, looked embarrassed at the noise she made then laughed again, "I needed that. One other question though, why did you do that?"

Gerold stopped and looked at her, "You look like you need the company. I get the sense you want to be around people but, for whatever reason, the town is too terrifying. I couldn't leave you alone like that."

She looked down at the road and kicked a rock, "Thanks, I appreciate it."

Gerold pointed his hand down the road, "Shall we continue."

Niitty continued down the road on a speed walk pace, trying to get as much distance from Wren's End as she could. The two made small talk until they reached the edge of the forest.

Instead of continuing the way he went earlier in the day, Niitty turned north and followed along the edge of the forest and the fields. Walking for a good mile, she stopped and turned into the forest. Just past the underbrush, she stopped and started to shimmy up a tree.

Looking up, Gerold noticed a tarp stretched between four trees by rope.

"Hold on, I have more rope. I don't figure you know how to climb trees," she shouted from above.

"You shouldn't invite a stranger into a camp like this," Gerold shouted back.

"Where would you even stay," she replied.

Gerold looked back toward the farms. The fields should be safe and he could probably get away leaning up against a barn, "I think I can manage."

"Nonsense," she shouted back after a rope fell from above, "You're a Paladin, what risk is there?'

Gerold couldn't believe the blind trust she was showing to a total stranger. Sure, he was a Paladin and, at least from what he understood, they were all honorable people - the Gods wouldn't select them otherwise - it was still a terrible risk. The stories of Paladins were so widespread and believed that this girl was willing to invite him up to her safe place.

Gerold grabbed the rope and gave it a few tentative pulls. He wasn't confident he could do this. He pulled himself up a few feet before gravity asserted its dominance and pulled him back down.

"Put your stuff in your bag," Niitty shouted down.

Gerold stopped and thought back. Did he ever tell her about his bag? He shouted back, "It won't fit in there."

"Oh quit it. I know it's a bag of holding. How else did you get all those ears in there without it leaking blood?"

Gerold cursed his new companion's crazy observational skills, at least out in the woods. He removed his chain hauberk and, along with his hammer, shoved it into the bag. He never tried it before and marveled at how the bag's opening stretched open to accommodate the shirt. He wondered what he could fit in there. Would opening it in a lake drain it?

Removing his hauberk dropped his weight by around 20 pounds. That was enough to help him muscle his way up the rope. Niitty was laughing at him during his entire ascent.

Rolling onto the tarp, Gerold took a number of deep breaths to calm his heart. He found the hard way that training some muscles didn't translate into strength with others.

After he caught his breath, he looked over at Niitty. The tarp was a secure leather construction with a large, three foot tall lip stretched along the edges to keep occupants and objects from tumbling out. It was tight with the two of them, barely larger than two inn beds. Thankfully, Niitty had the tarp strung so tightly that his weight didn't cause her to roll in his direction.

"Why were you laughing," Gerold said after he caught his breath.

Niitty snorted again, "You climbing. Why were you hoisting yourself up with your arms?"

"How else to I pull myself up?"

"Wrap your feet on the rope and stand on it."

Gerold didn't understand and his face betrayed that to his companion. Niitty slid down the rope and told him to watch. Taking a leap, she grabbed the rope as high as she could. She then pulled her legs up around her head, wrapped the rope around one foot and then held it between both of her feet. She stretched back into a standing position and repeated this process until she pulled herself into the tarp.

She wasn't breathing hard at all.

Gerold grunted at her efforts. She laughed while pulling the rope back up, "You held your entire weight in your arms all the way up. Using your legs lets you rest while you reposition yourself to climb higher."

If he decided to continue on with Niitty, Gerold figured he would get a lot of practice doing this. He looked over the edge again. This certainly was a solid setup for the wilderness, at least when there were substantial trees around. They wouldn't have to worry about monster attacks way up here.

"It's tight," Gerold said as he tried to find a position where he wasn't brushing too close to Niitty.

Wrapping some belongings in a sack, Niitty started stringing them up on a branch to provide more room in the tarp, "We are used to this. Families would each stretch a tarp when the band stopped and we would sleep in groups. It helps keep us warm in the cold. If you want, I could unfold the Parent's Partition."

"What's that?"

She pulled on one of the side barriers that kept them from falling out, "This one is a midpoint. There is more folded underneath. We can double the size of the sleeping tarp. It gives parents privacy for when they want to…you know."

Gerold grunted, he knew.

"I'd have to take this down and find another spot. This clearing isn't large enough to fold out the second half."

Gerold waved the suggestion away, "Let's not. The sun is almost down and we should get some sleep. We've had a long day."

Gerold pulled his fur blanket from the bag, curled up and faced the wall. Niitty rustled a bit from the other end of the tarp. He heard what sounded like her brushing her teeth and a few more rustles as she prepared for the night. Gerold found himself missing brushing his teeth, his curse ensured they'd never rot. Her weight shifted at the other end then went quiet.

In the few minutes after the sun fully set, Niitty whispered, "Gerold? You still awake?"

Gerold grunted an affirmation.

"I want to thank you again. I have had to spend nights alone these past few weeks."

"Don't mention it."

Niitty was silent for a while longer, "Do you mind if I tell you something?"

"Go ahead."

"I wasn't doing well. I wanted to quit today, go back home, tell my family my First Journey was a failure. It's not a big deal in my people, many of our tribe returned within weeks of venturing out. We do this to build up skills and bring back new knowledge to help the tribe. We recognize the hurdles that we face when we leave the tribe. It may sound strange, but my people like being around others, just not strangers. Cities are stifling. We need the trees or sky to be above our heads. It's not just fear, it's the extreme dread that is present in every one of my tribe. I saw you come out this morning only because I was trying to build up the nerve to come in for breakfast. I couldn't even manage that. I then spent all morning following you around trying to build up the nerve to even talk."

Gerold hummed to indicate he was still paying attention.

"There's something about you, though, that makes me want

to continue trying to succeed on my journey. Sure, you're nothing like the Paladins my Father told stories about. You don't enter the room as the shining beacon of attention, you don't speak loudly and confidently, you're grumpy, you're willing to push away those you dislike and annoy you and you seem to dislike yourself to the point you're trying to make yourself as ugly and unapproachable as possible."

Gerold snorted, "Thanks for the compliment."

Niitty gave a small, sleepy laugh and continued with a fading voice fighting the call of the God of Dreams, "Yet here you are. You gave up a room in town where you'd be comfortable, climbed a rope like a drunken rock and are lying yards above the ground in a tarp on a cold night just because you met someone who was scared and alone. You may not be my Father's Paladin, but you're one where it counts."

Gerold couldn't believe what he just heard. This girl had the worst naiveté he'd ever run across. Not even his children had this degree of blind trust in a total stranger. He wasn't sure if it was an odd cultural thing, her upbringing in a small, trusting community or his status as a Paladin. In any case, this was a dangerous behavior to hold. Just because he showed her a little kindness and she saved him wasn't a reason to invite a stranger back to a sleeping area like this. He hoped it was her fatigue making decisions and this isn't normal behavior.

He didn't want to spend any more time with this girl since she could get him into a lot of trouble by proxy. Parts of him were saying he should stick around and protect her, or at least be there so when she did learn her lesson about the world, it would be an experience she could live through to remember. He wasn't sure which argument to listen to.

CHAPTER 5

Gerold was awakened to a rough shaking on his shoulder. Groggy, he turned over and saw Niitty looking down on him with deep concern. After instinctually trying to wipe out non-existent gunk out of his eyes and sitting up, he said, "What is it? Are we being attacked?"

She shook her head, "No, you were having some kind of nightmare. You were moaning and crying."

Gerold felt fatigued. Looking east through the trees, he noticed the horizon was barely turning red and the day was still dark. He touched his forehead. He felt dry. Then it occurred to him and he touched the tarp beneath him and it felt damp and warm. The curse removed the sweat from his body and deposited it into a small puddle of liquid that pooled between him and the tarp. Gerold's brain stubbornly refused to recall what it was that set off his night terrors.

"Sorry if I woke you," Gerold said apologetically.

"Do you want to talk about it?"

Memories briefly flashed in his head, "No."

Niitty only nodded, "The sun will be up soon, what's the plan?"

Gerold pulled out the copper Adventurer coins from his pouch and laid them on the tarp, "We should go over our skills to see how we distribute these."

Niitty spent a few moments shifting the coins around. She

looked disappointed, "This isn't a lot, is it?" She sighed, "Not that I have the skills to work with. We seem to be on equal experience footing. All I have right now is Identify Weakness, which is useless since it's only effective on monsters at a lower power than me, which is nothing, and Snipe, which improves my accuracy. Both of them cost one copper to activate."

"My spells are Turn Undead and Simple Heal. I have no idea how effective Turn Undead is and, from my limited training, Simple Heal only staunches blood loss from smaller wounds and removes infection," Gerold replied, "Plus, I only have the capacity to cast six spells before I have a splitting headache."

"Better than me, I'm at five."

Gerold split out five coins and pushed them over to Niitty, "Here, for when you need them. If you don't mind, I'll hold onto the rest." Gerold then scooped the rest into his pouch where they would be safe from loss or roving pickpocket hands. He hoped he wouldn't have to cast any spells. They now had to buy provisions for two to reach the crypt at 1 silver and 60 copper and he didn't want to have to kill any more than the bare minimum 80 goblins to pull it off. Now that he thinks of it, he will need buffer for spell casting, so at least another 66 copper for three days of spells, moving the kill count to a ridiculous 123. This was going to take some time.

Gerold slapped himself in the head, startling Niitty with this sudden outburst. The crypt! He never told Niitty that was his goal.

Gerold stated gravely, "Before we get in too deep with partying, I intend to visit the crypt that opened up in the mountains."

She paused her preparations for the day, "What? Why would you want to go there? I don't think it's a good idea for new adventurers."

Gerold looked down at his chest and played with the amulet of Erinne, "It's something I was asked to do. Erinne told me there was something odd going on around here and the crypt is my only lead. It's unlikely she would insist I investigate it if it wasn't something important."

"You mean like a vision or a sign," Niitty asked.

"No, we had a conversation in my head."

Niitty stared at Gerold for a few beats, thoughts racing across her face. Then she said, "You're serious, aren't you? Gods don't talk to anyone, they just show vague visions at the best of times. If it wasn't for your aura and my Father's stories about the Gods' careful selection of their chosen warriors, I'd think you were crazy. You really believe Erinne came out of her seclusion to choose you."

Gerold shifted in his seat, trying to get a better position on the tarp, "She hasn't told me much. All I know is she is an eternal being that created the very universe we stand in. That, for some reason, my soul is unique in that it allowed her a conduit to the world. She isn't reclusive by choice."

A sad smile crossed her face, "I still don't buy that. No God has ever talked directly to a person, least of all the Recluse Queen. Assuming this is true, I have one question. How can she make the universe and not have ultimate power?"

Gerold shrugged, "She would only tell me she can't say."

"Can't or won't?"

"Can't," Gerold replied, "In any case, are you willing to remain in the party knowing I'm going to an undead crypt at the behest of a God?"

She fiddled with her unstrung bow, twisting the string in her fingers while she thought. "You know," she began,

"Remember how the administrator told us about how unlikely it is for our guild IDs to be sequential? Maybe that's a sign this was meant to be. Sure, I'll join you."

Gerold internally rolled his eyes at her overly trusting nature and visibly nodded in return. He had hoped asking her to go out into the wilderness to find a crypt would have changed her mind.

Niitty threw down the rope for him and showed off a technique where she rolled herself in the rope and then used it to descend in a controlled spin. Gerold had no intention of even trying that and slowly slid down, Niitty laughing at his clumsiness the whole way. Gerold took that time to put his chain hauberk back on and, after a moment's thought, retrieved his wooden round shield.

After climbing back up to withdraw the rope, she shimmied down the tree and they went to look for their prey.

Niitty was an ace in the forest. Gerold had wasted an entire day wandering the forest with his sense evil aura to find goblins and he only managed to stumble upon one band. With Niitty, this took 15 minutes. Moments after traveling west into the forest, she stopped, kneeled, waved her hand over the dirt and smelled the air. She pointed slightly more north and they went. Gerold then sensed the evil at the edges of his aura.

Gerold's crunching on the ground was heard by the creatures as he heard a howl pick up and the mob of disgusting creatures streamed at them through the trees. Like before, Gerold positioned himself to the side and prepared to run. Niitty got out ahead of Gerold and fired an arrow into the mass, hitting one in the center of the chest. The goblin dropped to the ground and skid in the dirt, snapping the shaft in its death.

Gerold took off at a jog. However, he saw Niitty panic and run in a different direction. Because she got out ahead of

Gerold, the mob went after her. It took a few steps to stop his momentum and turn around to give chase.

Cursing, he ran around a tree in the direction Niitty went. After dodging two more trees, he saw the goblins surrounding a tree and attempting to claw their way up. Niitty had jumped and scrambled up the tree and was sitting on a branch, watching as eight of the yowling creatures clawed the bark. She fumbled with her bow and was unable to stabilize herself to draw an arrow. She almost lost her balance, which caused her to drop her bow when she abandoned it to hold onto the branch to keep from tumbling to the ground.

Gerold ran in from behind and slammed the flat of his hammer hard on the crown of the head of the rearmost goblin, buckling it at the knees, dead. This caught the attention of two more that turned around and attacked. Learning his lesson from the day before, he held up his shield to catch the creatures as they dove for him. While standing, he was able to use his superior mass to shove the two down to the ground where he hammered one of the goblins while he stood on the face of the other to keep it in place. After smashing the creature's face, he flipped his hammer around and drove the spike into the other's temple.

Three goblins down, five more to go. Niitty grabbed a few pinecones from the branch and was throwing them down at the mass, hoping to distract them from Gerold as he worked from behind. Not that it did much since the din of the screams and yowls kept the rest from hearing his work.

At least until he took out the fourth. Gerold's slam to the monster's head rocked it to the side, causing it to topple into its four remaining compatriots. They all turned as one and paused, taking note of Gerold. He smashed one before the other three jumped at him. He was able to use the top of his hammer to hold one back and the shield to hold off a second.

The third proved more troublesome when it latched itself onto his leg and began chewing on his shin. The sharp, yellow teeth easily penetrated his cheap pants and into his flesh.

Gerold let out a scream, taking the full of his concentration to remain standing in addition to attempting to keep the other two at bay. He was considering activating Calm Nerves to hold back the rising panic when he thought of Niitty being slaughtered by the creatures after they got him when she thumped down from the tree in a crouch. Pulling her rapier, she jammed it clumsily into the one chewing on his leg. She penetrated it low on the torso, missing anything vital. She pulled it back out again and stabbed it into the goblin's neck, using the sharpened blade to saw its way out from the side, partially beheading the creature.

With the loss of the mass gnawing on his tibia, Gerold was able to drive the other two forward into the tree, forcing Niitty to dive out of the way. Holding them in place, Niitty was able to more accurately drive the rapier into the eye socket of the one held by the hammer, which allowed Gerold to drag the final goblin down the tree trunk, hold it down with his knee then hammer it into submission.

Gerold's attempt to stand sent a searing pain through his shin, causing him to fall back on his rump. He spent a few moments catching his breath, trying to ignore the pulsing pain in his leg. He felt another rise of panic as he worried about an infection from the disgusting yellow teeth and who knows what in the saliva. It subsided when he realized his Paladin's curse was, instead, a blessing in this situation.

Finally getting his breathing under control, he looked up at Niitty. She was quiet, looking down at the ground in remorse and fiddling with her bow in both hands.

Gerold stretched his damaged leg out and looked at it. There was a light trickle of blood flowing from the wound, the drips staining the dried pine needles crimson. The goblin didn't have enough time to do any real damage. While the cut hurt, Gerold's Paladin abilities negated any chance of infection and would heal it up rapidly. The gash from the day before had already closed and there wasn't even a sign it would leave a scar. He was, instead, more concerned with the fact that the creature had torn the entirety of the pant leg off below the knee. He lacked the materials or resources to repair or replace his trousers.

"That could have gone better," Gerold finally said after he examined his leg and pants. He looked up and took note of Niitty. Tears were streaming down her face and she had a pained expression while she tried to hold back in gutting sobs.

Gerold tried to stand to get a better look and buckled when his leg gave out a second time, "What happened? Did one manage to injure you?"

She shook her head and, through sobs, said, "I was so scared. I thought that I could get them through the trees. I was the best speed shooter of all the kids and I thought I could shoot them all. They moved so fast and I ran and they followed me. The scouts keep monsters away from the tribe and all I ever shot at before were elk and deer and this one time a rabbit that I missed and it's not the same when they run at you. I jumped in the tree and I was so scared I dropped my bow. Then you came in to save me and then that one got your leg and you got hurt because of me. I'm so sorry sorry sorry sorry." She dropped her bow, knelt into a squat, buried her face in her hands and started bawling.

Gerold propped himself up on his good leg and hopped over to her. Stretching his bad leg out, he sat next to her then pulled her shaking, crying form into his chest. He felt her tears drip down his body like a duck coming out of a pond as she let go. Gerold held her like that for a solid minute as she quietly calmed.

As she got her emotions out, Gerold realized that Niitty was still new to the world, barely out of childhood. She reminded him of his daughter, how she would rush into his arms at the howl of the wind or the crack of thunder, he ready to console away the fears. While he was no more experienced in the ways of fighting, Gerold had a lifetime of experience to draw on, decades of maturity, raising a family and…that thing he would rather not think about.

Niitty was thrust into an unfamiliar world alone to face her fears of going into towns and the mass of strangers. Now she faced, for the first time in her life, the mortal danger that adventurers face every day. And she, unlike Gerold, still wanted to live in this world, so her first brush with death wasn't muted by numbing depression.

Gerold began to wonder just how many newbie adventurers found their demise in these woods with inexperience their downfall. The only sign of their passing their guild tokens magically transported to the nearest Guild Hall as a sign of their fall and, if lucky, a survivor to tell the tale. Even this close to a town, the forest was too vast and too dangerous to risk a search for the bodies, which would be lost to nature.

Niitty's trembling began to calm. When her sobs quieted, Gerold said, "You know, for the first time in a long while, I was actually scared." Niitty said nothing in response while Gerold continued, "Not for me. No, I've lost all interest in living for myself. I could die here now and I wouldn't care. Seeing you up that tree, surrounded, made me fear that if I failed, I'd be failing you. Don't be sorry for my leg. It will heal. In a way, I'm thankful. It means I haven't completely lost all my humanity."

Niitty pulled away and sat cross legged on the dry pine needle floor. She looked around and took in her surroundings. Gerold followed her gaze and looked at the corpses piled up near the tree Niitty had taken refuge in. Eight of the monsters lay broken and bloody on the ground, a ninth a few yards away in the woods atop a snapped arrow shaft.

"When I saw that goblin on you yesterday," Niitty softly began, "it was so easy to kill. I took aim and fired, hitting it cleanly. At the time I thought, 'This isn't a big deal. My first kill, I can do this.' This is entirely different. I can tell this is how fights go."

Gerold pulled a dagger out of his bag and cut at his pant leg, "No, I don't think so. We went in blind. We didn't have a plan. We still don't know each other or how to work with each other." He wrapped the torn cloth around the wound while his brain applied some sort of filter that numbed the persistent pain to a low throb. He pulled a copper Adventurer's Coin out of his pouch and flipped it over in his hand. He hesitated, thinking this represented half an ear in income.

Niitty saw his hesitation, "You should use it. We can get more."

Gerold sighed. He gripped the coin and felt the strange, wordless arcane language come to his lips. No one could properly explain exactly how spells were cast. Sure, mages would have to study the mechanics of magic and clerics divine inspiration passed on by their patron God. They could, along with improving in power, impart the thinking patters and understanding of how magic works. Only when that understanding forms in the mind would the caster be able to use those silent words. Lips would move, producing a silent incantation that resisted all attempts at translation. Any attempts to read lips come back as empty gibberish. Any attempts to write down what is intuitively understood produced indecipherable scribbles. Every individual comprehends the magic in his own, unique way.

Like any language, it took time and reinforcement to master. The spell for Simple Heal solidified in Gerold's mind. He had only cast it a small handful of times since the Pantheon Temple and they were unwilling to waste too many coins on his training. After fumbling a half dozen times, the word finally passed silently over his lips. He watched as the Adventurer Coin dissolved into a disk of white motes of light. The light then spread its way into his hand and, apart from a gentle blue glow, vanished.

Taking his hand, instinct directed it toward his bandaged wound where his will released it over the cloth. He could feel an itch as the bleeding stopped and the pain subsided. It still pulsed and he knew that the wound was still present. A spell of this level wouldn't heal the wound, not completely. The spell accelerated the body's natural blood staunching properties and healed a small portion of the skin around the edges of the cuts. He could feel the scab now formed beneath the tattered brown bandage.

Gerold stood on his leg, which no longer gave in. He was lucky the creature didn't crack his bone, or he would have had to use up all six spells he could muster for the day, and nearly half the party's accumulated wealth, just to hobble back to town. He was also lucky that the area of the damage was, relatively speaking, not a major hindrance to movement.

He tested it a few more times before turning to Niitty, who had a look of wonder on her face.

"First time seeing magic?" he asked.

She nodded, "Our tribe never had much in the way of Adventurer's Coin, only what we needed for funerary rites and some for emergencies. Our scouts and hunters killed many monsters, but few of us were willing to make the long trek to a Guild Hall. It would take weeks to traverse to the nearest

Guild Hall, so we left the parts to return to nature. The forests and mountains would otherwise provide the herbs needed for healing poultices."

Gerold smiled, "And you can do the same too. With practice, you can do it without the risk of failure when the words are finally carved permanently into your mind."

Her wonder was replaced by confusion, "Goblin ears are only worth two copper, meaning we'd end up losing money if we had to use more than one ability on each. I also fear that our equipment will need replacement and these forests aren't rich in the resources I need to make new arrows. We have to decide whether that ability is worth not being able to afford new equipment."

Gerold could only nod. He had a wise statement about spending coin to save a life hung unsaid on his tongue after being visibly indecisive about closing the wound on his own leg. The young didn't respond well to hypocrisy.

"In any case," Gerold said, "I think I have an idea on how we can approach the next pack."

Gerold's basic training provided him some insight, tips and a few drills on five man groups and solo combat, both against equal and numerically superior opponents. Nothing taught him how to handle a two person team. There were many nuances and concerns present in just two people that weren't in a larger group or alone.

The first attempt was he tried to re-create his run and stretch method that worked alone. Two people proved inefficient since Gerold ended up doing all the fighting. Between his leg and Niitty's better speed in the forest, she ended up further ahead when the goblins caught up.

The second attempt involved having Niitty range ahead to draw a line, run them past while Gerold hid behind a tree.

Niitty would flash him a sign with the number of goblins in tow. After counting that number, Gerold would pursue from behind and attack the slowest while Niitty would hit the fastest. This proved a failure when Niitty ended up a tree a second time. Thankfully, the typical pack was only five or six members strong. There were only four in tow.

Niitty's weapon and skills weren't suitable to a quick turn and kill, forcing Gerold to take the brunt of the effort once more. While her rapier did have a sharp edge, her limited training from home was mostly focused on single combat with an intelligent opponent. Niitty had to stop and pivot to put enough force into her attack to kill the lead goblin, but removing the weapon took too long.

Worse, she couldn't fire arrows on the move. Gerold also thought the process was inefficient on resources since the arrows had a bad habit of breaking with each successful kill.

The only thing going their way so far was this area of the forest was so lousy with goblins that Niitty always managed to pick up and find a new band every 15 to 20 minutes. They were spaced out fairly reliably one mile apart. Any closer and the bands would clash, creating a natural buffer. This space is large enough that, without a trained tracker, running into a band is entirely luck, as proven by Gerold's aimless wandering the day before.

After taking care of the two remaining goblins trying to claw up after Niitty again, Gerold examined the tree. The trees in this forest were huge; the trunks would take three or four men holding hands to fully ring just one. Gerold sighed when an idea formed in his head.

"That one was a bust. We need to get you a short sword or a clubbing weapon if this is going to work," Gerold said as he went about his business cutting off ears.

Niitty protectively gripped her rapier, "This was my Father's sword. I'm not going to give it up."

"I didn't suggest selling it or disposing it," Gerold said after cutting up the goblins closest to him. He would backtrack for the other three later. He walked up to the tree and put his hand across the bark, "Having weapons for different scenarios is needed. In any case, here's my next idea. These trees are massive; we should use them as a backstop."

Niitty's eyes went wide, "Wouldn't that cut off a means of escape?"

Gerold smiled, "It would, but with goblins, the biggest threat we face is being surrounded. With a tree at our back, that won't happen. And it's not like we are abandoning the run method."

"I don't like this," Niitty said, "Turning and setting with my rapier is going to cause too much delay."

Holding up a finger, Gerold replied, "You don't have to worry about being set. I plan on being the rabbit to draw the goblins to us."

She pointed at his bare leg with the cloth tied around it, "With that leg? I'm faster than you are and can escape up a tree if I get in trouble. You can't even climb a rope."

"I don't have to escape when all I need to do is drag them enough to create separation. You will get the first one. I'll turn, we put our backs to the tree and we take them out one at a time as they come. This will allow us to reset our swings. You hit the first and, while you reset, I hit the next. We alternate like this to avoid getting in each other's way."

Niitty slid her hand over her face and sighed. She didn't look like she was excited about the idea. Huffing, she said, "I don't like this at all."

"Also, you're running low on arrows. Every time you kill a goblin, it falls over and snaps the shaft. Those can't be cheap," Gerold added.

That got through to her and she quickly replied, "I'll still have to identify the goblins and point you in the right direction. You'll also have to remember how to get back."

He waved her away, "I think I can manage."

"Oh? What was that you were doing yesterday out here," she retorted with a snort.

"Just lead the way."

After cutting the ear off the first goblin in the group that Niitty took care of, Gerold had a bright idea. Grabbing the goblin by the foot, he told Niitty, "I think I found a beacon."

She looked down at the goblin, a naked male with a snapped shaft protruding out of the center of its chest, with disgust, "Those things smell horrible and you want to drag it around? How is this going to help you?"

"I can sense evil. It's not detailed, I can only tell direction and intensity, not distance or individual. Another limitation is if I'm too close, it feels like the evil is surrounding me on all sides. This one should prove useful as a beacon out to 100 yards."

She looked at it and gagged, "Whatever. As long as I don't have to touch it."

Niitty made her way through the forest with Gerold trying to drag the body along with him. It was cumbersome trying to keep up while pulling the thing. Inspiration hit him and he opened up his bag. If it worked for his hauberk and shield, it could work with this thing. The bag accepted the corpse, yawning the opening wide to suck it in.

Niitty made another gagging noise, "That was nasty."

"And yet it's easier to transport than dragging it through the woods by its ankle."

A few minutes later, Niitty signaled Gerold to stop. She pointed further into the woods, "That way. It's a smaller band, six by the tracks I see."

Gerold looked around at the forest. He picked a thick tree at random, "Hold there. Let's see if this works better than the other attempts."

Gerold shoved his hand in the bag and willed the goblin corpse to it. He found himself gripping the thing at the wrist when he pulled it out. He laid it out against the tree and walked in the direction of the goblin group. He felt the evil seeping off the corpse behind him. Happy his idea had worked, he continued on.

50 yards out, he caught the sense of evil from ahead. He began stomping loudly and shouted gibberish into the air. The telltale scream of the goblins echoed in the distance. As before, he positioned himself toward the beacon he felt in the opposite direction, ready to run. When the pack streamed around a tree, he ran, his leg hurting far less now that he got used to the pain.

This time, Gerold didn't turn and look behind, less concerned with spacing and allowing a gentle approach to get back to the tree to ready himself as best as possible. The beacon proved true and he arrived next to Niitty with thirty yards to spare.

Gerold turned and pulled his hammer and readied his shield. When the first goblin got in range, Niitty thrust forward and penetrated the monster into the heart, the momentum pushing its corpse up the blade. The second was close behind and as Niitty was pulling back to reset her stance, Gerold smashed his hammer into its head.

This pattern proved perfect. Not only did the alternating attacks allow for cleaner, more measured attacks, the bodies of the first two goblins proved a minor obstacle that slowed the remaining creatures as they approached. In short order, five ashen grey bodies were piled at their feet.

Other than a short sprint, Gerold felt far less winded after this encounter. The battle was predictable, they were able to get into a rhythm and their movements were short, quick and efficient. And best of all, the bodies were all in the same place. They no longer had to range out over a hundred yards collecting ears.

After sheathing her rapier, Niitty held her arm cocked to her side with her fist up, looking expectantly at Gerold. Gerold had no idea what she was doing. After a brief moment, she grabbed Gerold's arm and put it up in the same manner then said, "Make a fist."

He did and she tapped her wrist against his.

"What was that," Gerold asked.

Niitty smiled, "A small post hunt ritual from my tribe."

Gerold shrugged, "How did that feel?"

"Much better," Niitty said pulling a dagger, "I still feel the adrenaline in my system and it was still frightening. Still, it's much easier when I knew the direction they were coming from and we had an effective plan."

Niitty quickly cut off the ears and they continued on. This method proved helpful throughout the day. After a while, Gerold started getting used to forest navigation and started practicing getting back without a beacon corpse, though he wasn't deluded enough to think he turned into an expert woodsman after a few hours of running.

If they could keep up this pace for a few more days, they will have collected enough bounties to make the trip.

CHAPTER 6

Niitty watched Gerold cut off the ear of a goblin in the latest pile they created against the latest tree, trying to hold in her laughter. He looked absurd kneeling in the forest in his one-legged pants. She found herself confused by the man. He was around her age; his combat experience, the way he moved through the forest and his appearance all indicated an 18 or 19 year old man. His beautiful features reminded her of a scion of a noble family and, she could admit, she found him very attractive.

It was other parts that confused her. When she saw his performance against the goblins, it betrayed a keen mind that, despite the lack of combat practice, displayed unusual maturity. When he was mounted by the goblin ready to tear out his throat, he barely fought back, was calm and even ready to give in to fate. Even when she saved him, he showed little emotion and acted as if a near-death experience was no more troubling than finding a rock in your boot.

Contrasted with her own near death experience, Gerold's mentality was that of a hardened combat veteran. His concern for her safety when she came down from that tree was the first time he showed anything more than a mild disdain for his surroundings. And when she lost her nerve and cried? She thought his embrace would have caused annoyance or arousal. What else would it feel like to be embraced by a crush, one she barely knew, when she was at her lowest? His touch was gentle and caring, one more suited to quelling the fear of a child.

Being comforted reminded her of a feeling she hadn't felt in over a decade when her Father had last embraced her before he went off and never returned from that final hunt. He even fussed over the meager coins their party possessed like her Father had, showing willingness to suffer a nasty wound to save a copper.

She couldn't believe that she brought him back to her tree refuge. She was fairly certain he was a Paladin and no one had ever heard a story of one of them harming an innocent. His weird cleanliness from walking the forest and lack of smell made her mostly sure of it. She wasn't aware of any magic that could keep a person smelling fresh like that for so long, or anyone willing to spend that many Adventurer Coins to maintain it.

Had Gerold not radiated that strange calm that brought her out of the deep panic attack she was feeling on the way out of Wren's End the day before, she would have thanked him at the gate and insisted he go back. All he did, other than make a fool of himself by clumsily climbing up a rope, was politely listen to her emotional outburst before she fell asleep.

Gerold did have some kind of delusion. He wasn't being dishonest with her and he fully believed everything he was saying. She felt he had some form of trauma in his past and he is trying to cover it up. He became extra prickly and cantankerous when she asked about it and he refused to elaborate on anything beyond the task on hand. It had to be bad to craft the insane story that he's really a 49 year old man. He went so far as buying and wearing tattered farmer's clothing, a ratty grey wig and a similarly ratty beard. Thankfully, his fake hair had been destroyed in the encounter where she met him, or he would be traipsing about the forest in them.

Plus, his Bag of Holding failed to match her expectations.

It was a powerful and expensive artifact, yet he stressed over each copper. Even the bag was equally as strange as possessing one. Every story she heard of a Bag of Holding involved a pouch that was a work of art, not a plain leather pouch. It took platinum Adventurer Coins to activate the enchantment, so attaching it to a well tailored bag would be a trivial expense.

That and he not only claimed to be the first ever Paladin of the Recluse Queen, he also claimed the Goddess talked directly to him. He believed he had received divine instruction that compelled him to investigate the crypt – Paladins and undead were eternal enemies after all – but it was excessive to claim it was a set of verbal instructions. He probably saw the posting at the Guild Hall where he signed up and figured it was a sign where to go next.

Niitty wasn't worried he'd do anything unhinged. The Pantheon was, to a God, dedicated to good. She couldn't think of any that were malicious, the worst being a little chaotic. Gerold would have never gotten his powers had he showed any indication to abuse it. Otherwise, he proved a keen thinker, dedicated, protective, competent and, the shallow part of her insisted on adding, easy on the eyes. If she was going to attach herself to a long term adventuring party, Gerold made for a great choice. She resolved to not ask him about his past again and let him tell her in his own time.

"How many is that now," Niitty asked Gerold. She was happy with his latest strategy. She was getting used to working with him and learning his habits. And, compared to the first few packs, the goblins proved an easy kill with this method. He also suggested she swap out her rapier for something easier for group combat, but it was the only thing of her Father's that came back from that hunt and this method proved she didn't need to switch out. She just couldn't see herself swinging around the war hammer that Gerold preferred to use.

Gerold's brow creased in thought for a few moments before he replied, "That was 68, so we have one silver and 36 copper in our party funds."

She smiled at his phrasing, "Party funds huh? Does this mean you're ready to make it official?"

As usual, his face was a mask of indifference. She felt her nerves rising when he didn't immediately respond and stared at her. Eventually, he replied, "We work well together and you did agree to travel to the crypt with me. Next time we're back, let's make it official."

"Do we have a goal with this hunt? If not, I suggest you buy some pants."

He looked down at his tattered trousers and bandaged leg, "I would need around five silver for that. We need to have eight days, each, for provisions just to get out to the crypt, which is a silver and 60 copper. It took us all day and we still aren't at that goal. And that's if we don't keep a few coins around for spells and abilities, which I'd rather not risk."

Niitty wasn't experienced in the ways of money. Her tribe, mostly, lived off the land. Her clothing was made of leather from animals they hunted and plants they foraged. Yes, there were finances, as her Mother regularly stressed over, and money was made from selling pelts, antlers and medicinal herbs. She lacked the context to price items since she was never included in the process. Mother had paid for her to join the caravan down to Wren's End and all her meals were either foraged from the land or, when she built up her courage, the free one at the Guild Hall.

How hard it was to earn money and how expensive things were to buy gave her a new appreciation for the work people did every day in the civilized parts of the world. They had to carefully plan their lives and couldn't just buy new clothing because it got damaged.

"I think I saw a patch of wild flax at the edge of the forest," she offered, "Do you know how to spin it? I have a small seamstress kit at the hide you could use as well."

He nodded, "Yes. Farmers grow flax every few seasons. We would make our own clothing with it along with oil then selling the rest. I had never bought clothing before, it's too expensive."

Niitty noticed his expression turn sad when he was talking about making flaxen thread and decided to cease this topic of conversation.

"I'll swing us by that patch on the way back to town. I think we should get going, we ranged out pretty far and it's a bit past noon. We have to turn in these ears and I'm famished, the hunting in the forest is terrible and there aren't any berries or nuts to forage this deep in."

Niitty led the way back to town. She had moved west and north and they would have to follow along the edge of farmland once they cleared the forest. Luckily, both the flax patch and the tree hide were on the way.

It took them two hours to get to the thick underbrush near the edge of the forest and she stripped a nice raspberry bush she found, sharing the snack with Gerold. Her traveling companion looked impressed that she led them directly back to town despite taking a meandering route in the forest. Even if he did manage to kill that goblin the day before, he would have likely gotten lost, wandered deep into the wilderness and died of starvation or exposure.

Niitty paused and looked out over the clean border into the farmland. She felt a sense of dread rising in her chest. Low spring sprouts poked their heads out of the tilled dirt in uniform rows. It was artificial and strange to her mind. She turned back and looked at the forest. The canopy formed at the top of thick trees promised refuge. She closed her eyes to calm her nerves. She took in the scent of decaying pine needles that were on the breeze as it gently moved through the trees. The odors of goblins almost ruined the experience, though avoiding the creatures was a simple task. She couldn't avoid the crowded streets of Wren's End.

She opened her eyes again. The forest was inviting with its pleasant dimness. Beams of light here and there cut through the canopy and illuminated small patches of thin grasses as they made subtle patterns that followed the path the light would take as the seasons changed. The greens and browns, along with the scent of decay, signaled a healthy ecosystem.

The only real problem she has identified is the limited animal life in the area. Hunting proved to be an issue, forcing her to venture into town to get Guild Hall meals. There weren't many small game animals while larger animals, like deer, were absent as were predatory animals. The only monsters she had so far identified in the area, goblins, are too stupid and loud to be a threat to rabbits or deer and were too weak to kill wolves or bears. She figured it was a result of the valley constrained on three sides by impassable mountains. Hunting would have wiped out the animals over the years and farming communities didn't like predators too close to their settlements.

Niitty led Gerold to the patch of flax she had found when she was looking for a good spot for her tree hide. Her training focused on combat, making her ignorant on plants beyond those used for healing or other alchemical properties. Other members of the tribe, who lacked the interest in going out to adventure, gravitated toward harvesting plants used in daily life.

Niitty watched Gerold as he waded through the patch and

waved his hand through the plants, small buds that would bloom into brilliant blue flowers in a few weeks peppered the top of the plants. The presence of the plants was another sign of civilization encroaching on the forest. While the border between farm and forest was clean, it didn't mean that plants like flax couldn't jump the border. The plants weren't native to the region and were encroaching on the natural undergrowth, only limited in its expansion by the lack of full sunlight deeper in.

Niitty noticed a wistful sorrow come across Gerold's face as he was lost in thought, staring at the flax while gently waving his hand through the patch. Taking a deep breath, he bent over and started harvesting the plants with his dagger. His soft hands with perfect skin moved with a trained deftness that indicated extensive experience in the practice that was held back by an inadequate tool.

Gerold's behavior continued to perplex Niitty. His skill at harvesting plants, how he only harvested the most mature plants, removed diseased ones and absentmindedly pulled out weeds as he went brought question to her assumption this was nothing more than an act brought on by delusion. Could he really be telling the truth that he's an old man made young again by his Paladin status?

No, that's not possible. He knew little about fighting and a God wouldn't have overlooked a candidate like this for so long. They were, according to the stories, always on the lookout for compatible souls and would snap them up the moment they came of age.

Niitty leaned against a tree to enjoy the feeling of the wood on her back while watching Gerold methodically move through the patch. After clearing a 10 foot by 10 foot section, she called out, "Gerold? How much do you need?"

He kept working and called back, "I'll need three times more than this to make a shirt or pair of pants."

Her eyes went wide. That much flax just to make one shirt? No wonder buying clothing was so costly. The amount of labor and time required was incredible. And it was just the plants, she had no idea what he was going to do to turn it into a shirt.

"And how long will it take to make new pants?"

"I'm not that good, so about two hours. I'm not going to make a replacement pair and I still have to spin thread, which is a few more hours of effort. Oh," Gerold stopped, stood and held his hands about a foot apart, "Can you help by finding a solid straight stick about this long? I'll need it to spin the thread."

Happy to have something to do beyond watch Gerold harvest plants, Niitty went into the woods to search for a stick. Gerold had spoken like finding a length of wood in a pine forest like that was a simple task. This forest didn't have a lot of fallen sticks. Most sticks she did find were too moist from the recent winter thaw while branches were too long and too thick.

Ranging back toward the farmland, she noticed a few younger trees. One had a small branch about a foot long and she severed it off of the main trunk with her utility dagger. She made sure to strip the small sticks and needles off of the small branch on the way back.

When she returned, he had finished his task and he nodded in approval at the stick. After making a small notch in one end with his dagger, he shoved it into the bag, "Ready to head into town?"

Niitty felt her pulse quicken and a sheen of sweat bead up on her forehead, "No. Do you think you can do it and I stay out here?"

A look of sympathy came to Gerold's face, "I wish I could. We need to form our party and you'll not get credit for these kills without your token."

Niitty knew she was trying to avoid the inevitable. Part of the purpose of the journey was not only to become more skilled to join the ranks of the hunters for the tribe, but it was also to assist with relations that required trips into a town. She was never going to reduce her anxiety without regular exposure. At least she had a friendly face to join her, one who could help reduce the fear.

"Can you at least do what you did yesterday? That calming feel?"

He thought for a moment, "Only if it gets bad. I can only use my Calm Nerves aura once a day and for 20 minutes. Plus, it paints a beacon on me that allows everyone inside the range to know exactly what I am."

Niitty had no room to argue his hesitancy when she, herself, had to fight with all her willpower just to walk through the town gates. "I understand, I'll try to keep it together long enough to turn in the bounty and get some food."

Niitty steeled her nerves and reluctantly led Gerold back to the road and back into town. The unnatural fields surrounded her and her dread continued to build as the town palisade came into view. The walls were a mockery of the forest. While her tribe wasn't against cutting down trees like some of the stranger races even more reclusive than the Mountain Elves, this wall felt like an insult to everything natural. Her instincts saw the wooden monstrosity as lining up the naked corpses of genocide to display a ruler's ruthless power. Tree trunks with sharp tops were packed together one by one on each other, closer than anything that could be found in the forest. The bark was stripped away and treated with weather-resisting resin. And, while only in her imagination, she could swear she felt a pulsing thrum from the walls as the Town Seed's enchantment bolstered the defensive effects.

The two town guards looked at her with a sinister sneer. Her logical brain tried to tell her this was just a trick of her imagination and that they were just bored of watching a gate that only saw the passage of locals going to market or adventurers returning for the day. Emotion had a way of beating logic bloody and shoving it into an unmarked grave.

The open gate, doors swung wide open and out, resembled the maw of a monster, that if she walked in she would be eaten alive and digested within until nothing, not even her soul, remained. A rumble in her stomach and the presence of Gerold at her side, who she noticed was standing quite a bit closer than usual, reminded her that this is a task that must be done.

She successfully passed through the gate and into the town. The buildings and the outer wall loomed over her, threatening to collapse in on her. The townspeople were plotting, planning an attack on her as they stared at their passing. Her logical brain had become a rotted living corpse, shoved its hand out of the grave her emotion had buried it in and told her that they weren't staring, that the boulevard was wide and not that crowded.

Something solid and warm was gripped in her hand. She looked down to find what it was. Gerold had somehow put his arm in there and forced her fingers closed around it. No, that's not right. She had unconsciously reached out and gripped his bicep, moving in closer to his body. This calmed her a bit, seeing his own lack of concern at walking in the town.

"Do you need me to activate the aura?"

His voice cut through her fear as she looked down at his face. His was a look of worry as he looked at her. Her brain had suddenly strayed into his eyes, ones that she found drawn to. His eyes were different from what she was expecting. While her own Father's eyes were brown like healthy soil one could find high quality herbs growing in, the eyes she now saw were like perfectly polished and cut emeralds surrounded by that deep limbal ring that further accentuated the green, the feel of looking into them was similar. She felt like a six year old girl again looking up at her own private hero, even though Gerold was shorter than she was. She was 6'2" and estimated he stood around 5'9".

While still terrifying and alien, the sinister air that the town was in her mind started to fade a little. Travel through the town became marginally more bearable as a result. Her logical brain, bruised and battered in the war against her emotions, found purchase and held its ground. It made no headway, but it at least defended what it still owned. The street suddenly felt a little wider, the surrounding structures less looming and the stares, she noticed, were directed more toward Gerold than to her.

Taking a deep breath to reduce her quickened pulse, she replied, "No. I have to get used to this eventually."

Gerold grunted in his normal laconic manner and continued on. She noticed he made no effort to extract her hand from his arm. As they approached the Guild Hall, she knew the stress wasn't fully gone. She was going to be rude, short and prickly with anyone who talked with her and she decided to let Gerold do all the talking. Making it this far a third day in a row was enough of a victory for today.

CHAPTER 7

When Gerold walked into the Guild Hall, Niitty was still gripping to his arm. She had calmed down slightly when he suggested using his aura and her grip wasn't crushing his bicep, but she was still dealing with severe issues with coming into town. He found himself thinking about helping her get over her fear so the competent and effervescent Niitty he was getting to know in the forest would present itself within a city. Not that he had any idea how to pull it off other than be present. Having a friendly companion seemed to keep her a bit more balanced. That was a concern for another time. A different challenge, one with a face plastered with disgust, awaited.

Karl's presence, along with his party, dominated the common room. He was surrounded by the usual boisterous crowd of adventurers clamoring for his attention. He immediately noticed Gerold and Niitty's entrance and then got up from his table and approached the two of them. After catching sight of Gerold's bandaged leg jutting out of tattered pants, his face changed to a smug smile. Stopping a few paces away, he said, "I see you're struggling with the whole poor adventurer thing. Didn't you bring enough to cover incidentals? This is the last chance to join us; we head out to the crypt in the morning."

Gerold felt Niitty's hand tighten on his bicep as she pulled herself smaller to try and get out of Karl's visible range. Gerold stared Karl in the eyes silently, making the other man nervous. After a few more moments, Gerold replied, "No, I don't think so."

Without waiting for a reply, he walked away toward the administration desk.

Karl shouted after him, "Fine! We could have been great allies in the Imperial court, but you've made me your opposition. Once I find out who your family is, I'll be sure to do whatever it takes to undermine your position."

Gerold waved his hand backwards dismissively.

As Gerold made his way over to the administration desk, he heard Karl's voice once more, "Friends! We must turn in for the evening. For a parting gift, I shall pay for one last round for you all! We must leave on the morn to quell an evil dwelling in these mountains. The undead walk the slopes among the rocks. Lest the evil spill out into the valley, cutting us off from help and besieging us within this fine village, we must venture forth. The journey will be difficult and fraught with danger. Fear not! We were chosen to dispatch these foes and cleanse the cursed crypt with our holy might. And when we return with both trophy and glory, I shall throw a feast worthy of the Imperial capital itself!"

Gerold rolled his eyes and he heard Niitty let loose an exasperated sigh before a roar of approval, applause, whistles and shouts filled the crowded room. Niitty went rigid at his side and pulled herself closer to him. Gerold turned to look and she had her forehead buried against his arm with her eyes closed tight. Positioning himself against a wall to help block the view, he bent his arm around the back of her head and waited for the din to die down.

It didn't take long as Karl and his party had ascended the stairs to their rooms above to turn in early. As the noise died down, Gerold whispered to Niitty, "If you want to stand outside, I think we're close enough to the desk to let me take your token."

She nodded her head against his arm and fished her token out of a pocket of her trousers. After handing it to him, she rushed away and disappeared through the door. Gerold walked up to the administration desk and found no one present. Popping a bell on the counter, he heard a voice from the back, "Coming."

From out of the back room came the face of Gerold's second favorite person in the entire town, good old Allan. His expression of neutrality turned to mild frown, "Oh, it's you. What do you want this evening?"

Gerold huffed and put the two tokens on the desk and his bag of holding, "Turning in a bounty."

Allan pulled out the box and device, "You know the drill. Ears in the box."

Gerold looked at the box, "I don't think that one will be large enough."

"Please, I doubt you got that much today," Allan said, rolling his eyes.

"Humor me."

Allan stared at Gerold, down at his bare bandaged leg, his eyes drifted to the tiny bag Gerold held in his hand then back up again. He smirked and put the box away and went to the back. He returned with a far larger box, "I'll be sure to laugh when your pitiful haul falls in."

Gerold was getting tired of his attitude. Gerold decided to risk sacrificing his identity to mess with the man. Gerold turned the bag upside down and shook it over the box. Since he hadn't willed anything, it dropped nothing. He gave it another shake and he willed just one ear to fall out.

Allan burst out in laughter, "Oh, my, what a powerful warrior. I am surprised...surprised you managed to only find a single goblin when they travel in packs of at least five."

"Hold on, there's more in here," Gerold said, shaking the bag. He then willed the remaining 67 ears to fall out at once. When the disgusting, shriveled grey ears started pouring out of the tiny bag, Allan's mouth went slack. He watched in shock as the box filled in with the ears and the deluge stopped.

He picked up the box and looked inside, "One moment please. I need to pass this by the Guild Master."

"What? Why?"

"To make sure you didn't cheat," he said and left through the back room door without letting Gerold get in a response.

Gerold mulled over what the problem was. Did Allan think Gerold had cheated and bought or stolen the ears? Considering that's very much likely what Karl and his group did, he would have words with the Guild Hall if they accused him of cheating.

He paused for a second and wondered why he suddenly felt like it was an absolute affront to his very soul to even think about cheating. He had been known to cheat before. Nothing major, he never cheated at cards or in business. He would, however, sneak playing pieces off the board when his son wasn't looking or change the rules on the fly when playing with his daughter. Now? That thought seemed to sicken him. Was it something to do with becoming a Paladin? Stories were quite clear about their honesty and trustworthiness. Gerold found his emotions were subtly altered to make unethical behavior more unpleasant. Still, he knew he could fight through the feeling if it proved essentially to a greater good.

His introspection was interrupted when Allan returned

with an extremely well dressed gnomish man. His thin musculature betrayed a profession sitting behind a desk or some other idle activity. He had sharp features in his face, was extremely pale and had a messy mop of brown hair. On his face perched a pair of silver wire spectacles.

The man looked up at Gerold from behind the desk, "You are new here so I'll get this out of the way. I am Philip. Yes, I am the Guild Master. Yes, I actually am an adventurer. No, I am out of practice. No, I am not a combat specialist, either in arms or spells. I am a Scribe because we can't have Warriors and Mages run a Guild Hall. There is too much paperwork, accounting and, here, school administration to take care of. Does that answer your questions?"

Gerold was taken aback by the unprompted rant. Yes, he was thrown off-guard to see a skinny man who doesn't look like he's seen the light of day in months announce he's the Guild Master. He wasn't sure if he was going to question it since he didn't have time to process the man's presence before the speech. Deception training kicking in, and his compulsion to not lie directing his thoughts, he hedged, "I didn't question your position in this fine establishment."

Philip squinted his eyes at Gerold, not sure of the honesty of the words. He held out a hand, "Show me a hand."

Gerold did as instructed and Philip grabbed his hand. Gerold allowed the strange Guild Master to inspect his hands. Philip ran a finger over Gerold's palm then flipped it over as he closely inspected the back of the hand. He hummed a few times, "Lean in closer so I can get a good look at your face."

Gerold leaned in and Philip got uncomfortably close, stared directly into Gerold's eyes and took in various features on his face followed by a deep sniff. He hummed again and backed away while rubbing his hand against his chin. "Come. And Allan? Bring the Guild Register with you," the Guild Master said before spinning on his heel and marched back into the back room.

"You heard him, come," Allan repeated, bringing the tablet and wand device with him.

Gerold stepped through the door and found a plain hallway with three doors on the left and one at the far end. He saw Philip standing at the door at the far end, holding the handle. He ducked in when he verified Gerold had come into the hall.

The door led to an office. A desk faced the door against a large window crisscrossed with diagonal lead bars to make a diamond effect in the thick glass. The darkness beyond the glass obscured the training yard that would be visible during the day. Filing cabinets lined the walls to the left and two bookshelves with orderly rows of books featuring esoteric titles Gerold didn't understand were organized by color on the wall to the right. Between the desk and the door sat an octagonal table with eight chairs with an enchanted light suspended from the ceiling to provide light to the room.

Philip sat at the octagonal table in the chair facing the door and pointed his hand at the seat opposite the table, "Please, have a seat. And Allan? Leave the box and Guild Register here and go about your duties."

Allan looked at Gerold, "Sir, he could be dangerous."

Philip laughed, "Trust me, you pose more a danger to me than he does."

Allan looked at Gerold again before putting the box and register down.

"Before he goes, can you tell me how long you intend to have me here," Gerold asked.

"Don't be rude," Allan snapped.

Philip waved his hand, "Calm yourself. I'm not sure. Why do you ask?"

"My companion is waiting for me outside and I don't want her to think I left her there."

He looked at Allan, "Please go fetch his companion and bring her here. And some wine."

After a minute, Niitty entered the room with Allan, who left a bottle of wine in front of Philip and then left. She looked extra nervous being in the smaller room.

Philip looked her over while uncorking the bottle, "Mountain Elf. I take it you're in a tribe that still follows the old ways, correct?"

She nodded in affirmation while keeping her eyes on the table.

Philip smiled warmly, "I appreciate your bravery then. Being in here can't be easy, so I'll keep this brief. Sir, you're a Paladin, are you not?"

Gerold frowned. He was getting the attention he didn't want. Unable to lie, he deflected, "What makes you think that?"

Philip sighed, "I'm quite a bit older than I look. I've met one that came through here years ago. Your eyes, your lack of odor and your lack of calluses are telltale signs. It also helped I got a missive informing me you'd be arriving."

Gerold only grunted in response.

Philip waited to see if Gerold would elaborate. When he didn't, Philip poured some wine into a mug. He stood up, walked around the table and then tossed the red liquid on Gerold's shirt.

Gerold bolted up out of his chair, knocking it to the floor, "What was that for?"

Philip pointed to his torn shirt, "Look. That wine stains cloth. Yet, on you, it fell right off. You're not even moist. And don't worry about the mess, I'll have Allan wipe it up later."

Gerold scowled at the man, "What's your point?"

He returned to his seat and sat down, "To prove your identity. No enchanted shirt would work if it was tattered like that. You have your reasons to keep your identity a secret. I promise not reveal it. I do, however, have a request."

Gerold returned his chair to its position and sat down, "You could have asked without the theatrics. What can we assist with?"

"The crypt, I want you to back-up Karl's Party," he said, "I want you to avoid interfering with him unless they get into trouble. And, yes, that's the formal name he registered with us, Karl's Party."

Gerold hummed, "Apart from developing my skills, I have another reason to be here. My God informed me of a pulse of necrotic magic in the area. Before I agree to this, have you noticed anything else odd in the region?"

Philip thought for a moment, "Nothing comes to mind. The crypt is the only unusual event happening in these parts."

"Hmm, I was going to head there anyway. Why do you want me involved and why do you want it concealed?"

Philip sighed, "Karl is the son of an influential Duchy. I've been told he's been harassing you thinking you're another noble. You're not one, are you?"

Gerold shook his head, "No, I'm not. My guess is he's assuming I'm a noble because of my looks."

"Figures," Philip replied, "He's not the brightest. Nobles like his family buy their children up the ranks in the Guild for prestige. It's technically illegal, but the Guild will turn the other way for a large donation. I am completely against the practice, not that I have any authority to override my superiors. The only limit is the parts needed to get past Iron are so dangerous to obtain that adventurers are unwilling to give them up."

Gerold nodded, "I thought the same thing. We happened to travel with the same merchant on the way from the capital. I've only gotten basic combat training with the Temple, so I'm no combat expert, but when we were accosted by bandits on the road, those five displayed a concerning lack of ability."

Philip leaned back and stared at the ceiling for a few moments, "As I suspected. He even brought in three of his friends from military and merchant houses and bought their way into Iron as well. The fool is even bragging about being a Paladin. The only outlier of the bunch is the Leopardia woman. She's still wood and, for some reason, Karl has refused to admit her to the party. They'll quickly learn that quality equipment will only get them so far. They managed to clear out four goblin bands in the last two days, so I fear they're getting big heads. And, unfortunately, after turning in the parts to get to Iron, they laid claim on the crypt quest."

"And why is this something I can help with," Gerold asked.

"Paladins have one key advantage against the undead, mainly your Turn Undead ability. Even as a rookie, the Turn Undead ability should weaken the crypt's residents enough to give you a fighting chance."

"What about the Cleric they already have with them?"

Philip shook his head, "That's not an ability clerics have until they're much more powerful. And, as you can imagine, clerics that powerful are rare. Focusing on healing like they do is a high risk and their survival rate is low. Most clerics only ever learn Simple Heal and Basic Heal before quitting to open healing dens."

The situation made perfect sense to Gerold now. Karl's party, while made up of four formal Iron rank adventurers, was, especially after today, even less skilled than Gerold and Niitty. Gerold wasn't confident he could beat any of them in a duel with the gap in equipment and the two of them would lose a fight against his party, the two of them would perform better against an unintelligent foe. Rolling over a few goblins in a party of their size would not have developed any coordination the way the trial by fire that Gerold and Niitty had gone through that day. And, while Karl and his band, save Gewa, were arrogant and haughty, they weren't evil and didn't deserve to die in a tomb. A strong instinct rose up in him to accept.

"I am willing to accept. Niitty, are you in agreement?"

Niitty nodded silently.

"Then that's it."

Philip smiled, "Good. I suggest you set off a day later. I suspect your companion is a skilled tracker and that should be enough space to arrive at the crypt soon after they do while ensuring they don't see you following."

"I could join them instead of holding back. That would be better," Gerold said.

"After that disagreement you two had? I fear if you suddenly change your mind, someone in the party will recognize I asked you to chaperone and they'll take it as an insult. We want to avoid that," Philip said as he poured another mug of wine. Gerold couldn't argue with that, realizing his prickly persona has caused him more trouble than he expected to avoid.

Gerold replied, "I can't leave without making preparations. We lack the funds for travel rations and we will need another day of hunting to get enough for travel. We will also need directions."

Niitty, to Gerold's surprise, quietly added something to his statement, "And there are few game animals to hunt."

"That and I'll need at least four hours to repair my pants," Gerold continued.

Philip stood up and went to his desk. He pulled out a leather sack that clinked with coin. Opening it, he pulled out two silver coins and put them on the table, "I can offer you an advance to cover the expenses of travel. This should cover the cost of provisions. Please take tomorrow to prepare and rest." He paused for a moment, reached into the sack again and pulled out two copper coins, "And use the copper for your leg. A pair of simple heals should accelerate the healing process down from several days to overnight. As for how to get there, it's easy. Go due west out of the town and into the forest. You'll find a stream and if you follow that, it should lead you near the crypt. It's up on a rise in the mountains. The herders don't know much more than that since they fled the area after finding it."

Gerold picked up the coins and immediately dissolved the two copper ones into sequential Simple Heal spells. Pulling the makeshift bandage away, he saw it mostly closed up, leaving an angry red line that he knew would be gone in the morning.

Philip smiled, "I have eight more of those silver coins for when you return. Before you go, we have a few more things to take care of."

Picking up the two guild tokens, he slotted them into the Guild Register, "You haven't formed a party. Would you like to?"

Gerold nodded, "Yes please. Let's do this."

Philip smiled, "I have to read you a disclaimer." He got up and walked back to his desk, pulling out a well worn piece of paper. Clearing his throat, he continued, "Be warned, adventurer, forming a party is not a step to undertake lightly. Doing so will tie your soul to your fellow members. Your fates will be linked as will your fortunes. You will develop a sense of loyalty to your compatriots akin to close family and you will be unable to raise a hand in harm. This will additionally allow the use of skills that only affect members of your party. Please understand that this decision is irreversible and only death will dissolve your party affiliation. Additional effects will be felt that are best discovered through trial. If you accept these terms, please provide your party name and confirm your decision with a thumb print."

Gerold remained silent as he digested what he just heard. Gerold had always thought it was just a loose affiliation. He had no idea it was such a grave decision.

He turned to Niitty, "Is this something you want?"

She remained quiet. Gerold watched as a flurry of emotions passed over her face. She then looked up and over at Philip, "This is really permanent?"

Philip nodded with a grave expression on his face, "It is. I find it concerning how newbie adventurers treat party formation with almost no respect. Despite receiving the warning, most adventurers disregard it and link themselves out of youthful enthusiasm. It frequently leads to heartache later."

Niitty turned her eyes down at the table again and her eyes darted back and forth in thought. Finally turning to Gerold, "We have only known each other for two days. There's something about you I can't explain. Our guild IDs, you being a Paladin, the weird feelings I have when you're around. Everything in my body says to take this risk. I will do it."

Gerold had a different thought. He really didn't care one way or another. The warning didn't mean much to him. However, he did have a protective instinct when it came to Niitty. Seeing her reminded him of Elli, of what she could have been in a decade. If it was for his own benefit, Gerold would have turned this down here after hearing about the conditions that came with it. Fate brought him together with a young woman who, while talented, still needed a companion she could trust in life.

"Let's do this."

Philip nodded and ran his finger along the line indicating the party is not registered and the screen changed. In the place of their names and guild ID was a new empty box with a series of boxes below. Within each box was one letter of the alphabet and one for each number. Below that were five blank boxes, two of them highlighted in a darker gold. He turned it toward the two.

"Put in your desired party name and place your thumbs in the indicated boxes."

Gerold hadn't thought about a name. He looked over at Niitty, "Uh, do you have any suggestions?"

She looked down for a moment and closed her eyes. Opening them again, she pulled the device over and tapped in two words: Divine Misfits.

Gerold huffed, "What made you think of that?"

She shrugged, "You're weird. I'm weird. I figure we'll be on quests sent by the Gods. It makes sense."

Gerold didn't really care. This was just a formality to him. "Fine by me," he said, putting his thumb on the square. Niitty did the same and they watched as the box filled in with a solid gold color over three seconds. After fully filling in, the box vanished and their information came back. The moment it did, Gerold felt a strange feeling build in his chest that was tugging itself in Niitty's direction. It wasn't uncomfortable or concerning, just an odd warmth before subsiding. That must be the magic taking effect, he thought.

Divine Misfits
Niitty of the Hirvi Clan, Wood Rank Ranger, ID 042778722526R92
Gerold of Hivastock, Wood Rank Warrior, ID 042778722525W41

Philip pulled the device back, read it and smirked, "Not the strangest name we've ever seen." He slid the box of ears over and prepared the wand, "And this is the last order of business."

"The ears," inquired Gerold.

"Not quite," he said, converting the box of ears and Philip poured out one silver and thirty-six coins out in front of Gerold. Gerold scooped them into his bag of holding.

"What is it then," asked Gerold.

He pointed at the box, "How did you do this? We normally expect new adventuring parties to kill one or two bands of goblins in a day. You just came back with, what, 11 bands worth of ears? Answering this is a formality that I have to apply to everyone, even a Paladin."

Gerold explained the tactics they developed that morning along with the close calls and mistakes made along the way. He made sure to emphasize that Niitty's tracking skills were the real winning strategy since he would only find a band by pure accident, making her cheeks go red in embarrassment. Philip nodded along the entire time as he listened to the story.

Philip then turned his head to the ceiling, closed his eyes and folded his hands over his chest. He sat there, silently breathing, for a solid minute.

"Uh, sir," Gerold interrupted after the minute passed.

"Sorry, thinking," he replied, eyes still closed. Opening them again, he said, "As I suspected. That's an obvious and correct tactic, especially with a small group and the opponents you faced. You learned something from your basic training."

This confused Gerold, "Why? Are we high performers?"

"Normally," he said, opening his eyes and looking, "You'd be above average. Nothing fantastic, we've had parties in the past pull in twenty bands in one day, though they only were able to keep up that travel pace for a day. Moving twenty miles and fighting is doable if you travel light. Unfortunately, things aren't the same as they were. As recently as two years ago, parties would trip over each other clearing out the forest every day. Now? The forest is overrun yet parties stumble around, running into two or three bands a day."

Philip sighed and played with the sack of coins, "The poor performance has impacted the town's income. We aren't doing too well."

This threw Gerold for a loop, "This is supposed to be a major farming community and a training center. Towns like this get big subsidies to operate."

Philip nodded, "The border wars out to the east have strained the Imperial coffers, resulting in budget cuts. This has cascaded into problems with banditry on the roads that have cut into the funds even more. I have managed to keep the town running by cutting corners. One corner has been eliminating wilderness survival and tracking classes. An adventurer can buy provisions and stumble through the woods, but a skilled woodsman that can't fight is dead. The cuts have led to a marked decline in performance that's exacerbating our problems. I fear this is a losing battle."

Sighing again, he dumped out the sack of coins. Twenty silver coins tumbled out, "This is the last of the Adventurer Coins. To keep the Town Seed going for another month, we need one gold. There is another caravan arriving the day after tomorrow. If that one is waylaid, we only have eight days left before the protection deactivates. Losing the protection wouldn't be the end of the world. Some people would leave and adventurers can shift to act as border patrol. The frontier towns have managed to survive for generations without an active Town Seed. Still, I hope it doesn't come to that."

The office went dead silent. Gerold wasn't sure how to digest this. A town as vibrant as this one, though small, was at the cusp of losing its Town Seed?

Gerold broke the silence, "Couldn't we have the adventurers focus on giving the coins to the town?"

He shook his head, "No. Not many here are altruistic and will leave if asked to chip in. It would also spark a panic. Besides, even if we performed at the level we did years ago, we'd have to pull in thirty bands a day just to feed the Town Seed, leaving nothing for food, Guild Hall maintenance or instructor salaries. It would also siphon off coin necessary to keep other things running, like at the bath house, street lights, the local healer and various enchanted items the shopkeepers who cater to adventurers have gotten accustomed to. While most commerce operates on mundane coin, the higher class residents would leave for the Capital without luxuries. The entire economy would be upended when an Adventurer Copper exchanges for a Mundane Silver."

"And have you discussed this with the instructors or the higher ups at the Guild?"

He belted out a short, bitter laugh, "The higher ups? I fought the budget cuts with them over a year ago. They told me it was an efficiency initiative and to make do. I can't bring this to the instructors. You haven't been here long enough. My entire support staff has been cut down to just five people while I only have four instructors left. I used to have twenty support staff and ten instructors. The layoffs haven't been good for the mood. If I mention anything about how close we are to insolvency, this Guild Hall is done."

Something wasn't adding up to Gerold. If things were so dire, why was he being sent off to babysit a noble's party? He needed to confirm this, "Why are you sending me off after Karl then? If Niitty and I focus all day, I'm sure we could help mitigate the budget problem on goblin ears alone."

Philip smiled, "Politics. While I appreciate the thought, I do have a caravan coming that will keep us afloat. If Karl is injured or killed, the political ramifications could guarantee the failure of this Guild Hall. We are expected to protect the nobility and his family could have just enough sway to ruin Wren's End."

Gerold frowned. He didn't like nor understand politics. In farming, the plants grew when they wanted and in conditions they preferred. You couldn't cajole or negotiate with the weather. Work wasn't up for a debate, it had to be done or your farm failed. Politics, to Gerold, was a pointless waste of time and he didn't have the energy to discuss it, "I understand. Help Karl and I keep the town from failing."

He stood up, retrieving the Guild Register, "Good. Now, unless you have any more questions or comments for me, I think I've taken up enough of your time and your friend seems to be at the limits of her willpower to remain in this enclosed space."

"Then we shall take our leave," Gerold stood up, gave a polite nod to Philip and left with Niitty following close behind.

After exiting the administrative area, he noticed a sudden silence come over the room. Everyone was staring at him. Allan, in particular, had a strange smug look on his face.

A whisper broke the silence, "Is that him?"

"No, it can't be. Look at his clothing. No way a Paladin would look like that."

"I thought it was Karl. Are there two here?"

"I heard they're supposed to be friendly."

"Look at his face. He's so perfect and clean."

"Do you think he would let us join his party?"

"I hear they can kill fifty goblins alone."

"I hear that vampires cower in their presence."

"Why do you think he even came here? Is there something going on?"

Gerold groaned and shot Allan a nasty look, who continued to smirk in response. The man decided to get his revenge and divulge his identity. He must have been standing outside the room and listening in. Gerold in that moment felt like Niitty and wanted to get out of the Hall.

Before leaving the Guild Hall, he noticed his favorite server. He walked over to her, "Hey. Sorry, we haven't been introduced properly. That's been rude of me. I'm Gerold."

She smiled, "Hi hon. Don't worry, trainees come and go through here so I'm used to never learning names. I'm Sandra."

"Hi Sandra. It looks like my secret got out. As you can imagine, neither Niitty nor I want to be in here right now. Can you get something we can take with us?"

She had a nervous smile on her face, "Of course, my lord. I

can get some fresh bread and a few water skins."

Gerold frowned, "Don't do anything special or use honorifics, I'm a normal adventurer like anyone else. Just the normal fare any other adventurer is entitled to."

"Are ya sure?" she asked, not quite certain what action she should take.

"Yes," Gerold replied, "I'm trying to avoid the attention."

"I'll be right back," she rushed off to the kitchen and returned with two loaves of stale bread and two water skins.

Thanking her, Gerold and Niitty left. They were followed by a dozen curious adventurers out into the town.

The small procession got the attention of the townspeople who were out in the main plaza. The whispers of the adventurers spread like a sickness to the rest of the population, who also started to stare and whisper. Gerold took a glance at McVatter's General Store along the perimeter of the plaza, reminding himself he would need to come by later to buy provisions. Right now, he didn't want to get trapped in the shop by a growing throng who wanted the once in a lifetime glance at a legendary Paladin.

The two picked up their pace as they headed to the west gate. The two guards were flabbergasted by the parade of people following two adventurers and could only stand by and watch. When the two exited the gates, they looked back and saw the crowd cease at the gates. Thankfully, the prospect of getting locked out of town for the night dissuaded the growing crowd from following them further.

Gerold hoped that getting into town tomorrow for provisions wouldn't draw this attention.

CHAPTER 8

Niitty was thankful for their turn of events with the Guild Master. Instead of having to venture back into the town again to collect another bounty, they could spend the day in preparation. Still, Gerold suggested they spend an hour or two in the morning practicing combat against goblin bands before he returned to town to purchase provisions. His incredible healing, along with the three spells he cast the day before, completely closed up the wound on his leg and any evidence of the damage to his face and head from two days prior was entirely gone.

Gerold had commented that he was thankful for his curse in that he had spent hours the prior day fighting goblins and he wasn't even sore. Niitty continued to marvel at the extent and consistency he had in maintaining his story that he's a middle aged man. He even developed little behavioral tics. He would roll his left shoulder and massage his right knee. The movements were habitual since his movements weren't otherwise hindered by his joints. Having an old childhood injury wouldn't be a surprise since the Paladin gifts, or the curse as he called it, would have healed them up. She decided not to ask given his reluctance to talk about the past.

As she caught sign of a goblin band to the south, she began to notice the effects of forming a party. She found herself having second thoughts about their name. She felt so out of place in town that it made sense at the time. She also noticed two other effects that the Guild Master didn't disclose in his little speech.

First, her feelings toward Gerold changed. She previously had a mild infatuation that was developing into a sort of affection based on his gentle patience with her condition. Now she felt an odd sense of protectiveness toward him in addition to her infatuation. Even the thought of him being attacked drew up a sense of ire in her bones.

Second, she had a vague sense of where he was at all times. Gerold had described to her how his Sense Evil aura worked and how he could feel the direction and intensity of an evil aura. The connection was much more detailed. She could feel his direction and a general sense of how far away he was. Not only that, she could sense his surface level feelings. This, she guessed, would help determine if her party members were in any sort of distress.

At the moment she got a sense of overwhelming sadness and depression. His face may be a neutral mask and his speech measured and paced concealed a darkness boiling beneath. She also felt a tiny little spark of light in there as well, one that threatened to go out at any moment. She could save pondering that for later, the goblins were close.

After a couple of hours, Niitty and Gerold had managed to kill five bands of goblins, collecting thirty ears. Gerold indicated that they didn't have a reason to turn them in right away, much to Niitty's relief. She felt a strange sense of refreshment and also a little stronger. Gerold reported that his came a few goblins earlier. They must have hit a threshold where they killed enough monsters to subtly improve their power. Adventurers had to put themselves at risk to experience this momentary bliss.

It was mid-morning when they returned to the tree hide. Gerold asked if she could prepare her sewing kit for him when he returned.

After Gerold left to go to town to procure provisions, Niitty occupied her time collecting firewood. Remembering how far the mouth of Gerold's bag had extended to accept his hauberk, she drug back larger branches and logs to bring along. She also found a few sturdy branches that would serve as tent poles. The trees going up into the mountains would be too thin and spaced too far apart to erect the hide so it would need to be used as a tent. Plus, it would take too much time since a hide was designed to be a shelter for an extended period of time.

Nearing noon, she completed her task and piled a good bit of wood at the base of one of the trees. Hopefully Gerold would notice it and understand the meaning. She climbed back into her hide and lowered the rope for when Gerold returned.

Turning her face to the pine canopy above, she watched as the breeze shook the branches, letting in a sparkling, ever-changing pattern of light through. She found it beautiful. She also felt a deep sense of fatigue building behind her eyes. The fatigue wasn't physical. The exhaustion didn't come from fighting goblins, which proved to be much easier once they found their combat rhythm.

This fatigue was emotional. She was feeling the weight crash down on her in this rare moment of calm.

She reflected on her Mother as they embraced before leaving with the trade caravan south. Her Mother had surprised her with her Father's sword, entrusting the family heirloom to her daughter for the long trip ahead. The journey from her tribe's winter settlement was thankfully uneventful. The caravan carried a Nomad Seed. It wasn't nearly as effective as the Town Seeds that sat at the center of permanent settlements, the radius measured only three hundred yards, it was only effective when stationary and it needed at least fifty people in its vicinity to function from their ambient magic generated by their life force. The Seed reduced the need for guards at night to a minimum since it kept monsters at bay. The effect created a small sanctuary in monster infested lands.

Once they arrived at the northern most frontier village of the Empire, Niitty struck out on her own. There, she joined the Adventurer's Guild in the very same hall that all the members of her tribe had done before her. The residents of the town were Mountain Elves that, over generations, had become accustomed to settled life and didn't have the same phobias that the nomadic tribes developed.

Thankfully, the residents of the city were familiar with their cousins that followed the old ways and were patient and kind. The village construction had many features that reminded her of nature. Live trees were grown to act as central pillars for buildings, creating a forested canopy overhead to mask the permanent structures that were built around them. The Guild Hall was the only exception since the Imperial Guild always built them the same, though the wood construction fit in well with the settlement.

When she registered as a Ranger, she thought of her Father and how, when he was her age, he stood in this exact spot and registered himself all those years ago. That thought reduced the pressure of standing in a cramped building, at least somewhat, when she resolved to make his memory proud.

She immediately left and traveled along the trade roads protected from monsters by enchantments that extended out from towns and cities. The Imperial Capital, which she learned was just called the Capital because it made no sense to name something everyone already knew, supplied the bulk of the Adventurer Coin necessary to maintain the trade network. The trip to Wren's End, where her Father had traveled to start his training as an adventurer, had no adventure at all, much to Niitty's relief.

She had never seen a live monster up-close until the day

she met Gerold and the first time one was close enough to do her harm was the day after. She had gained an appreciation of her tribe's Hunters and Rangers and the job they performed protecting her while she learned how to shoot a bow, free of monster harassment. It was one of these jobs protecting an older child that claimed her Father's life.

She was only six when it happened. The twelve years following it had dulled the pain of the loss. Now it was only a faded scar with mostly happy memories that remained. She felt melancholy about how he didn't see her off on her journey nor did he teach her to shoot a bow or to fence. Such was the way of the world. Nomadic people struggled more and were tougher as a result. At least she thought she was tougher before facing her first real danger, or venturing into a town four times in the past two weeks when she never set foot in one before.

Her eyelids felt heavy from all the accumulated stress. She closed them and breathed in deep, held it then slowly released it. Every breath took in the familiar odors of the forest, thick pine scent permeating the air with a minor undertone of the fertilizer of the nearby farms threatening to ruin the effect. Her mind drifted into a state of emptiness, melting the stress away.

She focused on the cool breeze passing over her skin, tickling her with the prickly sensation of the late spring morning. Her muscles slacked as tension she didn't know she had released.

She listened to the sounds of the forest. Birds, one of the few animals that were still in abundance in these woods, sang, filling the air with joy. The pine needles above rustled gently in the wind. Her Father had once said that, if the wind was right, the rustling of the branches sounded a lot like the waves of the sea. She wanted to see the ocean and feel the waves, to experience first-hand her Father's stories. As she imagined what a large body of water would look like, the feeling of hot sand on her feet as she walked slowly with Gerold down the beach, she drifted off to sleep.

She awoke to a swishing sound. Opening her eyes, she looked up at the swaying branches, the light shining through indicating it was past noon. The wound wasn't from the needles rubbing across each other. Turning to her side, she saw Gerold sitting cross legged in the hide.

Leaned up against one side of the hide was a wide bundle of fibers attached at the end of a branch and Gerold was leading a thin thread between two thick pinched fingers into a smaller stick in his other hand. She watched in silence as he clumsily converted the flax fibers into thread. She noticed he wasn't paying much attention to what he was doing as he stared blankly out into the forest. A sense of sadness permeated through their new connection as his hands moved on their own volition.

His eyes suddenly snapped into focus and he turned his head slowly to face her. She watched as he silently regarded her, continuing his pinch and turn process. After a moment, he said, "I saw the pile of wood at the base of the tree. Thanks for collecting that. I hadn't thought of it. Why the three long branches?"

Niitty sat up and stretched her arms to get a knot out of her back muscles. Yawning, she replied, "To make a tent. I'll have to take this hide down tomorrow before we leave. They're designed to work on the ground as well."

Gerold grunted and continued to spin in silence. After a while he said, "I hope I didn't wake you."

"No," she replied, "I was having a nice dream about the ocean. I have never been before and I'd like to visit some day."

He paused his work and looked up, "The ocean? Why?"

"My Father had told me stories of when he went. He said the waves sound much like the rustling of pine branches."

Gerold shrugged, "I wouldn't know. The largest bodies of water I've ever seen were the four rivers that pass through the Capital."

"Do you think we can go someday?"

Gerold silently went back to spinning. Niitty felt a war of emotion going on through their connection and she had no idea what to make of it. After she felt the strong emotion subside, he replied, "If we have the opportunity, I wouldn't mind."

"How did the trip in town go," Niitty asked, remembering with a shudder the throng of people pressing near them the night before.

"Thankfully, no one got a good look at me, so I didn't draw the same attention," he responded.

"That's good," Niitty said, silently thanking Gerold for taking that risk. He only grunted in response.

Niitty sensed he didn't want to talk anymore, so she watched in fascination as he finished making his thread. He picked up the small sewing kit her mother had given her and started working on his pants. He had left them on his body and started the process of rebuilding the leg.

"Wouldn't that be easier if you took them off?"

Gerold didn't look up as he continued sewing, "That wouldn't be modest in your company."

She blushed at the thought and realized what she just suggested.

"I think I should go take a walk, see if I can get a rabbit for supper."

Gerold stopped and reached into his bag, pulling out a sandwich with a large slab of meat and cheese on it, "I almost forgot. We had some extra funds and I thought you'd like this since you haven't eaten all day."

She gratefully took the sandwich and devoured it. While she knew it was a basic sandwich, it tasted divine after having subsisted on basic travel rations and, while here, the bland free Guild Hall food.

"Thanks. What's the occasion?"

Gerold shrugged, "You looked like you needed something good today. And we had extra money left over after Philip gave us those coins. I spent the 20 copper in change on two sandwiches after buying the travel rations. I already ate mine."

She was licking her fingers when he mentioned the cost and mumbled with her fingers in her mouth, "I' 'ouh 'ah 'uh?"

"Take your fingers out of your mouth, I can't understand you."

She pulled her fingers out, embarrassed at what she just did in his presence, "It cost that much?"

Gerold hummed an affirmative.

Like the day before, the concept of money continued to surprise her and how expensive things were. Two sandwiches had just cost ten goblin bounties. From what she heard from the Guild Master, new adventurers would normally only kill twenty of them a day. That wasn't enough to pay for a full party's meals. No wonder they congregated at the Guild Hall for free food.

After eating, she lowered herself down on the rope and went

into the woods. She shoved aside all thoughts and entered into a state where her mind was mostly empty. She allowed the forest to fill her senses. She saw more signs of goblins and the signs of other passing adventurer parties. She was able to avoid both with ease, finding no more than passing areas of battle, some that didn't go so well based on the drag marks. She found no adventurer bodies, so she was hopeful they all survived.

She failed to find any small game. There signs of passage were too irregular to reliably set a snare and catch anything. Even with a mile between the goblin packs, the density was too high to allow for animals to remain in an area for long.

She had been gone for a few hours and returned as the sun began to set over the mountains. Climbing up, and taking the rope up with her, she saw Gerold sitting in a cross legged position with his eyes closed, pants repaired with a mismatched whitish patch of natural flax, and talking to no one in particular out loud.

"I'm heading out tomorrow morning," Gerold said to the empty air above him.

He paused and looked like he was listening.

"And that's a bad sign? Setting that aside, it's getting dark and we can't travel right now. Another party is already en route."

He paused again and waited.

"Yes, the reports say the crypt is only a few weak undead wandering around outside. Even with their limited abilities, they should be able to handle it with the gear Karl has obtained. What's that? You heard something?"

Gerold opened his eyes and saw Niitty, "Welcome back. Did you find any rabbits?"

She looked at him in concern. She didn't feel anything off

with the connection this entire time, only a sense of minor annoyance. She had assumed he was having issues with his repairs, "No. The animals in this forest are too skittish because of the goblins and adventurers. Who are you talking to?"

Gerold cocked his head and said, "Is it forbidden to tell her?"

"Why are you asking me," Niitty replied.

"I'm not," Gerold answered in a matter of fact way. He waited a moment while listening to the air then said, "She said it's fine. She says the soul link, what she calls forming a party, has given her some insight and says you're good. I'm talking to Erinne."

Niitty felt worried. Gerold was acting extra weird now.

"Why are you talking to her out loud?"

"The way she explains it, Gods have no access to our thoughts. She says it wouldn't be right to judge us on our thoughts, so she blocked access to them. She can hear and see what I do, so I have to talk out loud," Gerold replied in a matter-of-fact tone. He continued, "That's all I found out so far. And, she just left. No social graces, her."

"She's gone then," Niitty said, playing along.

Gerold shrugged, "She does that. She has other duties to take care of and can't spend all her time occupying my head."

Niitty had more questions, but she didn't think continuing the charade was a good idea. He was deep into his delusions.

In the final daylight, Niitty handed possessions to Gerold to store in his bag for the trip. She was going to have to take the hide down in the morning. They could save time if they put away the gear now. After stowing everything except for a blanket, Gerold handed out two stale loaves of Guild Hall bread and they went to sleep.

CHAPTER 9

Gerold had another restless night. He dreamed about his family, this time it was winter. It was a sunny day and, in that part of the world, a cloudless sky meant it was extra cold this time of year.

He was walking the border fence around his field, trying to ignore the foul odor emanating from his winter clothing. The winter in these parts was so harsh that they had to sew themselves into their winter gear, leaving only openings to expel waste. Even though he did this every winter since before he could remember, he always hated never having enough money to buy firewood for more than keeping warm at night.

Even though it was cold, his kids loved the snow. He sat on a small stool out in the front of his farmhouse, shivering in the cold, as he watched Malrin swinging an old rake around. He was swing at pretend monsters that threatened the farmstead. Gerold found himself torn as he watched. If Malrin wished to become an adventurer, would Gerold permit him to follow in his Grandfather's footsteps or would Gerold insist he stay?

That day was still a few years away. For now, Gerold could enjoy watching his boy fantasize about being a hero. Looking to his side, he saw Elli rolling balls of snow in her knitted hands, patting them and putting them into a circle. He couldn't fathom what she was doing and, if he asked, he'd get such a rapid fire series of words from the energetic child that he would struggle to interpret the meaning. It made sense to her, though.

Then Gerold felt his pulse quicken and a fear rise. He noticed the world wasn't right. Everything was grey, as if he suddenly lost his ability to see color. His brown fence was grey, his son's coat was grey and the sun was grey. There was also a strange series of tiny black spots over everything, like a cloud of ethereal flies that covered his vision, flickering into existence and back out again.

He also noticed that one moment he was walking his fence and then, the next, he was sitting on a stool watching his son. He had no idea how he got from there to here. The circle of snowballs that his daughter had made was now next to his son and shaped like sun bleached skulls. His son was holding the rake at the ready, preparing to strike at an invisible foe.

The center of the now skull circle burst forth, throwing old tamped down snow and dirt into the air. A rotting hand had erupted from the soil and was now gripping his son around the throat. His rake was gone and he was now turning, looking at Gerold.

A whisper came to his ears that came from everywhere and nowhere at the same time, "Why didn't you save us?"

Elli poked him in the side.

"Why didn't you save us?" the whisper said again as his son turned and smiled warmly at him through flesh that began to slough off his skull. Elli poked him again.

"Why didn't you save us?" As his son was pulled into the circle, he now looked like a rotted corpse that tanned in the sun. He gave a friendly wave before he was pulled under. It's winter, he has more time. It didn't happen until autumn. Elli was now shaking him.

Gerold was then greeted by darkness with a slight red tinge that allowed him to barely make out trees above.

"Hey, are you well," a soft voice said to his side in the darkness. He felt a warm hand on his shoulder and realized Niitty had awakened him. He had a nightmare and rubbed his hand over his face. His curse had left his skin dry while his sweat had absorbed into the fur, making him feel both hot and cold at the same time.

He sat up, "Sorry, I had a nightmare again. Did I wake you?"

"I was going to get up anyway," she replied, Gerold picking up the lie through the tone of her sleepy voice and a stifled yawn.

"The sun isn't up yet. You can go back to sleep if you want."

Niitty sat up and began to roll up her fur blanket, "No, we need to get started. It'll take me a while to disassemble the hide."

Gerold put their remaining items into his bag and slid down the rope, happy he wouldn't have to navigate the accursed thing for a while. He sat against a tree and watched her dismantle the treetop tarp, or "hide" as she called it. He wondered if she called it that because it was made out of hide or it hid the occupants above the ground.

In the dim pre-dawn light, he watched as she reached out and pulled a rope. Wrapping her arm into a loop in the hide, she released a corner and let it fall. Gerold noticed she had tied the rope in such a way where a single yank would release the knot, making it easy to untie alone. After the hide stopped swaying, she repeated the act with the second rope, leaving just two corners connected to a tree.

Gerold wondered if releasing the rope would swing her into a tree, a question that was quickly answered. The third rope was longer and the knot holding it on looped back under the hide and was tied against the tree next to the fourth.

He watched as she shimmied over to a branch on a tree and released the third rope, allowing the hide to flop against the trunk. She then unraveled a long length of rope holding the final knot in place and threw it to the ground. After climbing down the now slack hide, she released the final rope.

After folding the hide into a compact square and stowing it in his bag, the two were off.

They traveled in silence. Niitty needed the silence to track properly and avoid any roving goblin bands. She was having a tough time as it is with his noisy tromping. He'd have to ask her how to walk more silently in the forest.

He took the time to recall the short conversation with Erinne the night before. It was not only the shortest time she had occupied his head, it was also the shortest interval for returning as well. He wondered if the time away and the time she stayed were correlated.

Erinne seemed worried. The necrotic signal pulsed again with a slightly stronger signal than before. Her vision lacked the clarity to find energy sources that came and went quickly. She explained that she looked at the world from high above the ground and when she looked in close, she was blocked from seeing anything else. She could only see people moving around and analyze magic. She was well acquainted with the tops of peoples heads and she didn't even experience what sound was like on Alios until she tapped into Gerold's ears. She couldn't even read a book unless someone left it open on a desk. She only figured out what language he spoke because the information was fed through her via his soul.

She would get updates on what was going on in Alios from the other Gods. Even then, she said they were imprecise and always focused on the domain that God governed. Rudo, the ebony skinned God of Love, would only ever talk about how well people who asked for his guidance interpreted his signs and how they did in their romantic pursuits.

Her vantage made it nearly impossible to get a bead on the brief pulse of energy. All she knew was there was a second pulse and it was a bit worse. Umieranie, the Goddess responsible for death, was too busy handling the broader strokes of her job to notice, not that she could identify the location of a brief pulse, either.

So Erinne had to turn to her very own Paladin. She also said the coincidence was just too strange for her liking. Fate, she said, is something beyond the Gods, even her. It was a force just as eternal as she was.

Gerold, like everyone else, was a slave to time and distance. He could only get to the crypt so fast and there was no guarantee that it was the source of the pulse. As the day wore on, he felt it harder to breathe. He mentioned this to Niitty and she said that they were going up the mountain where the air was thinner. Gerold picked up a sense of unease in her voice.

They continued to make slight course corrections as Niitty maneuvered them around monsters in the forest. They eventually ran into a small stream where they stocked up on water. Curiosity hitting him, he put his bag into the water and opened it wide. Instead of sucking in the water, the water flowed around the opening, forming a bubble underneath.

Not sure if he learned anything useful from the exercise, he removed the bag. They continued following the stream, only taking a few detours away as necessary to avoid confrontation. Karl's party had, at least, been following the correct path to their destination.

As the day wore on, the surrounding trees grew smaller and wider spread apart, allowing the underbrush to grow in thicker. Eventually, they came to a line where the trees stopped and the landscape grew rocky and was broken up here and there by small bushes and thin, low lying grasses. Thankfully, the upward slope had ceased and Gerold looked out over a long flat expanse before reaching the base of the mountain range's prominence in the distance.

Niitty looked at the sky and the sun was touching the mountain peaks, "We need to stop for now. The days will grow shorter this close to the mountains." She also looked nervous staring out over the rocky scrubland.

"Something wrong?" Gerold asked.

"You could say that," she said as she looked around the area from the edge of the thinned forest, "We are above tree line now and I'm not experienced in tracking in this terrain. Luckily, we can see a good distance. How long can you keep your Sense Evil aura up?"

"Indefinitely."

"Good, we'll need it. I don't have any faith in my tracking in this terrain."

Gerold pulled the tent posts and the hide from the bag and then acted like a glorified post himself since he had no idea how to put the thing up. Niitty had the conical tent up in fifteen minutes. Niitty nixed Gerold's suggestion of starting a fire since the night wouldn't be cold enough and that it would ruin their night vision and garner unwanted attention. Besides, three of the twelve moons would be full this evening, making it easier to see at night.

Gerold volunteered for the first watch of the night since they no longer had the safety of the trees. Gerold handed out the evening's rations and Niitty turned in. Activating his Sense Evil aura, he expanded it. Instincts told him that his recent power up moved the range out to 110 yards now. Getting himself as comfortable as he could, he sat crosslegged and closed his eyes.

He was once again alone with his thoughts, accompanied by the chill wind blowing down from the mountain. The moons were visible through the red glow glancing off the sky from the sun hidden behind the mountain. The shorter days shortening as they approached the tall peaks jutting into the sky came with the benefit of reasonable sleep when a watch was necessary.

The landscape should have hit him as empty, lonely and a little frightening. But instead of a sense of unease, he felt an empty pit. Gerold instead closed his eyes and thought of his family. The end of winter festival would have been two weeks prior. He realized the Capital didn't even celebrate it. He had left that day on the caravan and it felt like any other day.

He thought back on the last one he had with his family. It was not a lavish event in his village, not like the harvest festivals that marked the transition between seasons. It was a somber affair where the residents of the area came together, pooled their food and reallocated it to the people who needed it. Even though everyone took care to prepare for the long winter, not everything would go to plan for some. Emergency food for adventurers stumbling in from the wintry plains would happen and rats would sometimes damage stores. Gerold himself fell victim to preserved food that didn't properly disinfect, ruining a small barrel of pickled beets.

Still, it was a time for celebration, one where they survived another winter and gave thanks to the Pantheon for the conditions necessary to see it through. And it was a time for mourning for those who didn't make it, which was thankfully rare. And this was the first one that would not be held back home in generations.

A deep sense of sadness welled up in his chest that led to a numb tingling feeling creeping down his left arm. His father had reported such a sensation before he fell out of his chair, dead, just before the birth of his son. Gerold hoped that he would, too, fall dead then and there, not sure why he kept on going. Knowing his poor fortune, his curse would stop this as well and the feeling was something else entirely. Maybe this crypt and mysterious necrotic magic would be the end of him.

A sense of worry suddenly filled him from the direction of the tent. His own mental state was causing concern for his traveling partner. He reorganized his thoughts and pushed down his pain, realizing he was interfering with Niitty's sleep. Calming his mind, he took deep breaths. One of the Paladin trainers said meditation was an excellent way to commune with his patron God. It allowed your soul to open to better receive the vague feelings and premonitions on what your God wished of you.

Of course, for Gerold, that was silly since Erinne would show up and talk to him directly. He did find meditation, at least for a while, allowed him to empty his thoughts and take in his surroundings to their fullest.

It was dark now, the red glow fully faded away, as his reflection on the past and meditation chewed up some hours of the day. He focused on his aura, feeling it as it spread over the area like an invisible fog. Apart from a brief blip at the edges as something with an intense sense of evil entered from the direction of the rocky lands and into the forest, the night was mostly uneventful. It passed through so quickly that he knew it was at the extreme edge of his sense and he couldn't see that distance in the dark. Whatever it was either had no interest in them or didn't take notice.

He did have a wakeup call with his senses. While it would warn him of monsters, they weren't the only dangers in the wild. When he was deep in his meditation, he was brought out of it by the snapping of branches in a low shrub near the camp. Looking at the noise, he saw a large boar nosing itself into a bush some ten yards away. He had gotten lax in the forest around Wren's End where animal life was non-existent. Predators still existed in the world and even animals like a boar could be a danger if it was angered. Thankfully, this one had pressing business elsewhere and moved away from the camp to snuffle in more bushes.

He spent the rest of his watch on his feet, training his ears for additional sounds. As the night wore on and further darkened, he was able to make out a distant fire. This must be Karl's party and they were announcing to the entire flatlands that they were there. He couldn't bring up the emotion to accuse them of being fools. Gerold would have also started a fire had it not been for Niitty's warning and they lacked the experience and training necessary for wilderness travel. Not even Philip's Guild Hall training would have resolved that, having cut that out to save money.

His thoughts shifted back to the financial concerns of Wren's End. From what little he had gleaned in the Capital when he wasn't being run into the ground in training, farming communities like Wren's End were critical to feed the major urban center and the armies of the Empire. Wren's End, particularly, neither had powerful enough monsters nor a dense enough monster ecosystem to fund the Town Seed.

To maintain the territory of the Quellis Empire, a system was necessary where Adventurer Coins were funneled into farming communities to maintain their seed. Otherwise, they'd devolve back into the warring kingdoms to the East, with small fiefdoms centered on Town Seeds that had to maintain living, military and farming activity within a limited radius while using adventurer and military resources on regular monster patrols for outlying, unprotected farms. Villages like Wren's End were the secret to the Empire's domination of the lands to the east of the Bear Teeth Mountains. And here doubly so as it also served as a training center, though not its only one in the vast lands that stretched over four thousand miles West to East.

What could be going on within the Empire to see it cut funding like this? Emperor Quellis the 182nd was well into his elderly years and could be losing his touch. Though as per tradition, his heir apparent, who will take on the name Quellis the 183rd, won't take up the post until his Father dies. Gerold pushed those musings aside since a provincial farmer turned reluctant Paladin wouldn't solve the financial woes of a random village at the extreme western fringe of the Empire.

When the Moon of Early Spring reached its apex, he woke Niitty. She berated him for waiting until formal midnight and not waking her sooner. The sun would arise at the same time despite the longer nights. Gerold patiently listened to her lecture him about proper sleep, though he kept to himself that he didn't want to face what his dreams would bring.

CHAPTER 10

Staying up later into the night had some benefits. Gerold awoke tired as the first rays of light seeped through the cracks in the opening to the tent. For the first time since finishing Paladin training, he didn't wake up in a wet patch. He crawled out of the tent to see Niitty peering over the open terrain in the direction of Karl's camp with a look of exasperation on her face, "Those idiots had a fire going all night. I can't believe we're already a half a day behind. What are they doing?"

Gerold had to defer to her expertise on that. The fire looked a good distance off when he saw it the night before.

Niitty smelled herself, "That said, I need you to keep watch, and your back turned. I haven't cleaned myself in ages."

Gerold grunted in affirmation and, after requesting he get some water first, filled a small pot he kept from his home and handed her a cloth. He got himself busy starting a fire and putting the pot on to heat. The travel rations he purchased could be eaten either as a bar or thrown into a pot to make a soup. He figured they should take advantage of Karl's slow pace and heat up their meal. From the smell, it didn't help. Warm slop was better than cold sawdust all things considered.

Gerold was engrossed in stirring the terrible smelling ration stew when Niitty returned, looking refreshed. "Thanks for not looking," she said, though Gerold felt a sense of disappointment coming from their shared connection and there was a strange tone to her voice. Wiping yourself down with a cloth in a cold stream would leave much to be desired.

After eating and taking down the tent, they continued. Niitty slowed their pace compared to the day before. Gerold still hadn't gotten used to the thin air and they had to rely more on his Sense Evil aura for the trip. It was now up to Gerold to adjust their path as they followed the stream, which according to the intelligence, should lead close to the crypt.

Niitty would still adjust their path as she peered out over the scrubland. A blip here and there touched the rear of Gerold's senses; nothing stayed long enough to indicate something was following along. That is until he felt something to his left. It had entered into his range and, as they walked, it not only lingered but it also didn't subtly shift direction as they continued to move.

"Stop, we have to get ready. Something is coming at us," he said as he readied his shield and war hammer. Niitty took up her position slightly to his rear as they had with the goblins and waited.

"See anything," Gerold asked.

Niitty replied, "A few bushes are rustling. The thing is shorter than the bushes and is darting between them. I can't tell what it may be."

A rotting smell tickled Gerold's nose followed by a disgusting creature that stepped out of a bush and into the stream. It was a kind of rodent that stood three feet at the shoulder. Squat and round with short legs, it had a snub nose with two long incisors. This, normally, wouldn't be concerning. What was concerning was the rotting flesh, cloudy eyes and skeletal structure visible through the flesh. Its nose twitched as it turned in their direction and let out a strange gurgling squeak before charging with surprising speed.

Gerold stepped forward and caught the creature's lunge on

his shield. The thing was stronger than it looked, unburdened by the little mental blocks that keep muscles from tearing themselves apart in living creatures. The monster's incisors dug into his cheap wooden shield while its front paws grabbed the edges. It mindlessly chewed at the wood, trying to get through to Gerold's arm.

Niitty stepped around the side and stabbed the undead rodent. Her rapier slid in easily with a wet squelch, the rotting flesh offering no resistance to the blade. The monster didn't even react, finally breaking through the shield and clamping down on his chain protected forearm.

Gerold felt the pressure of the bite as the chain, and his bone, held, "I can't get leverage, you need to stab the brain."

This proved easier said than done. Not only was the creature surprisingly difficult to hold still, the brain on the rodent was too small a target to easily hit while clamped on Gerold's arm.

"Use your Turn Undead spell," Niitty shouted as her missed stab passed through the monster's neck and failed to put enough force to sever the head from the spine from the awkward attack angle.

Dropping his war hammer, Gerold nearly lost his balance as he reached in his bag for another coin. Instead, he used his now free hand to add to the force and he flipped the monster over on its back, Gerold falling on it and pinning the creature under his superior mass. This was short lived as he felt the bony protrusions of its foreleg toes scrape against his hauberk while the rear legs damaged his recently repaired pants and cut into his legs. He was, however, now able to reach into his bag and pull out a copper coin.

Gripping it in his free hand, he willed the Turn Undead spell to cast. Muttering the beckoned words, the coin dissolved into motes of light and he felt a pulse of energy fire out of him in every direction. At that moment, the monster went slack, allowing Gerold to get off of it.

The creature now moved sluggishly. It was struggling to roll itself over and on to its feet, power sapped from its body. Gerold took the advantage to retrieve his war hammer and smashed the creature's head flat into the ground, finally stopping it.

Using two more coins, Gerold stopped his bleeding between big gasps of air as he still wasn't acclimated to the altitude. He looked down at the undead rodent with the now crushed head, Niitty walking up to stand next to him.

"Sorry," she said, "I wasn't much use."

Gerold shook his head, "Don't apologize. We weren't prepared for this."

Racking his brain as he examined the monster, he had to admit his academic skills weren't very good. Little of what Gerold was taught in his rushed training remained in his head. Trying to focus on academic pursuits didn't mix well when your mind was distracted by other concerns.

Even then, he did remember broad strokes of undead types. Zombies were, generally, created in two ways: a burial site is forgotten and the bodies within corrupt from a lack of maintenance or they're intentionally created. Undead animals were always intentionally created.

Who would create a zombie out of a rodent in the middle of nowhere? The rituals or Adventurer Coin required to animate the dead was too costly to waste on a small animal like this.

Backing away from the body for a moment, he moved around to see if there was anything else that triggered his Sense Evil aura. Nothing came up and Niitty didn't report anything in visual range. Whatever created this creature intentionally left it alone since created undead would follow its master's orders and never get lost by accident.

"This is concerning," Gerold said when he recalled the intense evil blip the night before.

Niitty had knelt down and yanked out one of the incisors which she had held out to Gerold when he made his statement, "We need it for the bounty. What's the problem?"

Gerold hummed, "Undead animals don't manifest naturally like humanoids. They don't have gravesites. Something had to intentionally create this and I fear it ran past our camp last night into the woods."

Niitty's eyes grew larger, "What? That's back toward the village. Should we head back and warn them?"

Gerold pondered this for a while, "No, we need to press on. The village still has instructors and the Town Seed for protection. It would take a major siege to break it. We need to press on and investigate the crypt if that's where it came from."

They decided to abandon the mission to stay hidden and would try to catch up as best as they could. They had to get to that crypt.

The rest of the day was, thankfully, uneventful. After delaying their start that morning, they made it to the campsite that Karl's party had made the night before. As they got closer to the mountain, the days continued to shorten and they had to stop again. The area had lost all of its ground cover and the landscape turned into a craggy rocky terrain with the stream cutting through from the snow melt further up the peaks, all plant life had completely vanished. It was also getting notably colder in the shadow of the mountain.

Karl's campsite was selected for convenience. It was close to the stream, wide and flat. Niitty reported signs of five full tents were present and the party abandoned the fire to burn itself out as opposed to being extinguished. Gerold felt a sense of annoyance through their party connection as she groused over the poor state of their passing. The party's expensive ration tins were discarded by the fire, though there were only four of them.

They also found a few blood splatters nearby the camp. Niitty estimated it was from that morning and, while serious, it wouldn't be life threatening with a Cleric in the party. The evidence of what attacked Karl's party had already decayed back into its component mana.

Niitty didn't like the location. It was exposed and, after a short scout of the area, she found a small rocky overhang in the crags a little ways from the stream. It had a short rocky tunnel that acted like a useful defensive choke point and they wouldn't have to break out the tent.

They followed the same pattern as the night before. Gerold took the first watch, with Niitty demanding a promise that Gerold wouldn't wait too long to wake her for her shift. Gerold made sure to word his response carefully so it wouldn't be a lie when he let her sleep through to normal midnight, giving her eight hours of sleep.

Gerold took advantage of the easier defensive position to fashion a pair of coin pouches he could tie to the inside of his hands. He wouldn't have a repeat of the undead rodent fight where he had to dig through his bag for a coin to cast a spell. He would have to set aside money to afford the special gloves with coin pouches to make casting easier.

Before going to sleep, Gerold had to endure another lecture from Niitty about not waking her at the appointed time. He could sleep when he was dead, which he secretly hoped would be soon.

Gerold had a second night in a row where he had no dreams, too tired for his body to make them. They then quickly packed and ate their dry rations on the move.

The slope grew steeper as they moved on as they followed the stream that cut a natural path through the mountain. A few places required scrambling up rocks, which Gerold struggled with. As they climbed, they saw a corpse of some strange goat monster. It had sharp fangs and dagger-like hooves with one spiral horn protruding from its head, the other having been sawed off. Niitty found more splatters of blood in the area. She said it looked like two or three in the party were injured in the battle.

Gerold was worried. Their Cleric wouldn't likely have much more capacity at casting as he did and he had, maybe, three spells left for the day. Yet they were forging on to the crypt. Gerold hoped that they'd take a break for the day before entering.

It was getting late in the day and the sun was already setting over the close mountains and they had not run across the party. The path then abruptly terminated into a small cliff that could be climbed and as they approached, Gerold felt an intense feeling of evil past the lip.

"Go slow, something is up there," he said to Niitty. She paused, sniffed the air and then listened, "I'm not getting anything. Give me a second to check."

Gerold remained still while Niitty silently crept over and jumped up, grabbing the lip. She pulled herself up and peeked over the edge. After a moment, she waved at Gerold to come up then pulled herself over.

After he pulled himself over, Gerold saw a wide area. The area was too flat and uniform to be natural, which was supported by the ten foot high carved walls into the side of the mountain. Six pillars, arranged in two rows, led to an intricately carved entryway as if a road had led to this area in ages past. The pillars were weathered from unknown amount of time in the elements. As the two approached the entry, Gerold noticed that it had the same weathering. The artistic carvings on wall were long worn away by the elements, leaving a barely identifiable carved mausoleum entry in the wall.

Gerold didn't notice Karl's party anywhere. He did notice a pair of bodies stationed at the entryway and more blood splattered on the wall and ground.

When he got close enough to see the bodies, he was reflexively brought to his knees. A wave of terror welled up in him. There were two rotten bodies lying in awkward heaps at the entryway, one male and one female. They wore moldy, age decayed fieldworker garb. The sight of them triggered memories of his family. A terrible howling filled the space as he huddled with his wife and kids, his daughter screaming. The din was more like the wailing of thousands of people suffering from unspeakable torture than the tornadoes that pass over the plains during the summer and fall seasons.

He remembered the searing pain in his chest that touched his very soul followed by his arm swinging, swinging, swinging.

He felt a warm hand squeeze his. This broke him out of his panic as he looked to his side and saw Niitty, who was also kneeling with her eyes closed, her face sheet white. With enough sense returned, Gerold expended his day's Calming Aura to snap them out of their panic. He immediately felt his fear suppressed into a mild thrum as opposed to an overwhelming panic. The stress was reduced to a manageable background noise.

Niitty laughed, "Look at us, a pair of pathetic adventurers. The second I thought of going into that cave, I lost it. I had no idea you were scared of caves, too."

Gerold took a deep breath, held it a beat, released it and then pointed at the corpses, "It's not the cave, its them."

Niitty looked at him in the eye and gave his hand another squeeze, "You want to talk about it?"

Gerold thought on it, "Not yet. After we see if Karl and his party are safe? Maybe."

She gave him a small smile, "I'll take that as a promise. That aura of yours is amazing. The fear is still there, but it's not holding me back anymore. Let's get in there."

The two moved toward the entrance. As Gerold passed the bodies, his fear nearly vanished entirely when he got a better look at them. This close, he could tell that these bodies weren't real people. Their features were excessively generic. The bodies looked like they were pulled from the backgrounds of portraits he'd seen at the tavern where the artist couldn't justify detailing more than the main subject. One generic Elf and one generic Human were produced by whatever mechanism spawned monsters into the world, not an intentional reanimation of a real person's corpse.

Gerold pulled his war hammer and his hand gripped for a shield that was long left discarded along the stream. Thankfully, Karl's party had lit sconces in the wall and the passage leading into the mountain was illuminated. The opening was only wide enough to accommodate two people abreast with a ceiling so low that Niitty could barely stand at her full height and she reflexively ducked in preparation for entry.

"I have to turn my Detect Evil aura off," Gerold said before they went into the passage, "This place is so seeped with evil mana that it is like walking in a fog. I won't be able to use it to see if anything is ahead."

Slowly, the two made their way into the gaping hole in the mountain.

CHAPTER 11

As Gerold made his way into the passage with Niitty, an image of the mountain consuming him through this mouth came to mind. The sconces twinkled with orange flames that reflected off the surfaces of the constrained hallway. Even through his aura, he felt slightly nervous. Niitty was sweating, his aura barely holding back her fear of enclosed spaces.

The air turned stale and musty as they moved further. Looking back, the light of the entrance was a pinprick in the distance. He was concerned about how long this tunnel was turning out to be. Was this one of those dungeons he heard stories about or a human carved passage? He wasn't sure how much that would matter.

As they moved further, the floor started to become dusty with visible footprints breaking up the otherwise uniform layer. Niitty reported that she saw five sets, indicating that, at least at this point, the party was still alive. The silence concerned him; the only sound was from Gerold's boots echoing off the stone.

Then they started to see strange oval depressions in the walls on either side with piles of dirt spread on the floor. Niitty had a look of concern as she had to duck to clear the piles in the tight hall and said the number of footprints increased as they passed each hole.

They passed two dozen pairs of these depressions in the walls with so many bodies moving down the hall that it made it impossible to determine the number, though both of them would have bet the clothes off their back that it was 48 bodies following 5.

Gerold stopped and held onto Niitty's shoulder, "You don't have to do this. The number of bodies walking down the hall is tremendous and this could be a death sentence."

She stared at him in the eyes with a fear she was barely keeping in check, "You've been very good to me when you didn't have to. I don't think I could live with myself if I let you die."

Gerold felt warmth coming from her through the connection for a moment before subsiding back into a feeling of focus.

The hall came to a sudden 90 degree angle to the left in the distance. Gerold took the lead and crept up to the corner. Sticking his war hammer out to give him some distance, he moved around the corner. He was greeted by two things: an additional length of hallway and a small lump on the ground in a pool of blood.

Moving closer, he prodded the lump with his weapon. It was a small body with ripped clothing and clear chew marks on the exposed flesh. He flipped the body over and saw the gnome rogue that was with Karl, Ellen. Her red hair was mostly ripped from her scalp and was barely visible in the blood below her body. Her face had been torn, missing most of one side as the skin was stripped with a single eye blankly staring up at the ceiling. Her clothing had been torn mostly off at the front as whatever had killed her desperately gutted through her ribcage to carve out the inner organs. Even the pants were mostly ripped to shreds with clear bite marks on the calves and thighs. Whatever had killed and partially eaten her had stopped and moved on. For some reason, zombies lost interest in a corpse after a minute. The working hypothesis is the zombies are trying to get to the soul and lose interest when it moves on.

"More zombies," Gerold said to himself, feeling completely divorced of emotion while clinically looking at this young woman who was, just a few days before, vibrantly flirting with adventurers in the Guild Hall. He felt distress come from Niitty. He turned and saw her with a hand over her mouth, tears welling in her eyes.

Gerold saw her reaction, closed Ellen's one remaining eye and flipped the body back over on its chest to hide the gruesome immodesty. Standing, Ellen's blood sloughing off Gerold's hands as he continued to be reminded of his change, he gently put a hand on each of Niitty's shoulders, "We'll deal with this and make sure she gets a proper send-off."

Gerold remembered something from his training and bent over again, looking in her pockets.

"What are you doing," Niitty asked, a sense of anger welling up through their connection.

"Don't worry, I'm not going to steal anything. I'm seeing if her token is still on her," he replied.

"Why?"

"It'll give us an idea of how long she's been dead. When an adventurer dies, the token will crack and, after an hour, transfer itself to the nearest Guild Hall," Gerold said, remembering something he read in a book while at Paladin basic.

After checking her pockets he found nothing. She wasn't carrying anything beyond gear immediately needed for combat. No coins, no provisions and no token.

He sighed, "This isn't good. She's been gone for over an hour. I have a bad feeling about this."

Niitty stepped over the body, avoiding the blood as they continued. They started to run into a zombie body here and there. The dust and hallway lacked any sign of what happened. Had they panicked? Was Ellen the rear guard and surprised? The most logical course of action was Karl going in first so he could block the way with the shield. The narrow hall limited the ability for the party to turn and face a surprise attack, necessitating a solid rear guard. Why hadn't the Desert Elf Nader been the rear guard? He was their second sturdiest member.

Gerold forced his mind back to the immediate task when they came upon another body. This time, it was the Cleric Tulugaak who, like Ellen, was savagely ripped into and then the body was abandoned. Another turn in the hall back to the right brought more bodies and yet another party member, this time it was Nader, his broken short spear sticking out of a zombie's head. The armor on his torso kept him better protected, leaving his head and legs to take the brunt of the attack.

His retreating battle had taken 28 of the zombies that emerged from the wall, Nader's ultimate limitation the durability of his weapon. All that remained were Karl and Gewa. Neither body had been found yet.

The hall suddenly terminated into a large cavern. Gerold heard a chorus of moaning and hissing in the distance.

"Be prepared to retreat. Remember how we handled the goblins? This hall is perfect," Gerold whispered to Niitty who silently nodded in response, pulling her rapier.

The room was huge with pillars much like those outside, though more detailed as they were out of the elements, stretched 200 yards into the distance. For some reason, the sconces on these were also lit and, based on the situation, Karl and Gewa wouldn't have done so. At the end of the cavern was a raised dais with a stone sarcophagus on top with the lid laying partially broken across the front.

To the left, he saw a mob of twenty zombies gathered around a pillar. The ones against the pillar looked like they were trying to climb it and, on top, he saw a robed figure. It was Gewa. She had her knees pulled up to her chest and she was rocking back and forth in a catatonic state. Karl was nowhere to be seen.

They continued moving closer to Gewa to get a better idea of what they were dealing with. The zombies were making so much noise that they didn't notice the two adventurers. The Calm Nerves aura soon enveloped Gewa and she looked up at the two. Her eyes grew wide and she suddenly shouted, "Above! Beware of above!"

They didn't have time to react when Gerold heard a flop and a scream behind him. He whipped around quickly and saw a shriveled black creature with taunt skin ripping into the back of Niitty with long, disgusting claws.

Gerold snapped, feeling a rush of emotion that was held behind a dam. Dissolving one of coins, he cast Turn Undead. This caused a notable effect on the creature as it slowed down, leaving it only a little less deadly than before. Thankfully, Gerold got the creature's attention and it turned its eyes on him.

Gerold started swinging. The creature, even though slowed, was still fast and dodged the strikes. Gerold didn't let up yet the monster was just one step ahead. It swung a talon and Gerold leaned back to avoid a nail dragged across his forehead, the cut it left in its wake leaking blood. Blood and filth refusing to stick to his body turned into a liability as the blood freely dripped into one of his eyes, making it harder to see. He didn't care and he continued trying to hit the creature.

Gerold could swear the thing smiled at him, or what passed as a smile on a face that had no lips or eyelids with exposed sharp yellow teeth permanently plastered in its mouth. Gerold was feeling fatigue pile on from the combination of his wild swings and the effects of the altitude.

The monster hit Gerold two more times to his side. The chain only resisted a slash from the sharp talons, the force leaking through to crack his ribs. He still didn't care. His life didn't matter so long as he kept Niitty safe.

The monster was beginning to speed up again, the effects of Turn Undead waning. He cast it a second time and the monster staggered again. This time, when it staggered, a streak of fire came in from a downward angle and struck it in its face. The monster shrieked in pain as the flames splashed over its skin, creating an ember effect like hot coals. The effect proved limited when the creature quickly recovered and stared in the direction of the attack.

The distraction did its job when a sword sprouted through the center of its chest. The surprise attack in combination with the fire delayed the creature enough to allow Gerold's crushing blow to smash into the creature's temple. It crumpled on the ground, emitting squeals from the critical strike. Gerold followed up with two more bashes and popped the head with a loud crack, causing it to leak a strange black fluid on the ground.

Niitty was standing with her sword and she shouted, "More coming!"

Gerold turned and saw the zombies. His Turn Undead spell had caused them to take notice. Luckily, the nearest bunch was disabled, which caused the rearmost ones to trip. However, his spell was wearing off again. Before the zombies could regain their speed, Niitty and Gerold sprinted back to the hallway to avoid being swarmed.

The two turned and waited as the mob regained its composure and lurched forward. Gerold had enough time to pull out one more Adventurer Coin and, when the mob was in range, he released the spell again. The lot of them slowed significantly with a few falling again, tripping up others. This gave them time to get into their rhythm of alternating attacks they'd practiced a few days prior. Gerold noticed her strikes were sloppy and he would have to push zombies back here and there. Serving as Niitty's shield proved awkward in tandem with the necessary style of combat to defeat a zombie.

After bludgeoning his spike through the last zombie's head, Gerold took a breath. Somehow, they pulled it off. He looked across the way and saw Gewa standing on the pillar, her hand still out from her opportune cast of that fire spell, staring in shock at the sight. He also noticed a crumpled body against the pillar.

Investigating the identity of the last figure could wait. He turned and saw Niitty slumped against the wall of the tunnel with her face turning white. Her breathing was labored and her sweat was profuse on her brow.

Looking up, she smiled at him, "Ha, we did it. Though I think that thing that hit me from behind got the better of me."

Panic welled in Gerold. He pulled out three more adventurer coins and quickly cast Simple Heal on her. Her condition didn't improve. The damned spell wasn't strong enough. He wasn't strong enough.

"No, don't die on me," he pleaded.

Niitty weakly reached up her hand and cupped his cheek, pulling him close to press her forehead against his.

"It was an honor to know you," she said through shortening

breaths.

Gerold couldn't take it and, out of desperation, shouted, "Erinne! Do something!"

A peppy voice echoed in his head, "Hi, I'm so hap...," and was cut off. Her voice suddenly changed its tone, taking on a matronly commanding voice Gerold never heard before, "Do what I say now. Take out a silver coin. She will die if you don't follow my instructions. I'll explain the details later. Do you understand?"

"Yes," he said, thankful that he had saved up three silver coins, "I understand."

"Under...stand what," Niitty asked through closing eyes.

"Good," the voice of Erinne ordered in a tone that brooked no debate, "Hold that coin and think about using the entire thing on a Simple Heal."

Gerold gripped the coin hard, thought of Simple Heal and pouring the concentrated essence of the silver coin into it. The coin flared hot in his hand, like he picked up a steel ball from a blacksmith's forge, but he held firm through the immense pain. It dissolved and the searing pain migrated into the essence of his being, feeling like the magic was tearing apart his soul.

Then, from his hand, a blinding light emerged and settled onto Niitty. Her breathing stabilized and the last thing he remembered before he blacked out was a splitting headache.

CHAPTER 12

Niitty was feeling cold and weak as she slumped to the ground. She remembered saying a few things to Gerold. She wanted to confess her growing feelings. She found herself unable to fight through the embarrassment, even now. Her back hurt and she couldn't stand. She felt the warmth in her body leaving and her vision fading.

Then something odd happened. She had pressed her forehead to his as a final farewell. Then he started shouting at the air, pleading to the Recluse Queen for help. Her thoughts drifted to thinking that, even now, his delusions were still fully in hold of him. He then stared at the air for a few moments, acting like he was listening intently and then said, "I understand."

Her mind was going and she could only think to respond through a weakening voice, "Under...stand what?"

As her eyes started to close for what she knew was the final time, Gerold's entire body suddenly flared bright white. He thrust his hand over her torso and she felt an amazing warmth spread through her body. While she still felt tired, she didn't feel like she was going to die at any moment and her back no longer had the searing pain.

Looking down, she noticed Gerold passed out next to her on the ground. A panic rose in her body as adrenaline filtered through her veins that quickly subsided when she saw his slow, even breathing. Looking out into the cavern, she noticed nothing moving save Gewa, who was climbing down from the pillar. She stopped briefly and looked at the figure slumped against the pillar before making her way to them.

She made her way over to the duo and looked down at them before bowing to Niitty with folded hands, "I thank you for saving me. I feared this was the end for us all when that Lampreyer got the drop on you."

Looking down on Gerold, Gewa continued, "He's a Paladin, isn't he? A real one."

Niitty fought uncooperative legs in a failing attempt to stand, "Yea, he is."

"I knew it when he came close and I was able to think straight. I'm glad my fire bolt was able to turn the battle, though I feared for you. What did he do?"

Niitty wasn't sure how to respond. Then it hit her. He was telling the truth about Erinne. He wasn't delusional and he really did talk to the Recluse Queen. How else could she explain that bright flash of light that healed her wound? At his level of power, all he should have had access to was Simple Heal, which he had used on her to no avail prior to his surge of power.

The Recluse Queen had selected him. She didn't know what to think about this. She did know she had to keep it concealed. It wasn't her place to tell his secrets, even though he'd probably tell if asked.

"I couldn't tell you," she said, "I don't know anything about Paladins other than the stories. He healed me and then fell over. I'm still feeling weak from blood loss, though."

Thinking on it a moment, she reached for his bag. The enchanted item refused to cooperate with her attempts to open it.

"Is that a Bag of Holding," Gewa asked.

"It is."

"You won't be able to get into it. Only the owner can access it. This is a problem because Karl," her voice cut off after saying Karl's name. She reached into at a satchel she had at her side and opened it. Pulling out one of the fancy tins she saw discarded at the camp the day before and a water skin, she handed them to Niitty.

Niitty ravenously consumed the tinned meat and water. Still not feeling whole, she did have enough rest to allow her to stand. She saw that they were surrounded by the defeated undead and didn't think this was the best place for Gerold to rest.

After checking that the wound above his eye had coagulated, she convinced Gewa to help drag him away to the side of the cavern. It was a challenge moving his body in her condition. The two of them lifted him by an arm each and pulled him away from the entrance. Niitty was exhausted after moving his body to the wall. His bag held nothing that could be used to prop up his head. The two were unable to find a comfortable position on the ground, so they left him on his back with his hands folded on his chest.

All the two had in their possession was whatever Gewa had in her satchel along with six copper coins, five that were in Niitty's pockets and Gewa's last coin. Both Karl's and Gerold's bags locked away anything else of use.

Niitty also discovered that the items in Karl's bag were lost forever on his death. The bag would disenchant itself by the end of the day and the contents would convert into mana and disperse into the air. Gerold being incapacitated and making their gear inaccessible was a huge problem and she realized they couldn't rely on it.

Thankfully, nothing else approached them while in the

cavern. Niitty asked Gewa to watch over Gerold while she circled the room to ensure nothing else was in there and she discovered that the room was the last. She found nothing except for a mummified corpse in the sarcophagus with its hands held above it in a strange position, as if it were holding something in ages past.

After she ensured nothing could sneak up on them, Gewa asked if Niitty could help collect the bodies of her party members. Niitty verbally agreed to assist Gewa even though she didn't want to see the saved corpses again.

Starting with Karl, whose face was completely ripped off along with his lower jaw, they moved the bodies to the opposite end of the cavern and lined them up. They couldn't make a pyre until after Gerold woke up. Niitty found herself disgusted when Gewa started digging through the pockets of the bodies. Her people would burn personal effects with the bodies to allow them to take their favorite items and mementos of life to the next world.

Gewa looked disappointed that the gear was entirely wrecked. Even Karl's armor was dented and punctured with holes while his shield's leather straps snapped. The last thing Niitty even had energy for was to take a trophy from the Lampreyer to turn in. When she reached the crushed head, she took a closer look. The body lay in a pool of a mixture of thick, black ooze and her blood from the attack. She marveled that she was able to remain upright and fight after that. The monster's skin was dry and so black that if it got any darker, it would suck in surrounding light. She couldn't tell what the head had looked like, only that the mouth was round and filled with a circle of exposed teeth with a red, scaly tongue forced out by the hammer's impact. She decided to cut the tongue out and keep it as the trophy, shoving the disgusting appendage into her bag.

She also saw the long, yellow talons at the end of its gnarled hands. She did the best she could to get a glance at her injury through the torn opening in her back, catching a glimpse of her bare skin through her damaged armor. She felt her back and it was smoother than she had remembered it, as if the spell healed the wound and made the skin younger in the process. Her mind wandered to thinking that this spell would make for a great skin treatment in her later years.

Her thoughts returned to the wound and the talons, particularly the secondary effects of whatever disease clung to those yellowed appendages. She her initial worry about an infection from taking a cut from those putrid claws was squashed. The part of her body she could see had no telltale signs of putrification nor did she feel any pain. She was confident the spell addressed the wound in all its negative effects.

Gewa, too, was exhausted, especially after the effects of Gerold's Calm Nerves aura ceased. She did, however, suggest Niitty rest while she stood watch. Niitty took her up on the offer and settled against the cavern wall next to Gerold and took a nap.

Niitty felt better after what Gewa estimated was a two hour nap. She stood watch while Gewa took a short rest as well. As Gewa slept, Niitty grew concerned for Gerold. He had collapsed after healing her and slept through being dragged through a cave and showed no sign of awakening.

Gewa had only slept for a half hour or so.

"I'm going to collect zombie parts," she announced. She looked haunted after her short rest. Niitty figured the realities of the day's events had hammered down on her. She didn't feel like helping out and figured Gewa earned the parts, even those Niitty and Gerold defeated.

This didn't take Gewa long and she returned to her pillar to sit alone. An awkward silence descended on the cavern. In the quiet, Niitty realized that she was underground and the subtle fear of enclosed spaces started to descend on her again. She remembered watching Gerold when he thought she was asleep engaging in a strange breathing exercise. She felt through their connection at the time that it calmed his darkness.

She sat cross-legged and took slow, measured breaths and exhaled only after holding the air for a few beats of her heart. Focusing on this process helped push thoughts out of her mind. As she breathed, the feeling of the oppressive cavern withdrew. She felt the feeling leaving her body every time she exhaled, leaving only a small sense of persistent anxiety. She would have to talk with Gerold to see if there was more that could be done to improve her results.

Opening her eyes again, she looked around and her eyes landed on Gewa. She had her knees pulled up to her chest and her head buried in them, large paws with sharp claws jutting out of them clasped. Niitty picked up light sobs coming from her direction and her form was shaking.

Niitty went and sat by her. She held back on her instincts that told her to touch Gewa's shoulder. Niitty didn't think she would appreciate a stranger's physical contact. Instead, she asked, "Do you want to talk about it?"

Gewa nodded, "They weren't bad people."

She paused for a few beats, "They took me on in the Capital. I was, am, a nobody. My parents are poor laborers from the dockside. They are hard workers that never could earn much. I would occasionally find myself in the orphanage whenever times got tough while my parents worked through their financial issues."

She pulled her head up and looked ahead over the cavern

at nothing in particular, "I would frequently go through the garbage behind shops. Sometimes for food and other times to find things I could bring back to fix and sell. One day I found something that would change my life. It was a Basics of Magic book. The text taught me simple cantrips and magical theory. That's how I learned that fire bolt I used earlier, along with ice bolt and simple breeze."

"My parents found out that I had the book. They looked so happy. Here I was, their little girl with a talent that could allow me to escape," she stretched her legs out and folded her hands in her lap, "They sacrificed to allow me time to read."

Gewa moved her hand to the floor and began scratching the stone surface with a claw absentmindedly, "I wanted to learn more, but my parents were struggling. I had to put the book aside when I started getting older to start working extra jobs."

She got lost in thought as she continued scratching the floor. An artistic swirl was taking shape. Niitty allowed her the moment and patiently waited.

She then continued, "It went on this way for years. Then I came of age. I told my parents that I wanted to join the Adventurer's Guild and try out for the mage training. They were thrilled that I was on the path to escaping the slums."

She took a deep breath and closed her eyes again, "When I arrived at the Adventurer's Guild, I asked to register as a mage. They had me take a small aptitude test. I didn't understand what they meant and, in my excitement, cast the breeze cantrip. I was immediately marched into the Guild Master. I was terrified. He asked where I had gotten my hands on a Basics of Magic book because they were closely guarded by the Guild and only used as a study aid to see if someone had the mental capacity for magic. Thankfully, he was sympathetic when I revealed my parents' history and how I had found it in the trash."

Opening her eyes once more, she looked across the cavern where Karl's party lay, "That's where I ran into Karl. He was waiting behind this strange old vagrant registering for the guild next to me."

Niitty snuck a glance at Gerold. Did Gewa register at the same time? Her mind bounced to what Allan had said about their sequential Guild IDs and fate. Could Gewa be another one?

Niitty turned her attention back to Gewa, missing part of her story, "...told me that I was quite beautiful. He said, 'I can't make you a formal member, you understand. Your station forbids that I accept you formally in your party. What I can promise is fair treatment.' He was arrogant, a braggart and insecure. Underneath it all was a strong sense of honor. He was calling himself a Paladin. He was able to fool new adventurers with his claims. The pressure to succeed was heavy on him. He was a noble and his friends were the children of powerful people, so he had a lot to prove. None of them ever warmed up to me. They did keep their promise to treat me right and they never abused their station. Karl even financed my clothing and bag, saying I had to look the part of a follower."

At that moment, the bodies of the monsters started to dissolve into motes of gentle blue light. The process began in the same order that the monsters were killed, starting with the Lampreyer. Niitty hadn't seen the process before. It was strangely beautiful. Taking a glance at Gewa, she, too was enthralled by the process. The motes rose up three feet into the air, faded and then vanished like embers from a campfire.

Niitty felt a sense of sadness witnessing the process. She realized the world was filled with a dichotomy of beauty and terror. The three of them were now alone with nothing more than the bodies of four others that would never get to experience the event. All those hopes and dreams vanished without a haunting display of lights, their soul's final passing invisible to all but the Gods.

Niitty felt a tear stream down her cheek from the display and Gewa was stunned into silence.

Minutes passed before Gewa broke the silence, continuing with her story as if she didn't know what else she could possibly say to mark the event other than her own way of remembrance of the fallen, "When Karl decided to take on this quest, he had confided in his friends that this would convince his Father that he was a worthy heir to the Duchy. He had a sense of insecurity. He had spoken about how his family thought of him as a disappointment. He covered it with bravado borne of his own self-doubt. If he was able to speak that way to someone he thought of as an equal it would make it true. He was desperate to reach this crypt and cleanse it. He would use it as proof of his accomplishments."

She wiped an errant tear, "He had a sense of pride and he refused to allow others to do the work for him. He thought of himself as a peer and not a noble. When those bandits attacked us on the way to the village, he put himself out in front without hesitation. We were terrible. If it wasn't for that same old man from the Guild Hall in the group, we would have been in trouble. Karl put himself at risk to protect his party none the less. He did the same when we found goblins in the woods. He was always up front, distracting them to allow the rest of us to attack. On the way here, he took wounds from monsters we came across to protect the rest of us."

She shuddered before her next words, "His protective instinct proved his downfall. We never developed a sense of coordination. He would stand up front and the rest would fall in based on their social rank. His only insistence was I stay directly behind him where he could protect me. When we found this place, he went first as always. The hallways are narrow and he couldn't turn around, limiting our ability to turn and leave. Ellen ended up in the rear. I don't know what triggered the attack and we struggled to locate the origin of the scratching we heard. Karl assumed it was from up ahead. The echo made it impossible to tell where the noise was coming from. Karl prepared to meet whatever was coming. Then Ellen screamed. I turned and that's when Nader bumped into me. Tulugaak was panicked and pushing us forward. Ellen was overwhelmed by the zombies and Karl couldn't squeeze past me in his thick armor. Karl's thick armor kept us from running. Nader turned and attacked the horde allowing Karl and me to escape into the cavern. Only the two of us made it into the cavern. We saw nothing outside. Where did they even come from? Did I miss something and get them all killed?"

Her breath started to become erratic as her emotions were getting the better of her.

Niitty thought an interruption would help, "They were in the walls."

Her breathing stabilized, "What?"

"The walls. When we came in, we saw oval indentations in the walls of the tunnel and dirt on the ground. They clawed out from behind you. You couldn't have known."

She swallowed hard, "Still. I was terrified. I could only think of running in my panic. When we got in here, I continued to run. Karl tried to get me to stop and use the hallway as a choke point. He said I shouldn't worry and he would protect me. My legs refused to listen to his pleas. Then I saw the Lampreyer by the sarcophagus and it saw me. I ended up scrambling up the pillar. For whatever reason, the Lampreyer didn't climb up after me. The creatures have the intelligence of small children and are cruel. It left me up on the pillar to focus on Karl. The monster proved too powerful and too skilled for him. The equipment Karl spent a fortune on couldn't stop the creature from ripping into his head. He didn't want a helmet covering his head. He thought it would keep people from noticing him."

Her tears started flowing stronger, "He died protecting me. That arrogant noble playing Paladin died protecting me, a useless pauper. Then that Lampreyer started to toy with me. It would claw its way up the walls and drop at me from the ceiling. The monster would hide in the shadows and drop from above like a sick game while the zombies gathered from below. I don't know how long I was up there. My mind had completely shut down until your friend's aura touched me."

Niitty laid her hand gently on Gewa's shoulder, "Thanks for telling me. For what it's worth, I'm sorry we arrived too late to help. I'm glad we were able to save you. And I doubt you're useless. You did distract that Lampreyer at the right moment to help us win."

Niitty could swear Gewa blushed under her luxurious white fur, "No, thank you for listening to me babble on like that. It helped clear my head. I know it's strange to get this upset by the deaths of people I wasn't close to and barely knew."

Niitty found that she had grown comfortable with the Snow Leopardia woman and they chatted. Niitty told her stories about her people and her own childhood, which was admittedly far less interesting than Gewa's background growing up on the streets. Eventually, Gewa fell asleep on Niitty's shoulder. Niitty felt herself smile in what felt like an eternity, happy that there was a small bright spot in this gloomy day.

CHAPTER 13

One moment, Gerold felt the essence of his very being burning as bright as if dunked in the crucible in a forge. The next, he found himself lying on the ground, staring at a cavern ceiling. His thoughts briefly turned to stories set in caves. Things called stalactites would hang from the top and bats hung from them, dropping rich dung that could be used as fertilizer. He was disappointed, however, to see that it was a smooth surface.

Then his mind came back to him. Niitty! He shot up into a seated position, his pulse rising. It immediately calmed when he saw her a few yards away sitting against a pillar with a sleeping Leopardia woman leaning against her shoulder. She was blankly staring at the entryway.

His movement caught her eye. She looked excited and smiled brightly, "You're awake! I'd get up, but I turned into a pillow."

Gerold winced at the pain pulsing in his side from his broken ribs when he stretched out of habit, "How long was I out?"

"I'm not sure. It's hard to judge time in here. Around twelve hours maybe," she said, not entirely sure about the answer.

He grunted in response.

"As vocal as ever. How do you feel?"

He felt like death, his body ached and his ribs were broken.

He thought of a way to tell the truth and assuage her concern, "Better than before I got knocked out."

"Good. And thanks. I thought it was the end, but then you lit up with a bright light, healed me then passed out. What happened?"

He thought for a moment, "I don't know. I called on Erinne, she answered and saw you through my eyes then told me to use a silver coin for a Simple Heal."

Niitty looked confused, "What? What would that do? If you use a silver coin to cast Simple Heal, all it would do is cast Simple Heal and burst into 99 copper coins."

Gerold shrugged, "I don't know. I just did what she told me and my hand burned, then it felt like I was going to explode before I cast the healing spell on you. That's the last I remember."

She suddenly looked sheepish, "I have a confession and an apology. This entire time, I thought you were delusional. It was unbelievable that you'd be Erinne's Paladin or an old man. That's the only thing that can explain that miracle."

Gerold grunted, "Don't mention it. And I'm not old."

Niitty said with a serious note, "I'm serious. It's a big deal to me. You've been honest and forthright with me and you even saved my life. Yet I harbored distrust."

"Then apology accepted."

She yawned, "I lost a lot of blood and I'm hungry. We have to arrange for me to carry provisions if you're incapacitated like that again. All of our food is in your sack."

Gerold hadn't thought about it. The bag was so convenient in keeping weight down for travel that they had put the entirety of the party possessions within. They couldn't make that mistake again.

He handed her some travel rations and a skin of water, which she inhaled, "Thanks. I think I need to sleep. I've been forcing myself to stay awake to keep watch. Have you recovered enough?"

Gerold evaluated himself. He felt odd, like his soul was exhausted. He tried extending his Sense Evil aura to check the area now that he noticed the bodies had vanished and it refused to activate. He felt weak and strangely disconnected from the mana in the world. He felt like a simple farmer again, though young. He even noticed dirt had accumulated on his pants and a blood stain was on his shirt.

He decided to conceal his injury with a well placed truth, "I can keep watch. You get some rest."

She slightly adjusted her position, careful not to disturb Gewa, and immediately fell asleep.

Gerold stared around the cavern, taking in details that he had missed in all the stress. He had no experience to draw upon to determine the nature of the opening. The tunnel was straight and uniform, indicating it was intentionally carved. Here though? Apart from the flat floor, the walls and curved ceiling were uneven and random. Was it even possible for a space like this to form inside a mountain?

It was a mystery he would likely never solve. He stood and saw four bodies lying across the way. Crossing the open space, he noticed the monsters they killed previously had dissolved back into mana, leaving blood splatters from the adventurers as the only evidence of the altercation. He stopped and took in the particularly thick one that marked the spot Niitty was ambushed. His mind turned to wonder what he would have done had she not survived the ordeal, not sure if he could have held the burden of another loss on his conscience.

He arrived at the bodies and felt his stomach drop. Here were four more reminders of his inability and uselessness. He found himself squatting with hands folded over his knees and ignoring the pain in his sides, whishing that the monster before had killed him or that he would have never awoken from whatever he had done to save Niitty.

His attempt to store the bodies in his bag for later burial was rebuffed by the item. The bag wouldn't accept the bodies of people, only monsters. The item had its irritations to go along with its utility.

He stood and decided to at least provide a proper send-off. He emptied most of the wood from his bag, not concerning himself with making a campfire for warm meals on the return trip. After arranging the wood in a pyre, more of a thin bed now that he thought of it, he fought through the searing pain of his broken bones to drag the bodes on top. The wood he had in his possession wouldn't be sufficient to immolate the bodies. Still, he had to try.

He pulled the last two silver coins and stared at them. He didn't have enough funds to provide the customary silver coin send-off for the departed to pay Umieranie, the Goddess of Death, to guide the souls of the departed. He thought back on his own parents and how his Father had sold personal effects to obtain an Adventurer Silver for his mother and then how he did the same when his Father passed. He also considered keeping the coins since that would leave them with just 21 copper coins for the return journey and no more silver to repeat the feat he had performed to save Niitty, assuming he could even do it again. Then his thoughts wandered to his village and the kind adventurers that sacrificed their hard won silver coins.

"I'm sorry that this is the best I could do. We can't return you to your families," he muttered over the bodies as he gripped one of the coins by the edges with both hands and bent it, willing it to part. It burst into 100 copper coins that tinkled on the ground. He cursed himself that he didn't consider setting up some cloth to catch the coins first. Wrapping the second in some spare cloth he had sewn earlier, he converted the second silver into copper.

He evenly split the copper coins on the bodies in stacks of five. He would have to wait for Gewa to awaken to give her the opportunity to say the rites and any goodbyes.

His morbid task finished, he muttered to himself, "Erinne, why me? I don't know if I can keep going on like this."

To his surprise, she responded, "I'm sorry I can't do anything to help you when I'm asking so much for you."

"How long have you been here?"

"Since you woke up," her voice, soft and caring, echoed in his head, "I didn't find an opportune time to interrupt until now."

Gerold wasn't happy about being spied on. He could see her conundrum and she didn't make the decision with malice. He elected to keep that to himself, "What happens to them? After all this?"

"Sorry, I can't tell you that," she replied.

Gerold sighed in frustration.

"What I can tell you," she continued, "is you shouldn't worry too much about your offering. Umieranie understands the circumstances."

"Fate is cruel," Gerold said as he stared at the four young lives that were snuffed out just as they were starting. Gerold felt disgusted that he had lived nearly as much as three of them combined.

"This wasn't fate," Erinne responded, "Fate is exceedingly

rare. Even then, all it can do is nudge probabilities. Chance and free will rule the universe in the end."

"Then this was my failure. I was too slow. I should have ignored the advice of Philip and kept close. It was my inability against the undead rodent that slowed us down," Gerold said, falling into a spiral.

Erinne's commanding voice returned, "Stop that immediately!"

"But…"

"No! You did nothing wrong. Events move beyond the powers of mortals and even beyond the power of the Gods. There are even things I can't do. You have to accept that life is messy and chaotic. Affairs beyond your control have a habit of upending your plans. All you can do is face them the best you can."

"But if…"

"I said stop! If you dwell on how things ought to be, you will only find disappointment. Live your life around how things are. If you have the power to change things, then count yourself fortunate. Most realities are beyond even an Emperor to change. Turn around," Erinne thundered in his head.

Gerold was growing angry. His ire was rising and he wanted nothing more than to reach down to his war hammer and slam the weapon into her face. His hand gripped the head of the weapon, his knuckles turning white as he attempted to crush the solid steel object. Raging at his impotence to do anything to the Goddess, he turned. There, he saw Niitty and Gewa asleep against the pillar.

Erinne's soft and comforting voice replaced her Supreme Being persona, "Look. You are so focused on your failures that you missed the bigger picture. You didn't fail four. Had you given up all those months ago, there wouldn't be four bodies in this crypt. There would be five. That young Leopardia woman would be a rotting corpse. The corruption of this place would have turned their remains into the undead. The monsters would have remained and a different adventuring party would have eventually come along and put them down for good."

Gerold's anger started to deflate.

"Look at Niitty. When you created your party, I gained access to your link as well. I can feel her emotions. You're so caught up in your own mind that you have ignored it. That girl cares about you and relies on you. She is still young and her fears and insecurities extend beyond going into a town. While you're both inexperienced in adventuring, she's inexperienced at life. You haven't noticed the good you have already done and you can help her mature and grow."

Gerold slumped against a pillar across the cavern, still facing the two sleeping forms, his boiling rage now completely gone. He felt a deep sadness come upon him and he started to cry, "I don't know if I can. I can't betray my wife and kids. I can't replace them."

"No one is asking you to," Erinne replied, "While no one can be replaced, you can give someone else the opportunity to be part of your life. I have no experience in loss the way you mortals do; I have seen your souls after you pass. They're each special and unique, never to be replicated and replaced. Each a sight that I have only ever seen once and know I will never see again. You mortals have exceeded everything I've set out for you and more. So, in a way, I can understand your loss. You've had no time to mourn these past six months. And it pains me to ask you to wait a little longer."

Gerold took a few deep breaths, leaning back on the meditation technique he had used before to clear his mind. She was right. Something in this area had occurred that was concerning for the Supreme God of creation. He could wait a few more days to work through things he had delayed far too long.

"Before I take a look around, can you explain what happened to me," Gerold asked.

"You know that the Gods each have a core domain," Erinne started, "And that you assume that I do not?"

Gerold nodded.

"You know I can only see through you, right," she scolded in a teasing tone, the energetic girl persona taking over.

Gerold sighed, "I'm aware. Each of the Gods has a domain that is associated with a major concept of our lives."

"Have you found it odd that it's only concepts? There are Gods for things like Love, Invention, Inspiration, Trade, Defensive Wars, Offensive Wars and more. There are no Gods for the ocean, air, the stars or plants."

"To be honest," Gerold began, "I haven't thought about it. Everyone knows that there are no Gods over the land or animals."

"Huh, I'm confusing you with other cultures then. Many of the Gods come to me telling me mortals complain about things they have no control over like heat waves or rain," Erinne mumbled to herself, "In any case, you know how everyone thinks I don't have a domain?"

"That's what the priests of the Pantheon say, yes."

"Well," Erinne started, "They're wrong. My domain is magic. It's through my power that the underlying mana of the world originates."

Erinne said that last part like it was a major revelation. Gerold couldn't muster up the energy to care about something better left to scholars, "And that means?"

She huffed, "I just revealed a major aspect of the universe and that's your reaction? Anyway, a thing about Paladins is that they have a special ability depending on who their patron is. It's a powerful ability that can only be used once a week. Paladins of Destus, for instance, can dramatically increase the durability of defending allies in a siege."

"And?"

"Let me finish," she continued, "Because my domain is magic, you can supercharge your spells. You can increase the power of your spells twenty fold. Buuut, unlike the other Gods, I'm a little too powerful. The cost comes at a 100 fold increase in the mana requirements and it is so stressful on your core that it will knock you out for about a half a day and you'll lose your powers for a week. All of them."

This caught his attention, "Is this something that could kill me?"

"No, a soul is indestructible, but it can be stressed and harmed. Your real risk is doing it when you're in danger because you'll be out for half a day. My power is so immense that tapping into it beyond the peripheral powers of association will burn out your soul. As it stands, you're no different than you were when you were a farmer. You can now get poisoned by mundane sources, get sick and you will get dirty again. Your powers are also locked away. A big one, too, is you'll rapidly age back into your original body. You'll look like you did before, except your hair won't grow out and you'll look as if you lived a healthy life and never got sick."

So much for his inkling of a plan to go out in a blaze of glory. While he welcomed going back to an appearance he was more comfortable with, it did mean he had to hike through rough terrain and deal with monsters without the benefits of being an Adventurer. Maybe being younger had its benefits.

Erinne misunderstood Gerold's silence as concern, "Don't worry, in a week, you'll gain your abilities and powers back. All ill effects will be reversed and you'll have your same youthful looks back."

"A couple more questions," Gerold said after thinking a few moments, "Why do Gods only have aspects over concepts and how do you know about this power?"

She laughed, "Oh, those are easy. I don't want people getting lazy and trying to ask the Gods for handouts and I can read magic. I had no idea you'd get this ability until you agreed to be my Paladin."

Gerold grunted and figured this was a good time to quit this line of discussion. It was good to know he had a great emergency ability though. Deciding he had enough talking about this, he stood, fought through the pain of his ribs and scanned the room. His eyes landed on the sarcophagus, "Do you think that's the source of the necrotic pulse?"

He could feel the shrug through their connection, "I don't know. The pulse is so quick that I can't dial in on where it is, let alone what may be causing it. I can't even be sure if it hasn't happened before. Even someone with my power can't look at all of the infinite cosmos all at the same time."

"How many limits does a Supreme Being even have?"

She went silent for a long while, so long that Gerold had thought she left again, "A few, many I can't tell you about. And I have another admission I think I can let you in on. You know how I can't stay with you at all times?"

Gerold sighed, more talk, "Get to the point."

"So rude," she replied, "Anyway, this is just a piece of me. I have to split off my personality to be able to interact with you.

I only keep my memories so I can talk with you and have few powers in this form. This is why I can't look at everything all the time. I have to do this when looking over Alios as well. That's a big reason why I can't figure out what's happening. By the time I create an avatar to investigate, the pulse is gone. Further, an avatar only has enough energy for a few days. And before you ask, I can only create so many, so I can't perpetually blanket the planet to observe it and each avatar serves a specific purpose. I only have the one that can talk to you."

Gerold hummed, "That explains why you disappear without saying goodbye. I just thought you lacked social graces."

"You think so poorly of me. Yes, that's why. I don't have a good sense of time - I can remember an eternity in the past after all; the time limit just sort of sneaks up on me. I also need time to reabsorb the information, so I can't create another one immediately. The last time was shorter than usual, so I was prepared to create my avatar when your prayer reached out and caught my notice," she said.

Gerold thought that had Erinne done like she had over the past few months and showed up to chat, Niitty could have died since Erinne, for whatever reason, didn't fully disclose all of his abilities. He felt a wave of anger boil up, "I suggest you not contact me then."

Gerold wondered if she ran out of time again because she went silent for a long time. Instead of wasting more time standing around waiting for a reply, he started walking over to the sarcophagus.

"Do you really dislike being my Paladin this much," he heard a voice sounding like it was on the verge of crying echo in his head.

Gerold stopped and turned his head to the ceiling. He had allowed his anger to direct his actions again and a sense of shame welled up in him. He pinched the bridge of his nose, "I'm sorry, Erinne. I didn't mean to phrase it like that. Had you not been insistent about it, I would still be back on my farm and there would be more death here. Maybe this is one of those rare interventions of fate and had I rejected it something worse would happen."

"I understand," an echo returned in his head.

"I'll probably snap at you again in the future. My life has been in disarray and I haven't had time to breathe. I'll try to be better. Still, I do think we should limit our contact. I don't hate you, I don't want to be cut off if there's a pressing need," Gerold said in a consoling tone.

"That makes sense and I agree. I would appreciate it if you take the risk now and again to check in. When you called for me earlier, I felt so happy. I only ever get to talk to the other Gods and I made them too obsessed with their domains to ever have an interesting conversation. Only the occasional crazy person ever prays to me and I can't even hear it unless I happen to have an aspect observing the world. Their prayers are rarely coherent and those that are…you'd rather not know."

Gerold was taken aback that the Supreme Being herself struggled with self-worth. Being the creator of everything and, due to circumstances Gerold didn't understand, coming off as aloof couldn't be good for esteem, "I'll take that risk now and again just to chat. I promise."

"Thanks," she mumbled back. Did Gerold pick up a sense of embarrassment?

He chose to let that go and walked over to the sarcophagus, ready to get to work finding the source of the problem.

CHAPTER 14

Gerold had no idea what he was looking at. The sarcophagus was a stone box on a raised dais with a fragmented lid next to it. Inside he found a shriveled old mummified corpse. All identifiable features were long decayed. No clothing remained and he couldn't even tell what the gender or race of the occupant was. He found the face disturbing. Where there were once eyes and a nose were now holes with tight skin pulling into the open void leading into the skull. The mouth was agape in a permanent scream with teeth that had long fallen out. He could make the teeth out at the bottom through the open mouth. Its arms were crossed over its chest with the hands raised with fingers curled into a claw. It looked like it once held something.

Other than being a disgusting sight, he noticed nothing unusual about the body. It was dead in a box.

"Do you see anything," Erinne's voice echoed in his head.

"A dead body."

"No, I mean anything unusual."

Gerold sighed, "What do you expect? I'm a farmer. I've never seen anything like this before."

Erinne groaned in his head, "Let me try something. Scan your eyes over the body slowly from top to bottom."

Gerold did as she asked, "Anything?"

"Nothing. It's a dead body."

"I just said that," Gerold groused.

"No, I mean I see nothing. It's been in this forgotten crypt for ages yet it hasn't corrupted and turned. The whole place is filled with corruption yet this body hasn't animated. Good thing, too, older corpses are more powerful," Erinne said.

"It was holding something," Gerold said. He took a closer look. Two pinkie fingers had been broken off and there were stress cracks in the arms near the elbows, indicating an object was present at some point in the past. It was removed, but he lacked the expertise to tell when.

"It looks like something was taken," Gerold said out loud for Erinne's benefit.

"Can you get closer to the head," she asked.

He did as she requested. What he noticed was the distinct lack of smell. Whatever caused the stench of death had long ceased. All that remained was a slight musty smell like an old trunk of clothing he'd forgotten in the cellar.

As he stared at the shriveled face, he realized this wasn't disgusting him like he thought it would. He was mulling over his mental state when Erinne spoke, "You'll need to burn this body soon. It's starting to fill with corruption. By my estimate, the process has been going on for nearly a week."

That didn't make sense, "This body has been here for a long time. Why would it start filling a week ago?"

"I don't know. It's odd," she said, clearly confused.

"And even more mysterious are the zombies. Unless I'm mistaken, those zombies were the kind that formed like monsters and weren't summoned. I'm not familiar with the other monster though," Gerold said.

"Can you describe it to me," Erinne asked. He did to the best of his memory.

"Ah, that's a Lampreyer. They will attach themselves on a body like a leech and suck out your blood and are about as tough as fighting 25 zombies at once. They form like other monsters and aren't summoned," Erinne explained.

"I guess this is a mystery that we aren't solving then," Gerold announced.

He felt her shrug through the connection, "Can you look at the cover?"

He knelt over the rubble of the lid. It was the same stone construction as the box and it was plain with exception of a few designs carved into the top. There were three lines of the symbols and parts that hadn't been ruined when the lid crashed on the ground were scraped off. Someone had intentionally scratched out parts of the design and based on the coloration it looked recent.

He blankly stared at the broken stone, not knowing what he should be looking for, "Do you sense anything here?"

"There is faint magic in the stone, but I can't tell if it held an enchantment or it's residual magic from this crypt," she replied, "Can you stare at those symbols for a little please?"

He did so while he heard her humming in his head. She muttered for a few moments and then said, "There, I have it. Those are words."

Gerold looked at them, not seeing it, "How did you figure that out?"

She gave out a small laugh, "I'm a supreme being. My mind moves so fast that you couldn't comprehend. Deciphering writing is trivial."

"Uh huh," Gerold said, unimpressed with the arrogance,

"What does it say, Oh Supreme One?"

"Sarcasm doesn't fit you," she replied, "Let me see. 'Here lies Wren who…By the…of Quellis the…The curse shall…'"

"And that's it?"

"The rest of it is either broken or scratched out."

The only thing that made sense to Gerold was they found who the town was named after. This is Wren and he or she found his or her end here. The rest of it was a conundrum. Why was Wren entombed out in the middle of nowhere in a forgotten hole in the ground? What is the curse? And what was this reference to Quellis? It's obviously not talking about the Emperor. He's not that old and all of them in the history he knew about always referred to themselves as Emperor Quellis. None of them would have written their name down without the honorific.

"This sarcophagus is older than the Empire and the Emperor's ancestor is referenced on it," Gerold said out loud.

"Who are you talking to," a voice interrupted him from behind. Startled, he jumped up and tripped over himself as he tried to turn around.

"Oh my, I'm sorry. Um, sir? How did you get here? Did you see a Paladin fellow anywhere around," said the voice. Gerold looked up and saw the Leopardia woman, Gewa he remembered.

Gerold pulled himself up, finding it unusually difficult to stand, "I'm sorry, I've been here the entire time. How are you feeling?"

She looked confused, "You have? There were only two people, Niitty and the Paladin Gerold. I would have remembered an older man. Were you outside?"

Now it was Gerold's turn to be confused before he realized what was going on. He reached into his Bag and pulled out his mirror. He looked into it and saw his face. His real face, though the old signs of pox scars were absent and he had stubble growing in. His eyes were baggy from exhaustion, he was dirty and the wound on his forehead was an ugly scab. His hair was still cut in the neat style as before and was faded and streaked with silver. The aging came on fast.

He sighed, "I am Gerold."

Gewa looked concerned and backed away, taking a protective stance over the sleeping Niitty and pulled a dagger out of her belt. Her ears folded into a state of agitation and bared her fangs, "I suggest you leave or you'll have problems. We have a Paladin with us and when he gets back, he will punish you if you do us harm."

Gerold couldn't think of anything to say in response.

"Show her the bag," Erinne echoed in his head.

Gerold did as Erinne asked and slowly presented it to Gewa and put his mirror back in.

She waved her dagger, "What are you doing?"

Gerold realized how stupid that was. The mirror would normally fit in a bag this size. He reached his hand in and willed one of the long tent posts and pulled it out. As he pulled out the post that would be impossible to otherwise fit in a bag that size, Gewa subtly lowered her dagger in surprise.

Her dagger came up even more aggressively again, "How did you get that? Did you steal it from Gerold?"

Gerold groaned, "How is that possible?"

He could see the plow tilling the fields in her head as she worked over the question. She hit a rock however and she raised her dagger again, "You could have one, too." Gerold figured it was fair that she would be suspicious. Her suspicion went overboard when she assumed Bags of Holding were common items.

"Hey, before you get into a conversation, we should cleanse this place and I should get back. If I reabsorb the avatar now, I should be able to form another quicker," Erinne interrupted.

"What about the necrotic pulse," Gerold asked, much to Gewa's confusion.

"There's nothing here," Erinne replied, "Apart from that sarcophagus and the room has nothing other than the normal ambient necrotic mana from a tomb like this. The only oddity here is the ancient body."

"I didn't say anything about a necrotic pulse," Gewa said.

"Sorry, I wasn't talking to you," Gerold said, "What about my powers? I can't do anything like this and I didn't know I had a cleansing ability."

Gewa put her other hand up, "I...I know magic. And I'm not afraid to use it." Gerold, even with his suddenly blurring eyesight, could see she didn't have a coin in her hand. The worst she could do is an annoying cantrip.

"I promise I'm not crazy, I'll explain in a second," Gerold said to her.

"You don't. Cleansing isn't really a spell, you just act like a conduit to spread divine power that will erase necrotic corruption. And unless you properly send off the adventurers and burn the mummy, the corruption will return. This place will be safe for a time until wild mana converges here and turns it into a lair or dungeon," Erinne said.

"What should I do then," asked Gerold.

"I don't know," Gewa said, growing a look of panic on her face and she reached down and shook Niitty's shoulder. Gerold felt a headache growing from the stress of trying to hold a conversation while looking like lunatic.

"Huh, wha," Niitty said with a start as she woke up. She was facing the entryway, "Is something happening?"

"A crazy man is talking to the air," Gewa said.

She didn't even turn around, "Oh, that's just Gerold. He does that."

Gerold sighed and massaged his temples, wondering what he did to deserve this. Erinne was laughing uproariously in his head, "This is amazing! I love it. Oh, wow, now I understand the God of Humor's point of view better."

Erinne calmed herself down, "Hold your hands out and let my power flow through you. It should be over in a moment."

He did as she asked and held his hands out and relaxed. He felt a warm, comforting feeling pass through him like flowing water and disperse from his fingertips. As he did, a sense of foreboding that was so ever-present that his mind had ignored its presence lifted from the cavern. The warmth faded from his body and the cavern of undead horrors was now a mundane cave.

"I shouldn't dally longer," Erinne said. Gerold bid farewell to the empty air since the Goddess never stuck around for the formality. He found it remarkable how he was slowly getting used to the Goddess's presence and that each time he felt more and more alone with her passing, even now when he was with two tangible people.

"Did you activate your aura again," Niitty asked through a yawn and a long stretch, "How long was I out?"

"It wasn't me, I just helped Erinne cleanse this place," Gerold said as he worked a sudden stiffness in his wrist that he developed from the repetition of farm work. He found the pain oddly comforting since it was the first time in months he felt normal.

Niitty stood and turned, "What is wrong with your voiohwhahappeyou?"

"What?"

She jumped up and ran over to him getting close to his face, "What happened to you? You're all wrinkled and old. And you're dirty."

Gerold grumbled, "I'm not old, I'm 49."

"I'm serious. What happened? And why are you holding your side like that?"

He sighed, "Broken ribs."

She frowned and poked him in the chest, "I thought you couldn't lie."

"I didn't," he responded, "I told you a truth. I just couldn't evade it believably this time."

"Don't do that again," she said, "Now, what happened."

Gerold felt like he had enough of being berated by people and was getting angry. Before he blew up at her, he felt the party connection between them. He felt a sense of fear and concern pouring through. Erinne was right, he needed to pay more attention to it.

He took a few deep breaths to calm himself. Thankfully, Niitty took it differently and didn't notice the emotional spike. Gerold wondered if the link could be overwhelmed by the most emotional member. He felt her concern elevate and she said, "Do you want to sit? Broken ribs aren't anything to take lightly."

Gerold shook his head, "It'll just hurt worse trying to stand again."

Gerold gave a breakdown of what Erinne told him. Niitty watched first with fascination and then horror. She poked Gerold in the chest again, "Don't you do that again. You hear me? That's too dangerous."

Gerold growled to himself. She had some serious issues with how the world worked, "Look, I'm the elder here. It's my job to keep the next generation alive."

"Nope," she retorted, "Don't do anything reckless."

"Was I to just let you die?"

He could see her face at war with this concept. She looked like she decided against a weak retort to the claim, lacking any meaningful evidence to the contrary. Gerold found it amusing how she wore her emotions like her clothing.

She groaned, "Fine. I understand. It doesn't change the fact that I'm worried about you. Don't do that if you can avoid it."

Gerold shrugged, "I couldn't if I wanted to. We're down to 21 Copper coins."

"We have monster parts at least. And here," she opened her bag and pulled out a slimy black thing, "Here's the Lampreyer's tongue. I don't want it in my bag. You keep it."

Gerold grabbed the object and his skin crawled from the feel. It was still sticky with some sort of mucous stringing from the tongue to Niitty's hand after he took it. He shoved it in his bag and looked at the gunk on his hand, wishing his curse would come back, at least to get rid of this. Instead, he willed a water skin out and used a small amount to wash it away. He offered some to Niitty as well who also washed the slime off.

Gerold turned back to Gewa, "I hope this is proof enough that I'm not going to harm you."

She was watching the two with concern and curiosity. Her arms went slack as she allowed the dagger to lower toward the floor. Her eyes were pinned on Gerold though with a look of distrust crossing her face.

"I'll accept you say you are who you are." Gewa put away her dagger, "I'm sorry about my actions. You can't be too safe."

Gerold couldn't disagree. He wished Niitty would develop some of that distrust as opposed to inviting a stranger, Paladin or no, into her camp the same day they met.

"That's a fair response," Gerold said. He felt another twinge from his ribs and winced in pain.

Niitty saw it, "You need to sit and rest. How long did you say this would take?"

"A week."

"We can stay here a week. I don't mind."

Gerold looked at her like she lost her mind, "And how do you intend we do that? We only have four days of provisions left. We spent three days coming out here and in my condition it would take four or five days back. We barely have enough to get back. Unless," he looked over at Gewa, "Does your party have provisions we can, uh, take?"

She shook her head, "No. Karl would carry the provisions and gear for his friends. I didn't trust his bag and kept some provisions for myself. I barely have enough to get back, too."

To force the point, the two sconces on the pillars nearest the sarcophagus started to dim, whatever it is that fueled them for the last half day was beginning to fail.

"It looks like we're going to be forced out. I don't want to be stuck in here in the pitch dark," Gerold said.

He looked over at the four bodies, "Gewa was it? We should take care of your companions before we leave."

The three walked over and stood over the four bodies lying on the small bed of wood with the small piles of coins arranged on top.

"Did you put those there," Gewa asked. Gerold caught a strange look in her eyes as she looked at the coins. It wasn't sadness. Did she want to take them? He dismissed the thought as his inexperience and the dimming light talking.

"Yes," he replied, "I have it on good authority that this should be sufficient. Would you like to say the rites?"

She looked at the bodies for a few moments. Gerold got another set of strange impressions from how she hesitated as she looked at her fellows with a sense of detachment, much like how Gerold felt when he stumbled on Ellen's body earlier. The look passed and a frown replaced it. For some reason, he felt her change in mood was faked. The poor girl was probably in shock.

Finally, she replied, "I don't know the rites."

Gerold sighed. He'd said them enough over the years to last a lifetime, "I can do it. Do you want to say any goodbyes?"

She shook her head, "While they treated me well and Karl died protecting me, I don't really know any of them. It would be insulting for a stranger to speak."

Gerold shrugged, "I guess I'm the closest thing to a priest here. I'll perform the rites."

Gerold positioned himself at the feet of the four adventurers with Niitty and Gewa standing a few paces behind him.

Bowing his head, he began the rites, "Umieranie. We, your humble servants, beseech you to guide these departed souls to their next destination. We ask you protect them in your divine embrace. We blame you not for the fate of those before us. Death is another aspect of life, not something to fear. We have prepared a humble offering as thanks for your tireless efforts and appreciation for your role in this world."

He imagined the words were tangible things and he allowed them to slowly sink into and absorb into the bodies in silence. After a minute, he reached into his bag for his firebox. Frustration grew when the wood stubbornly refused to ignite. He cursed under his breath as he continued to fail to light the makeshift pyre and then spiked the useless thing on the stone floor in frustration, shattering the item. It had worked for the campfire a few mornings past and chose now to cease functioning to spite him.

"Let me try," a voice said behind him. He turned and through pained ribs stood, hissing as he attempted to hold in the signs of pain.

Gewa pointed a finger at the wood and her lips moved with a soundless incantation. A small dart of fire that looked like what distracted the Lampreyer jumped from the tip and landed in the wood. The wood smoldered, refusing to catch. Gerold kneeled down, once again trying to ignore the pain, and gently blew on the spot. The fire finally caught and began to spread, picking up speed as the trapped heat built within the pyre.

Still, Gerold worried that the amount of wood was going to be insufficient to immolate four bodies. He didn't want to allow the adventurers to turn into the undead and was preparing the prospect of either scouring the rocky mountainside for more fuel or dragging the bodies through the wilderness.

His worries proved to be unfounded. As the flames started to crawl up the clothing of the adventurers, the coins he left on their chests flared into a bright, gentle light that illuminated the cavern yet didn't hurt his eyes. Gerold watched as the coins turned into a liquid then absorbed themselves into the bodies. The liquid caused something to change in the bodies and the fire quickly spread over the flesh, armor, weapons and other gear. Gerold watched in fascination as the flames poured out of the bodies. The fire was a crystal blue color, like an artist carved ice into the shape of flame and somehow animated it. Further, while he could still feel the warmth radiating from the wood below, the flames from the bodies produced no heat, especially as the flames blasted ten feet into the air.

Gerold watched the process in fascination. Now he understood why Erinne had said not to worry, Umieranie did accept the offering. He felt a strange sense of comfort as he watched the bodies turn to ash, the skin never curling or blackening in the process. One moment it was tissue and the next it was ash. Even the bones and armor dissolved away. The process lasted less than fifteen seconds and, soon, the blue light faded and then winked out, leaving the dull orange glow of the wood as the only remnants of the display.

He knew in the core of his being Umieranie was sending a message that their souls were in her protection and she would allow no harm to come to them. It was a comfort that was bittersweet as it reminded him of his past and the same feeling he received when he buried his loved ones in the family plot, though this spectacular display was not present in those somber affairs.

He stood there for some time, lost in the experience. He didn't know how long he stared at the fire, thinking of his past and his own loss when a voice cut into the silence, "First time seeing this, huh?"

He turned and saw Niitty standing at his side also looking at the flame. She continued, "This is how all of my people are sent off. We place their favorite personal items from life along with the offering for Umieranie and the flames signal her final sign that the souls are now in her care. Our legends say the flames run cool as to not set the tree crowns ablaze, one of the Goddess of Death's many considerations for our pain and loss."

"In the capital," Gewa started and Gerold turned to look at her as she stared at the fire, "We cremate our departed. The ashes are then sealed in a ceramic urn with our offering and it is placed on the family mantle or into the city mausoleum, at least if you're rich enough to afford it. If you open the urn, you'll find the coin is gone. There isn't a display like this."

She looked over at the two and a look of surprise crossed her face and she quickly added, "Uh, I only know the coin is gone because I accidentally knocked over Grandma's urn and it was only ash."

Gerold found that addendum strange of her. He ignored it and went back to looking at the fire.

"What about where you're from," Niitty asked.

"We bury our dead. We normally can't afford an offering and bury our dead in a cemetery. It's overseen by the local Pantheon Temple to consecrate once a year to keep the bodies from turning. My Father refused to trust that and sold some of my Grandfather's adventuring gear to bury my mother with a silver coin. I sold the rest for my Father's burial and whe...," Gerold suddenly cut off and felt a pang in his chest. He couldn't talk about it. He couldn't handle the pain in the moment. In addition, the sconces were winking out and they'd have to navigate the passage in the dark if they didn't leave.

"You don't need to tell me now," Niitty said in a soft voice.

Gerold nodded, "I think it's time we get going."

Niitty and Gewa had no objections. Before they left, Gerold had Gewa immolate the mummified body and then the three headed to the tunnel that led out of the mountain.

CHAPTER 15

Gewa looked at her two new companions as they exited the crypt tunnel in the early morning light peeking over the distant horizon. The artificial plateau felt cold and intimidating as it looked out over the slope as it descended into a rocky scrubland then, in the far distance, the start of the forest surrounding the town. Gewa preferred the warm embrace of an urban environment while this open space made her feel exposed.

She didn't know what to make of her two companions. The Mountain Elf, Niitty, was easy. She was an open book and blabbed her entire life story to a stranger. She wondered if a close knit community like hers fostered a sense of intrinsic trust in others. She was surprised at how quickly the girl trusted Gewa and fell asleep in her presence. Gewa, in turn, had to fight her exhaustion and only went to sleep when she couldn't hold herself awake anymore. Her parents would have gotten themselves in trouble after robbing them and then trying to traverse days of open terrain alone.

Gewa knew she was different from her parents. She refused to fall into their lifestyle after she saw the ramifications as a child. The look of that merchant that had his shop burglarized was seared in her memory. No, she was going to follow a different path in life, one of honor.

Old habits die hard. Niitty was naïve and easy to fool. The Paladin was a completely different story. He didn't look like much now that his powers were temporarily disabled. He was a middle aged man with signs of wear in his joints in addition to the injury he sustained against the Lampreyer. He stood at a modest height and had a relatively plain appearance. His body was strong though, the kind fostered by a lifetime of labor. He had broad, thick forearms and large hands. While clearly human, he had features that she suspected indicated his Father was a Dwarf. The only things unusual about him were the complete absence of old scars or even tooth decay. Whatever blessings the Paladins received from their gods cured the ravages a body experienced during life.

He was a far cry from the impossibly handsome young man that radiated calm and faced down a Lampreyer with righteous fury. It was still hard to fathom that this injured, plain middle aged man was the same as the one that rescued her from her fate.

As the three descended the mountain, she had given him the same story that she had given Niitty to help pass the time. It also helped keep him engaged and not focusing on trying to travel down a mountain with broken ribs.

The trick to telling a believable lie is to alter the truth. By telling mostly the truth, it's easy to adjust your story to fit the lie and keep your lies consistent. The fewer lies included in the story, the better. It was true she was born in the Capital. It was true she was poor. It was true her family lived in the Docks. The parts about finding a Basics of Magic book, her parents happy she found it and that she wanted to better her life by becoming a Mage with the Adventurer's Guild were also true.

It was in the other details that she peppered in the lies. Her parents weren't poor laborers. They were poor thieves. They were members of the Capital's Thieves Guild who rarely ever succeeded in their schemes. The book was something she had stolen up during one of her parents' training missions. It was this book that sparked her desire to learn magic.

She poured over the materials. While most magic comes as inspiration from gaining power, learning the underlying philosophies of spell casting would provide a foundation. It also allowed her to cast simple cantrips that were able to make use of the weak ambient mana produced within the body.

And, of course, her parents were thrilled at the prospects of her learning magic. To them, when she formally joined the Thieves Guild, she would be able to track into the Shadow class, mixing magical ability with thieving skills. And, before she came of age, she could use her cantrips in their schemes.

Their plans to use her simple cantrips never worked out. Her parents weren't too smart and they hadn't accounted for the fact that simple cantrips were common. While not everyone was smart enough to learn magic, enough had learned that a person making a spark come from a fingertip, even a child, was no more impressive a sight than a horse dropping dung on the street. She found herself running from angry shopkeepers and guards when her mother or father tried to palm goods while she made light breezes move items around. They never bothered to check to see if the distraction worked.

The book she had stolen had changed her life in other ways. The memory of the details was too painful for her, but that book was the reason she decided that she couldn't live the life of a criminal.

When she came of age and she announced she was joining the Adventurer's Guild, her parents were livid. They were planning on taking her to meet the Master Thief to induct her into their ranks. She had to escape them when they tried to drag her into the sewers. That's when she made her way to the Adventurer's Guild. Trying to explain away why she already knew magical basics wasn't as simple as she made it out to be. Thankfully, the Guild didn't press the issue too hard. They had no evidence to link this book to a years old crime.

She had made an error when she embellished her story of the party. While it was true that Karl and his followers weren't bad people, she didn't feel much for them. She knew she was only there as a prized servant, not a valued member of his party. This didn't engender enough of an attachment to generate more than a surface level sadness for their loss. Adventuring was a dangerous profession and she knew she could be killed even by random chance. She was, however, inexperienced and had assumed that Karl's money and lavish equipment expenditure was enough to bail them out. Bad luck and powerful monsters, as she learned, can outrun money.

Truth can also get you in trouble if you're not careful, like how she inadvertently mentioned knowing that the offering coins in urns vanished since she, in her youth, had smashed a few to find coins. She hoped this would never come up again because she couldn't trust remembering the story, already forgetting which relative's urn broke. The truth was the foundation that lies will stand upon.

However, this Paladin was different in ways beyond his appearance. All the stories she heard about Paladins from the thieves down in the Guild Hall were of righteous men who were too honest and trusting for their own good. They were gregarious, magnanimous and had boundless charisma. They were also easy to fool and a well placed sob story would get them to part with their hard earned coin, both mundane and Adventurer.

Still, you'd also have to be wary. If they ever discovered your identity, they wouldn't hesitate to clap you in irons and march you down to the nearest guard post. They had a near obsession to uphold good and law. It was only providence that they were so rare that you'd go a lifetime not even passing within shouting distance of one that kept thieves safe.

This Paladin she traveled with now? He was none of

those things. Other than the looks, at least when he had his powers, everything else about him didn't present the image of the legendary holy warriors. He was a mess, wearing torn clothing, a cheap chain hauberk and a ridiculous amulet to Erinne that only Niitty believed was legitimate. He was surly, terse, and distrustful. He had none of the charisma she had expected. Had it not been for that unmistakable aura that banished her mental collapse, his ability that staggered the Lampreyer enough to allow her a distraction and the blinding white light that cured Niitty, she would have thought him a scam artist so bad it would make her parents look like skilled Confidence Men.

When she told her story, she could see him working her story in his mind like a master locksmith. She could swear he had picked up on her deception. He either didn't care or she was mistaken in her assessment. She was worried. While everything else about him turned out to be the antithesis of a Paladin, she couldn't risk him finding out her true past.

The Paladin called for a stop to rest. Between his age and injury, the party was moving slowly. She hoped that when they left the rough slopes of this part of the mountain it would speed them up. He got a look on his face and reached into his bag. He pulled out a recurve bow and five arrows, handing them to Niitty, "Here, I think you'll need these."

Niitty took them and stared at the items, "Are you sure we can afford this? We don't have the money to replace the arrows."

He shook his head, "They're expensive for us, yes. What good is money if we're dead? I'm not in good shape and it would be best if we can kill or weaken a threat before it gets to us. I don't have my Detect Evil aura, either. You'll need to be on your best and range out ahead of us."

Niitty's expression displayed one of concern, "You know I'm

no good in this terrain."

He gently pushed her forward, "And the way you get better is to do it. Unless Gewa here is a tracker..."

Gewa shook her head. He knew very well that she wasn't a tracker and his question was for Niitty's benefit, "No. Until I joined the Guild, I had never even left the Capital, let alone learned anything about wilderness survival."

"There you have it. You're our best choice on the matter. Be careful. We're right behind you, not that my presence can do much," he concluded.

She slowly moved ahead of the group and, after looking back, ran agilely down the path they were following. After she moved far enough ahead that they could barely see her, The Paladin turned to Gewa, "You're hiding something from us."

Gewa's ears twitched in agitation. He knew. How? She thought she had carefully crafted the story. How did he know?

"You're probably wondering," he interrupted her thoughts, "How I knew. Between being a father of two kids and some training, I've gotten good at picking it up."

She put some distance between the two and felt her fur stand on end. She knew she could outrun the injured man. Niitty, on the other hand, would be a different challenge. Besides that, she would likely die alone out here. She didn't know what she could do and felt a sense of panic rising.

Paladin sighed, "I'm in no position to force the issue. I've not told you or Niitty anything about myself. I don't sense any malice coming from you. Still, that girl up there is too trusting and I need to ensure nothing happens to her when she makes a bad decision."

Gewa's throat went dry and she swallowed some saliva. The Paladin noticed this and pulled out a water skin from his bag,

"Here. What you can be certain of is if you're no threat to us, I won't force the matter. We all have our secrets. Besides, you could make a future party member and I'd rather not push you away either."

Like everything else unexpected about the man, his healthy skepticism conflicted with the image of a Paladin. She was getting a better idea of who he was.

He thrust his large hand out, "We haven't been formally introduced. I'm Gerold."

Gewa tentatively gripped his hand, careful to keep her claws from digging into his skin. She didn't want to sully her honor accidentally by drawing blood, "Gewa. And I appreciate you not prying. My past is not something I'm proud of."

He gave her hand a brief yet firm grip and released it, "Let's hope we can be friends. I think we should get moving before Niitty moves too far ahead. I'm worried she could be ambushed."

Now that, Gewa thought, was a trait of a Paladin. Beneath the crusty and grumpy demeanor was someone who legitimately cared.

They continued down the path. The Paladin, no, Gerold, was trying to put on a tough exterior to obfuscate his injuries and the effects of the high altitude. She, too, had problems with the thin air and the ridiculous robe Karl asked her to wear. Gerold had her beat with the broken ribs that would elicit a quick gasp of air every time he took a breath.

Gewa found herself reaching out to help him from stumbling down the uneven and loose terrain. The worst parts were when he tried to get down small drops from rocks or scrambling on steep declines. He was clearly struggling but he forged on, more concerned with their provisions situation than his own comfort.

After sliding down some loose gravel, Gewa helped Gerold up from the seated position. He huffed and spoke for the first time in a while, "I'm sorry I was late."

Gewa was confused, "Late? What do you mean?"

A pained look broke his neutral face, "I wasn't able to arrive to help in time."

Gewa was silent for a while. They continued to travel down the mountain for a half an hour before she found her voice again, "Don't blame yourself. What could you have done?"

"More people and my Turn Undead spell could have been beneficial."

"I don't think so. Do you have an ability to have known the zombies were buried in the walls?"

He was silent for a while again. Another ten minutes passed before he replied, "No. Detect Evil was overwhelmed by the aura of the entire crypt. I would have missed them, too."

"Then if you came in time, there would be seven bodies back there, not four," Gewa said. "And I appreciate your arrival. It wasn't late. It was right on time. Any later and I think that Lampreyer would have gotten bored and climbed up after me."

He didn't look entirely convinced and something was weighing on him about the entire affair. He thankfully dropped the conversation.

As the two hobbled around a bend in the mountain, they saw Niitty hiding behind a rock. She saw the two and indicated to hold in place and keep quiet, "There's one of those goat things down the way in the path. It's just standing there."

Gewa stuck her head around and looked. She was impressed by Niitty's visual acuity. There was one of those spiral horn goat monsters two hundred yards down the mountain. She recognized it was in the same place that her party had camped previously and were attacked by the same monster. Looking up, she saw it was mid-day. They were making poor time on the trek back and this was something they didn't need.

Gerold also looked, squinting through poor eyesight, "How long has it been there?"

Niitty shrugged, "I've only been here a few minutes. It's milling around and hasn't shown signs that it's interested in moving."

He turned to Gewa, "I saw your party killed one of these a ways back on your way up. How bad is it?"

Gewa thought back on it. The one he was talking about was the second of the two goats that ambushed them. The first hit them when they were breaking camp and it wasn't that much of a problem since they saw it coming. The second was bad since it ambushed them and skewered Nader.

"They're dangerous, but they're worse if they see you first. We had to deal with two of them and the one we killed in the same spot down there wasn't too bad. We didn't have a ranged attack at the time. I think an arrow should kill it," Gewa replied.

Niitty looked at Gerold, "Should I try shooting it?"

He thought a moment, "Let's wait a while longer and see if it leaves. You should use that Snipe ability if it looks like the monster lingers too long."

Turning to Gewa, he said, "How many spells can you cast per day?"

"I think eight? I haven't found my limit," Gewa said in response.

Fishing eight coins out, he handed them to Gewa, who only

took seven since she had one already, "In case we need it. After what I learned about these bags, it's not a good idea to keep this stuff in there. And I should do this, too." He took out all of the rations he had in the bag and handed half to Niitty and put his into a cloth square he then tied off to his belt.

They watched the monster for another ten minutes. It had no inclination of leaving the area and only looked around and, now and again, stomped the ground.

"Let's shoot it," Gerold announced, a look of impatience crossing his face.

Niitty nodded and readied her bow after slipping a coin into the glove on the hand holding it. Gewa watched as she crept down the mountain to get into range. When she reached the halfway point, Niitty stopped and Gewa saw the telltale glow of an ability as the coin dissolved. She couldn't see any other effects, if there were any, from this angle.

Drawing the string, Niitty aimed into the air in the direction of the goat monster. She held it a beat and then released it. The arc was beautiful. The arrow sailed gracefully through the air on the way to its target. It was perfect. Except that the damnable goat monster decided it was time to move.

Instead of the perfect heart shot that the arrow was headed toward, the head buried itself into the flank of the monster. The creature let out a strange bleat, one that had undertones of a squealing pig. The monster's face turned toward Niitty and started to advance up the mountain.

It was fast, even with the wounded flank. The monster hopped up the mountain from rock to rock in a zigzag pattern. Niitty struggled to target the monster through its erratic movements, forcing her to jerk her bow back and forth as she tried to predict its movement. When the monster got too close, she dropped her bow and started to scramble back up the mountain toward them when she realized trying to shoot the monster was a futile exercise.

Gewa readied a coin to cast a spell. She figured a lightning zap would be a good choice since she had no spells that could outright kill an opponent. The lightning could disrupt the monster and give the party an opening to kill it. She would have to wait until it got within 20 yards to cast her spell.

Her plans were interrupted when Gerold sprinted down the mountainside, clumsily sliding and nearly tumbling over from the poor footing. She was initially impressed that the man fought through terrible pain to be able to move like that before being replaced with irritation when the man had upended her plan. Not that she could fully blame him since they didn't bother to discuss a contingency in case of failure. She would have to remember this lesson for later if they survived the encounter.

The goat was gaining on Niitty, who was panicking as she ran up the mountain. Before it was able to reach her, Gerold, defying his age and injury, dove off a rock and rammed his entire body into the monster. This stopped the monster dead in the air as the two crashed into the ground. Gerold wasn't able to gain purchase as he held the monster by one of its spiral horns and was wrestling it to the ground, the goat kicking him in the chest with its free hooves. This didn't last long when the monster's head wrenched to the side and pulled itself free.

Gewa was, thankfully, able to get into range. Unfortunately, the spell failed to activate when her inexperience led to an attempt to cast it in haste, her mouth fumbling over the unknowable words.

The goat pulled away from Gerold then quickly lowered its head. Coiling its body, it bounded forward. Gerold pulled his war hammer and was unable to bring it out for a swing. He impotently held it out like a shield to keep the head at bay.

Niitty was able to snap herself out of her fear when she saw Gerold sprint by and had turned and pulled her rapier. However, she was not able to find any openings with the two tangling on the ground.

Calming herself, Gewa focused on the spell. She held and waited for an opening, which was when Gerold managed to shove the monster away a second time. This time, the silent words came to her lips. The coin dissolved and from the tip of her claw an electric jolt jumped out and hit the monster.

The monster convulsed as the electricity coursed through its body. This delay was enough to allow Niitty to stab her sword through the monster's chest, piercing its heart. The monster continued to convulse after death while the electricity effect continued and then it went still.

Gewa saw Gerold kneeling on the ground, gasping for air. Niitty had moved in next to him after killing the goat and was fussing over his side. Gerold weakly tried to swat her away, but Niitty won out.

"Give me your extra cloth," Niitty demanded of Gerold. Gewa came closer and noticed that Gerold had a nasty puncture wound in his side. With her limited knowledge of anatomy, she thought it may have missed anything vital and it didn't penetrate all the way through the body, the chain proving useless as a defense. Still, it was bleeding.

He shook his head, "The provisions bag is the last of it."

Niitty growled and pulled a dagger and started to cut off parts of her already damaged shirt. She helped Gerold out of his chain hauberk and after evaluating it, found it was too damaged from their recent fights to continue wearing. He weakly shoved it into his bag to reduce the weight he was lugging around. Balling parts of her torn shirt, she put it over the puncture and used the rest to tie it to his torso.

Gerold leaned against a nearby rock and tried to catch his breath. The makeshift bandage seemed to have worked and the blood spreading through the cloth slowed. Gewa saw Niitty in tears, "What did I say about being reckless?"

"And what did I say about elders protecting the young," Gerold retorted. He reached into his bag and retrieved some thread and a needle. He then pulled the bandage away, causing the wound to bleed again.

Niitty gasped, "What are you doing?"

"I need to sew it shut first. That bandage won't last long," he said as he tried to thread the needle with shaky fingers that were too slick with blood to properly hold them.

Gewa stepped in, "Give those to me."

Taking the needle, she moved the thread through the eye and knelt down. She stared at Niitty, "You, help me hold this shut."

Niitty quickly grabbed at the tissue and pinched it shut. Gerold groaned as he fought through the pain. Gewa held him steady and pushed the needle through the skin and started to suture the wound together. This was not an ideal situation. They were in the wilderness, the needle was thick and the thread was rudimentary. Gewa was also not the best seamstress and her work was far from attractive. Still, it was better than shoving a wad of cloth into the wound and hoping it worked.

She managed to close the wound, which still seeped blood though the slit. Niitty moved to reapply the bloody wad when Gewa stopped her, "No. Use my robe."

"It looks so expensive," Niitty replied.

Gewa sighed at her behavior. She wasn't thinking straight in her distress. "It's just cloth. Besides, it's uncomfortable folding my tail in under this thing," she said as she took her dagger and ripped off pieces of it. Since her robes were still intact and it was that overly impractical design that Karl had demanded she wear because it made her look the part, she had plenty of cloth to work with. She cut out a rectangle to apply to the wound and a healthy length to tightly tie it off. The red color was going to make it hard to evaluate spread through the cloth.

It would have to do, though. They had nothing else to work with and Gerold's magic healing was locked away. After it was tied off, Gerold tried to stand.

"What are you doing," Niitty shouted, "You're hurt and need to rest."

He roughly pushed her aside and slowly levered himself up into a standing position against the rock, "We don't have that luxury. We're exposed, it'll get dark soon and we still have to worry about provisions. I'm a fool for not removing that chain earlier, we could have made better time without it."

"And you'd probably have taken a worse wound as a result," Gewa replied.

He picked up his war hammer and tried to use it as a makeshift cane. It proved too short and harder to use than walking unassisted. He sighed and hooked the hammer back onto his belt, "Come on, let's go."

"Stop," Niitty said.

"What did I say, we can't sit around," Gerold growled.

"Not that. Pull out one of the tent posts," she said.

"What for?"

"I'll break it and you can use that as a walking stick."

Gerold did as she asked and pulled a long branch out of the

bag. Gewa was astounded at how the bag worked and that a long item like that would fit in there. Her parents would have loved one to help steal stuff.

Niitty took the branch and leaned it up against the rock that Gerold was sitting against. Taking her rapier, she hacked at a spot to create a notch in the wood. After that, she kicked at the wood and snapped it at the cut point.

Gerold took the stick and after testing it, he started to move down the mountain. Niitty continued to fuss over Gerold, who pushed her away again, "I appreciate your concern, but we still need you to scout ahead."

"What about," she tried to start.

"I'm still here, you know," Gewa said, "I can help him along if he needs it."

Niitty relented after a brief hesitation and moved down the path after she rinsed her hands off in the stream to clean off Gerold's blood.

Before following along, Gewa bent over and, after a few moments, managed to pry a horn out of the goat's skull with her dagger and stored it in her bag then cleaned her hands as well. Afterward, Gewa followed along, Gerold hobbling down the path on his makeshift cane after her.

CHAPTER 16

Privately, Gerold didn't think he would make it back to see Wren's End again. He was happy that he would die soon, especially since it involved at least keeping two people alive. While he saw the logic in both Erinne's and Gewa's statements, he couldn't let it go that there were four more people who would never see a new day again.

Despite the pain, he managed to forge forward with the help of the walking stick. They somehow managed to make it back to the same camping spot he and Niitty used the night prior to reaching the crypt. He credited his Dwarf father for blessing him with tenacity in the face of pain. He wouldn't give up until he ensured his companions were back safe at Wren's End. After that? That was a concern for another day.

That night, Niitty refused to allow Gerold to take watch. Gewa agreed to help and she and Niitty split that night's watch. Gerold eventually relented and bedded down for the night. Returning to his original age added to his fatigue and he felt himself nodding off quicker than he had in the past few months.

He dreamt of being on his farm again, sitting in the main room of his house. He quietly sat at the table and watched a figure as it stoked the fire in the room's stove, a small pot bubbling away on it. Turning, it was his wife, Zelina. She was showing a small bump in her midriff. He smiled, his joy tinged with a sense of melancholy. His Father suddenly passed away just a few months prior. While Gerold was happy to be a father this late in life, he felt sad that his own Father would never meet his grandchild.

Zelina poured a thick lentil stew into a pair of bowls, set one before Gerold and sat across the table. She smiled at Gerold as they ate. He had always been a quiet man and had poor communication skills. When he reached his 30s he had feared he would never marry. Then he met Zelina at a harvest festival and he was smitten with her personality. He was lucky to find a woman who also appreciated the quiet moments where just being in each other's presence was enough.

He suddenly found himself alone in the room. The food was gone and the stove was cool. Worse, Zelina was gone. It felt cold and empty. The world was grey with rapidly shifting black spots dotting his vision.

Worried, he stood up from the table. He went to the sleeping room. Inside, he saw two beds and a loft above holding a third bed. The three were empty with sheets disheveled and not made for the day. Gerold groused at the poor state of the beds and tried to pull the sheets into position, finding the cloth locked in place by some unknown force. He then turned around, abandoning the effort.

Instead of exiting back into the main room, he found himself outside the house looking over the main road passing in front of his farm. It was a sunny day with only a few passing clouds in the sky. Turning, he saw the area where he kept chickens. In it, he saw Zelina selecting eggs from the coop and gently placing them into a basket.

Once again, he felt content. He was now leaning against the fence around the chicken coop having teleported across the space between his house and the coop area. While his wife was still there picking eggs, all of his chickens were now lying still in the yard, grey blood spilling out of their grey bodies. Zelina continued smiling throughout, oblivious to the carnage around her.

She turned around, her bump gone and blood staining her smock at the crotch. She smiled at him warmly, "Why didn't you come with us?"

"I don't understand," Gerold said. He was now inside the coop yard and the chickens were gone.

"Come with us. The kids are waiting."

Gerold tried to walk toward his wife, but with every step he took, she moved further away. No, she was standing still, but the space between them only got larger.

She frowned, "What's wrong? Why won't you come?"

He took another step and then another. The space continued to expand. The distance expanded faster when he attempted to close the gap by running. When he stopped running in hopes it would stop the growth, he was mocked by further acceleration. Nothing that he did mattered; he would never reach his wife.

Out of desperation, he sprinted hard. Still, she pulled away. He began to sweat and feel hot from the exertion and collapsed on the ground. Instead of impacting into a solid surface, he fell through the dirt and found himself in his cellar. He was surrounded by the familiar mustiness of the room. Shelves lined the walls that were stacked with glass jars holding preserved fruit and vegetables for the winter. Barrels sat around holding pickled vegetables. A lone bottle of wine, dusty on a shelf, sat waiting for a special occasion that Gerold had never properly defined.

The expected cool comfort of the subterranean room was replaced by sweltering heat. He looked around again and the jars were replaced with a gruesome sight. Within the glass containers floated rotting body parts. Hands, eyes, ears and noses from zombies were contained within. A pair of lips that looked like his wife's put on a smile. It moved like it was speaking, the wall visible behind, and bubbles emitted from the empty space between. The bubbles surfaced and popped, "Where are you? Why aren't you with us?"

He was outside once more. The sky was grey with clouds and a light mist of rain spread down from above. The moisture soaked his clothing and condensed on his skin. The mist was warm and tasted slightly of salt. Looking at his house, he saw it in disrepair. The door to the cellar was broken open from the outside and his front door sat open, gently swinging despite the stillness of the air.

Neither door was inviting. The door to his house, the place where he was born, where his children were born, the legacy of his family, was cold, empty and uninviting. The door to the cellar, instead, held a sense of terror. The broken doors looked like the teeth of a beast, waiting to consume him and pull him into the depths of the underworld that served as its stomach.

For some reason, he found himself drawn to the cellar door. A dim red light could be seen below, breaking through the persistent grey of the world and a terrible odor emitted from below as if the ground had a case of halitosis. Still, he felt compelled to walk in despite remembering the jars on the shelves.

Then, from the dark, a rotting arm erupted and grabbed onto Gerold's shirt collar. It placed him in its iron grip and no matter how he fought, it slowly dragged him down into the pitch black. He closed his eyes as a high pitched scream came from below.

His eyes opened again and he was staring at a stone ceiling. He was back in the cave and he felt hot. Turning to his side, he saw Niitty sleeping close to him and, near the entrance, he saw Gewa's back with the dull red light of morning filtering through the opening.

Gerold ran his hand across his forehead. He was sweating and felt hot. He had developed a fever. Sitting up, he silently checked under the ripped robes that served as the bandage over his puncture wound. The wound had scabbed over with a sallow tint spreading out from the edges. Worse, the wound developed a white film with black spots.

He replaced the bandage to hide the wound and, fighting through the pain, pulled himself up. Gewa heard his movements and turned, "You're up. How do you feel?"

He tried to find a way to creatively tell the truth about his condition to avoid worry and couldn't twist his way out of it, "Not good. Can I trouble you for fresh cloth? I need to go down to the stream."

She didn't complain and tore pieces of her robe of her sleeves, reducing the cloth from the wrists to the elbows. Taking the cloth, he hobbled down to the stream nearby, not caring if a monster discovered him. No, hoping a monster noticed him.

The ice cold water felt good on his skin. He used a little bit of the cloth to wipe his sweat off his brow and he drank the clear water to quench his dry throat. He made sure to fill up his water skins while he was here.

He took a piece of the cloth and wet it. Gingerly, he dabbed the wound. White pus streamed from the wound along with bits of black. He felt disgusted at watching the sight. The pain seared in his body as he repeated the process. Wet the cloth and remove the infection. Each touch burned him.

After doing his best to clean the wound and hoping no one downstream would inadvertently drink the contaminated water, he realized that it would be a struggle to survive long enough for his powers to return and heal his infected wound.

He wondered if the seven day waiting period was when he blacked out or woke up. In either case, he felt he would be reunited with his family soon.

The wound still seeped after the process was completed. He folded some of the remaining cloth and placed it over the wound and tightly tied the rest to hold it in place. He found it amusing that his bandage was an elegant red color with seams of gold filigree. He felt like the Emperor himself with this binding.

Niitty had awoken before he returned and, at least now, he had a good truth for her when she asked about him. He just said the wound has been cleaned and wrapped and he was ready to move. That was enough for her.

Gerold forced himself to move as quickly as he could. He was worried about running out of provisions before reaching town. The party eventually found themselves on easier ground when they returned to the flat scrubland at the base of the steeper slope that led into the forest in the distance. As they descended, he found it getting easier to breath as the air started to return to normal.

As they traveled, he mulled over his dream from the night before to distract himself from the growing pain and worsening fever. It had been many months since the event and this was the first time he had dreamed of his wife. In prior dreams all his dreams were dominated by his children with his wife a background presence.

What did it mean? Was she calling from the beyond, asking for their reunion? No, that couldn't be it. She was a wonderful woman and wouldn't wish for his death. Were dreams a real thing, another force like magic, or was it just an artifact of the mind? He remembered discussing this with his Father over beers at the tavern in his retirement before he died, among other esoteric concepts his Father occupied his time with. The man didn't take to retirement well and he needed to occupy his time with something.

Gerold's mind returned to the dream again as he wrenched his way away from reminiscing on his past. Either a force in the universe was suggesting he die and join his family or he was. In either case, the message was the same.

As the day persisted, he found his brain becoming fuzzy as his fever worsened. He wasn't thinking straight and he found himself regularly being guided back on track by Gewa who caught his stumbling movements or when he started straying off the path. Gerold brushed off her concern for his well-being and insisted he could continue. His honesty didn't extend to admitting how long he could keep moving.

Another night passed as they only managed to get half-way across the flatlands in his state. Luckily, monsters didn't accost them on the path. Niitty had improved her tracking in this terrain and managed to identify and direct them away from a threat in the way. What it was, he couldn't remember in his state.

The next night was equally uneventful. His fever had reached a point where his body no longer wasted energy on dreams. He was out and a moment later he was looking at a sunrise. He went to clean his wound again and noticed it had gotten worse, the tissue turning blacker and ugly lines of infection were spreading through his skin. Once again, he managed to deflect Niitty's concern, as he pushed the limits of masking his worsening condition and perpetual sweating behind well-structured truths.

The day went by in a blur. All that came to mind as he pushed on was his growing discomfort and that the daylight grew longer the further from the mountains they went. He felt hot and cold at the same time, especially as the wind blew.

"Gerold."

Gerold looked around. He thought he heard someone calling to him. Looking around, he saw nothing on the expanse of rocky scrubland and the forest ahead in the distance.

"Gerold."

He heard it again. He looked to his back and saw Gewa, who was focused on the surroundings and helping him along should he stumble.

"Gerold."

"Where are you," Gerold replied.

He heard Gewa's voice, "I'm right behind. Don't worry."

It was not the first voice.

"Gerold."

"What do you want from me," he said to the space ahead of him, the voice impossible to pin down since it sounded like it was coming from everywhere and nowhere at once.

"Are you talking to Erinne again," he heard Gewa ask.

"What's wrong? Talk to me."

It sounded like his wife. He felt weak and his vision blurred. He had, somehow, come up to the edge of the forest and the last few hours completely vanished from his memory. His legs felt weak and his eyes were feeling heavy. The heat and cold were unbearable.

"Gerold, I need you. It's important," the voice came from a tree, its voice honeyed and sweet.

"Yes, I need you, too," he mumbled. He dismissed a muffled voice that cut in from behind him. He hated that the sound interfered with the words he wanted to hear.

He looked at the tree and it felt inviting. The tree promised salvation and rest. Its branches extended like inviting arms, showing the way to the base of the trunk where he could sit and accept its offer. He trudged over to the tree. He felt a tug on his shoulder that he shrugged off on his way to the tree. The tree was calling to him. It was time to sit.

A strange thought came to his mind as he sat down. He reached into his bag and pulled out the party's cooking pot. He then pulled out the goblin ears, a rat tooth and a disgusting tongue and placed them in a pile next to the pot. In the pot, he dumped the remaining eight copper coins in his possession. Finally, he pulled out the remaining tent poles, Niitty's hide tent and the blankets. He kept his personal effects in the bag.

A voice said something. He could tell there was a sense of urgency or panic in the voice. He didn't care. The tree called him over. The tree was the priority. It talked to him first. The voice could wait until later.

Whatever instinct told him to do this faded and, his work complete, he leaned his head against the tree bark. He stared up at the tree, its pine needles gently waving in the breeze. A strange fluffy white cloud with black spots, yellow eyes and sharp teeth floated into view. It was a pretty face with a look of concern in its eyes. Then a look of shock and fear crossed over the cloud which was followed by a muffled thunder as it floated away. Strange, he never saw the lightning. Could there be thunder without lightning? No matter, it's not important to consider.

The tree was inviting, opening its arms to its bark. He smiled. It was time to see his family again. He leaned his head against the tree and closed his eyes. The gentle breeze blew over his skin, the conflicting heat and cool irritating. Sleep won out over the discomfort and Gerold fell into the darkness.

CHAPTER 17

Niitty worried about her party. Gerold was clearly not doing well. He was looking pale and was sweating profusely. He had evaded her questions so poorly that even she was able to tell he was trying to conceal his condition. As they traveled, she noticed a clog of pus in the stream that trapped in a small side channel. There was no doubt it came from Gerold and, based on the color, he was badly infected.

Gerold was right. They couldn't afford to wait out here in the rocky scrubland or on the mountain slope while he recovered. Gerold couldn't afford to miss a meal in his condition. Worse, the chances of monster attack and the general stress of travel dictated they return to Wren's End. He could get help back at the town and she resolved that she would march herself in there, fear be damned.

The only thing that kept her focused was Gewa. She had admirably stepped up to help Gerold continue moving along. Niitty knew Gerold didn't share her trust of the Leopardia. Niitty was still convinced Gewa was a good person. They had saved her life and with her humble upbringing, she had little to worry about.

One upside is that desperate need is a good tool for improvement. Niitty was highly motivated to keep the party out of danger and away from any more monster encounters. After Gerold put himself at risk and further injured himself, the group couldn't encounter another monster out here and have all three of them walk away alive. She focused intently on her surroundings, looking for the smallest signs, along with foraging in her brain for the lessons taught on mountain tracking from her tribe.

She was connecting her academic work with practical experience. She noticed both signs of monsters and normal animal life. Animal life in the scrublands was far more plentiful than in the forest, owing the thinner monster population in the area.

She turned and looked back every few minutes to ensure she hadn't moved too fast for her party mates. A few times when she looked back, she saw Gewa guiding Gerold back toward the stream. This was not a good sign if he was unable to follow the water and would wander off. His mental state was degrading from the infection.

The next night was particularly stressful. The area was too flat and open for Niitty's comfort and they had neither a convenient cave like they found up the mountain nor were there any trees to erect a hide. Not that they could hoist Gerold up there if she did make one.

Somehow, she managed to get Gerold to pull her tent equipment from the bag. He was so mentally gone that she wasn't sure if he even knew what he was doing. Setting up the tent was an awkward affair now that they had broken one of the three tent poles down to make a walking stick for Gerold. She managed and made a long lean-to after Gewa offered to dig a hole to support the smaller stick and then they tied the two longer poles to it. Afterward, she draped her hide over it. Apart from looking strange, she found it a good idea for the future since it didn't stick up in the air, advertising where it was.

That night was uneventful though Gerold's sleep didn't look restful. His breathing was short and fast. When she checked his pulse, his clammy skin felt hot and his heartbeat rapid. The only upside was that, unlike other nights, he didn't move or moan from nightmares.

While he slept, Niitty checked on the wound. She had to peel the square of cloth from the wound since it had adhered itself to his body from the infectious fluids. The wound looked terrible and the infection was spreading. She only had basic first aid training and little experience to inform her opinions. She suspected the puffy red state of his skin was an indicator of blood poisoning. At this point, without a cleric or regaining his powers, she wasn't sure he would survive. She wasn't sure if the town even had a cleric of sufficient ability to help. Becoming a powerful cleric was difficult since they didn't have many combat skills to survive as adventurers.

Niitty forced herself to pull away from Gerold when it was time for her watch to allow Gewa some sleep. Niitty somehow managed to push her concerns aside while she kept watch. She did find herself lightly crying as thoughts of laying coins on Gerold's body as an offering to Umieranie invasively wormed their way into her head.

The next morning looked a little more promising. Gerold managed to store the tent and equipment into his bag and even ate some of the rations that Gewa carried. They decided the higher quality tinned meat would be better for him than the cheap travel biscuits that Gerold had procured previously. It was worrying that he didn't even notice the sudden change in fare as he mechanically chewed and swallowed while his unfocused eyes stared into the distance. Niitty was happy that he still managed to stand and move on when prompted.

Niitty checked the wound again and, after apologizing to Gewa for her ever shrinking robe, cleaned the wound and replaced the bandage with fresh strips taken from Gewa's robe. The infection was getting worse. White pus with black spots continued to form in the wound and the red flesh failed to improve.

Niitty's spirits lifted later in the day when she crossed the threshold from the rocky scrubland into the forest. The air was noticeably easier to breath and while she was improving her tracking skills on the scrubland, she was far more comfortable with the forest. Even with the density of goblins compared to the sparse monster population in the scrubland, she was more confident they could avoid conflict on the way back to the safe zone around town.

They were now on the fourth day after Gerold passed out. By her estimation, there would be one more night out in the forest and, after that, if they could get back to town, she felt that they could stabilize him enough for his powers to reactivate and eradicate the infection. She was feeling quite a bit better. Not only was Gerold still mobile, their destination was getting closer.

The brief reprieve didn't last. As Niitty moved her way into the familiar coverage of the forest, she started to hear shouting. One of the challenges in the forest was identifying where a sound originated from. Noise echoed off trees and made it hard to identify the direction. There were some tricks to it and, after focusing a bit to regain her forest instincts, she recognized it was from behind her.

Turning, she saw a lone figure in red waving bright white appendages. It was Gewa and she was alone.

Niitty's stomach sank and, discarding all caution, she sprinted back to Gewa.

When she arrived, Gewa was also showing signs of fear. She waved for Niitty to follow her, "Come on. He's collapsed."

The two ran a dozen yards back the way they came. There, Niitty's fear grew into outright panic. She saw Gerold, white as a sheet, slumped against the trunk of a tree. He had, strangely, emptied the contents of his bag around him. The cook pot, a pile of monster parts, the tent poles, her hide and coins were strewn about him. Her panic worsened when she realized Gerold had thought he was going to die and didn't want to strand them without the contents of his bag.

Running over to him, Niitty checked his pulse. His pulse matched his breathing, shallow and slow. Pulling the bandage away, she noticed the wound was significantly worse than before. The red of the infection clashed with the pallor of the rest of his body and the wound oozed the disgusting white substance.

Niitty searched her memories. While she had been trained in identifying useful herbs, her entire memory was exclusive to the forests and mountains of her homeland to the north. She had no knowledge or experience of this region.

In frustration, Niitty smacked herself in the head. Stupid! She should have made it a point to buy information on local medicinal herbs and monsters. She was so focused on her fear of going into town and, later, the rush of meeting Gerold that she had completely failed to consider intelligence gathering. She knew she would never make this mistake again. She hoped the cost wasn't more than she could afford to pay.

Think! Think! Then something came to mind. An image of the request board in the Guild Hall came to mind. The big bright bronze plaque for goblin ears dominated the board. Surrounding it were requests carved on wooden boards hung on plaques. Those were the open-ended requests. Why was she thinking of them all of a sudden?

Then it hit her. Some were requests from the local healer for medicinal herbs. Niitty fixated on them because it reminded her of nature and it helped her walk into the Hall that first day in town. A small piece of nature, even a carved facsimile, reduced her fears somewhat.

What was it again? Yes! It was an herb the local healer called Refik's Breath. Refik is the God of Healing, so it must be something Niitty could use to help Gerold. All she had to work with was a carved image. The plant was a long slender leaf with a single stalk arising from the center. The stalk had a series of small flowers arranged in a conical shape at the end. The carved wood lacked details on the color, forcing her to rely on the shape alone. Thankfully, the leaves were emphasized, indicating that was the valuable part of the plant. She would have to figure out how to prepare the medicine later.

With a shape to work with, she indicated to Gewa that she was going to go searching for the plant. Niitty assumed that since the request was on the board, it meant that the herb was growing this time of year.

Niitty took off, ranging along the sunnier borders of the forest with the scrubland. The plant proved stubborn to locate, especially since she had nothing more than a carving to work with. It was getting late in the day when she finally located a patch growing against the trunk of a tree. She harvested as many of the leaves as she could find.

Niitty didn't return the way she came since the forest curved along the border with the scrubland. Taking a direct route through the woods, she headed to where Gerold was left. On the way, a small bit of fortune presented itself. She came across a small cave in a hillside, partially hidden behind some shrubs. She weighed her need for speed to return with checking this potential safe place to bring Gerold back to and checking won out.

After a cursory examination of the cave, it looked like it hadn't been occupied in a long while. There wasn't the telltale odor of an animal or monster den nor were there any signs of life within. Making a mental note of the location, Niitty quickly returned to where Gerold and Gewa were waiting.

"I'm back," Niitty gasped when she came into view of the two. Gewa was standing guard over Gerold who still looked the same as before, shallowly breathing.

"Did you find anything useful?" Gewa asked.

"Yes, I found some Refik's Breath leaves. Even better, I found a cave nearby," Niitty said and reached down to grab one of the poles, "Help me make a litter."

The litter they fashioned was awkward. The poles were long and they were using the heavy hide to move Gerold. They gingerly placed him on the hide, using the blankets to support his head. Gewa threw the coins into her belt pouch and picked up the pot. They looked at the pile of monster parts. Niitty had reduced her weight significantly by relying on the bag of holding, so she had plenty of space in her travel pack. Holding back her disgust, she swept the parts into her pack, thankful Gerold's bag had a preserving effect since the goblin ears had no sign of rot.

Dragging a body across the forest was no easy feat. Uneven terrain, soft ground, rocks and the underbrush near the borders of the forest bogged them down.

Every jostle threatened to dump Gerold off the litter and cause further damage. Niitty felt stressed beyond anything she had ever felt, even walking into town or going into that crypt. She snuck a glance at Gewa and she also had a strong focused look on her face.

It was getting dark when they reached the cave. After carefully laying Gerold down, Niitty quickly left to locate firewood. She piled it up at the back of the cave and Gewa used her cantrip to set it ablaze.

Niitty felt drained physically and emotionally. She took out one of her rations and mindlessly chewed it, not feeling hungry. Looking down on it, she sighed.

"Do you think you can go back and get help," Gewa asked through bites of her own ration packet.

Niitty set aside and forgot her partially eaten biscuit and thought for a while. She calculated in her head the time it would take to get there and the risk of leaving Gewa alone. Finally, she spoke, "No. I don't think that's a good idea. If I leave at sunrise, I will make it back by the afternoon. Then I'll have to convince people to come collect him, organize it and get back. By the time I get back, his powers will have returned and we won't have to worry. If I leave, neither of you have a good chance of surviving out here."

Niitty looked over at Gewa. Her eyes flared with anger and they then quickly shifted into shame. Dropping her own biscuit, Gewa buried her face in her hands. She didn't sob like Niitty had expected but, instead, screamed. Her hands muffled the sounds of frustration.

Pulling her furry hands away, she looked at Niitty, "I know I'm useless. I have no idea what I was thinking. Karl flashed all those resources at me and my mind went stupid. I was born poor and it felt like a life changing amount. He had strange ideas on what Mages are. He insisted I wear this robe. Why a robe? It's not like it's a uniform we're obligated to wear."

Gewa leaned her head back and hit it against the cave wall, "And it's partly my fault, too. The book I read warned me that the path of the Mage is perilous. Mages can be powerful and those who gain power are also extremely wealthy. Reaching those heights takes either a wealthy patron or taking extreme risks. Spells are what defines us and that requires coin. At this level, I'd have to expend four or five spells just to fell one goblin. You can do the math on why that's a bad idea."

Balling a fist, she pounded the ground next to her, "I fell

for the stupid stories of robed Mages and their wealth. The robes are what the powerful ones wear at the Imperial Court to showcase their ability. To get there, I have to wear armor and learn combat arms like a Warrior. And I won't have the benefit of abilities. My spells will never rise beyond an insurance policy because of how costly it is to use my abilities. I should just give this up and switch to something else."

Niitty didn't know how to respond to that. Her people focused on outdoor survival and she never had to stress over what she would become. She trained to be a Ranger and knew that's what she'd do. She didn't have an underlying dream behind her profession the way Gewa had.

"I can't say I understand, but I think you shouldn't give up. Having a dream and pursuing it is something amazing. Besides, you being a Mage has been helpful," Niitty replied.

Gewa looked over, "How? All I did was provide a couple of distractions to help you and I've been useless elsewhere. I could be replaced with a thrown rock."

A wry smile crossed Niitty's face. She had no idea what possessed her to set this up. It would be a shame if she didn't follow through, "If you weren't a Mage, we wouldn't have your robe and I'd be near nude."

Gewa stared blankly at Niitty. She turned her eyes to her own body and examined her ever shrinking robe with her modest grey pants clashing with the rich red cloth. Cleaning and replacing Gerold's bandage had slowly cut into Gewa's attire. The torn edges made Niitty think of her as a Noble that had fallen on hard times. Then, out of nowhere, Gewa started laughing.

Niitty couldn't help it and started laughing, too. Nothing about what she said was funny. After the stress of the past few days, a laugh to relieve the tension was something the two needed. Niitty wiped a tear from her face and took a deep breath.

She looked over at Gerold. Caring for someone in this condition was beyond her knowledge, "Do you know anything about this? Should we feed him something?"

Gewa shrugged, "I don't know. I think there is some saying related to this. Was it feed a fever starve a cold? Or was it the other way around?"

Niitty never heard it before. Since she couldn't remember, trying to get him to eat something would be better than not. She had to at least try getting water into him.

Taking the second to last tin of meats Gewa offered, Niitty put it into the pot and used the pommel of her dagger to mash it up. She added some water and boiled it to further break down the meat until it was meaty water.

"Can you help here?" Niitty asked. "Try holding his mouth open."

Neither of them had any idea what they were doing. She transferred the liquid to a bowl and blew on it to cool it down. Gewa pulled Gerold's mouth open and, trying to avoid choking him, Niitty poured a small stream in. Thankfully, he instinctually swallowed the liquid when Gewa closed his mouth.

They repeated this process for a few more sips before his body started to refuse to take more. Next, she took another bowl and put the leaves in it with a small bit of water and ground them down into a paste. She pulled the bandage aside and smeared the plant matter on the wound, hoping this would work. There weren't any other options without an herbalist to consult.

Afterward, she requested more of Gewa's shrinking robe

and, before applying this one, she boiled the cloth to clean it. She squeezed the water out as best as she could and dried out the cloth on a hot rock before applying it to the wound. Now all they could do was wait.

Niitty sat back and looked at her half eaten ration she left on the ground. That wasn't a wise move since she only had one biscuit left and so did Gewa. Looking over at Gewa, she said, "I'll take the first watch. I need to prepare to go hunting tomorrow. I saw signs of a boar out on the scrubland that I think I can track."

Gewa nodded, "Before you do that, can you bring back some branches?"

"Why?"

Gewa pointed at the entryway, "I'm thinking of making a few sharp stakes to keep things out. I don't think I'd be able to kill anything if it got in here."

Niitty thought about it, "Worst case, you occupy your time on a project. We're going to be here for upwards of three days, assuming he survives."

CHAPTER 18

Gerold awoke staring at a stone ceiling. His mind was cloudy and confused like he had awakened from a mid-day nap that was a bit too long. He wondered what was going on. Searching his memory, he thought he had left the cavern and spent days walking through the mountains on the way back to town. So why was he back in the cave?

His mouth was sticky and his throat was dry. He was also feeling terribly hungry. He also smelled smoke and his confusion worsened. He sat up and felt a jolt of pain from stiff muscles and he had two dull aches from both of his sides. He hadn't been lying on the ground that long, so why did he feel like he'd been immobile for a long period of time?

He looked around and, instead of the expected tall cavern ceiling and the sconces and carved pillars of the crypt, he was in a smaller, musty cave. Near the rear, he saw a fire burning and pouring out smoke. Suspended over the fire were strips of meat on a wooden spit.

He turned to the entrance and noticed a thick forest of sharpened branches facing outward with a thin, zigzag path available for a person to squeeze through. A figure with white fur and black spots wearing torn robes with simple tan clothing underneath was sitting inside the cave by the stakes, staring out of the opening. A white tail sprouted out from under the torn robes and slowly swished back and forth.

He felt a presence next to him and he saw Niitty lying on a fur blanket, sound asleep on her side facing him. When he looked down at Niitty, he noticed his shirt was missing and he had a rich red cloth tied around his side. Curious, he pulled the wad away and a green sticky substance was absorbed into it. None of it remained on his skin, only a thin red line with hasty stitching still sticking out of his skin was visible.

His memories started to slowly creep back. They had left the crypt and he had hobbled down the mountain. Niitty was attacked by a goat monster and he took a nasty wound to the side. Everything else from there went fuzzy, with only little snippets of looking at a terrible infection that he tried to clean in the stream and stumbling through rocks. He remembered nothing about how he ended up in this cave.

Gerold inadvertently groaned. This caught the attention of the figure at the cave entrance. It was Gewa. She jumped up and rushed over, "Oh my, you're awake! How do y...whoa..."

She looked amazed and confused at the same time, her words cut off mid-sentence.

"What? What's wrong?"

She shook her head, "Nothing is wrong. Wow. You don't look old anymore. When I woke up for my watch, you were a mess. Sweating, pale and we worried you were near death. Now? You just look like a ridiculously handsome, if tired, man our age. This is so weird." To punctuate it, she reached up and poked at his face. Gerold waved her hand away, not appreciative of her pawing at his face.

She pulled back, "How do you feel?"

He checked himself once more, "Sore, thirsty and hungry."

She reached for his face again, pulling back quickly when she realized what she was doing, "Can I check your temperature?"

Gerold nodded in approval and she laid her furry hand on

his forehead. She looked at her paw then back at him, "That's insane. Your fever is gone and it looks like your infection is, too. Those powers of yours are incredible."

Gerold didn't feel elated. If anything, he felt more depressed. For some reason, he had this deep expectation that he was going to be reunited with his family. He looked down at his hands, the early signs of the gnarling of age long gone and his skin was again smooth and perfect. He closed his eyes and sighed, "So the curse returned before I could go."

Gewa looked like she had no idea how to respond to that. Her face looked concerned and she reached down to shake Niitty. She woke up with a stream of drool pulling up from her blanket, eyes half closed as she mumbled something. Her energy reached its maximum when she saw Gerold awake and looking at her.

Niitty rocketed up from bed and pulled Gerold into a strong embrace and buried her face into his chest. He sucked in air when his ribs silently screamed in pain and gingerly tried prying the girl off of him. He was getting annoyed at this overly familiar behavior from her, only holding back when he recognized she didn't harbor ill intent.

"That hurts. Can you let go?" he grunted out.

Niitty pulled back and wiped her face, "I'm sorry. I was so scared. You stopped taking water yesterday and the infection kept spreading. Your wound refused to close and kept oozing and you kept sweating. Then you stopped sweating and I got even more scared. Stupid Refik and his stupid plant. It didn't look like it was working. I'm so stupid. I didn't even think to gather information on herbs or monsters to study the area and we just left. It was my fault. You couldn't know and we just left without preparing. You went to buy stuff and I slept in a tree. I'm such a screw-up and you almost died from me missing a shot."

"Stop," Gerold snapped, "You're babbling."

"But…"

"Quit talking," Gerold growled, "Why are you taking this all on yourself? You're young. You're inexperienced. You made some mistakes. You'll make more. No one is asking you to be perfect."

She sat back into a kneeling position and backed away, looking at the ground. She had a look of embarrassment and was upset. Tears were streaming from her eyes and she was holding back halting sobs.

Gerold remembered some of the words from Erinne when he was in his own panic spiral. "Niitty," he said, directly addressing her by her name for the first time he could remember and only the third or fourth time her name passed his lips at all. He realized how rude he had been to the girl since they met. The girl he saw with legs folded beneath her reminded him of his son the time he failed to close the gate to the chicken coop and a wolverine got in and killed nearly the entire flock. He didn't see the value in berating the boy and, instead, used it as a learning opportunity. He also made a similar mistake at that age that ruined a portion of a harvest and his Father approached him in the same fair manner. He thought he turned out alright, so it makes sense to pass the wisdom forward to the next generation.

"People make mistakes," he continued. "I've learned that it's not worth getting upset by even the big ones. Unless you've made the same mistake many times over or intentionally tried to harm another, the act doesn't justify anger or seeking blame. I only ask that you learn and improve. This is an attitude that is shared by all the reasonable people you will meet in your life. If anyone seeks to attack and blame you, it would be wise to reassess your association with that person."

Gerold paused. He hated lecturing and he had to allow himself some hypocrisy since he was angry at himself for his failures. It always felt uncomfortable for him to talk one-sided like this. Even the thirty seconds or so for that last string of words felt like an eternity. He looked over at Niitty who was listening intently to his speech. Oddly, even Gewa was listening in just as intently, as if she was also being addressed.

"You messed up. It happens. Coming of age doesn't mean you stop growing. It's another phase of life and you'll be presented with more opportunities to grow. When we get back, ask the Guild about information on monsters and plants. Maybe they have documents you can use. If not, save up and buy some. We should still have monster parts to convert for that. Work on your strategy. Identify your strengths, your gaps and work with your party to cover each other. Keep learning and you'll slowly find yourself becoming the competent person you wish yourself to be now."

Niitty quietly nodded at his words. Gewa replied, "I understand. I'll do better." He won't ruin the moment by pointing out he wasn't addressing her. Maybe she needed to hear this, too.

Gerold was tired of talking. He didn't think he'd spoken this much in a single go in ages and hated lecturing. He tried standing up and the pain hit him. He reached into his bag and didn't find what he was looking for. "Can someone give me a couple of coins? I need to take care of this pain."

Niitty handed him a pile of coins. Gerold took one to cast Simple Heal on his puncture wound.

He looked at the makeshift suturing. It had done its job of ensuring the ragged wound remained closed well. After enduring the pain of pulling the threads out of his body, he cast a Simple Heal. The exterior closed, leaving a minor ache from the interior injury. He cast it once more and the pain subsided. He was confident the wound wouldn't rip open even though it wasn't fully healed.

The ribs were a different matter. He cast the spell four more times before the pain subsided to a dull throb. It was his sixth cast and he knew from experience if he tried another that he would have a terrible headache. This would have to be sufficient. Still, he had to be careful to avoid taking any significant blows to his ribs.

He started to run numbers in his head. He paused and asked, "I don't remember much after leaving the crypt. Have either of you used any abilities?"

Niitty reported her use of Snipe and Gewa mentioned Lightning Zap, each of them using up a copper coin in the process. Niitty also reported she had time to whittle new shafts for the arrowheads she had saved and was fully stocked at twenty.

He sighed, "We only have 14 copper coins left. How far are we from town? We need to convert these parts to replenish our funds."

"We should be back to the edge of the safe zone by sundown," Niitty said.

Gerold looked over at the meat, his stomach grumbling. He went over and took a few pieces and devoured them. Despite his hunger, the meat tasted no better than the gruel at the Guild Hall. He decided to hold his tongue to avoid insulting whoever prepared it.

He drank some water and noticed something about Niitty, "I have to say, I'm proud of you, Niitty."

She blushed, "What? What for?"

Gerold waved his hands around the cave, "You're in here and

you're not panicking."

Niitty looked up and blinked. Her mouth slowly opened in surprise then a big smile crossed her face, "I can't believe it! I'm not afraid anymore. It took you almost dying, but it doesn't feel so bad anymore. I still don't want to be in here though."

"One step at a time." He peered out of the cave opening, "What time is it?"

"Early morning," Gewa responded. Gerold thought back on the time. Erinne's estimate of a week proved accurate. Six and a half days had gone by in a flash. He was in a fever coma for much of it and his brain refused to store many memories after leaving the crypt. This created a strange sense of his ordeal taking an eternity when his mind had no tangible minutes to recall.

He felt exhausted. His abilities returning couldn't cure the effects of days of minimal food and water intake.

He still hadn't finished his mission of helping his two companions return to the town and he couldn't make a day long hike in his condition. He looked over at the meat. It looked like they had enough to last a few days, "Where did that come from?"

"I found a boar the day after you collapsed. We didn't have enough food to last out here and I didn't want to leave Gewa alone. I was only able to bring back 30 pounds of meat and had to leave the rest," Niitty said.

That explains the arrows. Gerold remembered the boar he saw the first night after leaving Wren's End nosing through a bush in the scrubland. In case it was the same animal, he gave it silent thanks for giving its life for his companions.

With what they had left, they could comfortably live in the cave for a week or two weeks if they stretched it out. Gerold didn't intend to sit here that long.

"I'm still weak. If neither of you have objections, I would prefer to recover one more day before we return to the village," Gerold suggested.

Neither of them objected and Gerold decided that a little movement would be good for him. He stood up and, after squeezing through the defensive barrier, he exited into the forest. He didn't stray far from the cave and made sure to remain in sight of the entrance. He didn't want to worry Niitty too much since he knew she would follow if he went too far out. He also needed his space.

He realized he didn't say what he was doing. He announced they were going to stay, stood up without any further comment and walked out. He knew he wasn't enjoying life these days, but it was impacting his behavior toward others. Gewa and Niitty had gone above and beyond keeping him alive when they would have been better off leaving him to the wilds. It was risky moving him through the forest and fortifying themselves for days away from town. Yet his only response to it all was a lecture, one mild compliment and then wandering off without a word. He didn't even thank them.

He leaned against a tree and rested his head on the trunk. He closed his eyes and tried to clear his mind. It didn't work. His head was a mess. He couldn't contain his randomly firing thoughts and he no longer had a fever as an excuse. His heart rate started to elevate and tears came from his eyes.

He wanted this solitude and quiet and he got what he wanted good and hard. The forest was still with only a light breeze to puncture the air. He never bothered to pay much attention to the area. Trees were just a thing that provided wood and, to a farmer, were treated like a large weed that interrupted his fields. If it didn't grow fruit, he didn't have much use for them. The plains of his home didn't have trees like these. There were smaller, gnarled things that peppered the landscape through the low lying golden grasses that waved in the gentle hills.

These trees were, now that he stopped to look, magnificent. They towered high into the sky on thick, regal trunks and provided a cool shade to the ground below. Sunlight sparkled through the needles above in a strangely beautiful pattern. He understood in this moment why Niitty loved being here so much despite the goblin infestation. Zelina would have loved it, too.

His breath grew ragged as he imagined her here, the two of them seated against the trunk, shoulder to shoulder, just enjoying each other's presence. She would have looked up at the trees in awe at this sight and he would have focused on her expression of joy, her face far more beautiful than the nature around them.

He slid down the trunk and his tears intensified. He was fighting a losing battle. He was afraid of releasing his grief fully and showing emotion. A memory of his Father came at that moment. He was 14 years old and they had returned home from his Mother's funerary rites. His Father was holding his younger sister's hand when the two of them entered their home.

Gerold had stayed outside and went about doing his chores for the day. His Father never exited the house. Gerold had found this strange. His Father was a strict and dedicated man. He had never once remembered a day when he slacked on his duties around the farm. Even when he was deathly ill, the man would fight his Mother over his responsibilities. Despite his Mother being a thin and delicate human, she always tamed the gruff Dwarf and convinced him to relent.

Yet his Mother was no longer here to force his Father to stay in the house and shirk his duties. Gerold spent that day patrolling the border fence of the farm along the prairie. The farm was at the edge of the protective shield. He would see the occasional monster running through the grasses and the Adventurers fighting them for their income. While those monsters were no threat to them, the grasses were tenacious. Farmers at the edges had the extra responsibility of culling prairie grasses that encroached into the farm in addition to normal weeding and pest control.

It was a long day and Gerold felt annoyed that he had to cover his Father's duties. He hadn't even eaten, not that he had much of an appetite. He didn't have the time to take a break covering the job of two people.

Annoyed at being left to the task alone, he stomped into his house. His anger had quickly been replaced with shock when he saw his Father. He was sitting on a chair next to the stove, staring at the fire. He was cradling his younger sister, who had fallen asleep on his lap. What shocked him about the sight were the tears streaming down his Father's face. He was sobbing and wiping his eyes, snot dripping into the thick braided beard he was so proud of.

He was tall for a Dwarf, owing to Gerold's Grandfather being human, standing at around 5'4". The man was broad and had thick tree trunks for arms and massive hands that Gerold could swear could compress coal into diamonds. Yet here he was, weeping in the dark while gently cradling a girl in one of those immense mitts, the scene lit by a conflicting warm glow of the stove.

He looked up at Gerold and beckoned him over. Gerold felt confusion as he approached since his Father would be more assertive when he wanted something. Saying nothing, his father took him in his free hand and pressed him against his side in a warm, firm embrace.

It was the memory of the lesson about men crying. Many

times over the months this came to him. He had always pushed it away, refusing to confront his grief over the past few months. Gerold was stubborn and didn't learn easily. This time, his mind refused to acquiesce to his demands. It was going to remember it whether he liked it or not.

His Father silently held him against his side. Gerold felt compelled to speak, "Dad, why are you crying?"

He looked down at Gerold, "Why are you not?"

"You said men don't show weakness," Gerold had said, matter-of-factly.

His Father sighed, "Gerold my boy, when I said men don't show weakness, I meant we don't give up or complain when things are hard. What you're seeing now? This ain't weakness. A man should not cry because he lost a competition or because pests ruined part of his crop. He gets to work fixing it. When a man loses one of the great loves of his life? Not shedding tears would be a grave insult. It means he didn't really love her. Mourn and honor your Mother's memory. You can't heal until you do."

His Father was more naturally terse than even Gerold. He rarely spoke this much. And he never spoke with that kind of emotion. Young Gerold realized that forcing himself to perform his chores was him trying to avoid the pain of losing his Mother. If he went about the day like it was any other, her passing would be nothing more than a bad dream. That when he returned home at the end of the day, she would be there preparing the evening meal as she would on any other day.

His denial of his grief was his denial of reality. He had to accept reality and accept it he did. Then Gerold, both the young one in the past and the one now, finally allowed himself to let go.

CHAPTER 19

The universe was cruel. Time and events waited for no one and it didn't care about your feelings. Gerold was once again reminded of this reality.

"Gerold!"

A shout echoed in his head, interrupting his private moment. He tried to ignore the voice, his grief replaced with a rising sense of anger.

"Gerold! Has something happened? You haven't responded to me in days!"

Gerold got up from his position against the tree slowly, still trying to ignore the noise that was grating on his nerves.

"Your eyes are open! This is good. Gerold? It's bad."

"What," Gerold roared into the air, "What do you want? Why must you bother me at the most inopportune times?"

"I...it's...I'm...I'm sorry, you hate me," the voice started crying and echoed in his mind.

Gerold was doing it again. He was lashing out at people who had nothing to do with his pain. This time was Erinne.

Gerold growled, mostly at himself this time. His nerves were frayed and he needed to address his mental state soon. He wasn't sure if he could calm himself down before he did something more permanent and the constant stream of stress was not helping.

"Erinne," he started, "You caught me at a terrible time. What is it?"

The sobbing in his head slowed, "I don't have a choice. You spent a day babbling at me and then I couldn't connect at all. It's the necrotic mana."

"And? If it's just another pulse you can't find, what can I do about it? That crypt was a bust. There's nothing I can do. I'm blindly walking around and doing no good."

"That's just it," Erinne said, "It's not a pulse anymore. It's now a constant beacon. And I know where it is."

Gerold looked up in the air, "Where is it?"

"It's moving through the forest. It spent the last few days moving around the forest, now it's moving toward Wren's End and fast. Worse, the protective barrier has failed."

Gerold spit in frustration. His mourning would, again, have to wait until later.

He ran back to the cave and, instead of trying to weave his way through the stakes, he started yanking them out of the ground and throwing them to the side.

"What's wrong," Niitty asked, concerned at his suddenly frantic behavior.

"We need to go. Erinne just told me the necrotic pulse she tasked me to find is now a constant beacon and is moving toward the town."

She jumped up from the fire and started to gather up their things. Gerold quickly shoved everything they could into his bag. They had to move.

Gewa put up a paw, "Hey. Slow down. You need to recover."

Gerold's heat rose and he tamped it down, "I can't. We have to get back. Now. Something bad is about to happen."

"What makes you think that," Gewa replied.

"Erinne just told me, that's how," Gerold stated.

"What, a vision or a sign?"

"No, she told me."

Gewa rolled her eyes, "You're still tired. The Recluse Queen can't be talking to you. She doesn't talk to anyone."

Niitty caught Gerold's frustration and put up a hand to stop his outburst. "Gewa, I understand how you feel. When I first met Gerold, I didn't get it either. The stories about Paladins don't tell us much. Gerold may be tired and confused, but need to trust his premonitions. The only reason he was even in town was because of his…visions…telling him about something wrong here. We need to listen and move," Niitty said, gravely.

Gewa chewed on it for a few minutes while Niitty and Gerold busied themselves gathering up their gear. As Gerold was stuffing the meat into his bag, Gewa responded, "I'll go along with you. You seem motivated at the least. I can't say I believe what I'm hearing. Niitty's right, I know nothing about Paladins. In this situation, going with you and hoping I'm right is better than staying here and being wrong."

Despite the urgency, Gerold's physical condition was still weak and they were not making great time. They could have maybe made it in eight hours had everyone been in their best condition. Instead, Gerold held his companions back with regular breaks to allow his muscles to recover.

Erinne was keeping them updated on the movement of the necrotic mana. It had suddenly stopped, to the best of Erinne's abilities to observe the area, it was either in or near the town.

For some reason, she couldn't fully pinpoint where it was, like it knew it could be observed and was obscuring itself. She just detected an irregularly shaped leakage covering a wide area.

Gerold could barely travel an hour before taking a break. At this rate, they'd have to spend another night in the forest. On one of their breaks, Niitty came by with a serious look on her face, "We have a problem."

Gerold was having a hard time processing everything. The universe just kept throwing new problems at him. "Of course we do. What is it?" Gerold noticed his tone was testy.

Niitty looked a little hurt, "I found goblin tracks. There's something weird about them. Normally, their tracks are erratic. The tracks alternate between hard running in a direction before congregating in a spot and repeating. These tracks are long drags and they're not congregating anywhere. They're constantly moving and slowly."

"I don't know what that means. Are they tired," Gerold asked.

"No. They don't get tired. They're hyperactive monsters," she replied.

"Hold on, let me check something," he heard Erinne echo in his head.

Gerold relayed this to his group. Neither Niitty nor Gewa cared since they were waiting on him anyway.

Erinne returned to his mind, "Gerold?"

"You're back," Gerold responded out loud, getting the attention of Niitty and Gewa who listened intently, "What have you found?"

"I'm going to have to skirt right up against divulging things I absolutely can't. I think this is something that's not going to violate rules since mortals, technically, can figure this out on their own. Have you ever wondered why monsters never enter Town Seed zones and why most monsters never stray from defined territories?" Erinne asked.

"No, I never thought of it," Gerold said.

"Thought of what," Niitty asked.

"Why monsters have territories they never leave and why Town Seeds work," Gerold relayed for their benefit, realizing he had to clarify Erinne's side of the conversation for their benefit.

Gewa just shrugged, "I've lived in the Capital my whole life. I never thought about it."

Niitty said, "I did sometimes. It made it easy to know how to avoid certain areas and would give us a good idea of what else we may run into when tracking animals. No one put effort into knowing why, it's just something the world does."

"What I can divulge is it has to do with the world's mana. Mana isn't uniform. As far as you're concerned, mana is just mana. Mana has, what's a good word to use? Hmm, you haven't discovered this general concept yet, so you haven't developed a word. I know. You know how you can see color? The light that makes up each color has different properties than the light of the other colors. Mana is like this, too. The only real difference is that when you use 'white' mana, the coins are converted white mana, and 'white' in light is all of the colors at the same time while in mana it has no color. Your spell then defines what the properties of the mana become. This is the best I can do. I know it's confusing." Erinne explained.

Gerold relayed this and both of them felt the way he did, that this was a lot of information to digest and the way Erinne was talking signaled they knew very little about how the world worked. Erinne, however, thought this was important so he continued to listen.

"This is what defines the monsters that will form in an area. Monsters need it to live and they can't leave the area or they'll starve, for lack of a better word to describe what would happen. There is something wrong with these monsters though," she said.

"Wrong how," Gewa asked.

"Necrotic mana is a result of death and decay. Everything decays after death and produces it. The decaying needles on the ground produce it. With plants and animals, the amount is very small and dissipates as it breaks down the body to return to the cycle. It has corrupting properties. It can 'infect' surrounding mana and convert it into necrotic mana. Necrotic mana is normally short lived and it disappears faster than it can infect surrounding mana. If the concentration in a spot is high enough, it can infect the local mana faster than it dissipates, creating a self-reinforcing process," Erinne said.

"Get to the point," Gerold snapped.

"You need the context to understand. Normally, to get enough concentration to start this corrupting process requires the dead body. While your soul resides in your body, it builds up a tremendous amount of energy. This energy is what fuels your consciousness. Without it, you'd be no more than any other animals. When you die, your soul leaves and the energy that your soul gave off is still in you. In death, the necrotic energy begins and there's this immense power source that it infects and acts as fuel that begins the necrotic buildup. All this requires is one body and, over time, it will absorb into the dead body and cause it to reanimate, in addition to manifesting necromantic aligned monsters. The natural mana is eventually changed and the necrotic corruption takes over. This isn't a fast process and can take months to fully realize and would need to be interrupted by either the Rites to burn off that excess energy or a Cleansing to use divine power to force the mana in the area to reset back to the 'white' kind," Erinne droned.

Gerold summarized this for his companions and then said, "I still don't understand what you're getting at."

"This would require a spell on a scale that's incredibly expensive. We're talking Mythril coins to have this expansive effect to override an area's mana properties on a wide scale this fast," she replied.

He relayed this. Gewa followed up, "Couldn't a ritual do this?"

"Yes," Erinne said, Gerold repeating her words, "A ritual is the other way to cast spells. But absorbing that ambient mana takes a long time since it has to convert it into, hmm, the equivalent of white light which is every type of mana. It loses a lot of potency in this process and requires extensive preparation to accomplish. Monsters are more efficient at this process and why it's faster to kill them for the coins, which store the mana."

Erinne continued, "That, too, makes no sense. From the time I first noticed the pulse, it would mean that we somehow missed tens of thousands of people congregating in one place and intentionally directing their own internal soul mana generation for weeks into a vessel. And it's moving. An artifact would have to absorb necrotic mana for thousands of years and then have some conduit to eject it all in a burst. None of this makes sense."

"Niitty," Gerold said, "What I'm going to ask is going to be dangerous. We need to know what is happening to these goblins, which means getting close enough to get a look. In these woods, that's a big risk. You don't have to do this if you don't want to."

Niitty's expression was firm, "I can do that. You rest while I scout them. The tracks I found shouldn't be more than a mile away. I can be back in 30 minutes."

"Be careful and don't move too fast," Gerold warned as she silently bounded away.

When she vanished from view, Gewa came and looked into Gerold's eyes. She said, "You're really in there, Erinne?"

"Yes," Erinne replied.

"She says yes," Gerold said, "What changed your mind?"

"The things you were saying. I know you're a Paladin and you guys can't lie. When you were bent over that sarcophagus, I heard you talking. I listened for a while and you mentioned out loud you were a farmer. I know that can't be a lie. While a delusion could make you believe what you say is true, what you just said on magical theory? That's extremely advanced. I know I'm making a judgment here, but I can't see a simple farmer able to talk about spellcraft and artifacts to that degree of expertise. Some of that stuff was only hinted at in the Basics of Magic manual and the other parts are just too detailed to be made up," she replied.

Gerold snorted, "I'm not offended, Gewa. No, I'm a simple man. I can tell you when to plant tomatoes or how to drive gophers off your land. On the topic of magic? You might as well ask me what's on the other side of these mountains. My Grandfather was an adventurer, a Warrior, and my literacy begins and ends with seasonal almanacs."

"Do you realize how big this is," Gewa asked.

"I've been told. I neither have the inclination nor time to go through detailed proof with everyone. It usually involves nearly killing myself or discussing deep ideas I shouldn't know," he said.

"I can see how that would be a problem," Gewa said.

Gerold said out loud for Erinne's benefit, "I think I'll rest quietly for a bit. If I fall asleep, please wake me when Niitty gets back."

Both Gewa and Erinne indicated an affirmative to his request.

To pass the time, Gewa picked up a stick and, using her claws, started carving something. Gerold watched in silence, relieved she wasn't too talkative. Even though she sacrificed to help him, she was still guarded in his presence. He thought that was a good instinct to have for a total stranger. Growing up in a major city gave the Leopardia woman a different outlook on life. It could very well be a different sort of problem with trust issues in the future. For now, she didn't allow herself to get attached to strangers.

He worried about Niitty's future. She was vivacious and friendly due to her upbringing in a close knit community. She had imprinted on him far too easily just because he showed her some kindness and buying into the stories about Paladins. He was finding her attachment crushing. She looked at him in a way that made him uncomfortable and a sense of expectation he was getting from her through their connection was only adding to his growing stress.

He tried meditating again in his rest. The agitation was making it difficult to rest his body and the meditation proved only a minor relief. This technique was less effective than when he used it in the past. His mind was racing and unfocused and he couldn't calm it. Despite his fatigue, his body insisted he get up and move. His instincts pushed him to pace around and his mind kept bouncing between the town, Niitty and his family.

A sound interrupted him. The rhythmic thumping was

annoying him and his anger rose. He opened his eyes, ready to yell at Gewa for whatever it was she was doing. She was quietly sitting with her carving and the sound was coming from elsewhere. He followed the noise down and saw his legs crossed, his knee bouncing off the dirt unconsciously.

He elected to stand and started pacing around. He needed to do something, not stand around. Much to his relief, Niitty returned, her brow deeply creased with concern, "I found the goblins. Six of them are a little under a mile away. Erinne was right, they're different. They look like undead. The difference is they haven't rotted like the ones back at the crypt."

"We have to go," Gerold said. His fatigue could wait until later. They had to get to town to at least warn them that a potential disaster was on the way.

"It's getting dark," Niitty announced.

Gerold blinked, "What? I haven't been moving that slow have I? Did I fall asleep somewhere?"

Gerold looked up, his vision blocked by the canopy of pine needles above. It was getting noticeably darker.

Niitty walked over to a tree, "Give me a moment, I'll go up and see what's going on."

She expertly climbed up the tree and disappeared above the canopy. She wasn't up there long when she descended. She looked like she was in a rush and she was wide eyed and sheet white. She started waving her hands, moving them from the ground upward in a dramatic fashion and was struggling to speak.

"Take a deep breath," Gerold said to the agitated girl.

"Big. Cloud. Black," she blurted out.

Before she could clarify, a low whine began to build and

echo through the forest. The sound was faint and coming from a distance. Gerold instinctually knew it was from the town. The sound had a bone chilling undertone of screaming people mixed with a dog howling and scraping metal.

"No," Gerold muttered low. He felt his pulse rising and buried memories forcibly returned to his mind. "No, no," he had to move now. His fatigue suddenly vanished as adrenaline coursed through his body. He recognized voices yelling at him. He didn't know why or care. He just noticed he was running.

The forest blurred by. He stumbled as he ran, barely keeping his feet under him. He was compelled to. It was happening again and, again, he couldn't do anything about it. What was the point of these powers he was granted if he couldn't stop this disaster from destroying another community?

Something was ahead in his path that appeared from behind a tree. The close growth of the trees irritated him and he wanted to knock them all down so he could have seen these distractions earlier. The six figures were short and moved in a strange, halting erratic manner just 25 yards ahead. The shapes turned and snarled at his approach. His mind refused to process what they were, only caring that he didn't have time to delay. He tried to angle around the figures that moved to intercept his run. A tree was blocking his path now and he had no way to avoid the distraction.

Anger rose in his blood. Who were these things to dare slow him down? He pulled his hammer and sprinted into the mass.

He slammed his hammer down on one of the figures, crushing its head into its torso. The body folded in on itself and collapsed to the ground. A second figure reached out and grabbed his arm, its teeth sinking into his flesh. His only thought was his failure to put his hauberk back on.

With a surge of strength, he swung his arm with the figure

in an arc, slamming it into the others. The body released from his arm, tearing pieces of his tissue off in the process. Gerold still didn't care. One was getting up, prompting Gerold to grab the figure by the head and throw it into the rest, keeping them down.

He looked down and watched the tangle struggle to gain purchase over each other to stand. Grabbing at one of the five sets of flailing limbs, he pulled a figure out and dragged it away from the pile. Before it could turn and stand, he stomped hard on the head. Once, twice, three times, pouring his rage out on the thing. The head crushed under his boot like a rotting melon, a disgusting squelch reached his ears when he felt the solid skull give way to the force of his stomp.

It made him happy, a rarity in his life these days. The remaining four had managed to stand and started moving his way. He snapped a straight kick out and knocked one back on the ground again. He followed through with a swing of his hammer, landing on the shoulder of another. It, too, fell over. His off-hand lashed out and punched a third in the face. It rocked backward on its feet, remaining upright after stumbling from the blow. The fourth had leapt through the air and was a hair's breadth from ripping out his throat when it spontaneously grew an arrow shaft out of its face and harmlessly bounced off his body before flopping to the ground. He mentally dismissed the corpse and turned to the remaining figures.

Gerold grabbed the one he punched by the neck and held it at arm's length. Flipping his hammer around, he rapidly smashed the spiked end into the head, blood splattering on his own body before sliding off into the dirt below. He suddenly felt stronger and more refreshed. His brain couldn't process why and two new abilities found themselves nestled in his mind. He pushed them aside as they were not important in the moment.

Two figures remained. One rolled on the ground and attempted to rise, one arm hung limply at the shoulder as it struggled to stand. Gerold kicked it to disrupt its process before turning to the next. He palmed the crest of the figure's skull in his large hand and dragged it over to the nearest tree. He then started slamming its face into the bark, dragging it down from shoulder to chest on each impact. Pieces of tissue got caught in the bark and fluid dripped through the crevices. He repeated this process over and over again and saw white pieces of bone embed itself into the tree. The figure stopped thrashing and he dropped it, the form flopping on the ground against the trunk.

One more left to punish. He turned and pinned the remaining figure with the limp arm under a knee against the ground. He pounded it in the back of the head until he was no longer able to distinguish it from the muddy dirt below.

Everything was now still, Gerold's rage seeking more targets to release his ire. He heard voices. Two? No, three. Two were behind him and one echoed in his head. He turned and glared. He saw two more figures. One was bright white with black spots in red and tan. The other figure was a pale peach in brown. They stood still ten yards away. Gerold regarded them in a haze, not recognizing what they were. The third voice was shouting at him in his head, annoying him.

In less than a second, he regarded the white figure as non-threatening and something inside him refused to allow him to attack the pale peach one. Besides, town was the other direction. He turned and continued to run, a voice continuing to echo in his head.

He lost track of time as he sprinted through the darkening forest. He passed by two more masses of those grey figures that he was able to avoid with little effort.

His heart was pounding in his chest and as he rushed through thickening underbrush, he came across a wide open space where the trees and underbrush abruptly ceased. Something waist high was in his way and he leapt across. The moment he crossed the obstacle he passed into a horrible power. A sinister force felt like it was trying to tear his soul out of his body. His soul resonated as it fought back against the power, pushing it away.

He came to his senses. He felt this before. Only what he felt now was much worse. It brought him to his knees even with his Paladin protections.

He looked up and saw a sickly green glow emitting from behind the walls of the village in the distance. Through it poured an unnaturally black cloud that went into the sky and spread out over the land. He pulled himself up to stand and struggled as he tried to return back over the fence. Deep down, he knew that the fence marking the border of the Town Seed's influence was where this horrible pain stopped.

Niitty and Gewa came running through the underbrush. They looked exhausted from the exertion. Niitty must have noticed Gerold struggling because the next thing he knew, she was running again, ready to jump over the fence to help.

Gerold knew he couldn't let her cross that border. He knew that only his soul was able to resist the sinister power trying to rip it free from his body. As she tried to leap the fence, Gerold found his strength and ran, diving over and tackling her by the midsection. The two tumbled and rolled to a stop.

After disentangling himself, he helped her up. She stood and stumbled, holding her midsection in pain. Gerold reached into his bag and pulled out an Adventurer Coin and healed the impact wound he gave her. A splitting headache hit him when he cast it, having gone over the safe six cast limit for the day.

More attempts at magic would make the pain worse.

After casting the spell, Gerold silently turned and watched the town in the distance. He felt the pressure of the edge of the event at the fence start to weaken. Then a bright flash of blinding light flashed from the town, followed by a deep rumble that vibrated his bones.

When his eyes recovered, he looked up. He could still see the palisade around the town, a half-dome of glowing blue having replaced the previous black cloud and green glow. The blue looked like shattered glass suspended in the air, the shards each an irregular shape and different size. Then, as if a string were cut, the blue light in the shards fell and winked out. Everything was replaced by total silence.

CHAPTER 20

Gerold stared at the town in shock. The dark clouds undulated above in the unnaturally still air. How could this be the same thing? Why here, too?

"Gerold, this was it," he heard Erinne in his head, her voice a distant and soft echo, like she couldn't believe what she witnessed, "This is what made me take notice of you."

The dam broke in his head, "What? This is what happened to me? To my family? And you knew? Why didn't you stop it?"

"I didn't know. I can't see everything and I can't interfere," she hastily said, blindsided by his sudden accusation.

"Then what good are you? What kind of useless Goddess are you? You claim to have made all of this and then you sit there and evade responsibility. You hid this from me. The thing that ruined my life and it happened again," he continued to rage.

"But I…"

"No. No more. Piss off you useless thing. Piss off and don't speak to me again."

She was silent for a while, "You really believe that?"

"Yes," he shouted, "One thousand times yes! You spent a week nagging me about becoming a Paladin when all I wanted was to die. I let myself get dragged around by your words thinking that, maybe, I'd have some kind of purpose. That didn't happen, did it? I played along for half a year thinking that I could find meaning. I went tromping off into the wilderness for ten days just to find out the thing you were looking for this entire time was here, under your nose. The only good thing that came out of this was I saved one life. Just one. Balanced against the loss of four and…I don't even know how many now. You are useless. Your powers are useless. Take this curse and leave me be."

"I can't take back the power. It's part of you forever," she said, her voice sobbing softly which then, suddenly, cut off into silence.

"Good riddance," he spit. That damnable Goddess refused to lift his curse. He would be stuck like this for who knows how long. He looked down at his hands. Every muscle in his body was trembling and he didn't know if it was from rage, fear or shame. His headache pounded in his ears. He wanted to hit something. He wanted to cry. He wanted someone to embrace him and tell him this was nothing more than a bad dream. He wanted his wife and kids. He wanted to be back on his farm.

A rustling sound interrupted him and he spun around. He saw Niitty and Gewa standing there with Gewa having backed partially into a shrub in the underbrush. Both of them looked terrified and it wasn't just because of the terrible event that had just occurred in Wren's End. They were looking at him.

He stared back in annoyance, their eyes mocking him.

Niitty broke the silence and, awkwardly as she wasn't sure what she should say in the moment, said, "Do you want to talk about it?"

He tried to push his rage down and it fought back hard. There was no putting it back this time, "Why? Why would I want to talk about it? Especially with you?"

Tears came to her eyes, "Talking things out with a friend can help. I'm here for you."

His phrasing hurt her. He internally screamed at himself. What are you doing? His voice didn't care, "Friend? Girl, I've only known you for two weeks. What part of that makes us friends?"

Niitty started to move forward. Gewa put her paw on Niitty's shoulder to pull her back and tried to indicate this was a bad idea, but Niitty ignored it, "But we were growing closer. You saved my life. You put yourself at risk many times to protect me. I thought you cared."

Stop talking you fool. You're hurting her, "Closer? Haven't you figured it out yet? I don't want to live. I'm tired of this life. The only reason I did that is it would only make my life even worse had I not saved you. And your fawning over me is weird. I'm old enough to be your Father, yet you hug on me like I'm your husband. It's uncomfortable."

Niitty took a few steps back. The tears were flowing more freely and she couldn't talk. Gewa gave him a strange look, one of concern and understanding. She pulled Niitty away and whispered something to her. Niitty listened and then looked up at Gerold before turning her eyes down to the ground. The two turned and walked away, Gewa giving Gerold a last backward look before they disappeared back into the forest.

Gerold's headache pounded even harder. He found himself wandering aimlessly along the border fence around the town's farmland. He ran across the two additional bands of goblins he vaguely remembered passing in the forest when he was in a blind rage. The fights with them were a blur and, it weren't for new injuries on his body, he wouldn't have remembered they were there at all. How he had destroyed them failed to register in his mind.

He continued his slow pace. It kept getting darker. He couldn't be sure if it was because it was night or something was still happening with the strange dark cloud cover lingering above. It had taken days for it to dissipate the last time he encountered it, day only distinguishable from night as being less dark.

As he moved along the border, he saw hints of the aftermath of what just occurred. Here and there, birds had fallen dead into the fields on the other side of the fence which eerily contrasted with the vibrant life still on this side. Whatever happened had used the Town Seed to work its evil magic and destroy everything within.

As he moved further along the border fence, he noticed birds circling in the sky. He had a small spark of hope, thinking that the disaster missed a section of land. When he closed in, he found it was another sign of the aftermath. The effects had dissipated and the birds were some that came in from the forest. They were circling a dead ox, having fallen over on its side, still hooked up to a seeding machine. The driver was slumped to the side in the seat, the reins still in his hands. He knew from experience the driver was undead.

He found himself back at the road leading into town from the direction of the Capital. He neither had no idea how he returned to the town territory from the wilds nor how long he had been walking at this point. It could just as easily be early the next morning as it could be early evening.

He wondered what happened to the merchant he joined on the journey to Wren's End. It felt like an eternity ago. The road cut through farmland and to the main town entrance that was obscured by distance and darkness. He remembered the old nag he had ridden in on and left in the stables just inside the entry. He then thought of those two boys who were planning on scamming the rumored Paladin that was abandoned when they caught sight of Karl. Gerold had given them two silver coins anyway, using asking directions as an excuse to give the boys a small charity.

He thought of Sandra, the kindly overworked woman who, despite serving an entire Guild Hall dinner alone, did so with a smile on her face. He thought of Philip, the Guild Master that stressed over how to balance the finances and keep the Town Seed active. The caravan clearly didn't make it on time. He even thought of Allan, the arrogant and self-important Guild Administrator. While Gerold didn't like him, this was not a fate he would wish on the man.

All of them, save the nag, would be the animated dead. More failures to weigh on Gerold's conscience. He passed down the road and headed toward town. He would put the dead to rest, at least until they overran him. He didn't make it very far before he noticed a farmhouse attached to the first plot to his left. His eyes were attracted to a warm orange glow in the window. The hearth was still going.

He ran his hand down the fence along the roadway until he found the gate in the dark. He fumbled with the latch and, after opening it, he slowly made his way up to the house. Nothing accosted him on the way and the world was deathly silent.

He rested his hand on the door. The shapes he could make out in the dark reminded him of his own home. It wasn't the same but it gave off a sense of familiarity. The gently rubbed his hand down the rough hewn wood, taking in the feeling of the imperfections on his palm.

He tried the latch and found it open and slowly pushed the door inward. Inside, the hearth still burned with the flame dancing low on the coal. The table was set for the midday meal, the lentil stew congealed and cold in the bowls. He saw two figures in the dim room. One was sitting in a chair, slumped on the table while the other was standing before the hearth, slowly swaying.

The one before the hearth had taken notice when Gerold closed the door, the latch alerting the form. It turned and gurgled. The movements were stiff and slow as it shuffled in his direction.

He pulled his hammer and, when the figure got into range, he held the hammer out to keep the figure at bay. He remembered a snippet from his brutal training months before that zombies were at their weakest if a fresh body is raised. The muscles stiffened shortly after death. It would take two to three days for the muscles to slacken and allow the zombies to move with greater fluidity and threat.

He easily held the figure away from him with his weapon, the zombie impotently flailing in an attempt to reach past the extended hammer. He looked closely at the figure. It was a young woman, possibly in her early 20s with only the earliest signs of death on her. Her hands were a darkened purple and the pupils of her blue eyes were fully dilated. They stared off into space at nothing in particular as the body tried to get to the soul energy emanating from his torso.

She was an attractive Desert Elf. He wondered what brought her out here to a farm far from her southern home. He continued to hold her back as he took a look around the main room. Like most farmer homes, this was a single room that held the dining area, cooking, small family living space and a wardrobe to hold winter coats. On one wall in the living area hung an unusual curved sword that was out of place for a farmer's house.

"Were you an aspiring adventurer that found it too difficult? Did you find a true love and give up on it? Or is that sword an heirloom," Gerold asked the woman. His only response was a weak attempt to grab at him and a small croak. It was just another thing lost now, a story he would never know and a history that came to an end here, in a place that should have been one of safety and happiness.

Another noise caught his attention. His voice caught the notice of the body at the table. The head had turned toward him, showing a fairly plain human man roughly the same age as the woman. The arm closest to him tried to reach across the distance to grip him, held back by an inability to stand. The man's back muscles were too stiff to allow him to move from the table. Gerold imagined that he was trying to come rescue his wife from an intruder, adding to his sadness at the sight.

He didn't know when his rage dissipated. Everything about Gerold was exhausted. He was physically, mentally, emotionally and spiritually spent. He pondered letting his arm drop and allowing the woman to end it here and now. He had thought he would end his days on his farm. He knew that was impossible now.

"Don't give up."

A voice echoed in his head. He started to get irritated that Erinne had returned when he explicitly told her to leave, only holding in his shout when he realized the voice was not the same.

"Please, fight."

It was Zelina. He had only ever heard her voice in his dreams. Now he was hearing it while he was awake. Maybe he really was going crazy. Maybe the past half year was a nightmarish hallucination and he was dying in his cellar surrounded by family.

"Don't give up."

The voice was right. Now wasn't the time to give up. There was still more to do. He looked at the woman pushing against his hammer once more, "I'm sorry. I failed again. I failed you. Please, rest now."

Gerold couldn't bring himself to smash this woman's head in like he had those rotting corpses back at the crypt or a common monster. He pulled his dagger with his off-hand and, slowly, pulled the hammer closer to himself. The zombie got closer and it grasped at his arms, the puffy purple hands unable to properly find purchase. When she was in range, Gerold punched the dagger through her temple. The body immediately went slack and, before she could fall, he caught her and gently lowered her to the floor.

He then walked over to the man and repeated the gruesome process, stopping its movements permanently.

After putting his dagger away, he looked at the two bodies still in their positions, one lying on the ground and the other at the table. This was wrong. He walked over to the door leading into the next room. Much like the main room, this one, too, reminded him of his home. Instead of a child's bed, the loft above stored personal effects. There was one bed across the way under a window that was still open.

Gerold walked over and closed the shutters on the window and secured it. He pulled the sheets down on the bed and returned to the main room. He then moved the bodies to the bed. Looking at them, something felt wrong. He noticed they didn't look natural. He closed the eyes on the bodies and, as best as he could through the stiffness, arranged them to look like they were asleep.

The last thing that felt right was he moved their hands to a final embrace before pulling the blankets back up. He couldn't be sure if this was the state of their relationship, giving into his instincts to give the couple one final dignity.

He reached into his bag and pulled out all of the coins he had, coming up with just three. That was all that remained and there was no longer a functioning guild nearby to convert the collected monster parts for more.

He fanned the coins out in one hand and stared at them. He wondered if he could afford to lose the last of these coins on two strangers and if a single copper would even be accepted.

Erinne's voice entered his mind as a memory. He no longer felt the hate at it like before, only a sense of regret. This quiet moment, seeing what is going on around him and the loss in his midst had sobered him. He also felt that what he had done, his words and actions, were irreparable.

He placed one copper coin each on the bodies in the bed. He spoke the rites and he was once again tinged with heartbreak at having to speak these words.

He then added at the end, "I know I spoke harshly to your Queen. I know that what I did is beyond forgiveness. Please, Umieranie, do not hold this against these two young souls."

Gerold backed away from the bed and slumped against the wall near the door and watched. Minutes went by and his sadness deepened. He couldn't bring himself to ignite the bed and burn this young couple's possessions and, possibly, the entire house. It represented their lives. Or maybe a single copper was just too little despite Erinne's words.

The last possibility was that these two would have to wait for someone who hasn't lost favor with the Pantheon to provide the rites or given to a consecrated grave. Gerold was now too tainted for the Goddess of Death to respond to.

With spirits lower than they had ever been in his memory, Gerold slowly pulled himself up from the wall. Then a low blue light flared in the room. Looking up, he saw the coins burn bright. Like back at the crypt, they turned into a liquid then absorbed into the bodies. Instead of the eruption like back at the crypt, the bodies gently burned with a low blue flame and he watched as the bodies turned to ash. All that left was the bed and ash on the pillow that trailed to and then disappeared beneath the sheet.

Gerold looked to the empty space above the bed, "Thank you for not holding my transgressions against them." No response came, not that he was expecting one. He continued to look at the bed that once held the bodies of the couple. He wondered why the flame wasn't the spectacular display that he saw back in the crypt. Was it the coin he selected? Did Umieranie decide Gerold didn't deserve to see it?

He thought back to what Erinne said about soul energy. Maybe there was not much left to burn off, so it produced only a low burn as the residual energy in the body was denied to the corrupting process of necrotic mana. What he did know is he had cut off the one who could possibly answer him.

He was tired and his body threatened to give out at any time. His mission to cleanse the area would have to wait.

It felt wrong sleeping in this room. It was the final resting place of the owners of this house. He stumbled out of the room and closed the door gently. Getting memories of his Father and the feeling of familiarity in the room, he pulled a chair away from the table and set it up in front of the hearth. Remembering his Father sitting in a position much like this years ago, he repeated the memory of his lesson in his mind.

He was now finally, truly, alone and no one would interrupt him this time. Tears didn't come again like they had back in the forest earlier in the day. His mind wandered to Niitty. To the words he spoke to her at their parting. The look of hurt she had on her face when Gewa led her away.

Zelina would be ashamed of him at pushing away a child like that. Custom be damned, the young are still young and they still need guidance. His reaction at her contact was inappropriate. He didn't communicate well and he didn't even follow his own advice he had given to her just that morning. He shamefully allowed his emotions to take hold and nothing could justify his actions. He would have never exploded at his children like that.

Gerold leaned back and stared at the ceiling, taking in the tightly woven straw into his mind. Tears finally filled his eyes and blurred the details of the straw weave pattern. His fatigue then completely took over and he fell asleep.

CHAPTER 21

Gewa looked up surprise as Gerold started shouting over and over again and bolted into the forest. The man who was struggling to keep up a decent pace just moments before and had recently stopped for a rest had suddenly found a burst of energy and ran off after that strange screaming howl echoed through the forest.

Gewa tried to run after Gerold. Whatever possessed him made him fast. Niitty, who was out in the lead kept looking back at Gewa as she tried to keep up, her face showing her confliction at whether to keep chasing after Gerold or not to leave Gewa behind. Niitty attempted to do her best to split the difference.

At least dodging trees didn't slow Gewa down since she had plenty of practice sprinting through the crowds of the city. Gewa skidded to a stop after clearing a tree and saw Gerold. He fought with fury against strangely behaving goblins. The goblins were stiff and moving erratically, making them unpredictable in their attacks. He threw one that bit down on his arm without concern to his safety. Blood and gore flew from his savage attacks, the fluids sticking to everything with exception of the Paladin.

He brutally dispatched the undead goblin group with the help of Niitty who had to fire an arrow using her Snipe ability to keep one from ripping out Gerold's throat. He then stopped and breathed heavily, completely ignoring the carnage strewn about him. Gewa stepped forward and made a noise, causing

Gerold to turn around.

Gewa made eye contact with Gerold. The sight was terrifying. She had found those green eyes with the deep limbal ring alluring when she saw them earlier in the day. Now they were the eyes of a predator regarding her as potential prey. His eyes stared at her then darted to Niitty. He didn't seem to see the companions that helped him cross mountains and scrubland. He didn't see the companions that spent days scouring the forest for healing herbs, fighting to keep his infection at bay and keeping him alive until his powers restored. He didn't see the companions he had recently risked his life to save.

No, he appeared to regard them as a potential threat. He looked at them a moment, those eyes studying whether or not to attack. He then dismissed them, turned and continued running as if he didn't just fight a goblin band. Normal adventuring behavior forgotten, they left the bodies without taking any trophies. Twelve copper coins weren't worth the risk of losing sight of Gerold.

Gewa was too focused on running through the forest to pay attention to how long they ran. Her muscles burned and she struggled keeping her breath as she ran. The day was darkening. Mountain Elves and Humans didn't have the same dark vision she did, making the run risky for her companions.

The underbrush started to thicken as they reached the edge of the forest and it became somewhat easier to see, though the dark clouds were almost pure black this close to the village. As they cleared the underbrush near the edge of the tree line, Gewa saw Gerold in a position of agony on the other end of the fence, trying to crawl his way back to the forest. The expression of a rabid beast had been replaced with one of fear.

Niitty must have seen this, too, because she ran to help him. Gerold suddenly looked panicked at this and, with a burst of energy, intercepted her as she tried to jump over the fence, tackling her back into the forest. Gewa couldn't figure out what he was doing. She could puzzle out his sprint as a panicked desire to get to town to stop the black clouds billowing out of the green hazy light. If the town was his goal, why did he suddenly turn and stop Niitty from advancing closer?

He stood and used a healing spell on Niitty before turning around to look at the town. Gewa didn't have any additional time to ponder this strange behavior further when a sudden flash of light from the town blinded her and a rumble took her to her knees. She was stunned for a few seconds. She blinked and rubbed her eyes to try and remove the spots that had burned into her vision. They eventually cleared and she saw the village again. The cloud column stopped and she thought she saw something blue fall down beneath the edges of the palisade.

The following silence was disrupted by Gerold suddenly ranting at the air, yelling at Erinne about some kind of failing on her part and cursing her existence. She tried to stand and stumbled backwards into a shrub. The snapping sound caused Gerold to whip around.

Gewa saw an expression she had only once before ever seen. One she had caused. His face was a mess of grief, anger, despair and confusion. He reached an extreme low and was drowning in his mind.

All she knew is he was going to be erratic, unpredictable and dangerous. She had to get away.

Niitty broke the silence, "Do you want to talk about it?"

Oh no. That's not good. That's the wrong thing to say right now. Gewa's fears proved right and Gerold lashed out. He could tell he didn't want to say the words he was saying, his mind too lost in his turmoil to stop.

Niitty kept pleading, her emotional state deteriorating as a response. Gerold questioned their friendship but Niitty kept trying to engage with him.

Niitty stepped forward and Gewa had to act. Gewa grabbed Niitty's shoulder to keep her away. He was too volatile right now and Gewa worried he would harm Niitty. Niitty pulled through away from Gewa's grip and Gerold drove in the metaphorical knife with his harsh words, finally causing Niitty to reel back.

Taking the opportunity, Gewa whispered into Niitty's ear, "He doesn't mean this. Please, we have to go. We'll talk later."

Gewa led Niitty away back into the forest. Taking one last look back, she saw Gerold gripping his head with one hand before he turned and wandered away along the border fence.

Niitty was an emotional wreck. She could only stare forward as Gewa guided her through the underbrush in the dark. Gewa was afraid to move further into the forest with those strange goblins wandering around since she couldn't rely on Niitty to track them right now.

Gewa also couldn't return to the village. She had no idea what was going on beyond what Erinne had told them about the necrotic energy. Peering across the flat farmland through the underbrush, she was barely able to make out the town gates, even with her eyes. They stood wide open, absent the telltale movement of people. A steady stream of panicked residents should be pouring out of the opening after the previous display.

All the residents within must be dead. Whether those dead were animated or they were the normal sort was not something Gewa was in a hurry to find out. Right now, she had to find somewhere relatively safe for the two of them to rest.

The forest was out. So was the town. That left one of the farmhouses that dotted the landscape. Gewa knew dealing with potential undead residents of one house was better than the hundreds in the town and the unknown number of monsters in the forest.

Identifying the closest one, she directed Niitty toward it. Before crossing the fence into the tilled land, she paused. Gerold was showing signs of distress while on the other side and had tackled Niitty back before she could cross to help him.

Gewa looked at the fence with concern. She scanned the land and saw rows of dirt in long lines. Gerold could probably tell her what this was since it had something to do with growing food. To her untrained city eyes, it was dirt and nothing stood out as unusual.

Gewa then saw an object lying on the ground. It was a bird. Its wings were splayed out and its legs were folded beneath it. She had seen dead birds on the streets in the Capital before. This one had fallen out of the sky. The ones she remembered had wings folded in on themselves and they usually landed on their backs with their legs curled in the air. This one looked like it had failed its attempt at landing.

Something killed the bird and Gewa felt it was safe to assume that the power driving the cloud and light from the town was the culprit.

Gewa couldn't stand here pondering the mysteries of the universe. She had to act. Taking a deep breath, she put out a finger and slowly moved across the fence. She tried a few times to push so much as a claw over the invisible border but hesitated and pulled back. A second and third attempt ended the same way.

She looked over at Niitty and saw a dead eye shock on her face. Niitty's eyes were red and she stared out over the fields, looking little more alive than the zombies she had survived back at the crypt. Gewa couldn't dither further and pushed her claw across the border, relieved when she felt nothing. Then the finger crossed and she still felt nothing. She moved her full arm over and, again, felt nothing. Whatever had concerned Gerold earlier had ended when the effect coming from the village ceased.

She steeled her nerve and climbed over the fence and discovered she was fine. With some coaxing, she managed to get Niitty to cross over and they moved toward the farmhouse.

The landscape darkened as time ticked on toward a sunset they were not able to see. Gewa saw a figure off in the fields behind the house slowly swaying that faced away, not noticing their approach. A second figure closer to the house did, an old human woman.

Unlike the zombies that accosted her back at the crypt, Gewa noticed this one looked almost alive. The clothing was still well maintained, hair remained in place and the skin was not decaying and falling off the body. The only elements that gave away the unnatural state of the figure was the stiff and halting movements and the blank dilated eyes that looked at nothing.

It moved slowly and held its hands out, a far cry from the more nimble zombies that had ambushed Gewa's former party in the passageway. It was between her and the door to the house, the only obstacle between them and temporary safety.

All Gewa had was a dagger and she didn't want to get that close to use it. She shook Niitty by the shoulders, "Hey, I need you to snap out of this. I need you to kill that thing."

She looked at Gewa and blinked, "What?" Then Niitty looked at the zombie and sucked in air as her shock was dispelled.

"Ma'am, are you alright?" Niitty asked the zombie. The old

woman croaked in response and shuffled forward.

"Don't, it's not a person. It's the undead, you need to kill it," Gewa said, backing away slowly to keep her distance.

Niitty regarded the woman and pulled her rapier when she realized that Gewa's words rang true. She walked up carefully in a guard position before lunging forward and piercing the zombie through the eye. The woman dropped and went still.

Niitty stared at the body on the ground and didn't look happy with what she did.

"Come on," Gewa said as she walked past on the way to the door, "We have to get inside."

Gewa tried the door and found it locked. Cursing her luck and the situation, she went back to check the woman on the ground. She leaned down and patted the woman, looking for pockets.

"What are you doing?" Niitty said in alarm.

"Checking her for a key," Gewa replied. Luck was, again, not on her side when she came up empty. The old woman had nothing on her body and she didn't feel like risking safety to kill the other figure in the distance to see if it had the key.

Gewa now realized she had to risk exposing part of her history and pulled her dagger. Niitty watched in confusion at Gewa's behavior. Gewa imagined Niitty thinking she would bash the door down with the small blade, giving her a brief moment of dark humor to break the tension.

Doors like these weren't meant to keep motivated people out. The key was a glorified metal slab that moved a bar out of the way. Poor people couldn't afford better locks, not that they needed them to protect against losing their meager possessions. Besides, any lock could, with the correct tools, sufficient time and expertise, be bypassed. Putting a fancy lock in the slums only made that door a target.

Gewa first looked into the keyhole to see what she was working with. The lock was so simple it lacked any security features. The opening was wide to permit a thick, easily produced key to enter. The back of the opening was covered with a metal plate that served to act as a guide to allow the key to be turned. She didn't see any tumblers or disks to impede the wrong key from opening it. It was so basic Gewa could hand the dagger to Niitty and she would be in the structure no slower than Gewa. A part of her was not proud she felt disappointment in how easy this was.

Reaching her dagger into the hole, Gewa found the locking bar and pushed it into the open position. Pushing the door open slowly, she scanned the room through the crack between the door and the frame. Through the crack she saw an empty room with an inviting hearth glowing in the dark. She continued to open it slowly and scanned, finding nothing else in the room.

She waved Niitty to follow and they entered the house. Gewa turned and looked at the door as she closed it. She needed to check the other room before latching and blocking the door.

"Please watch the door. I need to see if anything is in the other room," Gewa whispered. She crept across the house and slowly opened the inner door. Inside was a bedroom, also empty. Back in the main room she noticed a small hatch in the floor under the main table.

She shoved the table out of the way and hefted up the latch. A ladder led into a dark cellar.

Gewa lowered her head into the opening slowly and looked around. She saw a food storage area that was depleted from a long winter. Long rows of empty jars were stacked along the walls with only a few filled. A couple of sacks that could be grains were on the floor. When she looked at the provisions, she realized she was hungry. Gerold took all the food in his sack when they left the cave in their haste.

"It looks like the place is safe for now," Gewa said and walked over to the door, Niitty standing aside. Gewa found the latch and, fortunately, the door had a wooden bar to block it.

"What was that," Niitty said to Gewa.

"Help me block up the shutters first," Gewa said, partially out of concern for safety and partially out of a desire to delay the uncomfortable conversation they were about to have. Gewa closed and latched the shutters in the main room while Niitty disappeared into the adjoining one.

Gewa noticed a pot bubbling on the hearth with a thick vegetable pottage in it. She found two small bowls on a shelf with small wooden spoons. She used a ladle in the pot to pour herself a serving when she heard a gasp from behind her, "What are you doing?"

Gewa turned and saw surprise in her eyes. She was pointing at her bowl.

"I'm hungry," Gewa replied and picked up the other bowl, "Do you want some?"

"What? No, that's stealing. How can we kill an old woman, break into her house then eat her food," Niitty demanded with an edge to her voice.

Niitty wasn't taking this well. Gewa put the empty bowl down on the stone lining around the hearth and then sat at the table with her back turned to Niitty. Gewa put the food down without taking a bite.

Gewa sighed, "I don't like what happened either, but we didn't kill a woman; we killed a monster. Whoever that woman was died hours ago. That was an empty husk animated by necrotic mana."

"We don't have to come in here and take their food."

Gewa spun her spoon on the tabletop, suddenly not feeling too hungry. This girl was too innocent for her own good. Gewa then put the spoon in the pottage and took a bite. Even though her body preferred meat, she couldn't let the woman's final meal go to waste.

After swallowing, Gewa said, "We have to. Our only choice was to stay out there and die or come in here and live. Besides, Gerold took all of our food."

Gewa continued to eat the food in silence. A few minutes passed when she heard the clatter of the ladle against wood and Niitty sat beside her. Niitty's expression was pained as she looked at the bowl, "Who are you? Really?"

Gewa licked her spoon and dropped it into the bowl, "A few days ago, I would have avoided that question. I'd have come back to town, said my farewells and left back to the Capital."

Niitty said nothing, so Gewa continued, "Seeing the two of you has made me think about the importance of trust."

"But," Niitty said, tears returning to her eyes, "Gerold doesn't trust me. He hates me."

Gewa shook her head, "No, that's not true. I have to tell you about the real me before what I say about him can make sense."

Gewa folded her hands on the table, "Most of what I told you about me was true. I'm a poor Docksider from the Capital. What I didn't tell you is my parents are members of the Thieves Guild and I was trained by them from birth."

Niitty's eyebrows went up in surprise and she let out a small gasp.

Gewa chuckled, "It's not that scandalous. Criminals aren't

rare in the Capital. Anyway, my parents are horrible thieves. They trained me as best as they could with their limited skills, which you can imagine didn't give me the best foundation. I'd regularly get caught when helping them out in their schemes. They never did manage much more than swiping trinkets and never advanced beyond Pewter rank at the guild."

Gewa paused to reach down in her sack. She rummaged around until she found what she wanted, an old, worn book. She put the book on the table. The book had a faded leather cover with slight hints of red flecked on the brown cover as the last reminders of the long lost décor. Branded in the cover were three simple words, "Basics of Magic".

"What's that," Niitty asked. Gewa smirked at her impatience.

"That," Gewa tapped the name of the book, "Is the item that changed my life."

"Oh," Niitty said, "That's the book you found to learn spells."

Gewa rubbed the back of her neck in embarrassment, "Found isn't quite the right word for what I did. I stole it and learning the lessons within wasn't what changed my life. I grew up in a thieving family and my parents were training me in the trade. I thought thieving was normal."

Gewa picked up the book and rubbed the faded cover with her thumbs, "This was one of my first successes at shoplifting. My parents noticed a merchant in the main Guild Hall square was receiving a new shipment of goods. We went into his shop pretending to browse. The workers moving crates into the shop was chaotic. I noticed that one crate was sitting near the door and the lid had popped open. It was easy. I walked by, reached in and pulled out the first item I could. It was this."

Gewa found herself giving a bitter laugh, "Hitting that shop was a horrible risk since it was the main general goods store the Adventurers used and the shop procured items for the Guild. My parents only managed to get a few trinkets before being seen and they had to run. This is the only reason I was able to walk out. No one pays attention to a nine year old girl when they're busy trying to chase down shoplifters."

"I see. How does a book tie into all of this," Niitty said through a spoonful of pottage, her hesitation forgotten as she listened to the story.

"I'm getting there," Gewa replied, "My parents were happy I had successfully made my first theft and so was I. My parents are terrible thieves. When they saw it was a book, they told me to keep it. They didn't think anyone would want a book of stories. What they missed is this is a Basics of Magic book. Magic is an exacting process. Diagrams, concepts and even wording must be perfect. The scribes copying them can't make the smallest of errors or the whole book is useless. Because mistakes happen, the pages are copied multiple times while pages with errors are burned to avoid one inadvertently getting into the finished product. They're immensely expensive. And the Empire controls the copies and reserves them for the Guild for new Mage training."

Gewa saw Niitty had a strange look on her face, "If they're that important, how did you end up getting that one? Why was it lying in a box on the floor of a merchant shop?"

"You can develop all the controls and protections you want, the one factor you can't control is people doing what they're supposed to. The box was one of many the harried laborers were trying to move and my parents provided, accidentally, a perfect distraction. No matter how well protected something is, there is always a flaw or mistake somewhere that can be taken advantage of," Gewa explained.

Niitty opened her mouth again but Gewa put a hand up, "I'm getting there. At the time, I thought nothing of the theft. He was a rich merchant and he could afford a few losses. I decided that we needed the items more so taking it wasn't a problem. As we passed through the area over the next few months, I noticed the shop becoming visibly more run down. It started small. The windows wouldn't get cleaned and rubbish built up on the front. Then a roof shingle fell out and it wasn't replaced. Then chain on the shop sign broke and the owner allowed it to hang. A few weeks go by and the next time I went by, everything was boarded up. Another month goes by and the shop is fine again with a different name hanging on the signpost."

A deep sense of shame welled up in Gewa, "In my childlike mind, I thought everything was good. He fixed the place up and changed the name and went on. It turned out that my imagination wasn't true. Some years went by and I was twelve. I was still engaging in petty theft, mainly market stalls for cheap trinkets or food. I was wandering a market street leading out of one of the city gates when I saw this dirty man casing some food. He was being obvious about it and was so bad he made my parents look like masters. Even they wouldn't have made the mistake of giving away their intentions."

Gewa hated this part of her story. Niitty was the first person she was going to tell this to and she had to take a deep breath to calm her nerves, "The man went for a meat skewer on a grill. It was so obvious that the guard was already there and they grabbed him the second his hand touched the skewer. He fought like a wild animal. Screaming, biting and yelling loudly how hungry he was. When he was thrown to the ground and secured, I saw his face. It was that merchant who owned the shop. He was gaunt and haggard. The worst part was the expression on his face. It was a man who lost everything. He was desperate, scared, and he didn't have anything to live for."

Gewa felt a pain rising behind her eyes and her pulse quickening. She wanted to run despite the lack of a threat and had nowhere to escape. She just had to power through. It was the only way to build any real trust with her new companion, "I asked one of the merchants what happened. It turns out he was contracted by the Guild Hall to procure items they needed for operations. One of them was a new copy of a book, Basics of Magic. He had to obtain a replacement at his own expense. Between that and his tarnished reputation for losing the book, his business was ruined and he ended up living on the streets."

Gewa took another deep breath. Her lungs were burning from her pressured speech. The thought of how she ruined a life was pressing on her, "I never knew what happened to him after that. Since that day, I've thought about how I could make it right. How I could fix what I did. The reality is that I can't. I have to live with my actions and strive to live a more honorable life."

Niitty listened on in silence. When she realized that Gewa had ceased talking, she asked, "Wow. Thank you for telling me. Hearing a story like this is different from the stories people in my tribe would tell. I am at a loss, though, as to what this has to do with now."

"The expression on that merchant's face is one I have only seen twice in my life. The other was a few hours ago," Gewa said.

Gewa could tell Niitty didn't understand. Niitty chewed on her lip for a moment then mumbled, "I didn't know he hated me that much. Was I imposing on him?"

Gewa looked at the ceiling in exasperation. This poor, sweet, naïve girl didn't understand at all, "Have you ever talked to people back in your tribe?"

Niitty's brow creased, "What? Of course I have."

"What do you talk about?"

"Oh, what we did for the day. The hunt, where animals are and the tasks we perform around our camp."

"Have you ever talked about the past and people's hopes and dreams?"

Gewa saw that this idea was foreign to Niitty. Gewa had suspected that a close knit Mountain Elf tribe knew each other so well that talking about the past was redundant. They were all there to witness it, after all. And everyone knew each other so well that talking about dreams and hopes was unnecessary. They already knew each other deeply.

Gewa waited while Niitty blinked and moved her mouth silently, like she was trying to form words. She ended up at a loss for which ones to use. Eventually, she relented trying to form a more complex explanation, "No. I never really have."

"And have you ever thought about what brought Gerold here? Listened to him or observed him?"

"Sure. He's cute, dedicated and helped me out a lot since I got here. After we formed our party, I did see a little sadness in him. We were already on the way out to the crypt so I haven't thought much about it," Niitty replied.

"And when he lost his powers and turned into a middle aged man, you never wondered why someone like that was a new adventurer," Gewa stated flatly.

Niitty twiddled with her spoon, "No."

Gewa could tell Niitty was struggling with this line of thinking, "Someone with an established life doesn't drop it to become an adventurer, even if chosen to be a Paladin. He let something slip when talking to me before he got his injury from that goat monster. He knew I was hiding my background and briefly mentioned his kids. Did he ever mention he was a Father?"

Niitty silently shook her head. She was visibly getting more and more upset.

"He told me when you went on ahead to scout. I don't think he meant it to be intentional; it just came out when he recognized that I wasn't being honest. Then when he spoke to you after he woke up about mistakes, I knew it wasn't an act. Even though it lacked eloquence, he spoke in a way that I wished my own parents would speak," Gewa said.

Gewa felt bad about what she was about to say, "Something horrible happened to him. It's made him confused, reckless and he is lashing out. He saw your close contact as inappropriate and he was too overwhelmed to address it correctly. There is a good man under all that. He cares about people and cares about you. He is willing to throw away his safety to ensure yours."

Niitty was sobbing, "I was so lonely and he was so supporting. When I was panicking in the village he relieved my fear, even without that aura of his. Are you saying I was wrong and that I was a burden?"

"If he thought you were a burden, he would have just left you," Gewa started, "I don't think you were wrong. I don't think you did nothing wrong, either. If circumstances were different, maybe he would have addressed his discomfort with your behavior. Between the loss of my party, my rescue and now all of this, he couldn't take it anymore. I find it interesting to see, after all those words he had for the Recluse Queen, that it was his only problem with you. It's a small miscommunication between you two that was elevated by everything else."

Niitty nodded, "What can I do?"

"I don't know," Gewa said, "I'm not used to the idea of people caring about me like that. Sure, my parents weren't completely terrible people, but they were willing to let me be caught and sent to an orphanage. The guard is easier on kids than adults, so I was willing to go along with it. I have no idea what it's like to have someone in my life willing to lay down theirs for me. You said you formed a party, right? Have you checked on him?"

Niitty shook her head, "I can't feel anything through the connection. All I can tell he's off to the East and I think he's on the other side of town. I'm not able to get a good read on him."

Gewa searched her memory, "You know, my party had a minor argument that got pretty heated. They were arguing when Tulugaak noticed that he couldn't read anyone's emotional state anymore. They all got worried that the party link had broken and when they stopped to focus on each other again, they could feel each other. You're too focused on yourself to notice the connection."

Niitty thought for a moment, "I have an idea. It's something I saw Gerold doing and it worked back at the crypt to calm my fears."

Gewa watched her stand up from the table and sit in the middle of the floor with crossed legs. She closed her eyes and started to breathe in a slow and deliberate manner, holding her breath and slowly releasing it. Gewa saw how her muscles relaxed after a few minutes.

Gewa felt she shouldn't interrupt this. She finished her food and her body rebelled at the thought of getting another bowl. The woman's food would have to join thousands of other meals that were destined to rot.

To pass the time, Gewa flipped through the Basics of Magic book. She had read it cover to cover many times. Most of it was diagrams on rituals, basic information on artifacts and instruction on how to structure her thoughts to better cast spells. Even if the inspiration came from an unknown source and, outside of rituals, they couldn't craft their own spells, they still needed to know how to stretch their minds to allow the undecipherable mystic words to flow.

The book wasn't much use to her now and a lot of it was speculation on how magic operated and why no one could write down or comprehend spells. Still, it was a comfort to review the pages she already knew by heart.

After about 30 minutes, Gewa looked up at Niitty. She was still sitting in that position and still breathing in the same rhythmic pattern. Had she fallen asleep? This went on for a few minutes longer when Niitty opened her eyes. She had a look of concern on her face that conflicted with her calm body language.

"He's in the direction of the town," she said.

Gewa felt herself frown, "That's not good. Is he in trouble?"

Niitty shook her head, "No, I think he's on the other side of town. He's not angry anymore. He's just…barely there. It almost feels like he's feeling shame and sadness. He's regretful of something."

"I'm going to wager that's a good thing," Gewa replied.

"Why?"

"Because I don't think he's given up. It's late. We can't do anything about it right now. Let's just hope he works out whatever it is he's going through. We'll check on him tomorrow."

CHAPTER 22

"Wake up. Do you intend on lazing around all day?"

Gerold awoke with a start. He rubbed calloused hands over his eyes to remove the gunk that had built up during his nap. He looked down at his dirty fingernails, a reminder of his hard work that morning.

He looked around and saw the pot bubbling on the stove. It was an unusually cool summer mid-morning day, though it wasn't cold enough to worry about frost harming the crops.

He looked up from his chair and saw Zelina giving him a friendly scowl. He looked from her to the stove and back again while his mind churned. It dawned on him and he stood and moved the chair back to the table to make room.

Zelina waved a ladle at him, "You are a lot like your Father."

Gerold looked at her smiling face and tried to parse out what she was talking about. As usual, she had expertly read his thoughts, "That was his favorite spot. He'd spend evenings sitting in that chair and stare into the flames."

He thought back on his Father. Ever since the day they returned from his Mother's Rites, his Father would spend nights in that chair where he comforted him and his younger sister. While he got over his grief, he never forgot his wife. He struggled for a few months after her death. Even after his Father recovered and got most of his admittedly gruff energy back, he would always sit there every night. Even after he finished mourning, he always acted like his life was incomplete without her.

His Father only ever talked about it once when Gerold came of age. His Father told Gerold that now he was an adult, he could confide in him his feelings. That his wife was always on his mind and a piece of him died that day. He also explained that her death wasn't his death, that he had much more to live for and that Gerold had nothing to worry about.

And he never spoke about it again. He busied himself about the farm with Gerold. He showed happiness when Gerold announced he would take over the family legacy and when Gerold finally found a wife. Even with the loss he endured decades earlier, he never let it hold him back.

"You still haven't let him go, have you," Zelina asked, her ability to read Gerold's thoughts was eerily accurate.

Gerold shook his head, "No. I long ago came to terms with his loss. I think it's good to remember your loved ones. Not at the expense of those who rely on you now, though."

She smiled, "That's good advice. Just be sure you don't forget it."

Gerold found her phrasing odd. He walked over to the window and peered out of the back of his house. He looked over his fields and saw the crop was coming in good. In his fields grew corn with vines of beans climbing up the stalks. Spaced around the ground between the corn stalks were squash plants.

His neighbors always thought he was odd for doing this. It was a practice that his Grandfather picked up in his adventuring days in a region beyond the Empire's eastern borders. He claimed the combination kept the soil healthy. There may have been something to it because their farm's yields had always been good. He could have moved out of town into the wider prairie and become wealthy with this method, but that would require hiring employees and retaining an adventurer party to protect the land. He was happy with the smaller, safer ancestral plot within the borders of the Town Seed.

"What do you plan on doing today," Zelina asked him.

Gerold looked out of his window over the farm, "I'll go out and check on the crop."

After giving Zelina a kiss on the cheek, the put on his boots and stepped outside.

As he walked the fields looking for signs of pests, he recalled some stories his Grandfather had told him about other parts of the world. One he found amusing was about city people. According to his Grandfather, people in the city thought farming was easy. Put some seed in the ground then sit around for weeks on end watching it grow. He even said they'd talk about taking trips to farms for holidays. Even more entertaining, some of them thought that food came from shops.

Gerold smiled to himself at the thought. Even if they did recognize it took effort to till the soil and plant the seed, it wasn't as simple as waiting for plants coming out of the dirt and then picking it. You had to monitor the land constantly. You had to check the plants for disease and remove it before it spread. You had to identify and kill pests. You had to remove weeds that would compete with your crop for nutrients. Land maintenance between harvests involved mixing accumulated compost back into the soil. His Grandfather said the city people disposed of their valuable composte by throwing it out of their windows into the street.

Even knowing what to grow was important. It wasn't just the season, either. He had to keep an eye on the soil condition to know which plants to crop. Different crops would help improve soil condition and he would leave portions of his field covered in alfalfa, which he would plow under instead of harvesting to replenish the land.

As he walked the paths in his fields looking for signs of insects or disease, he rubbed his sore shoulder. Age was starting to catch up with him. Thankfully, Malrin was already proving to be a dedicated apprentice. He had aspirations to go off and adventure though. It pained him thinking that his son didn't want to take over the family farm. His Father had given him and his siblings the choice and Gerold was the only one to take him up on the offer. His older brother went off to the Capital and he never heard from him again and, after a few years in her 20s adventuring locally, his younger sister disappeared beyond the Imperial borders.

That was a risk Gerold had to take. Gerold had no inclination to leave home and was perfectly happy to take on the farm. Had he decided to leave as well, he knew his Father would have sold the place in retirement and accepted that his children had a different goal in life. If neither Malrin nor Elli had any interest in taking over the land, Gerold would not fight it if they were fulfilled.

His examination of the plants didn't come up with any concerns for the day. Malrin had already taken care of weeding along the border fence and the colder weather reduced insect activity. It was looking like it would be a good harvest.

It was early afternoon when he returned home. Everyone had gathered around the table for the midday meal. He loved this time of year. He was presented with a bowl of fresh vegetables with a boiled egg. His children were eating with gusto while his wife smiled at him. He sat down and joined in.

After finishing, he thanked Zelina.

She smiled at him, "Did you get everything done you needed

to?"

She used a tone that implied he had forgotten something.

"I don't know, let me go check," he said and stood up to head back out.

He wondered if he'd checked on the cistern lately. His Grandmother had insisted on building it to store water to help during dry periods. He grabbed a lantern, lit it and then descended into the root cellar where she had constructed an access. Past the shelves holding their building winter preserve stock was a door cut into the wall. His Grandmother was a Dwarf and had an excellent engineering mind. The stonework was solid and impressive.

He rubbed his hand over some childlike artwork carved into the stone frame. Visitors would have wondered how his kids managed to carve the stonework. Those designs were also a product of his Grandmother. She, like many Dwarves, had assumed their engineering skills also made them skilled craftsmen and artisans. Gerold had inherited the same thick, imprecise fingers that carved these rudimentary designs.

Opening the thick door, he walked down a hallway that sloped downward a dozen yards before opening up into a large stone pool. A series of pipes and collectors exist on the surface that capture the water and store it below. A hand pump allows for users to extract it above.

He stood on a wide platform that was separated from the pool by a steel railing to keep people from falling in. The cistern's sturdy stone construction allowed it to double as a tornado shelter, evidenced by benches carved in the walls. He hung the lantern on a hook from the center of the ceiling, banishing the darkness from over a long pool of water.

Even with all the genius of the design, it still needed to be maintained. Tools hanging on the walls allowed pipes to be removed and replaced. Crimpers, threaders, wrenches and other tools lined the walls. His eyes landed on a particular one. It was a pipe expander that always came off to Gerold as sinister with its long conical spike. For some reason, looking at it today made him uncomfortable. Above the tools was a long wooden pole with a flat paddle at the end that reminded him of a gardening hoe. On the ground below the tools were five buckets lined up next to each other.

He peered into the water below and noticed detritus was beginning to accumulate at the bottom. The system didn't have a reliable means to filter out dirt. Taking a bucket, he attached it to a rope and dropped it into the water. Using the long hoe, he pressed the bucket into the water to fill it. When it sank, he directed it into a sloped recess that ended in a cavity that was designed to fit the bucket.

Using his wooden hoe, he began carefully slide the dirt in his direction. He had to be slow and deliberate to avoid stirring up the debris. Go too fast and he would have to wait for the material to settle before going again. When the dirt reached the slope, it slid down into the bucket.

He slowly performed this task until the dirt displaced the water in the bucket and raised it up. It was heavy and still water logged. He would have to let the water evaporate before trying to heft it up to dispose back into the yard. He repeated the process and pulled out two and a half more buckets of silt.

He looked into the water, seeing only small bits of debris that were effectively impossible to extract. Feeling the job well done, he pulled the lantern and returned home.

It was dark. Gerold didn't realize he had been down in the cistern for so long. He worried his wife would be mad at him for coming back late.

His family was around the table with fresh salad and egg

again. It was turning into a great day to have this meal twice in a row. His family had already finished and his kids were playing a game in the open space in the main room.

He sat down to eat his food that was waiting for him. Zelina was working on a patch for some clothing and looked up after he started, "Did you get everything done you needed to?"

A multitude of chores he could get done around the farm flooded to his mind. The roof needed to be mended. He had to check the harvester to make sure it was still in good condition. He could check the water pump. He thought he saw a loose fence post when he was checking the crops.

"No, I can hold those tasks off for tomorrow," he replied. Before he tucked in, he thought he saw a strange sense of annoyance mixed with sadness in Zelina's face. He had also noticed the silence. He turned to his kids, but the moment his eyes landed on them, they were playing again. It was a long day and he should finish up and get some sleep.

He awoke the next morning to a dark, overcast day. Zelina had already gotten up for the day and took Elli with her. Up on the loft, he saw Malrin dangling his legs off the side.

He waved and smiled, "Hey Dad, what are your plans for the day?"

He looked up at his son, "Morning, Malrin. I need to fix the roof and look after the harvester."

He hummed and waved his legs, "Are you sure that's what you're supposed to be doing?"

That boy was getting sassy, a change in attitude that came with his puberty. Gerold huffed, "Boy, I know how to operate a farm. Do you know what you're supposed to be doing?"

Malrin only grinned in return. Then he leapt off the loft to the ground, ignoring the ladder. Gerold winced. He hated

Malrin doing that, "What did we talk about using the ladder? If you can't do that, we're moving your bed back down here."

He bounced up and down on his legs as his energetic nature made him want to move, "You don't have to worry about me anymore, Dad."

Before Gerold could reply, he bolted out of the room with a laugh. Gerold shook his head, wondering what the next few years would bring as his son grew up. That phrasing was odd, though.

After dressing, Gerold passed through the main room and saw it empty. Everyone was already out and about for the day. He grabbed some hard bread for breakfast before exiting the house. He looked over and found the storage barn on the property and went in. Inside were neatly tied off bales of materials. He passed his stocks of flax and had a strange impulse that he had to fix his clothing. He looked down at himself and he was fine.

Ignoring that, he went past some straw to a tool rack and pulled down a wooden mallet. On the way out, he hefted up a cube of straw and returned to the house.

Climbing up to the roof, he went to a spot that looked a little ragged. He got to work weaving in new straw and fixing the wooden supports. He would take care of that leak before working on the harvester.

He had found himself in that special place where all thoughts exited his mind as his hands performed the work. He was blessed with his Father's awful Dwarven dexterity that made making tight weaves necessary to keep out the rain a challenge.

"Are you sure that's the best use of your time?"

The voice broke him out of his fugue state. He saw Zelina

staring at him from below, a look of concern on her face.

Gerold was confused. He pointed to the sky and said, "I'm trying to get ahead of the rain."

"You know that's not rain."

Gerold frowned. What was wrong with her? It was an unusually cool summer day with a persistent cloud cover. Rain could be here any moment.

"Look at me."

He was getting annoyed at being nagged. What could possibly be more important than keeping their house dry? He reached for his mallet to adjust the supports, grasping air instead of a wooden handle. He looked over and the mallet was gone, along with the straw he as using for the repairs. Everything had turned grey with those little black spots flashing in his vision.

"Look at me."

Gerold didn't want to. He tried to continue repairing the roof, but every time he tried to move straw into position, it refused to budge. He'd have better luck pushing the entire house to the other end of the property.

"Look at me."

Gerold hung his head and closed his eyes, "I can't."

"You have to."

Opening his eyes, he turned his vision down to the ground below the house. Zelina stood there, looking up at him. The vibrant and beautiful woman he had married was replaced by a pale woman with cloudy eyes and a caved in head looking at him with a soft, mournful smile.

Gerold felt his hands tremble and he looked down at them

and saw them covered in blood.

"Stop that."

He looked back down at his wife. She looked at him with a strong expression that showed her disapproval.

"I can't," Gerold said, "I don't want to remember this."

"You can't keep refusing to address it. You need to stop blaming yourself."

Gerold pounded the immovable straw of the roof, "I can't forget."

He heard her click her tongue and he looked down. She was shaking her head, "I never said to forget. I said to begin moving on. You have forgotten something more important."

He blinked, "Forgotten what?"

She pointed off into the distance, "Look there and focus beyond yourself for a moment."

Following her finger, he saw a town in the distance. Instead of the familiar open design of Hivastock he saw a tall wooden palisade. It was quiet and the sky covered with a thick, dark cloud. Taking her advice, he imagined his focus exiting his body. He stopped and allowed the surrounding air to absorb into his skin.

He noticed how artificial everything was. It was dreamlike and ethereal. Had he not been so inwardly focused, he would have noticed this was a dream immediately. Through his core he felt the party link and Niitty. She had a sense of sadness and determination in her as she moved. He felt her beyond the town moving in his direction as she skirted it along the south.

He looked back at Zelina. She was back to her normal self and smiling, "There are people out there that still need you. And there is one you can start amends with now."

Gerold felt a hitch in his voice, "I don't know if I can move past your deaths."

She shook her head, "I'm not asking you to move on. I'm just asking you to take the next step and stop allowing the past to destroy your future."

"I don't think I can do it," he replied, "I'm just some farmer."

"That's wrong," she replied, "You're not just a farmer. You're a Paladin and, more importantly, you're a good man. There is no guarantee you'll succeed, but you still need to try."

Gerold was grasping at straws to find an excuse to stay, "I don't want to leave."

"Nothing says you can't come back later."

He knew she was right. There were people who needed him now. Coming to terms with his past could wait.

She smiled, "There's the man I know. Now, it's time to wake up."

CHAPTER 23

Gerold awoke in a dim room. His eyes passed over the remaining remnants of the coals in the hearth, the heat no longer able to keep back the cold air. The cloud cover was so thick that he felt frost building up on his chair.

He looked around and found the charcoal stores in the house and fed additional fuel to the hearth. Using the nearby poker, he was able to stoke the fire, the light banishing the darkness into a small sphere around the hearth.

His soul felt drained and numb while the sense of anger was gone and along with it his desire to sit around and do nothing. He returned to the chair and paused. On the floor below the chair he saw moisture stains in the wood in circular splashes, the color transitioning from clean wood to a layer of dust through rings of dried mud.

What felt like an uncontrollable sinkhole before that threatened to swallow him whole was now a smaller hole that was reinforced by stone. What remained was a manageable emptiness that he suspected would never vanish entirely, only fade with time.

Taking a deep breath, he took heed of the words his wife told him in his dream. He had spent the last six months refusing to take control of his life. He allowed circumstances and others to direct his actions. It was time to start being proactive.

His first order of business was Niitty. He couldn't imagine that she and Gewa would have separated after he abandoned them in his mania. Pushing his self-centered concerns aside, he focused outward on their connection.

He was able to sense her location. Like in his dream, she was quite a distance away. He estimated that she was on the other side of the town and they were swinging around the south in his direction.

He couldn't be sure if it was an attempt to return to the Capital or they were coming in his direction. Her emotional state was neutral and focused with a hint of sadness.

Inspiration hit him. If they could feel each other's emotional state, maybe he could use it to communicate. He called up a feeling of regret, apology and a desire to see her and then imagined pushing it into the connection. He waited a few minutes and, after nothing happened, he tried it a second time.

Then he got a response. He felt from her a sense of apology and remorse along with acceptance and happiness. He would have to assume it wasn't his imagination and would wait.

His next course of action was another he wronged. He had no idea how he did it before. The only time he tried directly contacting Erinne was when Niitty was critically injured. He called out in a panic back then and couldn't remember if he did anything special to accomplish it.

Not knowing what else to do, he sat and closed his eyes, "Erinne?"

Silence reigned in the dim room. He waited a few moments longer, "Erinne? Are you there?"

Silence refused to abdicate its throne. Gerold hadn't expected the Goddess to just return because he asked her to. She was the Supreme Being after all. These were words he still had to say.

"Erinne," Gerold began, "I have to apologize. My life has been in complete disarray for the last six months and I've had no time until very recently to stop, breathe and think. At first, I resented you and these powers. I wanted nothing more than to stay back home and die from some wandering monster. While I'm still not comfortable in this young body, I have come to understand this opportunity. My wife would be ashamed of me for my behavior and my refusal to help. I can't guarantee I'll be an ideal Paladin, but I can promise you that, starting now, I'll try."

He paused and listened. Once again, he heard nothing in response. He stoked the fire some to get more air to the charcoal, his skin happy that the air was finally starting to warm.

"I'm not sure if I've irreparably broken our connection or you're not able to hear me. Even if you never return, I can tell you that I will see this mission through. I'll do what I can to best represent you as your chosen warrior. I know I haven't shown gratitude for the opportunity you've given me. Without it, I don't think I'd even be alive today and no one would even be aware of this horrible event," Gerold finished.

He stood and held his hands over the flame. He could feel Niitty coming closer and it would still be a few hours before she arrived. As much as he wanted to stay in the warming room, he had to move toward Niitty and Gewa to avoid wasting time. Whether they agreed to come with him or not, he was going into town to see if he could find any clues as to what caused the disaster.

Before he left, he turned on his Sense Evil aura. He wasn't expecting the good results that came. When he activated it, he felt the range had grown to 120 yards as it expanded out. He also felt an underlying sense of evil permeating the entire area that didn't drown out his senses in a big black mass like before. It, instead, felt more like a dull grey that he could see evil through. He felt that his abilities had improved to a point where the aura wasn't completely useless in places like the crypt.

"I must have gone past a threshold yesterday," he mumbled to himself as he respectfully closed the house door behind him and faced toward the village in the gloom.

"You did," a voice echoed in his head, "You can now create an aura to protect against necromantic magic and cast a spell to help in fights against evil beings. That and you should be stronger, faster and more durable."

Gerold stumbled, "Erinne?"

"Yes, I'm here."

"I need to apologize to you for my behavior."

"Stop," she said, "I already heard it. I was listening in quietly and Umieranie also told me what you said last night."

Gerold nodded.

"I still can't read your mind," she said, though not in the usual playful manner.

"I know this won't make things better," he started.

"No, it doesn't," Erinne interrupted, "Until I met you, I never knew what it felt to be hurt before. It was a concept that was foreign to me. Your annoyance with me brought emotions that I had never felt before. What you said to me yesterday caused me a great deal of distress."

Gerold hummed out loud in response to indicate he was listening.

"This isn't something I can ever forget. To be honest, it's not something I'd want to forget, either."

Gerold was thrown off by that, "What do you mean?"

"Before I met you, emotion didn't mean much to me. Afterward, I started to recognize how lonely I was. An eternity with nothing is something no one can comprehend, even the other Gods. It's probably why I created everything. Even then, I didn't understand how empty it was. The other Gods are too simple to hold meaningful conversations. Mortals, though, are different. I can't imagine losing you to talk to and the prospect of it hurt the most," she replied, her voice quavering.

"I won't ask you to forgive me," Gerold said, "My behavior was unacceptable and I spent the past few months throwing your gifts back in your face. I had a realization last night that this is not a curse and these powers can be used for good. I still don't like looking like a young man. What I ask for is we give this another chance."

"I can agree to that, but only if you also accept my apology," Erinne replied.

Gerold felt confused, "What, why?"

"I've been pushy. When I found you, I was excited and could only think about myself. I didn't comprehend what you were going through until recently. I was too focused on pushing you to do things for me to recognize your pain. I treated you like a puppet, directed to do things at my behest without your input," she said.

"We can call this a miscommunication then. I accept your apology and let's start things fresh today," Gerold said as he started walking toward town.

"With that out of the way, why are you walking to town," Erinne asked.

"I'm heading toward where Niitty is. It would be faster to move to her than wait here," Gerold responded.

"Why would that be faster? The house back there is already warm. It looks cold out there," Erinne's voice was tinged with a lack of understanding.

Gerold trudged away from the house toward the gate, "I intend to investigate the town."

"What!" Erinne's shrill voice caused Gerold to wince, "I just said you don't have to follow my orders anymore. Why would you go in there? Even with your improved power, you can't handle hundreds of zombies."

"The population inside the walls is closer to two thousand," Gerold stated as his boots crunched the frost buildup on the road, "And I'm the one making this decision. I have to know what happened. This is the second time I've witnessed a village destroyed and I need to know why to keep it from happening again."

Gerold walked in silence down the main road toward town. He passed more farm holdings with the occasional body standing still in the fields like macabre scarecrows. The cold humid air cut him to the bone through his ill-suited clothing. He thought of furs in his bag then dismissed it since they would make it difficult to move in an emergency.

Gerold had reached the final house before the main gates of the town. At this distance, he could see bodies standing still around inside the main thoroughfare leading to the center. Niitty was still about an hour away at this pace and he decided to prepare the house for their arrival.

In front of the house he saw a family of four: A mother, father and two boys, one a young teen and the other around the age of ten. He felt a pit in his stomach at the sight. It was different this time. They didn't remind him of his own family anymore. He recognized deep down that they were truly gone. This feeling, instead, was a sense of sadness at all the potential erased. What they could have gone on to do and accomplished was now forever gone.

He wondered why all four were congregated at the front. Maybe they met for the midday meal before entering the house. It was another mystery that would remain unsolved with the loss of the family's lives.

A thought came to mind. He pulled out his final copper coin and looked at the four. They were no threat to him with how stiff and slow they still moved, impotently shambling in his direction over the ground. He flipped the coin over in his hand, wondering if it was worth the test.

"Erinne, can you tell how powerful my Turn Undead has become," Gerold whispered.

"I can't tell how powerful it will be until you use it. What are you thinking," Erinne replied.

"I need to know how effective it is if I go into town. If my ability isn't strong enough to have an impact, I won't take the remaining coins from Niitty since they'll need them to get back to the Capital," Gerold said.

It was a risk, but it was also an investment in the future. He could assume it was a bad idea and lose a powerful weapon to navigate the city. It could also be a mild delay like back at the crypt. Those undead were far more powerful. His advancement would unlikely cause a major change then, but against these fresh ones? He had no idea.

Gripping the coin, he knew he had to try. He pulled his hammer and approached the four undead. His boots crunching on the ground caught their attention and they stiffly and awkwardly turned to engage.

He knew from the crypt he had to wait for the monsters to enter a 10 yard radius. He allowed them to get well within the estimated distance and, after a brief hesitation, dissolved his final coin and engaged his spell. He felt the ability pulse out of him in a sphere. The results were impressive. The four zombies silently turned into ash, clothing and personal effects dropping to the ground, and he watched as the pulse carried the ash away in a spherical shape as the force pushed it out to the maximum distance. There, the ash slowly rained to the ground.

Gerold found it disconcerting that the entire process made no sound, conflicting with the spectacular results that completed with no fanfare. He made a few calculations in his head, "I wonder if I could clear the entire town if I gather the zombies up in bunches."

"That wouldn't work," he heard Erinne interject in his head, "While this is impressive, remember the zombies are at their weakest. In a few hours, the stiff muscles will start to relax and the necrotic magic will begin to strengthen them. The zombies are too slow to gather up fast enough to clear them all. Also, I analyzed your spell and that pulse is as strong as a single copper coin can produce. Even with your improved potential, you'll need more mana if you want a stronger effect."

Knowing the effect, he would have to ask for a few coins to delve into town in case of emergency. The need for more money to produce bigger results added a time limit to his investigation. He couldn't afford to use the ability on more powerful undead. He mulled getting closer to town to get a better look, but he risked alerting the zombies and decided against it. For now, he wanted to get into the house and start up a fire.

Gerold found a key in one of the piles of clothing that he used to unlock the door. The house had a similar arrangement to the one he just left. After a quick examination of both rooms and finding them empty, he stoked up new flames with some fresh charcoal in the hearth.

Taking up a familiar spot with a chair before the hearth, he mulled over how he could approach the town. He thought back to the day he arrived and those two boys again. When he arrived, he noticed that they had climbed up to the roof before falling into hay bales. Next to the wall were some barrels that they had likely used to climb up to the roof. He could use those and, with the narrow gap between buildings along the main thoroughfare, he hoped he could climb up and follow them along to the town center.

When he got there, he had no idea what he could do. He'd have to jump down into the clear area in the center to the Town Seed and, somehow, get back out again. He didn't have the same urge to go out in battle like he had the week before, his new responsibilities giving him a better outlook on life. He would have to scout the area when he got there to make further plans.

He checked Niitty's distance again. The whole process of eliminating the zombies, checking the house and mulling over his plans had only taken about ten minutes. He decided he should relax in the slowly warming room for the time being. He wasn't sure when, or if, he could have a quiet moment again.

"Erinne," Gerold called out.

"Yes Gerold?"

"I'm going to sit here quietly for a while. I think I need to clear my mind for a bit."

"I see. Why are you telling me?"

"I don't want you to think I'm just ignoring you. I've had a bad habit of ceasing conversation out of nowhere."

Gerold heard her hum in his head, "Thanks, I appreciate it. I'll try to do the same as well when I have to disconnect back to my real self."

Gerold hummed his agreement, remembering to do it loudly this time so Erinne could hear him. He reached his hands out over the hearth and rubbed his hands to clear out the stiffness from the cold. Now, it was time to wait.

CHAPTER 24

Niitty's mind was a tangle of emotion. On one hand, she got a message through the connection from Gerold signaling a sense of remorse and apology. She at first thought it was her imagination until it came through a second time. She was happy he reached out and tried to send her own sense of remorse back. She also wondered how their relationship would grow going forward. They were stuck together through the party link for life and she now fully comprehended the warning Philip had given them. Parties that had a falling out would drift apart, their connection a permanent reminder of their hasty decisions.

She suspected that it wouldn't be an easy road. He had made many valid points about her behavior and she would have to endeavor to improve. Gewa had warned her to temper her expectations and, more importantly, don't make it one sided. He should also be open to change and communication as well. Niitty didn't want the two to grow apart. She knew he was a good man and she wanted to grow their relationship. She would have to push down her infatuation, though, since that clearly made him uncomfortable.

She changed her focus to navigating the farms. The undead out in the fields weren't concentrated and, usually, easy to avoid. They weren't always conveniently swaying in the open fields and, after a close call with one lying against a piece of farming equipment attached to a dead horse, she maneuvered to navigate through wide open spaces.

The silence was eerie. She tried to fill it with small talk with Gewa, who had abandoned her torn robe back at the farmhouse and was now wearing simple city attire, the girl too guarded about her past to get much more than a few surface level talks. Niitty found talking to someone who was her polar opposite frustrating. She could understand the reservation. It took courage to admit her past like that. Niitty had told Gewa that she wasn't a bad person with Gewa responding that she wasn't a good person, either.

By late morning, they arrived at a house near the east gate into town. After making a wide berth around the structure to ensure nothing would surprise them, they approached the front door. Niitty saw clothing strewn on the ground outside the entrance followed by a line of grey ash. She felt her connection to Gerold and he was inside and not in any distress. If she remembered, she would ask about it later.

Arriving at the door, she knocked. Gewa gave her a strange look, "What are you knocking for?"

"I don't want to barge in on someone's house," Niitty replied.

Before Gewa could remark on her statement, the door opened into a cozy, warm room. A face with brilliant green eyes and a limbal ring peered out. The face belonged to Gerold, who invited them in.

Gerold pulled a chair away from the front of the fire lit hearth and swung it over to the table in the room before sitting in it. Niitty noticed a sense of deep fatigue in his body language that clashed horribly with his appearance. She would expect bloodshot eyes with dark lines marking their sockets. Apart from the distant look in his eyes and his hunched over appearance, he looked like he was well rested and alert.

He gestured with his hand out, palm up toward the chair across the table, "Please, I have a few things I'd like to say."

Niitty looked over at the chair and decided to sit. She wanted to say a few things as well. Gewa, instead of sitting, decided to poke around the small farmhouse. Gewa didn't notice the look of disapproval that Niitty sent her way.

Niitty sat and Gerold started talking, "I owe you an apology. To do that, I also have to make good on a promise to tell you about myself. Please don't take this as an excuse. My behavior was unacceptable, but it should provide some context if you're willing to listen."

He folded his hands on the table and tapped his thumbs. Niitty thought a moment and responded, "I would like us to continue traveling together and I also want to apologize."

Gerold unfolded his hands and drummed his fingers on the table, "You have nothing to apologize for."

Niitty felt frustration rising and she slapped the table with her hands, "I do and I'm going to." She immediately felt embarrassed at her outburst.

She saw a brief smile cross Gerold's face before it returned to neutrality. She wondered what that was about since she couldn't recall him ever smiling.

Gerold laid his hands palm down on the table, "You convinced me. Now, how should I begin?"

He stared at the table, deep in thought. Niitty felt a sense of conflict within him as his eyes blinked and looked at the backs of his hands. Niitty also noticed Gewa had given up on her search of the small house and decided to lean against the wall near the door to listen.

Then he started, "I am from a small community to the southeast of the Capital in the deep plains called Hivastock. Neither of you will have likely heard of it. While it was a good place to farm, it was far removed from trade routes or the river system. Up until my Grandfather changed things, it was one of those communities that didn't even have a Town Seed."

"I didn't know those still existed," Gewa interjected.

"They do," Gerold said, "They're a dying breed. Town Seeds are expensive to create and maintain. Despite having a good place for intermediate adventurers to train, including a small dungeon a few days away, we weren't on the way to anywhere adventurers could move on to without taking a lengthy detour. We had a guild and some adventurers looking for a place to train without hassle would come by now and again. Because of that, our Town Seed would frequently fail. We didn't worry since the monsters weren't dense outside the zone of influence and the adventurers could keep monsters in check. Apart from mid-summer where we would activate the seed once to keep it from completely decaying, we saved up our Adventurer Coins to set up the protection for the winter when the adventurers left for the year."

Gerold adjusted himself in his seat, "Back in my Grandfather's day, everyone would become an adventurer when they came of age. It was the only way to gain enough power to reliably protect your property. My Grandfather decided to change that. During his travels, he saved up a tremendous amount of Adventurer Coin and set up our Town Seed. He didn't lose his thirst for adventure because he set up the seed so that our family farm would be at the very edge of the shield. He would sneak out from time to time to fight monsters with my Grandmother."

Gerold paused for a few breaths, "He returned with my Grandmother, a fellow adventurer, a Dwarf woman, and started a family. Dwarves are strange in those parts since it is almost entirely made up of Humans who settled there. She loved it and so did my Grandfather. Needless to say, Father was also a Dwarf and, looking at me, mother was another human.

I had two siblings, a brother ten years my senior named Eirik and a sister four years younger named Cassandra. My older brother was a troublemaker. He would regularly get in fights and would ram heads with Father. He was good to me though, always coming up with games or making toys for me. When he came of age, he left for the Capital and I never heard from him again. He would write letters that my Father would read and, after sending a response, he would always burn the letter. He always looked ashamed at what he had read."

"Did he ever write to you?" Niitty asked.

"Apart from a wedding gift and a gift for the birth of each of my two kids, he never contacted me," Gerold responded, "I don't even know how he knew since I had no way of contacting him. After my Father died, the letters stopped. I don't know why he didn't send anything beyond those gifts without so much as a return address. My Sister was different. She was a firebrand who wanted to help people. She didn't hesitate to join the Adventurer's Guild when she came of age. She had some excellent talents and ended up as a Spellblade."

"What are Spellblades like?" Gewa asked, her curiosity piqued.

"From what she told me," Gerold said, "It was a big risk. All their spells amplify their swordplay. She also said it took longer for her physical growth to manifest. As she grew more powerful, the effects became more useful. I'm not sure what she's like today. She returned home in her mid-20s to train for a few years in the local area with her party. They left to continue their growth and I would get letters from her over the years. At least until I got her last one about 15 years ago. She told me that she was going to explore beyond the borders of the Empire. As you can imagine, communication out there is near impossible. I don't even know if she's still alive."

He sighed, "That's something adventurers always risk. She

knew that and I know that so I haven't thought much of her. Until I find out otherwise, I assume she's still exploring the world."

"And I'm guessing you were different," Niitty said. From everything she knew of him, she didn't take him as someone interested in excitement.

He snorted, "That's an understatement. Until six months ago, I never even left my home village. I had no interest in adventuring. Taking over the farm was all I cared about. Both Cassandra and Dad were relieved. Cassandra since she wouldn't face the pressure of being the last in line to accept it and Dad for having someone willing to keep up the family trade. My life is nothing interesting to talk about. I quietly worked the farm with Dad. I didn't meet my wife, Zelina, until shortly after I got my last letter from Cassandra. A few years later, Dad died, a few months after that my son, Malrin, was born and eight years after that came Elli."

He went silent and Niitty noticed tears forming in his eyes. He seemed to be struggling to talk further.

"You don't have to do this," Niitty said as she started to reach across the table, pulling back when she remembered his earlier statements on unwanted contact.

Gerold wiped his face, "No, I need to. It was about six months ago. It was a normal day. My son and I were going to maintain the grounds while my wife went to collect eggs at the coop with my daughter. It was early autumn and our Town Seed was down until the winter. From spring through autumn there were almost always a couple of adventurer parties in town to keep the monster population down."

A tapping sound distracted Niitty that was coming from under the table. She looked down and saw his leg bouncing against the wood. Gerold noticed her looking and placed his hand on his knee to calm it, "That's when the howl came across the plain and the cloud erupted from the town. You experienced it for yourself, so I don't have to go into the details. All I was thinking of was getting my family to safety. My Grandmother was quite the engineer and had built a large stone cistern under the farm to collect water for the dry season. It was a sturdy structure that we used for shelter in case of tornadoes and had a thick door in case monsters managed to get onto the property."

Gerold took a few deep breaths to calm himself, "We barely made it in and I blocked the door. I thought we were safe. Then it felt like something was trying to rip my soul right out of my body. My soul then, for some reason, fought back against the unspeakable pain. The best I can explain it is it felt like a gold glow, for what that's worth. The last thing I heard before passing out was the screaming of my family."

He put his elbows on the table then buried his face in his hands. He was having a hard time with the story. Niitty decided not to fight her instincts this time and, instead of waiting, she moved to the chair next to him. She gently laid her hand on his shoulder and left it there. After a moment, Gerold reached his hand up and put it on hers. She was expecting him to push her away but, instead, he gently gripped it once before pulling his head up.

"Thanks," he said, "When I woke up, it was pitch black. The lantern had fallen over and gone out. Something disrupted the ambient mana enough to disable the light. I was able to get it lit again and I saw my family just standing there, quietly, between me and the exit. They were blankly staring down the tunnel toward the door. I wasn't sure what they were looking at and I called out to them. They all turned and they had a dead look in their eyes. I had no idea what was going on. They started to stiffly and strangely walk toward me. I knew something was wrong when my daughter hissed instead of crying and jumping in my arms."

He paused again before pressing on, "I went over to check what was wrong and that's when they gripped on and started to bite and scratch. I panicked and didn't know what was going on. They pressed me up toward the tool wall and I reached up and grabbed one. It was a pipe expander that I used to maintain the cistern piping. I lost my senses and the next thing I knew, I was hitting my wife, my kids, with the spiked end. Then they stopped moving. I was covered in their blood and I blacked out."

Another pause before he continued, "The next thing I knew I was wandering my farm, covered in blood, hearing shouts from someone. I looked up and saw a party of adventurers. They were out at the dungeon and saw the black clouds on the horizon. They had returned to investigate and were asking me what happened. The clouds had cleared by this point, so I have no idea how long I was wandering around the farm. I noticed I was holding repair equipment for the fence. All I could do was tell them what happened. Thankfully, they went into the cistern and retrieved my family and donated some of their Adventurer Coin for the rites. I was a mess and couldn't even talk."

"The town was a loss and I was the sole survivor," Gerold said through heavy sobs, "The entire area had started to spawn the undead and, luckily, there were four skilled parties in the area, one with a cleric, who were able to clear the undead and cleanse the village. They had no idea what caused the disaster. They only reported that the Town Seed had been shattered and strewn about the center of the village. The whole village was dead and couldn't be recovered. One of the parties, the one that discovered me, tried to get me to leave with them. I refused. Eventually, they all gave up and left but not after leaving me with a few mundane silver coins in case I needed them."

He stopped and listened, "Yes, I'm getting to that."

"Was that Erinne?" Niitty asked.

"Yes"

Niitty felt herself warm. "I'm glad you two made up."

"She said she's glad, too. A sentiment I share," Gerold said, "The day after the adventurers abandoned the town, I started hearing a voice in my head. At first, it was asking if I could hear it. I thought I was going mad. I spent a few days going about my day like nothing happened. I did my chores, checked the crops and even talked to my family's headstones. I'd set the table for four and say goodnight to empty beds. The voice kept speaking, telling me it was Erinne. I couldn't believe it was the Recluse Queen herself and I had completely lost my mind. It was insistent, saying it wanted me to be its Paladin. I felt like if I was mad that I might as well completely embrace it and agreed after a few days. It wasn't until I felt the link in my soul when I understood I wasn't crazy. I eventually traveled to the Capital at Erinne's behest since the Pantheon Temple trains Paladins, then here to investigate the necrotic mana after I finished."

Niitty didn't know how to respond. She knew it wasn't the same when she lost her father. She was young and had a support system to rely on. Gerold not only had to put down his own undead kids, he spent the last six months in a constant state of action with no one to help him. She noticed that Gewa was also struggling with something in her head. Gewa had previously indicated that he was not justified in his behavior. To Niitty, this all made sense and she couldn't blame him.

"However," Gerold said, startling Niitty, "None of this justifies my behavior. You had nothing to do with what happened nor were you being cruel or inconsiderate. I am sincerely sorry for this and I submit myself to whatever you deem appropriate recompense."

"I'm sorry, too," Niitty started. Gerold looked like he wanted to interrupt, forcing Niitty to press on, "I was so caught up in thinking I had made a friend that I didn't pay attention to your discomfort. I was being overly friendly and I promise that I'll change my behavior in the future."

"I appreciate the thought, but don't let that ruin who you are," Gerold said, "There's a lot of good about you and I don't want you to think you have to fundamentally change who you are. Instead, strive to be a better you."

"I'll try. What you went through? That's horrible. I've been a burden to you on top of what you went through," Niitty said, feeling a sense of shame building up in her.

"Don't do that to yourself," Gerold interrupted, "I failed to tell you any of this, so you can't hold yourself responsible. Besides, you've helped me."

"What? How?"

"People need a reason to live. I had lost mine and now, I think, I've found a new one. I'll probably still be a mess for a while. At least I have something to strive for again," Gerold replied.

Niitty scratched her chin, "I can accept that. Does this mean we can go back to how things were?"

Gerold shook his head, "No, I don't think that's possible.

Niitty felt her heart sink. After all he said about purpose, how could he not want things to go back? Was he getting ready to part ways? She felt her head drop, "Oh. I see. Thanks for at least telling me about all this."

"I didn't phrase that right," Niitty heard. She looked up and Gerold had a sheepish look on his face as he continued, "We can't go back, but we can move forward. We have to learn from that, grow and evolve our relationship."

Niitty felt herself smile. She could work with that.

"Now that's out of the way," Gewa broke in, "Do you think I can get some of that meat in your bag and then we can get out of here?"

Gerold slapped his forehead, "I took all the boar meat, didn't I?"

"You did, now hand it over. I can't stand this pottage stuff," Gewa waved her fingers with her palm up, indicating she wanted the meat deposited there.

He pulled out some meat and gave it to her. He also offered some to Niitty, who accepted it. It tasted good after that bland food from the night before and she didn't have to resort to stealing it from a house.

As she chewed, Gerold continued, "We need to take stock of what we have left."

He pulled out the meat and piled it on the table while Niitty and Gewa put their coins there as well. Nine coins and a week's worth of food sat on the table.

"We can make it work," Gewa said, "Maybe we can get lucky and find a boat down at the river to speed things up and get back to the Capital in a week. We can decide where to go from there or part ways."

Gerold stared at the items on the table and then poured out all the monster parts on the floor. He then pushed the food across the table along with five of the coins, keeping four for himself.

Niitty stared at his behavior, "What are you doing?"

He pointed at the pile, "That should be sufficient to get you back to the Capital and inform the Guild of what happened. You can convert the parts when you get there. I'm keeping four coins since I intend to go into the village to find out what happened."

"What?" Niitty jumped up from the chair, "That's crazy! There are thousands of undead in there."

"Seriously," added Gewa, "It's risky enough to get back with just the two of us."

Gerold looked like he was getting overwhelmed with talking. He was looking at the ceiling, "One at a time please. Erinne, you're not making me. I'm doing this because I have to find out what happened. It's the second event that I know about and I need to know why it happened. Maybe that can help prevent another event."

He looked back down from the ceiling, "And you two don't have to follow me. I can't ask you to take on that risk."

Gerold stood up and walked to the door to exit the house.

"You're leaving now," Gewa asked.

"Yes. I don't have much time before the zombies loosen up and become more dangerous," Gerold said as he gripped the door latch.

Gewa darted over and held the door shut. "That's nuts! You can't do that! We need to get back to the Capital to report this."

Gerold's knuckles went white as he gripped the latch, "And then what? By the time we get there, get help and come back, a whole month will have passed. Adventurers showed up a few days after what happened to my home and no one found any clues."

Niitty stood up and went over, putting her hand on his shoulder, "Please, hold on a moment."

"I said I need to go now," he said.

"I know," Niitty told him, "We need to have a plan."

Gewa let out a frustrated groan, "We? You intend to go as well?"

Niitty felt herself flush, "Yes. I owe Gerold for saving me many times over."

"Don't do that," Gerold groaned. "Please don't think of life like a transaction. You don't owe me anything."

"Then I'm doing this for myself!" Niitty barked back with more energy than she thought she had. "Besides, if I can't help a friend now, what use am I to my people if I return?"

Gerold nodded, "As long as it's your decision, who am I to tell you otherwise?"

Gewa sighed, "I guess I'll come along, too. What's the plan?"

Niitty looked over, "What changed your mind?"

"My options are to travel alone with rising banditry on the road or come with you," she said. "Sticking with you two, as crazy as your intentions are, is the safer choice."

"You could always stay here and wait for us to come back," Gerold said.

"And if you die in there," Gewa scolded, "I'll be in the same situation. You could use a third set of eyes to help keep you alive."

Niitty felt relieved Gewa was coming along. No one present was experienced at this and more hands should lighten the load. She also felt awful for putting her in a terrible position, one where she had to choose between an intense risk of death or a slightly less intense risk of death.

Gerold shared her thoughts, "I'm sorry I'm forcing you two into this. I can't let this one go."

Gewa shrugged, "That's life. It throws bad options at you and asks you to pick. Now, what's the plan?"

CHAPTER 25

Gerold wasn't comfortable with the decision by Niitty and Gewa to follow him into the town. He appreciated the sentiment and, more importantly, the backup. He felt like he was forcing them to take this path by refusing to leave. Gewa, in particular, was a big risk since she didn't have a viable weapon to fight against the undead and they were limited to their nine remaining coins.

He suggested navigating the town via the tightly packed rooftops via the barrels he saw against the stables. Gewa agreed with this plan and said she could guide them. Apparently she had spent nights scouting the town, a habit she had picked up from her thieving upbringing, which Gerold was surprised to hear about after a brief explanation of her past for his benefit. Gerold had to quell her fears he would turn her in to the authorities. As far as he was concerned, she had a questionable upbringing and she was attempting to be a better person. He also didn't feel compelled to uphold any laws. Besides, he felt no evil coming from her, though she insisted she still isn't all that good either.

After scooping up the coins and divvying out three to each of them, he decided to leave the monster parts and food at the farmhouse. He couldn't risk keeping them in his bag if something happened to him and it was unlikely anyone would stumble by to steal them. Then they headed out toward town.

As the trio approached the gates, Gerold took note of the guards. The two were still dressed in their standard issue armor and helmets, their spears fallen to the ground. He couldn't imagine how hard these things would be to kill if they had the wherewithal to carry and use weaponry. Their appearance was eerie in the dim light under the thick cloud cover. They swayed slightly and stared off into the distance, barely distinguishable from well-trained town guards. Had it not been for the fact that a number of people visible on the other side of the gate also stood completely still, nothing would feel wrong.

Gerold marveled at the power of whatever it was that caused the effect. The townspeople were killed and converted into the undead at such an alarming rate that most of them didn't even have time to fall over. They died on the spot and remained standing as the undead. He had hoped that they were at least spared from the intense pain that he felt boring into him the day before.

The dark clouds pressed down on them hard. Gerold struggled to tell the time of day without the sun. All he could tell is it wasn't night since they could still see through the dense gloom. The clouds hung so low that they felt like they were going to come down and crush them in a dark black fog. Nothing moved, even the ever present breeze that Gerold experienced since arriving had ceased. The day refused to warm as the trio shivered and expelled visible clouds of breath.

As they approached the town gate, Gerold noticed the dilapidated state of the palisade. It had only been a day and it looked like the town was abandoned for months. The wood looked dried out and was cracking while dried weeds popped up out from under the road. One of the two large doors that protected the entry into the town was starting to rip out of the rotting frame, threatening to collapse and crush one of the zombie guards in the process.

"What's going on," Niitty whispered as she looked at the gate in the distance.

"I don't know," Gerold replied, just as confused as she was.

"This is bad," Erinne echoed in his head, "Whatever caused this was so intense that it not only corrupted the ambient mana in the area, it is accelerating decay. Objects in the area are aging at a rapid pace. Worse, I think it's turning into a large outdoor dungeon and it will begin to spawn undead soon."

"Will this have an impact on us?" Gerold asked.

"Not for the time being. I'm seeing indications that it's getting thicker toward the center of town. You will be fine, but I fear your companions can't spend long in there," Erinne said.

"I felt a new power come to me, a Protection from Necrosis. That could help," Gerold suggested.

Erinne hummed a negative, "Not a good idea. Like Calm Nerves, Protection from Necrosis will light a beacon on you. It will attract the undead within twenty yards of your location."

He relayed the other end of the conversation to his companions. They couldn't dally when they arrived at the epicenter, or they would risk too much exposure to necrotic energy or attracting a mob of the undead. Worse, the undead would be loosening up later in the day and grow faster and stronger as a result.

Gerold groaned at his options. They had to move fast. As they got closer, the two guards took notice of them and began to shamble in their direction. While still stiff, they were already moving with greater speed and coordination than the farmers from earlier.

"I'm going to draw them off," Gerold said, "I'm going to move into town a ways and get as many to follow me as possible. You two jump up on the roof of the stables."

Niitty tried to argue him down, "Are you sure about this? I'm faster and I'm a better climber."

"I'm the one with the emergency spell," Gerold rebutted, "If you get surrounded, you're done. I can still use my turn spell."

Gerold didn't wait for her response and took off at a light jog. He pulled his hammer and smacked the guards as he passed into town. When he crossed into town, he dropped the hammer's head down to the cobblestones and dragged the metal as he ran, the squeal of metal on stone broke the silence in the plaza. He ran a way into town, swerving to get the attention of the deceased townspeople near the entrance. He was thankful for his experience dragging goblins in the forest since it helped him maneuver the zombies into a chain.

Gerold took a quick peek down the street, finding his view of the main square blocked. All he could see through the dead clogging the street was that the previously ever present blue orb was gone. He would have to climb the buildings to get a better view.

Turning back, he saw Gewa and Niitty dart into the town behind the zombies and began to climb up the side of the stables up a barrel placed against the wall in front of an open window. Niitty bounded up with ease, a wall posing little challenge compared to scaling trees.

Gewa struggled with the climb. She extended her claws and dug into the roof of the stables, the now rotting wood making it hard to gain purchase. Niitty reached down to help her up when a different pair of arms emerged from the window and grabbed Gewa by the ankles.

Niitty squatted down for greater leverage to fight against the hidden foe trying to pull Gewa down. Worse, as Gerold trained the zombies around in a circle on the way back to the stables, Niitty started to slip as the roofing tiles began to separate from the structure. She was losing the fight with the monster as she moved closer to the edge, threatening to fall off.

Gerold accelerated into a sprint. Noticing he lacked a good angle to remove the hands from Gewa's ankles from outside, he moved into the stables proper. A foul odor assaulted his nose when he entered. Turning toward the window, he saw the young stable hand he had tipped days prior trying to chew through the thick leather boots on Gewa's feet.

He ran over and, after taking a solid stance, swung his hammer hard down on the head of the stable boy. He crushed the head like a rotten melon, his newly enhanced strength apparent when the follow-through of his fully powered strike terminated in the torso.

The released grip, along with Gerold's assistance, helped Gewa reach the roof. Turning to exit, Gerold found his escape route cut off. The zombies he distracted had followed him into the stables. He turned and saw that there were no other obvious exits and he didn't want to risk running deeper into the building in hopes of finding a new one. The windows, similarly, proved a poor exit since they were too small for him to quickly squeeze through before the mob caught up to him.

Turning, he saw the stalls where the horses were kept. There was a solid wood gate separating the walkway from the inner compartment. Gerold dove over the gate into a stall, hoping the thick wood designed to hold in a powerful animal would be sufficient, even in a decaying state, to hold back the mob.

Gerold landed in something sticky and, turning, he had fallen into the body of a dead horse, its flesh rapidly decaying in the unnaturally dense necrotic mana. He saw it was the old nag he had ridden into town on. Giving a silent apology, he stood up and, for the first time in memory, he was truly thankful for his Paladin's gift of cleanliness. He couldn't imagine walking around covered in the rotting gore.

The mass of bodies piled up against the gate and, apart from the sound of cloth brushing against the beams as the arms reached through, it was completely silent. The zombies' limbs shoved through the openings of the gate like a forest of grasping trees as they tried to push their way through the barrier.

Keeping his distance, Gerold observed his mini prison. Floor to ceiling walls separated the stall from its neighbors and the back wall had no openings. There wasn't much room for him to stand between the horse's caved-in body that, now it was smashed open, was expelling a horrid stench of decay into the air. Worse, the gate swung inward, designed to keep horses from smashing out, not keeping things from getting in. The latch was already showing strains. The bolts holding it into the frame were pulling out as the bodies pressed and shook the structure.

Gerold heard a quiet voice whisper over the sound of rattling wood, "Hey, over here."

He looked around and saw Niitty's head upside down looking through a window across the way. She waved and said quietly to avoid attracting attention, "There's a small gap on the other side of that wall. Do you think you can break through?"

Gerold decided to be a bit louder to keep the attention on himself, "I'll try."

She waved and rose back up out of sight.

Turning, Gerold gripped his hammer and flipped it around to the spiked side. He never expected to use a weapon of war like a carpenter's tool. Drawing on his farm maintenance experience, he took a quick look at how the boards fit together. Finding a knot in one of the boards that had left a small gap, he aimed and swung. The spike bounced off the wall and scraped through the outer rotting layer, revealing still hard wood beneath the immediate surface.

Gerold realized he would have to stand in the corpse of the horse to get proper leverage to break down the wall. Putting one foot into the smashed in cavity, he swung again. This time the spike lodged itself between the boards. He heard a crack from behind. Refusing to waste time looking, knowing it was the latch giving out, he levered the board back and forth. The board pulled free after a few moments of pulling as it split in two and into the room. Removing this board made it easier to pound out a few more now that they no longer had a neighbor for support.

A louder crash caused him to turn and he saw that the latch had finally pulled from the frame with the gate swinging open from the force of the bodies shoving the gate open. He pondered using one of his coins to deal with the oncoming throng. However, the bodies had collapsed onto the ground into a pile and gave him a few extra seconds to react and save on wasting a coin. While the zombies fought to stand as their compatriots were attempting to climb over them, Gerold squeezed himself through the gap. He had forgotten to wear his hauberk, making the process easier. When he was mostly free, he felt a hand grip one of his boots. Thankfully, a kick with his other foot managed to free the hand and, after he passed the leverage point, he allowed himself to fall backwards out of the hole.

Gerold found himself in a small gap between the wings of the stables. He looked to one side and saw it terminated in a dead end and the other led to a small alleyway that would only return him back to the main street or, in the other direction, an unknown path.

"Up here."

Gerold looked up and saw Niitty and Gewa. They had

dropped to their stomachs to reach down to help Gerold climb up. He looked at the wall and saw a zombie reaching through, trying to get to him. He hung his hammer on his belt and pulled out his dagger. He reached in and grabbed the zombie by the shirt collar and pulled it partly through the hole then punched it through its head. Happy with his makeshift plug, he jumped up and grabbed his companions' hands by the wrist. Using the zombie as extra leverage, he managed to pull himself up to the roof with their help.

"That was fun," Gewa said after Gerold rolled onto the sloped surface.

Gerold could only grunt in affirmation. He stood up, walked up to the crest of the roof and looked out over the town. Now that he had a moment, the weight of what happened sunk into him. Men, women and even children that hadn't joined the throng currently trying to push its way into the stables quietly stood around, staring off into space. A once lively town that had been, in a moment, desecrated into this abomination that filled Gerold's sight.

Gerold felt sadness as he looked over the street below. Instead of a crippling depression, he felt instead a sense of drive and purpose. He couldn't let this happen again. Turning and feeling the spring in the roof, he knew they had to move. The rot was undermining their plan to navigate the rooftops.

"Let's get moving," Gerold said.

Gewa nodded and started to move toward the palisade to the east. Gerold was taken aback, "Where are you going? The center is due west of here."

"Two reasons," Gewa said as she prepared to jump across the gap Gerold had just climbed up from, "First, the buildings down the main lane have rooflines that are too steep to climb, so we'll have to circle around. The palisade has an elevated walkway around the city and we can make better time walking that instead of jumping around. Second, I've realized we are horribly underequipped for this and we need to make a stop."

"That makes sense," Gerold replied, "The decay is happening too fast for my liking and a solid walkway will improve our time."

The three jogged along the walkway along the edge of the town. The residential areas they passed were, thankfully, mostly empty. The population had been working or shopping along the main central artery when the disaster happened. Gerold took the lead on the run and body checked a couple of undead guards off the walkway to the ground below.

Gewa indicated a point about two thirds of the way around the perimeter to the north. The area was wealthier than the east end of the city where residences with flat, rooftop patios were situated. The buildings were still tightly packed, making it easy to traverse. The stone didn't rot like the wooden buildings though they were weather aged and had dead vines growing up the sides.

Jumping from the walkway to the first building was jarring. He noticed that both Gewa and Niitty bent their knees and rolled with the fall. The rooftop patios showed an opulence that, despite being in good condition a day before, looked like they had rotted in the sun despite the dark cloud cover. Dry rotted cloth seats decorated the patios and flower beds featured brown flowers that would easily snap if touched.

They easily avoided a few zombies that were caught on rooftops and made their way back toward the town center along the rooftops. They approached a three storey wooden building across an alleyway after jumping along the rooftops for a few minutes. Gerold recognized it as the back end of McVatter's General Store. They were level with a balcony leading into a second floor door.

Gerold made sure to jump first. He leapt over the railing and clipped it with his foot, breaking the rotting wood as he passed. The balcony also lurched to a steep angle as he landed, forcing Gerold to grab at the door. The door refused to open with his push, the lock holding it firmly shut.

Gripping at the windowsill next to the door, he steadied himself and smashed the handle, throwing the latch into the room beyond. He put up a hand to his companions to ensure they didn't jump immediately and went inside. He was in a sitting room with a fireplace and bookshelves. It was empty and he motioned his group to carefully jump over.

When in, Gewa immediately started to search the room, pulling open drawers, knocking sun bleached portraits off the wall and pulling moldy books off the shelves. Gerold felt uncomfortable with her searching a man's house, dead and decaying or not.

She opened a box she found on the bookshelf with her dagger and looked inside. She upended the box on the musky desk and five silver coins poured out. She picked one up and frowned. Gerold looked as well. Instead of the telltale mystic marking that was unique to each person, a mechanism that ensured no counterfeits could be passed, each was stamped with the Imperial seal. They were normal silver coins. Gewa swept them into her pouch.

"What are you doing," Niitty demanded with a harsh whisper when she saw Gewa pocket the coins.

"What?" Gewa asked, confused.

"Those coins. You just stole them," Niitty accused.

"This town is dead and that's what you're worried about?" Gewa whispered back in an equally testy tone.

"I could say the same thing," Niitty retorted and pointed at

Gerold. "Besides, you just stole in front of a Paladin."

Gewa's eyes went wide and looked over at Gerold. She looked terrified, but Gerold felt nothing at her actions.

"I'm not feeling any impulse," Gerold said. "Erinne? Why is that?"

"Hm? Why is what, I was monitoring the energy in the town," Erinne replied after a brief delay.

"These two think I should feel compelled to apprehend a thief," Gerold said.

"Oh, that. While you may feel compulsion to uphold laws, those are higher laws. Mortal laws don't concern Gods very much," Erinne started, "Part of that reputation, I hear from the others, is because the Gods want to ensure the best representation they can muster and don't select everyone with a compatible soul. They prefer to take righteous candidates. Any distaste you feel is your own personality. We don't override free will, just sort of nudge your emotions. We don't use that for mundane things, except the lying thing. That's a strange effect of the divine touch."

He relayed the words to his companions, "In any case, let's not take anything we absolutely don't need for survival. Mundane coins are useless for us."

Gewa shifted in thought, causing the coins to clink. She sucked in air. "Damn, I forgot about that. My Mother got caught once because she forgot to wrap the coins she pocketed."

Gewa ended up putting the coins back into the box and leaving it to avoid excess noise. The party exited the room after finding nothing immediately useful with most items rotted or molded beyond use. Gewa offered to sneak up to the third floor of the building while Niitty went down since Gerold lacked the grace to move silently.

As the two scouted, he moved across the hall over a molding lush red carpet toward a landing overlooking the town. The glass had fogged over with some sort of white film, blocking the view outside. He went over intending to see if he could scratch some of it off to see out. When he approached the window, his Detect Evil aura screamed at him. At the extreme edge of the aura he felt two large evil auras, a second larger one and a fourth monstrous one. The fourth one was so immense that it made his legs weak.

"Erinne," he whispered through pained breaths, "I'm picking up something awful. I thought this aura only pointed out direction and how evil something was, not its power."

"It upgraded, you should be able to get a general idea of how powerful something is if it's evil," Erinne replied, "What's wrong? Why are you kneeling?"

"Something at the edge of my aura is so immense that I'm terrified. With it are two that feel slightly more powerful than me and a third that's more powerful than those two. It's the last one," Gerold gasped, struggling to get the words out.

"I can't tell what it is," Erinne replied gravely, "All I can tell from up here is that a giant mass of necrotic mana is covering the Town Seed's former border. Be careful and I'm telling you to retreat if it's beyond your ability. Don't fight it on my behalf. I'm not fool to throw you away on a suicide mission."

Gerold shuddered as he regained his wits, backing up a bit to get that evil force out of his aura's range, "You have no argument from me."

"What's wrong," he heard Niitty behind him. Turning, he saw her in a crouch as well, with Gewa coming in behind her soon after.

"Upper floor's clear," Gewa said, "The balcony there is more stable and it has a ladder to the roof. As long as we don't jump on it, it should be fine."

"Thanks," Gerold said, "Change of plans. I just felt an aura from something so powerful it would easily kill us. I'm not going to risk you two to investigate the Town Seed."

"We went over this," Niitty whispered in an argumentative tone, "I'm not letting you go in alone."

"You didn't let me finish," Gerold said, "I'm not going in either. We'll go up on that roof and see what we can see in the distance and then sneak back out as fast as possible. Going in there will be lethal. Whatever that is must be what caused this."

Gewa smiled, "Finally, sensible words."

"Before we go, how is the first floor looking," Gerold asked, "We will still need support for our journey back."

"The shopkeeper and two customers are down there. One customer is looking in the direction of the opening into the room while the other two have their backs turned. All the windows look like this one. I can't tell the condition of the wares," Niitty replied.

"Does this side have a way to hid on the other side of the door," Gerold asked.

"No, it leads immediately into the stairwell."

Gerold drew his hammer, "Then we make a bit of noise and draw them up. We can use the stairs as a chokepoint. Back me up in case this goes bad."

Gerold went over to the top of the stairs while Niitty pulled her rapier and positioned herself against the railing looking down the stairwell. Gewa backed away to the room leading to the collapsed balcony. Looking over at Niitty, Gerold nodded.

Niitty returned the nod to indicate she's ready.

He began banging his hammer on the stairs. He didn't want to shout in case anything outside the building could hear but loud enough to attract the monsters below. Through the door stepped the first zombie, the owner, Mr. McVatter. Gerold barely interacted with the portly, balding man he had bought the provisions from the week prior. He frowned internally at what he had to do, finding it harder to put down a zombie of someone he had known in passing as opposed to a total stranger.

The zombies were moving even faster now as the three came through the door one after the next. They struggled to navigate the stairs through the rapid decay, their feet punching through the wood between the supports. Gerold swung downward hard and smashed the proprietor's head in while Niitty reached over behind the stalled zombie and stabbed the second through the top of the head. Both bodies immediately collapsed and rolled down the stairs, bowling the final one over. Gerold walked down the stairs to finish off the last one that had been pinned under the bodies of the other two.

Gewa came and helped drag the three corpses out of the doorway. Gerold looked down and felt like he should provide rites, but the critical lack of coins made that impossible. They would have to be left to decay in the necrotic mana.

The main storefront looked terrible. Goods on the shelf looked to have rotted or otherwise gone bad. Gewa opened the cash box under the counter and, apart from normal coins, found nothing. The one that looked like an Adventurer should have had some Adventurer Coins on her since she was in the shop.

"This is strange," Gerold said out loud, "Where are all the Adventurer Coins?"

"That means the area has become a dungeon," Erinne said in his head. "It took the coins to fuel itself as a source of easy mana to access."

Gerold huffed in frustration as he relayed this to his party. At least the coins on his body would be safe since their natural life force would resist attempts to take their remaining coins. The risk of continued exposure to necrotic mana on their health, on the other hand, continued to weigh on Gerold's mind, in addition to the massive evil force he was able to sense again at the edges of his aura.

Other items in the shop were similarly decaying. He checked the barrel of travel rations, which he thought should have resisted the rot due to its preserved nature. He found a few that were still in good shape, though most had started to show signs of mold. He was able to salvage four days worth for the group, which he stuffed in his bag.

Gewa was looking over the limited selection of weaponry a shop like this would carry. The general store was more geared toward farming needs, with tools, nails and other gear for the local community. Adventurers were an afterthought since the local monster population wasn't lucrative enough to specialize. Plus, the adventurers coming through here were new and didn't need powerful equipment.

Most of the equipment had molded and decayed beyond use. The cheap iron short swords were pitted with rust, the leather armor had cracked from a lack of oil and the wooden hafts on the spears had dry rotted and splintered. Gewa was able to find a well crafted short spear that had a lacquered shaft and a steel tip, two materials that held up well to age. She also handed Gerold a small steel shield, a buckler he recalled it was called, which was barely larger than his hand. While it was not an impressive device, it was better than having bare hands. On the inside of the buckler were four metal brackets sized to fit

Adventurer Coins.

Niitty, who looked uncomfortable looting the store, dug through a box with arrows lined in it. Every one she pulled up had rotted feathers with most of the cheap iron tips having rusted or the wooden hafts were too decayed for use. She found a similar result when reviewing the limited armor selection to replace her damaged chest piece.

Gerold checked out the clothing and like everything else it was unusable. Not only were they sized incorrectly, the cloth was brittle and snapped at the touch. It was wishful thinking to see if they could replace their shoddy attire. Gerold's clothing was a mess of holes and old bloodstains while Niitty's attire was down to a leather chest piece with a large hole in the back as most of her clothing had been torn to provide bandages for Gerold's injuries. The only one in relatively good shape was Gewa, who had abandoned the remains of her robe at some point in the last day.

Still, something rubbed Gerold wrong about taking the materials from the store. He knew they would rot away to nothing and, eventually, the mundane coins would be a prize to some future adventuring party. Opening his bag, he reached in and pulled out his silver mirror. He took one more look at his flawless face and decided that he wouldn't need the object anymore. His new appearance was only the skin he wore, not the person he was. He would keep the disguise kit, which would still be useful even though he lost the wigs.

He looked over at Gewa, "Gewa? Can you get those coins you found earlier in the reading room?"

"Change of heart?" she whispered back.

Gerold laid his mirror on the main counter and took three dozen copper and four silver coins from the change box, "No, just a fair trade."

Gewa rolled her eyes in response.

They would have to make do with what they had. Realizing there was nothing left of value in the place, the trio head back upstairs to the third floor and up to the roof. Crouching low to minimize visibility, they crawled to the peak to look over.

Once again, Gerold was finding himself thankful for his new abilities. In the plaza 120 yards out he saw the remnants of the Town Seed. The marble pillar, cracked with dead vines weaving through the structure, stood with a dull blue crown of jagged glass. Littered around the plaza were multitudes of the same blue jagged glass in different sizes and shapes.

The buildings ringing the plaza showed a more accelerated state of decay from the rest of the town. The higher concentration of the necrotic mana originating from the central point had made the buildings there look even worse. The Guild Hall looked like a stiff breeze would knock it over.

The four evil pulses at the edge of his aura were present along with the dozens of weak signals originating from the 30 or so zombies milling about the plaza. It wasn't too hard to identify the source of the evil.

In the distance, standing next to the remains of the Town Seed, were four figures. Two of them stood in a hunched, feral stance and flanked a short figure with his back turned to him was wearing clothing that looked like formal wear. The two flanking figures wore remnants of some sort of clothing, but they were rotted so badly that the figures were near nude. From his vantage, Gerold saw that their skin looked like baked leather with a color similar to the armor worn by Niitty.

In front of the three was a figure in a hooded cloak. Gerold instinctively knew it was the source of the intense evil aura. The face was obscured in the gloom under the hood and its stark white arms with taut skin were clearly visible from the sleeves of the robe. The arms had places where the flesh had fallen off and bleached white bone was visible beneath. Thin white legs came out from under the robe and ended in bare human feet. It moved with an unnatural grace that conflicted with the jerky movements of fresh undead.

The shorter figure was moving its arms in an animated fashion, like it was talking to the hooded figure, its words lost over the distance.

He whispered, "Can either of you make out what they're saying?"

"I can barely hear them," Niitty said as she cupped her hand behind her long pointed ear to improve her senses.

She listened for a moment, "The hooded figure is saying it's time to deliver the artifact to the Master. The smaller one is demanding a reward. The hooded one just told it to not make demands of their Master"

Erinne came into Gerold's head, "Something is going on between the small one and the hooded one. There's a swirl of necrotic mana like a whirlpool. From here, it looks like the energy is drawing into a spot between them."

Niitty frowned, "The small one says there are unwanted visitors. I think we need to leave."

The smaller figure turned around and looked directly at their building. All three gasped when his face came into view, showing Philip, the local Guild Master. In his hand was a black cube that Gerold estimated was six inches a side.

"The necrotic energy is flowing into that box," Erinne informed Gerold, "Hold on, something is happening."

Philip ran a finger across the surface of the box and turned it over. He then held it aloft over his head. Gerold wondered what was going on. He noticed that the ground around him began to crack and decay at an accelerated pace that radiated out from him in every direction.

"Activate your Protection from Necrosis Aura now," Erinne shouted in a panic.

Gerold did so and almost immediately after his new aura was erected, he felt a wall of energy crash into him. The aura held and he felt the energy wash over and around the sphere it formed over him, his companions and the building. The neighboring buildings, one the stone bathhouse, rapidly decayed. He heard a cracking sound and the rush of water as part of the bathhouse gave way, spilling its contents into the open. The wooden building to the other side collapsed in on itself as the support structures rotted beyond their ability to hold up the mass. His aura had not only protected his companions, it also protected the building beneath them from falling in on itself.

A similar cacophony of noise erupted around the perimeter of the plaza as the invisible energy washed over the area. The stone pillars ringing the Pantheon Temple broke away from the structure and fell, some of them landing on the next door town hall, smashing through the roof and folding the building in on itself. The Guild Hall's top floor gave out and fell into the next one down, causing a cascade failure where the structure imploded down to the bottom floor like a sinkhole had opened up beneath it. The wood was so rotten at this point that it didn't even spray debris outward.

Worse, the zombies milling about the plaza also underwent rapid decay. Hair fell out of skulls, eyes rotted and turned white while skin peeled away to reveal putrefying muscle mass and bone beneath. He also noticed the bodies began to move in a more fluid manner. They were no longer the weak, newly minted undead. There were now 30 zombies at their most dangerous in addition to the four distant figures.

Then, just as quickly as the energy washed over them, it came to an abrupt stop. Gerold looked across the plaza and saw the hooded figure with its hand clamped over the box with Philip looking up in terror.

"What just happened?" Niitty asked. "He held that box up and everything started to collapse. Now that hooded guy is telling Philip that the Master would be displeased to waste his energy on small fry."

"I don't know," Gerold responded, "Erinne told me to erect a protection aura and then I felt corruption slam into it."

"That box is the source of the energy," Erinne said, "Philip was it? He released a massive concentration of necrotic mana. That's the pulse. It's that box. Now it's absorbing energy again."

Gerold relayed this information for his companions' benefit.

"That looks like an artifact," Gewa said, "How did it collect that kind of energy?"

"I have no idea," Erinne relayed through Gerold, "That would take at least a Mythril coin to fuel or a ritual lasting hundreds of years."

Gerold thought for a moment and the image of the corpse of Wren they found in the crypt, particularly the gap under the mummified hands that looked like it held something. He asked out loud, "What would happen if you left an artifact to absorb necrotic energy on a corpse for thousands of years?"

Gewa and Erinne simultaneously let out a shocked, "No."

"Are you saying," Erinne began, "You think that thing was intentionally left to absorb necrotic energy for thousands of years?"

Gerold nodded, "Yes. It makes sense. What better place to hide an ancient corpse but at the far end of the empire deep in an impassible mountain range? The corpse looked like it was holding something that was removed when we looked at it and it showed no signs of absorbing energy and turning into the undead. That artifact was intercepting the energy and storing it."

"Why would anyone set that up," Gewa asked.

Gerold was about to indicate he had no idea why when Niitty interrupted them, "That hooded guy finished admonishing the Guild Master. He says he's going to deliver the artifact now."

Gerold looked over and watched as the hooded figure slid the artifact inside its cloak. He heard a sickening crack of bone as the thing's knees bent backwards and the figure dropped down onto all four limbs like an animal. Then, with terrifying speed, it sprinted East down the main road out of town, disappearing behind the buildings that were spared the rapid rot.

No one had any time to ponder what just happened when a voice shouted over the plaza, "I know you're there, Paladin. I can sense the stink of good flowing from you. When I saw that idiot noble's token show up at the Guild Hall, I was expecting yours to follow soon after. You surprised me that you not only survived, you also saved that Leopardia woman."

Philip snapped his fingers and the zombies in the plaza converged on the general store, the two figures flanking him remaining at his side, "And what's this? I smell another stench of virtue coming from up on that roof. That must be the damned Mountain Elf. I see you've gotten over your fear of towns, not that it will do you any good. Where's the Leopardia? I don't sense her anywhere, she must have left. That was a wise decision."

Gerold frowned and looked over at Gewa. She shrugged and whispered, "I told you I wasn't good."

Peeking back over, he saw Philip point toward his building.

The zombies responded by running toward the entrance and they disappeared from view beneath the roofline, "I suggest you come out. You've clearly gained power to resist the wave of decay. We can have a chat or you can stay up there and die of exposure. I have a thousand more of these townspeople shambling our way as I speak."

Gerold shouted, "We'll come out. Give us a moment to climb down."

He slid back below the roof and turned to his companions, "This is bad. When I had my Sense Evil aura up, I caught an idea of Philip's power. He's extremely dangerous. Worse, those two figures down by the Town Seed are more powerful than he is. Now we have thirty fully fledged zombies down there."

"I think Gewa should get out of here," Niitty added, "It doesn't make sense for you to die, too, and Philip isn't aware you're here."

Gerold looked over at Gewa who was removing her boots, revealing her padded cat paws from within. She stretched her toes out and flexed them once they were free from the confines of the footwear.

"What are you doing," Gerold whispered.

"I think it's time to earn your trust," Gewa whispered back. She shoved the boots at Gerold, "Can you store those in your bag? They're nice and I don't want them to decay out here."

"You don't have to stay. You'll need these boots for the road," Gerold retorted.

"Remember what I said before? My chances of survival are higher if I stay here with you than try and travel the road alone," Gewa replied, "Do you think you can keep them occupied while I swing around behind?"

"If you don't mind," Niitty said, "I have a new ability but I'll need five copper coins to activate it. It improves my agility for a minute and I think I'll need it."

Gewa slid her three coins over to Niitty, but Niitty only took two, "Keep one in case. My single coin abilities are useless here and we only have nine coins between us."

"Are you sure you want to do this?" Gerold asked.

"If they're as dangerous you say they are, you'll need all the help you can get," Gewa said, adjusting her spear in preparation to move.

Gerold couldn't argue with that logic.

"Hey," Gewa said, "You can sense evil, right? Why didn't you notice him earlier?"

Gerold thought on it a moment, "I never had my aura turned on in town. In the Capital, it constantly triggered evil and I couldn't tell where or who it was. It was distracting so I deactivated it and kept it deactivated in town." Gerold privately endeavored to keep it on, just in case he ran into situations like this in the future. Advanced warning was worth the irritation.

Gewa wished the two good fortunes as they parted ways. Gerold knew they couldn't delay this further. He and Niitty gingerly descended the rickety ladder back to the third floor balcony and then headed down to the bottom floor.

CHAPTER 26

Before Gerold exited the shop, he made sure to slot his coins into his buckler. Niitty slipped hers into a glove and they wielded their weapons and exited. Philip arranged the thirty zombie townspeople like an honor guard to mock them. The dead formed a path leading toward the Town Seed. The odor of their rotting flesh now apparent as they sloshed through the mud that formed from the water pouring out of the collapsed bathhouse wall.

When Gerold and Niitty reached the midpoint of the two zombie columns, all thirty turned in tandem and marched in step with them as they moved toward Philip and the two mysterious forms. Looking around, Gerold noticed the plaza was starting to fill in with more of the less decayed zombies that filtered in from the side streets.

Their boots crunched on shards of the dull blue glass as they otherwise silently traversed the distance. At twenty yards out, the zombies fanned out and created a circle around the remains of the Town Seed. Standing before it like the Emperor himself was Philip, back turned to Gerold with his hands clasped. The two figures stood like a protective detail at his flanks.

They stood there silently for a while. Gerold was beginning to lose patience, "Why have you asked us to come out here?"

Philip put up a hand, "Hush. Do you hear that?"

Gerold listened and heard nothing, "No."

"That's the point," Philip said as he turned, a smile plastered on his face, "It's glorious."

Gerold stared at him blankly, "I don't get it. You killed everyone because you thought it was too noisy?"

Philip groaned, "No you buffoon. I gave them all purpose. The silence is proof of that deed."

Gerold felt himself trying to compress his hammer's handle, "I still don't understand."

Philip dramatically waved his hand across the plaza, "All of this was pointless. Every young adventurer collecting meager coin in the woods and villagers performing simple tasks impeded greater things. They refused to deploy their lives to a greater purpose. My Master gave me a great privilege to finally give these lives meaning."

"What's that purpose," Gerold said as he took a step forward, but he stopped when Philip held up a silver coin between his fingers and pointed at Niitty.

"Nice try. I'm not some storybook minion that will tell you the plans of my Master," Philip scolded.

"Then why are you doing this," Gerold asked, "What do you want from us?"

"Oh," Philip started, "I figure I owe you this much. After I sent you after that Duke's son, I expected you to die in that crypt. If the trap didn't get you, then the Lampreyer definitely would. Then you didn't come back to town. You must have survived some kind of ordeal."

Gerold smelled the lie, "I don't buy that."

Philip snorted, "Fine, I wanted to gloat. I did send you out to die but I am glad you didn't. I couldn't have you here in town to potentially interfere with my plans, but what's the point of victory if no one is around to see it?"

"What made you this way," Niitty pointed her rapier at Philip for emphasis.

He laughed, "What? Were you expecting some sad story? I have ambitions. I was stuck in this dead end post babysitting ignorant children. When I was approached by the Master, I was elated. In exchange for ensuring the failure of the Town Seed, I was made a Necromancer. It was surprisingly easy. I would leak the caravan schedules to ensure the subsidy money was stolen and a few compatriots up the chain made sure the budget for the town was cut. Then I made sure to eliminate courses to reduce adventurer efficiency."

Philip wagged the finger on his other hand at Gerold, "Then you came along. A Paladin showing up was a wrinkle in the plan as were those herders stumbling upon the crypt. It turned out fortuitous. You gladly wasted even more of the town's resources for payment and I was able to draw you away. I'm quite proud of my financial management. This coin in my hand and one more in my pouch are the last ones in Wren's End, save for whatever it is you have on your person. It was timed flawlessly."

His smile turned sinister, "Now I have the bonus of killing a Paladin. I can't stand your type. The one that came by here long ago was smug and arrogant. Everyone loved him but I knew the reality. He existed purely to stoke his God's ego. The way you walk through the mud like it's no more an inconvenience than air disgusts me. I'll be a legend when I kill you and raise your corpse as my minion. Then that pretty face will finally look like how you really are underneath."

His outstretched hand with the coin in it pointed at Gerold. He watched as the coin dissolved itself and Philip moved his mouth in a silent incantation. Distorted air, like heat rising off rock in the summer, erupted out of his finger in a thin ray. It hit

Gerold's protection aura and most of it, like the earlier pulse, dispersed along the edges. However, while his aura worked well against a wide effect like the pulse, it couldn't handle a concentrated drill and some of the energy made it through. He felt it punch him in the gut and he felt it war with his inner being, trying to rip his soul out of his body.

Not knowing what else to do, he dissolved one of his coins and cast Protection from Evil and directed the effect inward. A coin disappeared from his buckler and he felt the effect help his willpower push back the spell. He knew that, without the protective layer from the aura, he didn't have enough coin to push back the full effect. He couldn't afford to drop the protection nor risk getting too far from Niitty. He couldn't counter that spell and Philip gave away that he had a second coin.

Philip's face screwed up in anger, "Damned Paladins. Let's see how you handle this."

He snapped his finger and the zombies started to close in. The thirty faster zombies bolted forward while the slower ones pressed in. Gerold had to quickly react and dissolved his last two coins to cast Turn Undead. He hoped doubling the power would work on the more decayed ones beyond a minor delay like back at the crypt.

The pulse rushed out of him and the 30 zombies collapsed to the ground while the other 100 or so that were called into the plaza exploded into dust. Unfortunately, the two undead flanking Philip only showed a mild rocking in response. Gerold hoped that wasn't an ill omen.

Gerold couldn't tell if the more decayed zombies were killed or just disabled. He couldn't risk focusing on them with Philip still holding onto those other undead.

Philip was angry, his face screwed up in a sneer. He pulled

out his last silver coin with a cloth and used it as a sack to split it into copper coins. He dissolved half of them and placed a hand on one of the undead then repeated the process with the other. He then pointed at Gerold and Niitty, "Go my ghouls, kill."

The two figures spun with a terrifying speed. Gerold saw looking back at him the horribly warped images of Allen, the arrogant desk administrator and Sandra, the affable server. Gerold's blood boiled at seeing two familiar faces corrupted into these monstrosities.

Sandra growled through a lipless smile and launched her form at Gerold with Allen targeting Niitty.

The ghoul swung a leathery arm with finger bones protruding from the ends of its hands like talons. Gerold punched out with the buckler to intercept the attack. A squeal erupted from the contact of unnaturally reinforced bone against the steel. Gerold felt the shock reverberate up his arm when he failed to properly deflect the strike, stressing his newly enhanced strength.

Gerold was forced to take a step back and the follow-up swing missed by a hair, cutting into his shirt. He cursed forgetting to put on his hauberk but simultaneously knew that if he wore it, it would have slowed him down enough where the attack would have connected. He barely backed out of range of another strike and he pushed down his random thoughts. This would take everything he could give to survive.

Taking another step back, he stumbled on the body of a zombie. This proved fortuitous as the next swing was aimed at his head and he stumbled below the strike. He took the opportunity to punch out with the buckler and connected with the jaw of the monster. He wasn't sure what was worse, blocking the strike or hitting the jaw. He got an image of the time he had to break a boulder that was thrown into his farm by a tornado.

Gerold's arm went numb from the impact as the ghoul was repelled, the remnants of the wavy brown hair flopping over its face and covering the milky white eyes in the process. The distance was enough to allow Gerold to follow up with a side swing with his hammer, which connected against the ghoul's temple. The monster staggered backward as it resisted falling over.

Before Gerold could make another attack, the creature bounced backwards to recover its footing then launched itself into him. The monster was properly leveraged for the attack. Gerold noticed this and he pivoted to lean back with the attack since he knew he couldn't absorb the full force of the blow. He attempted to use his buckler to deflect the force to the side to reduce the impact.

He was only able to deflect one of the creature's hands. He barely held the attack back when he braced on his leg. The talon-like fingers on the other hand slipped past his defenses and punctured into his torso. The talons penetrated one finger bone length deep into his body and brought searing pain.

Gerold used the monster's momentum to twist and throw it away. Gerold took the brief reprieve to see where Niitty was fighting. This sort of fight was one that Niitty was best suited for since she was trained as a duelist. A single opponent to focus on was her specialty outside of archery. He saw her dancing around with an unnatural grace and deflecting Allen's attacks. She, like Gerold, was in a stalemate. Her power was insufficient to breach the ghoul's defenses while on the move and her enhanced agility was dedicated to deflecting attacks.

He turned back to his ghoul. It launched itself up even faster than before as the effects of his Turn Undead were wearing off. It swung at him with even more devastating power and speed, forcing Gerold to try and deflect the attacks with punches from his buckler and impotent deflections with his hammer.

The only saving grace for Gerold was the ghoul lacked any strategy or intelligence. He was learning to predict the movements of the monster and was able to hit the creature here and there as he redirected attacks. A punch to the jaw with his buckler followed up with a strike to the spine with his hammer.

The ghoul was beginning to slow from the accumulated damage. With every strike, Gerold took hits of his own. He was bleeding from cuts on his torso, arms and face. Worse, the intense pace the ghoul was forcing on him was sapping his stamina. The undead didn't have this limitation and continued to press the attack. It was only a matter of time before he suffered a more grievous wound.

Gerold heard a pained scream come from Niitty. When his ghoul attacked next, he dug down deep, caught the monster and threw it as hard as he could. This bought him precious moments to check on Niitty. In her fight, she had moved out of his aura's range and it resulted in her ghoul becoming more powerful. She had taken multiple cuts and gashes as well from the fight.

Gerold rushed closer to Niitty to move the ghoul back into the effects of his aura. It visibly slowed back down to a manageable opponent to the Elven Ranger.

Gerold felt his spirits dip. He wasn't sure they were going to survive this engagement as he continued to struggle trading blows with the powerful undead. They were out of coins and they were tiring. Just then, he saw a streak of white across the plaza running along the perimeter behind the ruins of the collapsed buildings. It was silently circling around toward the collapsed Guild Hall.

Gerold caught a brief glimpse of Gewa moving into

position to attack Philip, their only hope that disabling the Necromancer would disrupt the ghouls. He felt a renewed sense of energy surge in him as he dug deep. It was just enough to keep himself ahead of his opponent's attacks.

He punched away another attack by the ghoul aimed at his side and took a step back to smack the monster across the face. His hammer was met with the same rock hard surface as it impacted the creature, snapping its neck to the side. His rush was fading fast and his arm was starting to feel like a loose rope attached at the shoulder. He wasn't sure how much longer he could keep this up.

The monster struck again and Gerold's parry was off-target. Instead of directing the claws away from this body, four of the fingers raked across his chest, adding to the multitudes of injuries. He lost his balance and the monster had already spun to make a more substantial attack.

Then a scream rang out and the monster halted its movement. Gerold didn't pause to see what happened and took advantage to hit the creature's head with an attack that was able to connect with his full force. The sound of a splitting stone rang out over the plaza. The strike finally showed a substantial effect. He hit it again, knocking it to the ground and followed it up with one more overhead slam to end the creature.

The monster had gone still and lay broken on the ground. Gerold examined his buckler. Deep rents marred the surface and the thin, cheap metal was dented and wouldn't survive many more blows intact. Gerold removed the reminder of his own close call and threw it aside.

He took a closer look at the body of the former server now that he had a moment to take it in. Her skin had browned and turned into thick leather and, what he could make of the remains of her head, had lost clumps of hair as if she were afflicted by a terrible disease. The clothing had mostly rotted away, revealing a disgusting nudity that looked nothing like human anatomy that ended in thin arms. The bones on her hands were distended and sharp, making for perfect weapons. Her terrible smile and milky white eyes, now flattened into the ground, were permanently seared in his memory.

He turned to check on Niitty and he saw that she had separated the head from the ghoul's body before she had collapsed into a seated position in exhaustion. He wanted to ensure she wasn't too injured, but he had one more thing to take care of. Turning next to see Philip, he was collapsed face first in the ground with blood spreading across his back. Behind him stood Gewa with her spear trained on his form.

He looked at Gewa, who understood the look in his eyes and said, "Go, I have him covered."

Gerold rushed over to Niitty to check on her. Her leather armor was shredded into tatters, exposing bleeding cuts beneath. He kneeled next to her to get a better look. The bleeding gashes weren't immediately threatening, but the specter of infection from the ghoul's talons still loomed. His visible inspection was limited to his poor knowledge, "How are you feeling? Is there anything you're concerned about?"

She waved her hand, "I need to catch my breath. That agility spell takes a lot out of you. I'm feeling blood trickle down my stomach and I think my ankle is twisted, but otherwise nothing life threatening."

That relieved Gerold. He was glad he didn't need to stabilize Niitty or carry her out of the town with more zombies in the area, "Good. Rest up while I check on Philip."

Gerold didn't feel much better than Niitty looked. He was wobbly when he stood back up and had to use his hammer to assist his rise. He walked over to where Gewa still had her spear trained on Philip's body. He noticed that her feet were bleeding, a trail of blood leading back to the former Guild Hall through the field of broken glass littering the plaza.

Gerold winced as he pointed, "I'm sorry you had to go through that."

Gewa shrugged, "While wearing boots makes me quiet, I really hate stepping in horse shit or walking on the streets where people throw their bedpans with my bare feet. Plus, getting cuts isn't fun. Besides, you look way worse than I do."

Gerold reached for his bag, "Do you want your boots back?"

"No," she responded, "The last thing I want is to get blood in them. Let's wait until we get out of here and I can clean my feet first."

Gerold nodded then he walked to the body on the ground and knelt by it. The blood staining his shirt came from a puncture wound low on the back near the kidney. He couldn't imagine how unpleasant that must have been. He flipped it over, causing Philip to groan in pain.

"Ah, gentle, you're being too rough with an injured man" he complained then looked up at Gewa. He started to laugh, "Now how did my Sense Good Aura miss you?"

"Oh, she's not all that good," Gerold responded which triggered a wry smile from Gewa.

Philip barked an even louder laugh, "Now that's original. I thought you Paladins couldn't lie. I smell the faint stench of good coming off of her. How did you manage to keep it concealed until now?"

Philip's statement got a look of surprise from Gewa, her ears twitching in thought. She recovered her senses and waved a spear at the man, "We're the ones who will ask the questions here."

Gerold dragged Philip over to the remains of the Town Seed, the man complaining the entire way about his rough treatment. He leaned him up against the pillar and stood back, looking down on the man, "Would you like to tell us anything about your Master?"

"Now why would I want to do that," he cackled in response.

Gewa thrust her spear at his face and stopped a hair short, "This is why."

A look of fear crossed his face, "That argument lacks weight. I won't betray the Master. You're wasting your time."

She pushed it slightly into his throat, drawing blood, "Your Master isn't here, I am."

Philip reached up and pushed the tip away, "If I do that, he'll resurrect my corpse and do unspeakable things to me. Like I said, you're wasting your time with these threats. Nothing you do will be worse than what betrayal brings."

Gewa pulled her spear back a few inches and looked over at Gerold, "What should we do with him?"

Philip put up his hands and crossed his wrists, "I surrender. There's a patrol post four days downriver where you can turn me in."

Gerold glared at the small man, "Why would I want to do that?"

"Because it's the law," he responded, a smug look on his face, "If you Paladins are famous for anything, it's your slavish loyalty to righteousness."

Gerold looked down at the man and then at the hammer hanging in his hand at his side. He raised the hammer up and gripped the head with his other hand. He took his eyes off the gnome and peered around the devastation surrounding them.

The twisted and broken forms of Sandra and Allan lying in the street crossed his eyesight as did the rotting zombies that circled their makeshift arena.

He scanned the town square and took in the unnaturally decaying buildings and ruined structures. All that time and labor along with the associated dreams lay collapsed on the ground, their collective future potential erased from existence. In the distance, zombies that didn't heed the call of the necromancer still milled about the side streets feeding into the plaza along with many more out of view.

The entire town, once a sign of the start of life for a multitude of starry eyed adventurers and a safe haven to raise families for the residents, now sat silent, a graveyard that stretched for miles in every direction. His eyes returned to Philip, the architect of this destruction. Yes, he was doing the bidding of some higher power, but he did so with gusto and glee. There was something off about his request to be turned over to the authorities. Why would he want that? What was his angle? Gerold knew he couldn't give the man what he wanted.

Gerold rubbed the head of his hammer and looked deep into his being, seeing if some sort of compulsion attempted to drive his behavior. What came was not righteous anger, a sense of vengeance or even a sense of mercy. What came was a sense of duty.

He let the hammer fall and allowed the head to drag along the ground as his hand loosely gripped the haft. He looked back at Philip, who was waiting for his bindings.

"You know," Gerold began, "Someone close to me said something. She told me that I make a terrible Paladin. I think she's right."

Then Gerold's arm reached back and a look of shocked fear

crossed Philip's face. It was the last expression it would make as Gerold's hammer smashed it between his hammer and the Town Seed's stone pillar, blood and bone splattering out and sliding off of Gerold's clothing.

Gerold extracted the hammer from the caved in face. He neither felt remorse nor satisfaction when he looked at the former gnome slumped over in the center of his sin. Instead, Gerold felt like he made a small contribution toward redeeming his failures.

Not sparing an additional moment in thought, he signaled to Gewa that he was going back to check on Niitty and then the three could finally leave this depressing ruin.

CHAPTER 27

Gerold was happy that Niitty's injuries weren't life threatening, but her twisted ankle proved to be an issue. He didn't want to use the last coin on a Simple Heal until her wounds were cleaned to avoid secondary infection.

They still had to navigate their way out of town and the rooftop method was no longer viable. Gerold and Gewa bought the party some time when they went around to ensure the zombies that Gerold previously disabled were dead, but he didn't feel safe sitting in the epicenter of the necrotic zone.

Even though he couldn't see mana the way Erinne could through his eyes, he could feel the corrupted magic pressing down on his protective shield. It was originating from the remains of the Town Seed though, thankfully, he could sense that its effects faded away the further they were from the epicenter. He also couldn't be sure when the ambient necrotic mana would start to coalesce and form monsters, so they needed to hurry to leave the area.

Gerold pulled out the makeshift crutch he used on the way back from the crypt and gave it to Niitty. Gewa rifled through Philip's corpse, finding nothing of use, and then took up a position to help Gerold. Gerold then took point and led the party east toward the exit.

Philip's call had drawn in the zombies at the edges of the plaza that were taken care of with Gerold's Turn Undead spell. Thankfully, his threat that a thousand zombies were on the way turned out to be an exaggeration when no more bodies entered the plaza.

When they were twenty yards out from the nearest bunch of zombies, Gerold called for a stop. He was worried that the zombies had become faster in the time they fought Philip and his ghouls. He would need to be careful until they left the town proper.

Examining the street, he saw it was lined with various businesses and shops. He moved down toward the nearest zombie bunch while trying to peer through windows to see if he could use anything inside. The windows, like the General Store, had clouded over from accelerated decay. Noting a back alley access point between the otherwise tight packed buildings, he picked a bakery storefront and pushed the door open. Inside he looked toward the back and saw clear through into the kitchen area where it led to a closed back door and another cloudy window.

A plan formed in his mind. He went into the store, careful to not get ambushed by the employees. He found one on the ground behind the counter and a baker standing before a cold oven that held molding bread. He quickly dispatched the two and went up the stairs. The second floor was empty as was the third. He returned to the main floor and went out the rear exit. No bodies greeted him out back and the back of the shop was wide enough to run if needed. He checked the small alley to ensure it was clear, finding it free of obstructions.

He returned inside and blocked the back door before smashing out the back window. He would draw the zombies into the store and squeeze out of the window before swinging around to close the front.

He was still exhausted from the battle with the ghouls, so this plan had little margin for error even with the slow monsters. Pulling his hammer again, he walked down the street dragging it on the stone like he did back at the stables. He wanted the sound to draw attention but not make his presence known to the entire town the way a shout would.

The noise successfully attracted the attention of around fifteen zombies. They were faster than before, showing a reduced degree of clumsiness than the crowd that followed him into the stables. He had to bunch the group up to make sure they would follow him in a tight group and not lose some in the process, so he weaved around some to get them all in a tight mass. He then he drew them toward the open door of the bakery and walked inside. He walked back toward the kitchen, continuing to hit surfaces with his hammer to keep their attention.

As the main room started to fill and the first zombies reached the kitchen door, Gerold squeezed himself out of the back window. He had a slight scare when his hips caught on the frame before the rotten wood pulled away and allowed him to fall out. To ensure the group made its way into the building, he rapped the hammer on the back door.

Gerold then swung around to the side of the building and looked through the gap to the street. He didn't see anything and moved to the next corner. Looking to the side, he saw the last of the zombies push its way into the bakery. A quick look the other way showed the street clear for around fifty yards. As silently as he could, he crept up behind the throng and pulled the door shut, trapping the zombies within.

The next bunch of around twenty zombies would prove much more challenging. This stretch of the town became a more tightly packed residential stretch without any alley access to perform his trick. Worse, as he tried doors, they were locked. He asked Gewa if she had any knowledge on lock breaking. When she tried, she reported they were too complicated to pick with a dagger.

Gerold attempted to use the rotting wood to his advantage

since the trapped mass would hold the door shut, not the latch, and hit one of the handles like he did at the shop. The door held against his attack, sending an unpleasant vibration up his arm on the impact. It felt like it was barred from the other end. He tried a few more houses to the same result.

He looked back at his party. Niitty was hobbling on her crutch and Gewa showed growing discomfort with her cut feet.

Gerold sighed, "I'm going to have to kill this next batch. Hold back for a bit."

Gewa stepped forward, "I can help."

"Are you sure?" Gerold pointed at her feet.

She grimaced, "I'll be fine. I have to walk over there either way."

"I appreciate the backup. I think we should move slowly while I tap the cobblestone. Hopefully, we can draw them in a few at a time," Gerold suggested.

Gewa nodded, "Should we split to speed it up?"

"No," Gerold shook his head. "The risk of getting surrounded is too high. They're getting faster and we'd do better together. Hand me that last coin in case I need to use a Turn Undead."

Gewa handed her last copper coin to Gerold and, lacking a place to put it, gripped it between his palm and his hammer. Gerold then explained the alternating attack method he had developed with Niitty against the goblins, which Gewa suggested she modify by using Gerold's shoulder as a support. Gerold liked that since, which he kept private, he would serve as a shield to his companion.

Gewa situated herself behind and laid the spear against his offhand shoulder. Gerold then slowly stepped forward, tapping the cobblestone with each step. He drew a pair of zombies near the side of the road, which turned and moved at a brisk walk in his direction. The two were moving in tandem as they arrived.

"Take the left one," Gerold whispered back and readied his weapon, spike side out. When the two came into range, he swung the weapon into the temple of the monster while he felt the haft slide along his shoulder and punch into the eye of the other.

They slowly moved down the street against a line of housing to reduce angles of attack with Niitty trailing behind. Their slow and deliberate pace proved almost as stressful as the fight back in the plaza. He was on constant guard to doors even though he rationally knew that these creatures didn't have the wherewithal to open them.

They managed to clear out the zombies as they moved down the street without more than the exhausting worry that something would go wrong. At the final building before the open area around the gate, Gerold peered around the corner toward the stables. Their luck held and all the zombies he had drawn in the building were still choking the stables entrance. They were facing away and they had ceased moving now that Gerold was no longer in view.

Gerold asked Niitty to use his shoulder instead of the crutch for this stretch of the walk to avoid the sound of the wood tapping on the ground. Helping her move, they successfully exited the town and made it back to the small farmhouse from before.

"Take a seat you two, I'll see if there is anything that can help clean your wounds," Gerold said when they entered the farmhouse. He looked at the table and the meat was still there.

Niitty removed her bow and set her rapier aside before she

sat in one chair and stretched her injured ankle out to avoid putting pressure on it. She looked down at her torn chest through the leather armor and winced at the touch.

On the other side of the small table, Gewa pulled a second chair in front of hers and put up both feet, sighing in relief to finally get off of them, "I can go a lifetime without ever experiencing that again."

"I don't have any arguments to the contrary," Niitty said as she tried to move her arms to undo the armor but her expression indicated it was too painful to move in that manner.

"Hold on a moment, I'll help," Gerold said as he dug through the remains of the coal stores to refresh the low fire and warm the room. He went over and pulled the monster parts he left on the floor back in his bag and picked up a slice of smoked meat. He gave it a sniff and it smelled fine. He then tentatively took a bite and it didn't taste wrong. Either the smoked meat kept well or the necrotic effect was significantly weaker outside of the walls. He couldn't tell since the pressure he felt on his aura had disappeared when they left the main plaza.

"That should still be good," Gerold pointed at the meat before entering the sleeping room. He checked on a chest he found in the room and in it was stored a few spare sets of clothing. The farmer was taller and thinner than Gerold, so the attire wouldn't work as a replacement for his ever disintegrating shirt. The woman's clothing was too short for Niitty. He thought he may be able to do something with it if he had enough thread left in his bag.

Grabbing the children's clothing, he tore them into strips for rags and returned to the main room. He set the rags on the table before picking up the cook pot. He was able to locate a water pump outside, wash it out and return to boil some water.

While the water heated, he looked at his companions. Gewa had her head leaned back over the chair and had her eyes closed. Niitty was taking short quick breaths to deal with the pain she was going through.

He walked over and kneeled by her, "Let me help you out of this."

He felt a strong sense of shame and embarrassment flow through their connection from her when he reached up to the ties to remove the mangled armor, "Something wrong?"

She looked flushed when she responded, "I don't want you to see."

He frowned, "What? They're just cuts. We survived a terrible ordeal. There's nothing to be ashamed of."

Gerold examined the armor and it was a two part design that tied together at the sides. He untied the armor and levered it off her chest gingerly. Niitty sucked in air when he pulled it away from her skin as the congealing blood underneath pulled away with a sound that reminded Gerold of when he helped a neighbor birth a calf. The blood left small trails between her skin and the underside of the armor as he pulled it aside. After supporting her with a hand on her collarbone, he helped her lean forward so he could extract the remaining armor. She had avoided taking any injuries to her back this time, allowing her to safely lean back on the chair back.

The leather was in terrible shape. The old hole from behind in combination with all the new slashes and shredding rendered it functionally useless. He held it up to Niitty, "Is there any reason you'd want to keep this?"

She looked down on the item and shook her head, "No. It's a cheap thing I picked up after I joined the Guild. It obviously didn't do a good job."

Gerold looked around trying to decide where to discard it. He worried the blood could attract attention if he threw it outside and he didn't want to leave it in the room. He found a trap door to the root cellar and threw it through the hole.

He turned back to examine Niitty's injuries. He looked over her torso and saw it was ragged with cuts and punctures. Some blood still seeped from the larger cuts but they had mostly coagulated over by this point. He needed to clean her wounds to evaluate the risk of infection since he didn't want to waste their final coin unless it was absolutely necessary.

The blood mixed in with days of road grime and marred her otherwise pale white skin. The blood morbidly accentuated the well developed musculature and was staining into the wrap she had around her breasts. Gerold winced at the sight, "I'm sorry you have to go through this. The water should be ready in twenty minutes."

She laughed, "You don't look much better. Did you let that ghoul use you as a chew toy?"

Gerold looked down at his chest and through his torn clothing. The reminder caused the throbbing pain to manifest itself, "I'll manage. The bleeding stopped and you won't have to worry about me falling into a fever coma."

"Good, because that will add a debt on the ledger you'd owe me," she responded.

Gerold frowned, "What did I say about keeping track?"

She grinned back, "I know. You said you wouldn't keep track of what I owe you. That doesn't mean I won't track what you owe me."

Gewa laughed while keeping her eyes closed and head back, "What brought on this snark?"

Niitty shrugged, "I needed some levity after what we just went through over the past few days."

Gerold was happy to allow himself to be the butt of a joke for the two immature kids in his party and he groaned for their benefit. This got them laughing even louder, though Niitty interrupted it with a few pained grunts when she laughed too hard.

After the water came to a rolling boil over the hearth, he let it sit for a couple of minutes. Gerold couldn't remember how long it should boil to be safe, so he let it go for five minutes before letting it cool. He found a bowl as a rinse dish and, after allowing the water to cool some, used a ladle to fill the bowl.

He pulled the pot over next to Niitty and used the ladle to dip a strip of cloth in and, after letting it cool some in the air, he started to clean the blood off of Niitty's torso. He carefully wiped around the open wounds to remove the fluids and grime, periodically dipping it into the bowl to rinse the cloth.

After clearing the area around the wounds, he ran his hand across her ribs. Niitty let out a small gasp and he felt a torrent of confusing emotion explode through their connection. He quickly pulled his hand back, "Sorry, I think it may be broken."

"No, no," she shook her head, "Your, uh, hands are a little cold."

Gerold held his hand over the steaming pot to warm his hand, "Sorry about that."

Gerold heard Gewa chuckle.

"What," he asked her.

She smirked, "Oh, nothing. You're kinda clueless."

What was the girl talking about? He looked at her feet, "These cold hands will be examining your wounds next."

Her eyes went wide, "No, I think I can do that myself."

"That's not happening," Gerold responded, "You'll struggle to clean both of them and I need to make sure there aren't any signs of infection. We only have one coin left and we have to be sure to use it wisely."

"But," she began before Gerold cut her off.

"No arguments, I'm going to check them," he said.

Gerold turned back to look at Niitty's wounds. Other than some continued seepage from the worst of them, nothing looked like it would need any stitching to keep closed. He saw a deep red forming on her pale skin around the edges of each of the cuts along with some white pus building in the larger gashes. He dabbed gingerly at the white substance and Niitty grunted in pain.

"Yea, it looks like an infection is already building. I'll have to use Simple Heal on you," he said, "I need to check one last thing."

He reached down to her foot and started to untie the boot. She started to take in deep breaths and releasing the air slowly in preparation for potential pain. Gerold gently slipped the boot off followed by the woolen sock beneath. The terrible odor of road travel assaulted his nose as it was removed.

He looked at her ankle and it didn't show any signs of puffiness. He gently touched it, "Does this hurt?"

"No," Niitty shook her head, "Nothing."

He slowly flexed her foot back and forth, "Now?"

Again she shook her head, "No, it's just a bit stiff."

"Good. You just need to rest it and it should be fine," Gerold said, "I'll have to use my Simple Heal to take care of that infection. It should also close up the wounds a little. You'll still need bandages to protect the scabs from pulling out."

He moved over to Gewa who twisted her feet at his approach. "I don't like my feet being touched," she complained.

"Don't be a child," Gerold scolded as he kneeled by them to examine the pads on the soles. The cuts looked minor with bits of road debris stuck in the wounds. He spent some time cleaning the injury, Gewa's tail flicking in irritation the entire time, before using some cloth to wrap her feet. He also noticed how matted her fur had become with mud and grime starting to stain parts of her brown. The tangles couldn't be pleasant.

"You two need a bath," Gerold stated flatly.

"Sorry we can't be high and mighty Paladins like some people," Gewa retorted.

"Don't take me wrong," Gerold explained, "It's not an insult. You're both filthy and I can't imagine it feels pleasant."

Gewa pulled up a sleeve on her shirt and examined her ratty fur, "That's true. I'll need some time washing to untangle this. Thankfully, I brought a comb along."

He turned to Niitty, who he caught smelling her underarm. She blushed and dropped her arm back down to her lap, "I won't say no to a more thorough cleaning."

"I'll go look for a washtub, a house like this should have something around to use," Gerold said.

After dissolving their last coin to take care of the infection developing in Niitty's wounds, Gerold went out of the house and noticed that it was, again, getting notably darker. He hated not knowing what time it was and assumed that the day was once again coming to an end. He searched the area and noticed a small storage shed a ways from the house. Inside, he found a wooden wash tub that was still in good condition.

Gerold hefted the tub into the house and left it in the middle of the sleeping area after pushing the two beds apart and against the walls. The room had a cheap enchanted lantern on an end table next to one of the beds. Testing it, he was happy to see that the ambient mana in the area had stabilized enough for the device to absorb and use it. It looked like even necrotic mana was sufficient to power passive enchanted items.

He took the hot water and poured it into the tub then ferried more back and forth before putting another pot up to boil. After he was satisfied with the temperature, just a hair short of being too hot, he announced, "Who wants to go first?"

"Niitty should go, she's had a worse day than I have," Gewa announced.

Niitty stood up with help from the table and picked up her crutch, "You don't have to ask me twice. I'll call if I need help. And that means Gewa."

As she passed, Gerold put his hand up and made a fist. She looked at it in confusion. Gerold grabbed her free hand, made a fist and tapped his wrist to hers. Realization dawned on her and she smiled, "You remembered."

Gerold shrugged, "How could I forget our first successful hunt?"

She then walked away and disappeared into the other room, closing the door behind her. Gerold shook his head and pulled the last chair up to the table and sat with Gewa. He folded his hands on the table and looked over at her, "You have my deepest gratitude."

She hummed in a mixture of embarrassment and confusion like she wasn't used to getting compliments. "What do you mean?"

"You had every opportunity to escape. Philip had no idea you were in the area and you could have slipped out unnoticed," Gerold explained, "You put yourself at risk to sneak alone through a dangerous area to help us. Without you, Niitty and I would be dead."

Gewa's finger went to the table and she gently dragged the claw in a circle on the surface with enough force to make a soft scraping sound but not enough to damage the wood, "I already said that my chances of surviving on the road were lower without you."

"We both know that's cow shit," Gerold said, "Don't devalue what you did for us. If you ever decide to, I am more than willing to accept you formally into our party."

A meek but genuine smile crossed Gewa's face and the gentle swishing of her tail gave away her emotions. He suspected that her skin was flushed under that white spotted fur, "Thanks."

"You know," Gerold continued, "Philip said something interesting."

She looked up at him, "What was that?"

"Remember how you said you aren't all that good," Gerold asked.

"Of course. That's because I'm a thief's daughter," Gewa replied.

"You shouldn't let your past define you," Gerold said, "Especially after a necromancer accused you of having a faint stink of good."

Gewa sniffed and looked back down at the table, "Oh, that. He could have been lying."

Gerold picked up the adult sized clothing he found in the trunk. He evaluated the lady's shirt and figured that the shoulders could fit Niitty, though it would need an extension to cover her torso. Gerold dug into his bag and willed the needle and all the remaining thread into his hand, "I don't think he was lying. That act of saving us tilted whatever scales measure our souls over to the side of good."

Gerold heard a hitched sigh, like Gewa had caught herself beginning to cry and stopped it. He looked up and she was smiling even broader with glistening eyes, "I know I still have a long way to go."

He went back to his task. He worked his dagger to cut the bottom part of one shirt and lined it up with the other. It was clunky and the flare at the bottom of the garment would look odd, but it would have to suffice.

"What are your plans from here," Gewa asked.

Gerold looked up at her and thought a moment, "I can't let that monster get away with this. We have to do something."

She frowned, "I know you asked if I'm willing to join your party, but if you intend to chase that thing, I respectfully decline. I won't rush into a suicide mission."

"I don't intend to track it down. If you asked me a month ago, I would have chased it without a second thought," Gerold paused his work and looked up at Gewa. "Now I have a reason to live and people to protect. Besides, my wife would have killed me if I did something that stupid."

Gewa cocked her head to the side and the smile returned to her face, "We'll see. I recall protecting you today."

"Give and take," Gerold shrugged, "That thing, though, is way beyond our means to defeat. We barely survived today and, had Philip noticed your presence, none of us had a chance of surviving. The thing that ran off with the artifact scared him. I won't give chase and, if Niitty catches its tracks, we'll take a different route."

"So how do you intend to stop it?"

Gerold went back to his repairs, moving the needle through the cloth and making rough stitches, "The Pantheon Temple in the Capital trains Paladins and has a registry. I'll see if I can convince them to put out a call to bring more experienced ones together. I still want to be there when this is resolved, I owe my family that much, but we'll do it the right way."

"That's a sensible plan," Gewa said, "I'll come along and see how this plays out. Maybe then I'll take you up on that offer to join." Gerold smiled and returned to his work.

Gerold was engrossed in his task and, after finishing, he started with working a shirt for himself. It would be more complicated since he would have to cut the shirt in half and splice more cloth in to make it wider to fit his shoulders. It would look ridiculous, but what he had on now was little more than going bare-chested like some fringe region barbarian.

His plans were interrupted by the door opening behind him. Niitty stuck her head out, her brown hair moist and loose as she stuck it around the corner, "Gewa? Can I get some help with your comb?"

Gewa sighed and moved her feet to the floor. Gerold pulled her boots out of his bag and, as she passed, he handed her the boots, some cloth strips for bandages and the shirt. She took them and nodded as she passed.

Gerold continued to work for a while when Gewa asked if Gerold minded changing out the water. He hadn't thought about moving the heavy tub back out and decided to use the window to toss the water with the pot. Niitty was sitting on a bed with her new shirt that hung tightly on her frame.

After he refreshed the tub with warm water, he said to them, "You two can go to sleep after you're done. I have a few more things to do. You can each take a bed, I won't need one."

"Are you sure," Niitty asked, "Gewa can always join me in this one. It's big enough for two."

"That's not a good idea," Gerold stated, "You need a good night's rest and avoid any chances of aggravating your injuries, so you should have a bed for yourself. I doubt Gewa will be thrilled to share one with me."

Gewa snorted, "That's right. I barely know you. Who shares a sleeping space with a stranger?" Niitty blushed at Gewa's words.

"What about a watch," Gewa asked.

Gerold hummed, "Let me ask. Erinne? You still there?"

"Yes," her voiced echoed in his head, "What can I help with?"

"Do you think there's a risk of something spawning on us in the night?"

A few beats of silence followed his question, "I think you should be safe for now. You don't have to worry about it until after the dungeon starts to form new buildings in the town to replace the decaying ones."

Gerold would have to see if he can locate any information on how dungeons operate when he was back in the Capital. He was approaching adventuring like trying to farm without an almanac. Gerold reached to close the sleeping room door, "I'll drag the table over to the door and use it as a barricade just in case."

After dropping the security bar across the door and shoving the table against it, he moved a chair to the familiar space in front of the hearth. He stared in the flames and reflected on the past few days. He reached over to a pile of clothing and continued working on the shirt he was making for himself. His chest itched as the wound scabbed over and bits of blood flaked away from his passive cleaning aura.

He worked the shirt for a while when he called out, "Erinne? Are you still there?"

"I am," she responded.

"I need to thank you as well," he started, "Your warning helped us avoid an untimely burial. Worse, without you, no one would have witnessed what happened here."

"What brought this on?" she asked.

"I've not been someone my family could be proud of lately. Now is always the best time to start improving," he replied.

He felt a sense of warmth fill him, "Thanks. It's nice to feel appreciated. Is there anything else you'd need from me? I think I should pull back to my core self and recharge the avatar."

"No. More importantly, do you need anything?"

"I just got it," Erinne's voice joyfully tinkled in his head, "I'm pulling back now. Farewell."

Gerold whispered a farewell even though he knew she was already gone. He was alone again and he stared at the low flames flickering across the coals in the hearth, his sense of loneliness significantly reduced. He still thought about his family and that he would have completed planting his spring harvest by now. The feeling, though, was more distant.

He pushed the spare thoughts aside and got to work on the clothing. He would finish up and get some rest for the night. They would need it. The trip back to the Capital wouldn't be easy, but that was a problem for tomorrow.

AUTHOR'S NOTE

If you're reading this right now, thank you very much. I appreciate the time you took and I hope you enjoyed the book. A writer, after all, is nothing without a reader. This has been quite the journey getting to the point that I have managed to not only finish but put out my first novel. I had no idea how hard it would be to produce a story that you could feel happy releasing to the world to read.

I plan on continuing this story later. When that is? I don't know. Still, I fully intend to complete the story of Gerold, Niitty and Gewa, along with new companions.

Once again, thank you very much. If I successfully made just one person happy, I can call that a win.

If you have any questions, comments, critiques or anything else, you can reach me at https://www.facebook.com/JustinMurrayAuthor or justinmurrayauthor@gmail.com

Have a wonderful day and I hope to see you again soon.

Made in the USA
Columbia, SC
13 November 2023